21st Century Ghost Stories

Wyrd Harvest Press

21st Century Ghost Stories

ISBN: 978-0-244-69169-1
Durham. UK. 2018

Edited by Paul Guernsey.
Proof Editing by Paul Guernsey. Grey Malkin & Andy Paciorek

Cover © Andy Paciorek. With thanks to Erin Sorrey. x
Typeset in Sylfaen.

Both Standard and American English spelling is utilized in this book.

Book design and production © Wyrd Harvest Press / Lulu. 2018

100% of sales profits of books bought from –
www.lulu.com/spotlight/andypaciorek will be charitably donated to different environmental, wildlife and community projects undertaken by The Wildlife Trusts. www.wildlifetrusts.org

Contents

In Memoriam

This volume of *21ˢᵗ Century Ghost Stories* is dedicated to the memory of JL (Jeffrey) Schneider, a man who invested his life in the craft of writing. Jeff, who died in January 2018, is the author of the story "Bubs & Johns" which won the fall 2016 Ghost Story Supernatural Fiction Award competition and appears in this anthology. Among his many other publications, Jeff was the winner of the 2015 *Fiction Southeast* Editor's Prize. His fiction has also appeared in *Snake Nation, The Newport Review, The MacGuffin, International Quarterly, New Millenium Writings,* and *Bacopa Literary Review*. He was nominated for a Pushcart Prize for fiction in 2013 and for nonfiction in 2014. In addition to his writing, he was a carpenter and an adjunct professor of English at a small community college in upstate New York. It is an honor to have known him.

Introduction

Dear Reader,

You have in your hands an anthology of 29 short stories penned by fine writers from around the English-speaking world, all of whom drew their inspiration from the supernatural. Every tale collected here was a winner or honorable mention in one of The Ghost Story Awards contests: The Ghost Story Supernatural Fiction Award, which honors full-length short stories of up to 10,000 words, and The Screw Turn Flash Fiction Competition, which recognizes excellence in fiction of 1,000 or fewer words. Both contests are administered by the editor of this collection.

Although guidelines for our two competitions strongly suggest that submitted stories incorporate a supernatural theme or element, we leave the door wide open for writers to make what they will of that relatively ghostly requirement. Invariably, what impresses us most about the fiction we select is the lyricism and originality of the writing, along with the accuracy and incisiveness of the author's insights into the human condition. As a result, as you read through this book you will encounter an astonishing range of approaches to the supernatural. Only ten of the pieces actually revolve around ghosts - and even then, each writer has her or his own unique take on what a ghost is, *why* it is, and what it can or cannot do. The other nineteen stories offer a variety of uncanny experiences and elements, including, but not limited to, demons, zombies, spirits in the Voudou pantheon, out-of-body episodes, doppelgangers, shape-shifters, hallucinations, dreams, imaginary people, mythical beings, and Things You Just Can't Explain. While you'll find little here that falls into the conventional Horror category - that's just not our interest - many of the pieces may be considered as strong examples of *Folk* Horror: stories that produce their uncanny effect through the incorporation of the myths, legends, superstitions, folk beliefs, and overall atmosphere of a particular landscape and its inhabitants. Several of the pieces are aimed at producing a laugh.

You will find the writers represented herein to be delightfully diverse. They are men and women from a number of countries and regions, and of different ages and perspectives. A few are professional writers who have had a great deal of commercial success. Others can boast of a long list of publications in well-regarded literary journals. Several achieved their very first publication with a win or an honorable mention in one of our contests - and in all cases, these first-timers had to best quite a few more experienced, even much better-known, writers in order to end up as one of our picks for an award. As I mentioned earlier, the things that matter most to us are originality, and insight.

The Ghost Story Awards got their start about four years prior to this writing, and they were rooted in a hunch I had. Having myself been a novelist and an editor for many years, my informed belief was that the fiction community unquestionably included a cohort of superb writers who regularly crafted polished, provocative, socially relevant stories - only to run into problems in publishing them due to their incorporation of a ghost, a demon, a spirit, or some other element of the supernatural that all too frequently resulted in their being dismissed as "genre" work unsuitable to a "serious" literary magazine or internet publication. I wanted to find those writers, I wanted to bring them together, and I wanted to create an appreciative online home for their work.

We started building The Ghost Story website (TheGhostStory.com) in late 2014, and by the spring of 2015, we were publicizing the first Ghost Story Supernatural Fiction Award contest, with its $1,000 first prize for the winner, and smaller cash prizes for two honorable mentions. The initial response, though not overwhelming, was encouraging, at least among American writers, and the submissions included three pieces that really took our breath away - "Guédé," "A Ghost of a Smell," and "A Nearly Perfect Five by Seven," all of which you'll find in this collection - and these we proudly published on Midsummer's Eve. After that, word of our competition spread quickly, and when we ran it again in the fall (for Halloween publication), we found that we'd already begun to receive entries from outside the U.S. In fact, one of the honorable mentions that second time around was the unsettling story "The Tattibogle," written by Kristin J. Cooper, an Australian living in Scotland.

Not only did the contest continue to grow both in prestige and in the number of submissions that poured in each time we announced it, but The Ghost Story Supernatural Fiction Award quickly blossomed into a truly international event - so much so that in early 2016 when we launched The Screw Turn Flash Fiction Competition, our separate annual contest for "flash" or "sudden" fiction, the winner and honorable mentions *all* were from England and Scotland - it was a U.K. sweep. Our fall 2017 Supernatural Fiction Award Winner was a Canadian (A.J. Rutgers, for "The Salish Sea Zombie") and, as I write this, we are preparing for the Midsummer's Eve online publication of our first U.K. winner in the full-length fiction contest: English writer Rowan Bowman's "The Beast of Blanchland."

When things have gone well for an enterprise, the question of "what's next?" invariably arises. In our case, the answer was to seek even broader recognition for the wonderful stories in The Ghost Story Awards contests by arranging for *print* publication - something that even in our unrelentingly digital era still stands as the most coveted literary showcase for many writers. To that end, we've teamed up with Andy Paciorek, creator of the online Folk Horror Revival community, as well as publisher of Wyrd Harvest Press in Durham, U.K., to bring you this paperbound anthology containing all the winning and honorable mention stories in The Ghost Story Awards contests, from the inception of The Ghost Story Supernatural Fiction Award in the summer of 2015 through the most recent set of Screw Turn Flash Fiction Competition winners, which appeared on The Ghost Story website in February 2018. Mr. Paciorek, by the way, in addition to his publishing collaboration, has crafted a wonderful custom illustration for each of the stories in this book.

This is Volume I. We expect to have a Volume II for you to enjoy in late 2021. Meanwhile, however, you've got plenty of terrific reading right here - 29 stories that are chilling, or funny, or a bit of both, and all of which will continue to turn in your imagination long after you've finished them. Below, I've provided a brief overview on each of our pieces, in order to help you decide which of them you might want to experience first:

Our collection starts out gently and gracefully with Maura Stanton's bittersweet and wryly humorous **House Ghosts**, in which a disparate and occasionally squabbling group of disembodied spirits makes repeated attempts to influence the sale of the suburban home they collectively haunt.

Next, we step right into the icy grip of uncertainty with Australian writer Melanie Napthine's chilling **A Community Service Announcement**. In this story, set at night in a lonely, half-finished housing development, a new mother's maternal anxiety seems to take on flesh in the form of three mysterious waifs who show up on her doorstep and seem to want ...*something.*

Another waif - a ragged homeless boy - is the protagonist of Northern Ireland-based writer Daniel Soule's flash fiction piece, **The Lostling**. The nameless boy, shuffling along a dark and deserted street on the way to his cardboard bed beneath a bridge, hears the ring of a pay phone and must decide whether to answer. His fate hangs in the balance.

In **The Donegal Suite** writer Lisa Taddeo, who has published an extensive amount of nonfiction on the subject of sex in *Esquire* and other magazines, serves up biting and funny social commentary concerning America's dispiriting dating-and-mating culture, as well as on our national obsession with sexually appealing celebrities. Taddeo treats us to the jaded and despairing perspective of one such celebrity - a Scottish-born, self-mocking "supreme sex god" with "flowy & fiery hair" - as well as to that of Denise, an otherwise seemingly sensible hotel manager who is more than desperate to hook up with him. Although the hot Scot's far out of Denise's league, the resentful help of a scheming and jealous Italian ghost increases her odds considerably.

Edgar Award-winning novelist Mindy McGinnis tackles the flash-fiction form in **Solitude**, the tale of woman spending some alone time in a cabin at the edge of an isolated lake. Anxiety builds as the protagonist begins to observe various creatures swimming to the center of the lake - where they all disappear with barely a ripple. This quiet story ends with a shock.

Explosions and cave-ins are the least of a coal miner's worries in **The Coal Mape**, Kurt Newton's unsettling flash fiction story about a Paleozoic demon set free from its deep imprisonment within the darkest rocks of the earth.

The scruffy, dissipated, grown-up incarnations of a man's two imaginary childhood friends face off against his comely and seemingly accommodating (twin!) adult fantasies in the late JL Schneider's story, **Bubs & Johns**. Guess who comes out on top?

In Gene Bryan Johnson's jazz and soul infused **Negroes Anonymous**, the disembodied spirit of Louis Armstrong serves as the Ghost of Christmas Past to "Skullcap Dashiki," an angry and alienated young black man who meets him in a New York nightclub. Together, they revisit periods of Skullcap's half-forgotten 1960s childhood, along the way encountering vicious white racists of all ages and witnessing societal racism's corrosive and heart-breaking effect on young Skullcap's struggling middle-class family.

Holy Rollers is Helsinki, Finland-based American Kevin McCarthy's hilarious short story in which a well-intentioned youth minister attempts to help a very disturbed young man, and for his trouble ends up getting taken hostage at knifepoint. Then, just as the reader thinks things can't get any weirder, along comes a sinister invisible entity whom the boy insists on referring to as "The Lef-tenant."

A Brief Respite, English writer CL Dalkin's Screw Turn Flash Fiction Competition-winning short-short story, gives us a working-class protagonist who heads off walking to his sister's house following a "bitter row" with his long-time girlfriend that turned a bit physical toward the end. She was an abusive alcoholic, and he feels relieved to have made a final break from her. But wait - why does he keep hearing footsteps?

Repressed memory plays a powerful role in **Fog**, by Petra McQueen. The setting is a quiet, somewhat eerie English village, through which a woman named Maggie anxiously pursues her young granddaughter and a mysterious, red jacketed little boy as they gleefully dodge in and out of the dense fog that has swallowed the town. As she listens for the laughter of the unseen children, Maggie also hears what sounds like someone digging a grave - and seemingly with each scrape of the shovel, she recalls a bit more about a long-ago tragedy.

In **The Tattibogle**, Kristin J. Cooper does for Old World scarecrows what the Stephen King novel, *It*, did for American clowns. One of the scariest pieces in this anthology, Cooper's story follows a family with two young boys to the remote, rundown, and blighted Scottish farm where, for generations, the mother's ancestors had scratched out a meager living. Now, the only one left is poor, old Aunty Morag, who had summoned them all for just one little visit before she dies. However, it soon becomes all too apparent to the boys, if not their parents, that a brief family reunion isn't all that Aunty wants. She's got a *plan*, and it involves telling them terrifying family stories, making them memorize unsettling incantations, and introducing them to the tattibogle - an animated, putrefying scarecrow that stalks the land at night, and sometimes slithers through windows. And laughs...

Ridge Carpenter's two pieces, **The Haunted Still** and **Yamanba**, both are "frame" stories written very much in the vintage style and diction of the "golden age" of ghost stories - roughly from 1880 until around 1920. It would not be wrong to call them homages to such masters of the genre as M.R. James, Henry James, and Algernon Blackwood. By "frame," I mean that they are both "stories within stories" which, rather than being told directly, are presented as oral tales that have been spun on the spot by a fictional narrator for the entertainment of a fictional audience. Narrator and audience for this type of narrative all tend to be upper-class Englishmen - though in "The Haunted Still" they are very pointedly Americans - and the setting, invariably, is a cozy "drawing room" where tobacco pipes are smoldering, a blaze is crackling in the fireplace, and beverages are being liberally dispensed from crystal decanters. In the inner story of "The Haunted Still," a federal revenue agent in the era of Prohibition tramps the dark and forested hills of Appalachia in search of stills for making illegal liquor; what he finds are spirits of quite a different sort. In "Yamanba," a detachment of U.S. troops, accompanied by a British doctor, stumble upon an impoverished and very spooky village in the remote mountains of post-war Japan. A bizarre statue dominates the center of town, all the adults in the place are starving, sick, and dispirited - and most of the kids seem to be missing. The doctor and his companions soon are seeking answers to the question, "where have all the children gone?"

In Scott Loring Sanders' **Moss Man**, dead, grotesquely mutilated wild animals have been turning up in the New Jersey Pine Barrens - and of course, the prime suspect is the Jersey Devil, a legendary, half-human swamp monster from the region's colonial past. The Newark *Star-Ledger* newspaper dispatches a reporter to find out what's really going on - and before long our man is squishing his way through the lonely barrens in the company of a local hermit and orchid thief named Bill who has tales to tell, and secrets to keep. While friendly for the most part, quirky Bill is especially insistent that the reporter *not* take a peek inside his house…The ending to Sanders' story is deeply haunting, and totally unexpected.

Rebecca Ring introduces us to an elderly gravedigger named Horace in **A Nearly Perfect Five by Seven**. Horace is a man who enjoys his work, taking great pride in excavating a properly proportioned final resting place, and reveling in the peace and solitude of the cemetery, where except for the occasional funeral party, he is usually alone with his thoughts and his balky backhoe. Then one day his tranquility is shattered when a school bus disgorges a pack of children who run laughing and screaming through the tombstones. His distress doubles as a strangely dressed little girl homes in on him with some unwelcome attention just when he's attempting to work a massive boulder out of the ground - and things turn truly horrific after he loses sight of her for moment, only to spot her tiny, red shoe at the bottom of the fresh grave he's been digging…

Art therapy plays a role in English writer Barry Charman's flash fiction piece, **Palette**. In this brief story, a woman named Suzette struggles to paint her way back to emotional equilibrium in the wake of a tragic and irreversible mistake. After becoming obsessed with capturing a particular landscape on her canvas, she finds herself baffled by the enigmatic figure who keeps turning up in the scene.

In **Tongues**, Irish writer Emma Murtagh packs a ton of terror into a brief flash fiction story. The protagonist is Maria, a talented polyglot text translator who's still at her otherwise empty office after hours because she works best in peace and quiet. A strange-looking, apparently mute, old man appears seemingly out of nowhere, shows her some indecipherable writing on a wrinkled sheet of paper - Maria doesn't know if it's even a language - and then, as she struggles to tell him she can't make sense of it, begins backing her into a corner…

Writer and rap artist **Dessa** focuses on the social and romantic challenges faced by an anomalous ghost in her wistful and bittersweet story, **Left of**

Heaven. Dessa's protagonist is different from the rest of her kind in that, as the product of a forbidden love affair between two other ghosts, she's never existed as a person - and as a result, not only is she shunned by much of the afterlife community, but she has no living lover left on earth over whom to obsess. So instead, she begins to invisibly haunt Matthias, a gentle Swedish man who doesn't know her, and may never get the chance.

In John Reaves' **A Ghost of a Smell**, a mild, middle-aged homemaker named Holly belatedly learns to stand up to her know-it-all bully of a husband through the guidance of her deceased Uncle Mike, who deploys an arsenal of odors to make his opinions known.

A Well-Urned Talent by J.P. Egry begins with the death of 47- year-old jazz pianist and composer Bernard. His grieving wife, Betty, brings home his ashes in the perfect receptacle: a miniature grand piano containing an electronic music box that plays recordings of some of his songs. Shortly thereafter, Betty discovers her own previously unsuspected talent for playing the piano - a boon that turns out to be quite a mixed blessing as she begins to understand that the urn is haunted, and that she owes her amazing new skills to a case of ghostly possession. When Bernard's old band invites her to take her late husband's place at the keyboards, Betty must decide whether to continue serving as his spirit's musical marionette - or cast his ashes to the wind.

Opposites attract - and then separate - in Scottish writer Ailsa Thom's **A Rational Explanation**. Thom's scientifically minded narrator works as a professional skeptic on a TV show called *Ghost Gumshoes*. Her job is to good-naturedly debunk the supernatural claptrap spun by Colin, the superstitious fellow who serves as her co-presenter - and secret lover - whenever they're filming on location in a purportedly haunted house or castle. One night, right in the middle of recording a show at "the most haunted castle in Ireland," our protagonist suddenly finds herself alone in the ancient, abandoned building, with not a trace of Colin or their crew anywhere to be found. But she's only a little bit worried, because she knows there's got to be a rational explanation...

Rebecca Emanuelsen's **Wilbur** is set in post-World War Two America, and its protagonist is Helena, a young girl with a couple of large preoccupations. One thing she spends time fretting about is fire - and that's understandable given that her cousin, Wilbur, and his father perished is a blaze that was sparked by her aunt's carelessly discarded cigarette. Her other worry has to do with the unexplained loud noises that emanate from the attic every night. As Helena's story progresses, the strong connection between these two concerns grows increasingly clear.

Rachel Wyman's steamy coming of age story, **Guédé**, features a struggling young dancer in New York City who falls in love with all things Voudou. Not long after she draws the image of a Voudou fertility spirit named Guédé and tacks it to her bedroom door, she meets Sugar, a much older man who not only bears a passable resemblance to her drawing but seems to know just what she needs - or at least, just what she needs to hear. But as befits a spirit, Sugar's presence in our protagonist's life remains frustratingly ephemeral, and her enchanted passion begins to give way to more complicated emotions.

What's spookier than meeting your own doppelganger? Meeting your own doppelganger on a crowded highway, driving a car that's identical to yours, right down to the scratch on the trunk. And what's spookier than meeting your own doppelganger on a crowded highway, driving a car that's identical to yours, right down to the scratch on the trunk? Meeting your *two* doppelgangers on that busy highway, both of them not only driving photocopies of your car but trapping you between them as you all go zooming along. After that, things *really* spin out of control in Carie Juettner's flash fiction piece, **Hindsight**.

When is a dream not a dream? When it's a *vision*. In Scottish writer Stuart Riding's flash fiction piece, **Kitsune**, our protagonist feels such powerful empathy for wild animals - his therapist tells him he suffers from a disorder called "empathepsy" - that no sooner does he fall asleep at night than he finds himself projected into the bodies of various creatures being pursued by hunters. As a result, not only does he repeatedly experience the trauma of being chased down and killed, but upon waking he feels terrible guilt for not having tried harder to escape.

Along with being a clever slice of metafictional magic realism, South Korea-based American Robert Perchan's flash fiction piece, **Compression: A Very Short Story**, is an extended literary joke. In order to fully appreciate it, you might need to review a few things about Ernest Hemingway, the pioneering literary stylist, short story master, and novelist. Mainly, you should understand that Hemingway was famous for a "compressed" literary style that involved writing tersely and omitting significant information that his readers were then compelled to infer from the pared-down text that he *did* leave on the page. Hemingway described many of his early works as literary "icebergs" in that most of their meaning lay "below the surface." So ...in his *own* story, Perchan sets a writer named "H." in a Parisian café and, through a delightfully compressed conversation with Perchan's narrator, shows him to be so obsessively consumed by compression that ...but, wait. I don't want to give it away. You need to read the story!

Yet another literary homage is **The Salish Sea Zombie** by Canadian A.J. Rutgers. In this case, the writer being honored with emulation is Herman Melville, author of *Moby Dick*. However, instead of a sperm whale, Rutgers' vengeful cetacean is a young bowhead named Y'bo'm K'ic'd. Oh, and Y'bo'm K'ic'd is *dead* - though still very active and glowing like a lantern, thanks to the incantations of Native American shaman Cal-my-Ish-met-al. Finally ... our zombie whale is extremely angry at humankind in general because of our pollution and pillaging of the Pacific Ocean, and he's especially furious at fishermen in particular because of having died a slow and agonizing death entangled in some carelessly discarded commercial fishing gear. Inevitably, the full wrath of the late white whale falls on one specific fisherman - though it's hard to feel sorry for Rutgers' version of Captain Ahab.

God Appears to the Fisherman by Matthew Stephen Sirois is the closing story in our anthology. The protagonist is Bob, a middle-aged man who is married to Heather, with whom he once shared a barnful of passion. Now what they share is a couple of grown and distant daughters, a lakefront home in Maine, and an around-the-clock alcohol habit. Bob amuses himself with fishing, while Heather amuses herself with the local fuel-delivery man. One morning prior to a visit from a daughter and her family, Bob follows his usual routine of heading out onto the lake with his boat, his fishing rods, and a bottle of Irish whiskey. But the fishing's poor, and when he hooks a series of yellow perch - "trash fish" - rather than the trout he's seeking, he executes each one by slamming it against the boat's engine. All at once, the fisherman's luck turns immeasurably worse as he finds himself lying stricken, semi-conscious, and quite possibly dying right there on the deck of a boat that's turning mindless circles in the water. Helplessly awaiting his fate, he flashes back over the highlights of his time on earth, and after he's finished, he "wonder[s] why there wasn't more." By this point, an immense being so majestic and terrifying that it "could only be God" has made a dramatic appearance - and through the very form it takes, confronts Bob with the irredeemable error of his ways.

For more information on the writers in this anthology, see **About Our Authors** on page 384.

Paul Guernsey
June 1, 2018
Unity, Maine

HOUSE GHOSTS
By Maura Stanton

USA

Meeting Time

The house was for sale. The house ghosts gathered in the basement that night to discuss what to do about it.

Emeline, a murder victim whose bones were still hidden in the backyard, sat hunched on the old futon, clutching her ragged shawl. She never talked, but she had large expressive eyes. With one other exception, the ghosts had been buried in coffins, and they sat on the moldy sofa, or on one of the folding chairs, just the way they used to sit in life. The other exception, Chloe, who'd been cremated, drifted about.

"Why are they selling?" asked Herbert, who always wore a fedora.

"The usual dissatisfaction." Jill swooped up one of the passing ghost cats. She thought it was the striped one but it was hard to see the cats. They were more transparent than human ghosts. The cat squirmed and wouldn't settle. Jill knew it wanted a warm human lap but she kept stroking it anyway until it fled.

"No, it's greed. It's always greed." Nikolas, who'd fallen off the roof when he was twenty-seven, went on to tell them that he'd heard the phone call to the real estate agent. Ostensibly, the current owners wanted a house with more land where they could raise a family. But the real reason was clear - they wanted a Jacuzzi and a three-car garage. He sounded scornful. He'd been a communist sympathizer in the '30s.

21

"I was hoping they'd have a baby," Chloe said. She glittered like sequins. She was more a shadow than a ghost, and the rest were glad they had bones somewhere.

Gladys, Herbert's wife, shook her head. "A live baby would be heartbreaking for little Oscar here." She was holding her grandson again. He'd choked on a rubber ball at the age of fourteen months. She held him up under his fat little arms and got his legs pumping up and down on her lap.

Herbert cleared his throat. "Look, here's the big question. They're selling the house. So, what do we do? Do we interfere? Scare off the buyers?"

"I'd hate to get some new people who fought all the time like that last bunch," Jill said. "They drove me crazy."

"Me, too," Herbert said. He rubbed his forehead with his fingertips as if he still had the headache that had predicted his aneurism. Gladys noticed. She stood up and put the baby down on the floor so it could crawl away. The floor was dirty, but the baby's nothingness could not be sullied by spider webs or cricket legs or dried up moths.

"Look," Gladys said, glancing around to make sure that everyone was listening, even Emeline with her glittering eyes. "We're ghosts, right? We should be able to control who moves in here. Here's what we'll do. We'll scare off the ones we don't like."

"Who do we want to move in here?" Chloe asked.

"We want a nice young professional couple who both work, like Bob and Suzanne. We want the house to ourselves most of the time, right? We don't want people with hobbies, or retirees, or teenagers. How would you like a garage band practicing down here?"

"I don't know," Chloe said. "Maybe some drums would be good for us."
The others looked at her with horror.

"Meeting adjourned," Herbert said.

Jill's Dreams

Jill had lived in the grey two story house when she was a teenager. She could have returned to several other houses or apartments or locations - even a beach - the instant a speeding car ran into her bike and killed her at a busy intersection, but she remembered being happiest in the house on Spring Street in the small town of Wander, now a bedroom community for the big city. The day she arrived, the house had looked almost the same, except for the new Pella windows. And the Norway spruce in the front yard was huge!

Herbert had met her at the front door that day. He'd put his arm around her. "I remember you," he'd said to her. "You're Jill Parker. You lived here for about four years. I'm sorry to see you here so soon - you're just in your late forties, right?"

Jill had nodded. "Will I always feel so cold?" she asked. She was shivering.

"You get used to it," he said. "But I have a surprise for you. Your cat!"

He pointed down at the black shape that was rubbing against her shimmering new legs. She stooped and lifted Ali Baba up against her shoulder. She looked into his wild yellow eyes and he looked back. He squirmed - he'd always hated to be picked up - and she let him down. He'd disappeared one day when she was fifteen and she'd searched the neighborhood for weeks.

"He was run over," Herbert said gently. "Just like you."

That day, after the meeting was adjourned, Jill drifted upstairs to see if there was anything she could do about the young couple's dissatisfaction. Suzanne, wearing a headband to keep her dark, curly hair out of her eyes, was doing Tai Chi in her bathrobe. Bob, wearing only boxers, was standing in the bathroom doorway, texting.

The couple had remodeled one of the bedrooms, the bedroom that used to be Jill's, into a walk-in closet. The room now contained built-in white pressboard shelves and drawers. There were two sets of sliding doors, his and hers, where they hung their clothes, and a big wall mirror. The old acorn-and-leaf wallpaper, which had pre-dated Suzanne's time in the room, had been torn off, and the room was painted pale peach. Jill looked out the window in her old room. The Norway spruce was scraping against the house. A squirrel sat on a bough eating a nut. One of the nice things about being a ghost was that you never scared off wildlife.

She waved at the squirrel, but it kept gnawing and chewing. She turned and waved at the mirror but once again she saw nothing but the room. Jill knew she didn't exist but it was hard to get used to. She had to keep testing.

Jill had a dream that she kept from the other house ghosts: she wanted to make a difference in death the way she never had in life. As a ghost she could do almost nothing, but ever since Bob and Suzanne had moved in she'd been breaking the rules of non-engagement and in secret ways encouraging them to be better and healthier people. She opened their magazines to articles about poverty in the Third World. She arranged their mail so that envelopes from Doctors Without Borders would catch their attention. She'd organize their digital TV channel lineup so that Nova would come on when Bob hit the control button instead of old reruns of Two and a Half Men. When Suzanne started gaining weight, Jill spoiled the milk (Suzanne was always making cocoa) and hid a box of chocolates in the recycle. One night she broke a full bottle of gin when Bob, already tipsy, tried to make himself another martini. He thought he'd done it himself, and in remorse gave up drinking for a month.

But she hadn't been able to do anything about the young couple's inchoate longings for something more. And they had so much! Good jobs, a nice house, vacations, a fridge stocked with yogurt and fresh fruit, veins pumping with blood.

They talked about having a baby. They talked about going to Australia. Bob thought he'd like to try scuba diving. Suzanne took up oil painting. She painted a still life with tulips, and a beach scene copied from the Nature Conservancy calendar, and a big jimson weed flower a la Georgia O'Keeffe. But she had nowhere to hang her paintings, she told Bob. That's why a larger house would come in handy.

Remembering this, Jill had an idea. She entered the bedroom and ducked under Suzanne's churning arms. Even though she could have drifted right through Suzanne as she did her Tai Chi, Jill always discreetly allowed the living to have some private space. The other ghosts laughed at her, but it was just something she felt sensitive about. Now she quickly knocked off the foam-backed poster of Maui that hung on the couple's bedroom wall.

"Here's some space," she shouted soundlessly.

Suzanne stopped her routine, her hands outspread in Passing Clouds. Then she dashed over and grabbed the feather-light poster and carefully rehung the scene of waves and surfers over the bookcase in the corner.

"Bob!" Suzanne called. "I want our new house to have a swimming pool!"

"Fine by me," Bob shouted from the bathroom.

Showings

When the real estate agent pounded the For Sale sign into the yard, the house ghosts joked about how they felt stabbed through the heart, but they were all feeling pretty grim about it. You expected life to change, but wasn't death a permanent state? Apparently not.

A lock box now hung on the front door.

Bob and Suzanne were at work when the first prospective buyers arrived. Herbert and Gladys stood in the living room by the fireplace, holding hands, watching anxiously as the perky blond agent, Marley, ushered an older couple through the door.

Retirees! Herbert and Gladys exchanged glances.

"This house was one of the Sears kit houses built in the 1920's," the agent was explaining. "It's never been added on to, so the shape is traditional. But it's been completely remodeled. Look at that staircase. Look at the exposed wood. And these floors! Aren't they great? Look at the proportions of this living room."

The old man had short grey hair. So did the woman. They were dressed alike in pale washed blue jeans and running shoes. The man wore a grey t-shirt. The woman wore a blue t-shirt and a padded vest.

Herbert hurried out to the kitchen and dripped the faucet. Gladys fanned a breeze across the bare neck of the woman and was gratified when she shivered and pulled up the collar of her vest.

Marley, the agent, chatted away. The couple said nothing. They stood in the middle of the kitchen, looking blankly at the big steel Sub-zero refrigerator. The man turned the handle on the faucet and stopped the dripping.

Upstairs, they scoffed at the bedroom-cum-walk-in closet. "Who has this many clothes anyway?" the man asked. The woman shook her head and zipped her vest higher. They looked at Bob and Suzanne's bedroom, at the

26

coverlet covered with shellfish, the Maui poster, and the bedside table lamps with conch-shell bases.

"They sure must like fish," the man said.

"Those stairs are on the steep side," the woman said.

Gladys and Herbert smiled.

At the next showing, a middle-aged businessman took pictures of everything to show his wife. He admired the Sub-zero refrigerator and spent a long time in the basement measuring to see how much space there was for his exercise equipment and his wine cellar. Chloe favored him, but Nikolas shook his head and made the lights flicker. He grinned when he heard the businessman tell Marley that it would probably cost a fortune to rewire the house.

Emeline

Emeline made them all nervous. She'd been murdered and buried on the lot before the house was built so technically she'd never lived in the house. Her bones were still out there under the forsythia bushes in the back yard. She wore a long dress and high-topped boots and a ragged shawl. Once she had opened the shawl, unbuttoned her dress, and shown Jill her stab wound. Jill had been shocked that she'd elected to keep such a horrible mark, for it wasn't necessary. The rest of them had chosen to resemble their favorite photos, so they saw each other as youngish and vital, which helped keep their spirits up. But perhaps Emeline had no photos of herself. She'd grown up in the 19th century. Luckily she spent a lot of time by herself in the furnace room. She'd sit with her back to the warm furnace for hours at a time. In the summer she roamed about rubbing her hands. She always brought a chill into a room when she entered. Back when Jill was alive and used to the live in the house as a teenager, she'd feel the chill but didn't know what it was.

Jill didn't know if Emeline just couldn't talk, or if she had chosen not to talk. But Emeline always came to the meetings, and she'd listen, and nod, and vote with the majority by raising her hand.

Venice

On the morning of their fifth wedding anniversary, Suzanne got out the album of honeymoon photos and sat down next to Bob at the table in the breakfast nook where he was eating his Cheerios and drinking coffee. Jill happened to be in the kitchen looking out the window, and she floated over to take a look.

Bob had to move his bowl aside so Suzanne could open the big leatherette album.

"Look, there we are in St. Mark's Square," Suzanne said.

Bob nodded. He pointed to another photo. "That's the café where we had Aperol spritz the first time, right?"

"And there's our gondolier. What was his name?"

"Luigi? Marco?"

"Don't you wish we were going back to Venice?"

Bob shrugged. "Not really. I think we used it up. I'd like to go back to Maui."

"Well, I'd like to go back to Maui, too. But Venice! That was a great trip."

"Did you make reservations for dinner tonight?"

"Yes, at Chez Charles. 7 p.m."

Bob got up to get dressed for work. Suzanne continued to look at the pictures and Jill looked over her shoulder. She'd never been to Venice, but she'd always wanted to go and she regretted not going now that she was dead. You were not allowed to go to places you'd never been before. You could only return to places you'd been. If only she'd known that when she was alive!

She stared at a picture of Suzanne standing by a canal. She was wearing a light skirt and sandals. She looked younger and happier than she did now.

Suzanne must have noticed, too. Abruptly she slammed the album shut.

Good News

Jill and Nikolas were reading in the living room a few days later when Suzanne, who'd just come in the front door from work, got a text message from Bob.

"Oh, my God," Suzanne squealed. She called Bob back. "Is it true? The loan's approved? We've got our house? So now all we have to do is sell this one. Why is it taking so long? Should we stage it?"

Suzanne continued on to the kitchen, still talking.

Nikolas shook his head. He was reading one of his own books, an invisible copy of Thorstein Veblen's *The Theory of the Leisure Class*. Jill was reading an early John Le Carre that Bob had inherited from his father. She'd stuck it hastily under a sofa cushion when she heard Suzanne at the door. She would have to sneak it back into the bookcase when she got a chance.

"We're screwed." Nikolas got up, stretching and frowning. "Some family with three noisy kids will move in here now."

29

"Kids mostly play video games these days," Jill said. "It's not that. I just feel bad for Bob and Suzanne. This is the perfect house for them, and they don't know it."

"Greed, greed, greed," Nikolas muttered. "Everyone wants more. They're destroying the earth, or haven't they noticed."

"They've noticed," Jill said. "But they can't stop."

She'd had this conversation with Nikolas before, and urged him to do something if he was so worried about capitalism and global warming and all that. But he'd insisted that since he was a ghost, he could do nothing. He was the past. He was there to be interpreted, but he could not act. Only the living could act.

"Can't we make *them* act?" Jill had asked.

Nikolas had laughed. "Shall we go *whoo*ing through the graveyard tonight? That'll get them moving."

Best Friends

Chloe and Jill had become best friends. They liked to sit out on the deck at night in the summer looking at the stars and talking in quiet voices about way, way back when they were still alive, and so dumb, so very, very dumb. It wasn't that they ever truly believed they'd live forever; they knew they wouldn't, it was just that somehow or other they'd gotten the notion that it didn't matter. Jill told Chloe about her messy divorce, and how her new vegan boyfriend from California had cheated on her, too, and how champagne, even real French champagne from Reims, could not compare in any way to a delicious cold grape Mr. Misty at the DQ on a hot summer night. She told Chloe about going green and riding her bicycle to work (yes, she always wore a helmet) and how she'd felt so tough and righteous when she sailed by cars stuck in traffic. And Chloe told Jill about the pills she took that made her feel calm and invulnerable, and how she had always loved driving fast on the freeway with the lights of other cars and big rigs streaming around her. She'd thought she had plenty of time to lead a life, or else that it didn't make much difference whether she died early or late. But she'd been dismembered in a car accident at nineteen, she told Jill, and cremated, and now she was stuck in the Midwest for eternity. No New York. No Paris or London or even Miami Beach. There was a house in Indianapolis where she'd once lived, so that was an option, but the house was crowded with disappointed Pentecostals. This house, which her parents had rented for a few years when she was a kid, was the best she could do.

"This house is pretty nice," Jill told her. "My first choice when the paramedics couldn't revive me was the beach on Marco Island where I once spent a week. But I've never seen so many doleful ghosts wandering along the edge of the water. There were thousands and thousands in bikinis or Hawaiian shirts or Speedos. There were so many they were passing through one another, hardly noticing each other, and all of them moaning and groaning louder than the sea. There was nothing to do but wander up and down looking at shells. And there was no point in picking up a shell. Where could you put it? And I couldn't get warm - you know how the sun doesn't penetrate us. So, I came here. Much nicer."

"This is okay," Chloe said. "I'm glad Bob and Suzanne like to watch House Hunters International. I hope the new people will, too."

Open House

The house was staged for the open house. Bob and Suzanne filled boxes and put many of their things into storage - extra pots and pans, linens, winter clothes. Jill was dismayed when Bob emptied the bookcase - the books had all belonged to his father - and carted the books to the library book sale so he could write them off on his income taxes. Jill had just discovered John Le Carre and now the books were gone. Nikolas told Jill that she could read

31

some of his invisible books, but they were all off-putting, out of date tomes like *Trade Union Wage Policy* by Arthur M. Ross or *Man's Worldly Goods* by Leo Huberman. Jill felt discouraged. Her quality of death had diminished.

Bob placed a bottle of French champagne on top of the wet bar and set out a few inviting glasses. Suzanne ordered a cheerful bouquet of yellow roses and daisies for the dining room table. They walked about, admiring their gleaming almost empty house.

"I'd buy this place," Bob said.

"Me, too." Suzanne grinned.

"So why are we moving?"

They both laughed. They went out the door. An Open House sign stood beside the For Sale sign on the front lawn.

The ghosts gathered in the living room. They sat down on the sofa and the love seat and the chairs. Emeline sat in the rocking chair.

"Why don't we open the champagne," Chloe said. "Somebody should drink it."

"Against the rules," Herbert said, adjusting the brim of his fedora.

"What rules?"

"You know what I mean." Herbert put his arm around Gladys. She was holding the baby. One of the striped cats and Jill's cat, Ali Baba, padded into the room. Various hands stretched out longingly to pet them but the cats undulated out of reach.

Gladys handed the baby to Herbert. She sat forward with a take-charge look on her face. "Listen," she said. "Somebody coming today is likely to make an offer on the house. We just have to make sure it's the right somebody. We've got to discourage the ones we don't like. Why don't we each take a room?"

"Good idea," Nikolas said. "I'll take the study. If I see somebody I don't like I'll make sure they see that big crack in the corner Bob keeps hidden."

"And I'll take the downstairs, the living room and dining room." Gladys pointed at the front door. "I'll evaluate them as they come in and let the rest of you know what I think. Herbert is good in the kitchen with drips and pipe-banging."

"I'll handle the bedroom," Jill said. "I'll open the window so they can hear the traffic noise if they're the wrong sort."

"And I'll take the walk-in closet," Chloe said. "It's easy to keep that light switch from working."

"Emeline?" Gladys looked to the rocking chair where Emeline was rocking back and forth, her hand on her chest wound. "Can you handle the basement?"

Emeline's eyes widened. She stopped rocking and nodded vigorously.

Summer Clothes

Jill rested on Bob and Suzanne's bed. She was waiting for a prospective buyer to come upstairs. Her eyes were closed. She pretended she was fifteen again. It was a summer afternoon with fresh breezes, not air conditioning, blowing across her brow. She had new, small breasts under her red tank top, and strong legs in short shorts, and a whole life ahead of her. So, what should she do differently?

33

Jill thought about it. Would she trust a condom and let Keith go all the way in his parent's basement? Probably not. Would she study harder for the chemistry test? Maybe. Maybe not. Would she try to be less sullen when her mother asked her to do the dishes? She hoped so. And maybe she'd try out for the swim team this time.

Then Jill sat up, feeling angry with herself. The life she was imagining wasn't that much different from the life she'd actually led. If she was going to do everything just about the same, what was the point? But there was no point, of course. She didn't have a second chance.

"Look, Jill," Chloe whispered. "Aren't I beautiful?"

Jill looked at Chloe, standing in the doorway wearing one of Suzanne's sundresses that she'd gotten from the walk-in closet. For a moment Jill only saw a colored rag and some dust floating in the air. Then she squinted and smiled until she'd forced herself to see a pretty girl with shapely arms pirouetting to show off the low back and the tiny straps.

Fire

It was Nikolas, looking down from the study window, who first saw the smoke. It seemed to be pouring out a basement window. He hurried downstairs to warn the others just as the alarms on each floor of the house blared and shrieked. Several prospective buyers were in the house, and Nikolas heard steps behind him on the stairs.

"What's going on?" someone cried. The real estate agent in charge of the open house, a friend of Marley's, began to scream.

"People, people! There's a fire. Get out, get out!"

"Did somebody call 911?"

34

"Yes, yes! Get out, get out. Is there anyone in the kitchen?"

Soon fire trucks were parked outside. Flames were shooting out of windows on the first floor, and firemen in masks were running in the door. The real estate agent and the prospective buyers were huddled on the lawn next door. Bob and Suzanne, contacted by the real estate agent, pulled up in their car.

"Oh, my God!" Suzanne screamed. She ran up to one of the firemen but he ordered her back. Something exploded inside the house. Two firemen were training a hose on the roof.

The ghosts were gathered in the street. They were all standing so close together that a neighbor looking out the window next door saw a strange cloud on the ground.

"We should have left her out of this," Jill said. "Emeline never lived in the house! It means nothing to her."

"She thought she was helping by setting the fire," Gladys said. "Oh dear, oh dear. Where will we go now?"

Soon the house was a shell. The main floor had fallen into the basement and only the top of the stairway dangled over the smoking damp hole. The upstairs rooms had only suffered water damage, but the windows had been blown out by the force of the water, and the contents were ruined. Suzanne sobbed while Bob talked to the insurance agent. The insurance agent talked of cutting them a check for temporary living expenses. The firemen surrounded the house with yellow tape and drove away.

Homeless

That night the ghosts wandered around the backyard. They all stayed away from the forsythia bushes, where Emeline was huddled with her bones.

35

"She just didn't understand the consequences," Gladys said, when the others muttered and glanced at Emeline angrily. "I don't think she was ever quite right in the head."

"Don't worry, they'll rebuild the house," Herbert said to the group as they floated through the tulips or rustled the maple trees. "They always do. If you don't mind hanging around a ruin for a few months, then all that construction noise, you can stay on here."

"But it won't be the same house," Jill said. "It won't be MY house."

Nikolas laughed. "You're dead, and you still call it MY house? Nobody owns anything. The living think they own things, too, but they're wrong."

Herbert cleared his throat. "Gladys and me and the baby, we're thinking of going out West. That's an option for us. We rented this apartment in Arizona once, and the baby visited. It's kind of small, but we don't need much room anymore. Less and less, actually." He looked down at the baby. "You know, when I was a kid I used to listen to Frankie Laine singing *Ghost Riders in The Sky* - and it never occurred to me I'd be one of those ghost riders myself one day."

"And what if the apartment gets torn down," Nikolas said. "Then what will you do? Live under a cactus?"

"Now we've always gotten along in this house," Herbert began, "in spite of different political views, and I think ..."

Jill cut him off. "Ali Baba! Where's Ali Baba?"

"There he is," Chloe said, pointing to a shadow near a bush.

Jill swept up her cat. She buried her face in his coolness. She thought about the shoddy apartment on the Washington beltway where she'd once lived with her husband, torn down only ten years after it was first put up, and the beach cottage in Santa Cruz that had been damaged in an earthquake. She'd spent a year there surfing with her rich and dippy but faithless boyfriend, and never wanted to see that cold ocean again. Her mother was still alive in a nursing home. Her father had gone back to Ireland after he died, but Jill had never been there so she couldn't join him.

"I'm staying here," she said, sitting down in the wet, dewy grass. "I'm not leaving Ali Baba again."

Chloe looked at her, nodding. "I'm staying, too. Suzanne's summer clothes are still up there in that walk-in closet. They just fit me, don't they, Jill?" She grinned. "They smell like smoke, but so do I." She laughed.

Nikolas pointed up. "And that's the roof I fell off."

Herbert and Gladys looked at each other. Then they looked at the others.

"OK, OK, I guess we'll stay, too," Herbert said. "You guys are family now. It'll be like camping out for a while."

"At least it's summer," Gladys said. "For now."

Herbert pointed up at the sky. "Look at those stars, will you."

Jill looked up. She was going to have to get used to living outdoors for a while and eventually forever, because someday there wouldn't be any houses left on the earth. She was glad that her sharp after-death vision cut through the light pollution and the foggy cloud cover. She marveled at the sky. It looked like it did not long after the Big Bang, the stars vibrating and singing on their way to the black edge of the universe and beyond.

37

A COMMUNITY SERVICE ANNOUNCEMENT
By Melanie Napthine

Australia

When the knock came, my first thought was for the baby, only just gone down. It wasn't till I had my eye to the peephole and registered the darkness on the other side of the door that it occurred to me to wonder who on earth could be calling at 11:30 at night. Not Darren, who was in Sydney for the week for work, and who I'd spoken with not twenty minutes earlier. Unfortunately, the globe in the porch light had blown a week or so back. Our house was also at the end of a court in a housing estate still under development. Half the houses on the street were nothing but framework and the street lights were up but not yet functional. So I could make out only a shapeless shadow through the peephole.

I opened the main door. The screen door was locked.

Two children stood there. One looked about fourteen - or perhaps gave the *impression* of being around fourteen might be a more accurate way to put it. He was probably only the size of an average ten-year-old, but his face was years older than that. There was no shyness in the eyes that met mine. Beside him was a small girl of perhaps seven or eight. She was staring past me into the hallway, like a possum stunned by the light.

"I was wondering if we could use your phone," said the boy calmly. "We've just gotten off the train and our parents were supposed to meet us, only they weren't there."

He spoke just a shade quickly, perhaps worried I'd close the door on him. His sister continued to look elsewhere, with a touching docility, as though he'd done a good job so far of hiding from her the fact that they were in any kind of trouble.

"Don't you have a phone?"

"It's dead." He took a blank-faced Galaxy from his pocket and held it up to show me.

"But ...do you live around here or ..."

"We live over there." The boy waved a vague hand.

There were a few inhabited houses on the estate, even three or four on our street. But we were the last house in the unfinished court and several streets away from the railway station. Which anyway I didn't think had trains passing through past 11 on a weeknight.

But they were just children. The girl's legs were bare and though it wasn't especially cold - early April - the air was sharp.

"What's your parents' number?" I asked. "I'll call them."

The boy said, "That's probably not a good idea."

"Why?" I glanced behind me. I'd fancied a small noise might have come from Milo's bedroom but in the silence that followed, it wasn't repeated.

It was the girl who said softly, "They'll be angry."

"Angry! Why?"

"Because you're a stranger."

I had to laugh. "But you knocked on *my* door," I pointed out.

The boy shrugged. Hard to tell in the dark, but I thought I saw a bruise-like shadow beneath his left eye, and a new possibility occurred to me.

"Why were - where were you anyway, that you're coming home this late at night? You weren't - were you - running away?"

I said it smilingly, and glanced away at the end of the sentence, so as not to frighten them by suggesting I attached much importance to the answer. Though already I was canvassing options in my mind: police, social services, my friend Immy who worked with homeless teens. It really was too cold for the girl's legs to be so uncovered.

But the boy answered me no. "We've been at our grandmother's."

Which, in the darkness, sounded almost too fairy-tale to be true. It was ridiculous to be wary of children, cold and lost. But their being at my doorstep at this late hour was so inexplicable, I had to look past them to the street for a car containing villains for whom they were the decoy. Or wonder if the well-spoken boy could possibly be a thug using his small sister for cover. If only Darren had been home! It wasn't my own safety I was worried about of course. I was newly enough a mother that everything seemed a threat to small Milo, so insecurely asleep in the room closest to the front door. But also, newly enough a mother that abandoned children tugged at my sympathy in a wholly unprecedented way. If that had been my lost son begging for help...

"Here you go." I turned the key in the screen door with one hand and cracked it; with the other hand I held out my phone to the boy.

He hesitated; it was the girl who took a quick step forward. For a wild moment I imagined she was going to charge past me and into the house but she stopped just short. She snatched the phone, then stared at it as if she didn't know what to do with it. The boy took it from her and began pressing buttons. The sounds the numbers made as they were pressed were startlingly loud in the silent night. I glanced down the road: our nearest neighbours were about five houses up and on the other side of the street, but all was dark at their place and there was no way of knowing if their car sat on the other side of the garage.

The boy had the phone to his ear. I could hear the ringing at the other end. It seemed a long time that the three of us stood there, listening to the amplified ringing of a phone who-knew-where, while a stiff wind stirred up dust from the construction site next door and sent a shiver up my bare arms.

"No answer?"

The boy shook his head.

The girl said, "I need to go to the toilet." Her knees were pressed together so as to catch her thin dress between them. The pattern on the dress was familiar: the Osh Kosh leaf dress from that autumn's range. This was not, then, a neglected child. But in between the intention to take a step back and hold the door open a little wider that she might pass, and the execution of this intention, a thought occurred to me.

"Where are your bags?"

"What?" A quick little shiver passed over the boy's face, which I read as irritation directed at himself for having been surprised into impoliteness, since he immediately corrected himself. "I mean, what bags do you mean?"

"That you took to your grandparents' place."

"We left them there," said the girl. Her trembling legs stilled, she straightened her dress with one hand.

"At your grandparents'? Why would you leave them there? Where do they live anyway?"

42

Like the girl's dress, the boy's sneakers looked expensive, though Milo was so many years from teenage footwear that the brand was unfamiliar to me. But if they were taken care of in the matter of clothing, their parents seemed cavalier about their children's physical safety. The question about their bags was like a link in a chain: it led to another and then another question, that I found myself firing at the pair in tones of equal wonder and exasperation as the extent of their parents' remissness started to become properly clear to me.

Because the looseness of their arrangements for their children, and their subsequent failure to seize their phone in a panic of worry and readiness for rescue, was beginning to look like conferring responsibility for those children onto me. And I was tired. Alone, but for a fractious, teething baby, for almost a week now, with a chaotic house not even completed yet (there was the new oven still to be put in, and the tiling in the bathroom, that had been shoddily done and needed replacing, and the driveway paved).

"Shepparton," said the boy, and the answer seemed outrageous.

"Shepparton! You've come all that way, just now? But you must have had to change trains. Why couldn't they pick you up from the city? Or put you on an earlier train? It's not safe to be travelling on this line, this time of night."

"There's only two trains. Early or late," the boy explained patiently. "Our mother works. She couldn't meet us if we arrived in the day." His calm answer seemed a rebuke to my spurt of irritation. But I wasn't out of questions, though the girl was shifting from foot to foot again.

"But why would you leave your bags?"

"She meant at the train station. They were too heavy to drag all the way out here. By ourselves."

The obvious question - why my house - was yet to be asked, but for whatever reason I was reluctant. Instead I wondered why they didn't try the other parent. Both looked at me oddly, as though I'd said something stupid.

I explained, "Whose phone did you just try? Your mum's? Or ..."

"Dad's."

"Well, can you try your mum's phone then? Maybe your dad has his switched off, or it's out of charge or something."

The girl looked at her brother. He must have confirmed something in some hidden way because she said then, "We don't have a mum. Just Dad."

Which put a totally new complexion on the matter. You didn't, obviously, expect of a lone father what you might of an intact family, or even of a mother alone. I thought how certain friends would cringe to hear me say it, how even Darren would argue that I was being sexist, but that was just how it was. I saw, now, how the girl's dress sat too high above the knee, that the boy's sandy fringe obscured his eyes.

"Well then. If he's not answering his phone, I suppose I should really call the police."

I didn't say it to frighten them. It was only the obvious solution. I imagined a distracted man, who worked long hours to buy expensive shoes for his children, who kept track of them as best he could, but who was liable, absent a wife or a secretary's help, to mix up dates and times, to forget to listen to phone messages. Possibly he wasn't even expecting them till the next day, or week.

But the children both said, "No," so quickly that my image of the man had instantly to be refined. The money was not strictly well gotten perhaps, or he was apt to forget himself in drink.

"Well," I said helplessly. "What then?"

"You could walk us home," the girl suggested quickly.

"We have a key," reassured the boy.

But then –

"You could bring your baby," the girl added, as though guessing the reason for my hesitation. But this wasn't the whole reason, and anyway -

"How did you know I have a baby?"

"Um." The girl chewed at the inside of her cheek.

The boy said, "I can hear him crying."

I listened: the wish of the wind, the faraway purr of traffic on damp roads, the tiny plash of one drop of leftover rain falling from the guttering.

"He's …"

Then it came, but as though from farther away than I knew he was, or else he was tangled in blankets perhaps - the sound of Milo sobbing. There was no explaining the dread that came over me then. The riot of images that tumbled in my head like a film I'd never consented to watch. Milo taken, Milo hurt - worse. It was just the surprise of it I suppose, in the quiet night and when I'd been just about to say -

"You can go and get him," said the boy.

"Can I use your toilet?" wanted to know the girl.

"I'll wait here," said the boy, as though to reassure me. To the girl he added, "But you'd better take Stinky James too. He must need to go."

"Who's Stinky James?" The words were out before I'd properly thought them, most of my mind on Milo, every nerve in my body attuned to his cry. I felt the very hairs on my skin bending toward his room just off the hallway. But wondering also what to do with these unusual, difficult children on whom I was somehow reluctant to turn my back but whom it would be strange and cruel to lock out in the cold while I cuddled my own child close. The boy took a half-step sideways; the girl looked down. I was stunned to see between them a smaller child, not more than two or three, wearing only a t-shirt and a nappy, mouth plugged by a dummy. His hazel eyes - nothing like his siblings' - were narrow with sleepiness, his shoulders slumped low. He swayed a little as he stood there. I couldn't understand how I'd missed his presence. It may have been dark, but the child's skin was pale as paper. And was any child so small so quiet for so long? Milo -

"That's what we call him," the boy explained.

"Oh God. Bring him in. He must be freezing. I can't believe - just wait in there," I pointed to the lounge room just off the front hallway, "while I get the baby."

If I'd been nervous at their apparent desire to get into the house, once the door was opened properly to them and I stood back to make way (glancing behind me towards Milo's room, still pierced by his cry, which was somehow louder with the door pulled wide to the bare, empty street), then their slowness to seize the invitation should have been reassuring.

The boy came first, the girl behind him, holding the hand of the youngest. Whose nappy, I noticed, sagged troublingly.

46

In his crib, Milo was scrunch-faced and feverish-looking. He'd worked himself up to the point that even my lifting him made no hitch in the rhythm of his screaming. I held him against my chest and felt my heart slow, just to have him safely against me. I shushed and rocked, and his crying seemed to float somewhere beyond me, a distant buzzing I barely heard and which thrummed the nerves not at all. I closed my eyes.

I don't know how long I stood there, rocking. I didn't forget the children but, with them out of my sight and Milo safely in my arms, the uneasiness I'd felt earlier seemed silly. It was odd, inconvenient, and a little sad, and I'd have been happier had Darren been there. But as tales of neglect went, really it was one of the milder, as opening the paper any day of the week would prove. They were fed, they were clothed - mostly - they spoke with the crisp diction of the well-educated. A father not coping - the loss of the mother was perhaps recent? - was really to be pitied rather than condemned. As Milo's screaming slowed to sobs, and then to a shuddering, even breathing, I felt my own shoulders loosen. I would lay my baby back down, go back out there and offer the children something to eat, a hot drink, have them try their father again and if that failed, call the police. I felt ashamed of my prior prevarication. My only excuse was the late hour and accumulated tiredness. But I would not want the world to know that three lost children had come to my door and almost been turned away into the cold night.

Milo flung his arms wide as I lay him down but then was still. I returned to the lounge room, quaking inwardly at every creaking floorboard, grateful for my visitors' quietness.

But they were not there. The house was aggressively quiet. I imagined them silently opening the bathroom cupboards, running dirty fingers along the labels of the bottles. But the bathroom was dark and empty. I moved down the hallway toward the kitchen, where I thought they might have gone in search of food. But I walked quickly, nerves alert, and somehow was not surprised to find that room, too, in darkness. I circled back to the lounge

room. Still empty, and I had to assume that they'd taken fright, or perhaps only gotten bored or restless while I took so long tending to Milo, and abruptly left. Or maybe I'd been had: I scanned the lounge for missing valuables - not that we had many - but everything seemed as it had been.
I thought to take a quick peek out onto the street, to see if they might be still standing uncertainly on the doorstep, or else hitting up any other houses further down the court. A black corner of my heart was grateful to have been relieved of the burden of dealing with the unwieldy problem, and if they had moved down the street, I didn't intend to call them back. If they pinned me to it, I'd help, but if they were willing to slide out from under my responsibility, I wouldn't hold myself blameworthy.

But when I put my hand to the front door knob, I found it locked. I knew I'd not locked it, had not even closed it, letting the children in. I'd been in such a hurry to get to Milo, I'd left it wide open for them to come in, and I'd moved down the hallway before the last of them had.

There seemed a thudding in my chest, strange echo of the knocking that had begun all this. I turned around, but the hallway behind me was still. I looked through the peephole to blackness but kept my eye there several long seconds. Because the next place I had to look was the one I couldn't bear to. My heart's knock slowed with my reluctant footsteps, pulled back down the hallway as though I were on a string. At the door to Milo's room, closed now, though I had left it open, I paused and listened, just listened, to the quiet reaching a crescendo.

THE LOSTLING
By Daniel Soule

Northern Ireland/England

A streetlamp flickered. Under the lamppost stood an old red phone box. In the old red phone box a black telephone was ringing.

Down the street came a boy. No one knew his name, or if they ever did they had forgotten it along with the boy. His clothes didn't fit him well - his coat was too big, his trousers too short. Dirt tried to gather under his fingernails, even though he had bitten them to the quick. He was filthy. He scratched from lice and carried a newspaper for packing under his clothes if the weather turned cold.

He was heading to one of his spots - a cardboard box and a plastic sheet, hidden beneath a tumbledown railway bridge as forgotten as he was.

The boy heard the telephone. The ringing grew louder and more insistent the closer he got. Overhead, the streetlamp flashed an orange warning against the night sky.

The boy stopped under the lamppost. He had nowhere to go, other than his cardboard box. There was no one waiting for him at the tumbledown bridge. He looked up and down the street. There were no cars with somewhere to go. No one walked their dog, picking up its mess. Teenagers didn't kiss on the corner, already ten minutes past their curfew. Only a rat was there to watch him disappear and reappear in the stuttering orange light. No one saw him. Nothing had changed.

His dirty, bitten fingers curled around the brass handle of the telephone box as he checked the street once more. Even a boy such as this, a forgotten soul, a lostling, knows to answer a ringing telephone. For if no one else was around, then surely the call must be for him as much, if not more, than anyone. Who else would a call be for, in a telephone box no one used, if not for the boy that no one wanted?

The red door swung shut behind him. Out of habit, he slid two fingers into the change slot, checking for unwanted coins. But no one used telephone boxes much anymore and in a few more years they would pass out of memory like so many things, like so many people. His other hand curled around the receiver, lifting it to his ear, to answer the call that must be answered.

"Hello?..."

The streetlamp stopped flickering. Beneath it, the old red phone box stood empty, the phone's receiver swinging in the silent night.

The Donegal Suite
By Lisa Taddeo

USA

Perhaps you want to know what happened in this room. I can tell you it was dreadful for me to watch, but I had to make sure it went as planned. Now my stomach is turned. My guts are runny like *stracchino*.

The room will be haunted from now on, and nobody will guess why. There will be multiple children conceived, but they will end in miscarriages. They will have been baked at too high a temperature. I did not get to have my own child. I did not get all the things you are supposed to have, so that you can leave this world in peace.

I'd thought the woman I chose was going to be easy on me. It took years to find her. The nice thing is that she looks like me - a bloated, American version. Kind, big and sad, with poo poo eyes. With her cat and her books and her collection of copper pots. Part of it was, I felt sorry for her. I talked to myself, I said, You are also doing a service for her. *Questa povera cagna.*

But let me tell you what I know now. Even the fat sad ones - especially the fat sad ones - they have spent so much time dreaming of the moment they will have the man they covet. They watch *pornografia* and on top of touching themselves and thrusting like lonely cows, they are also learning. They are becoming *dee del sesso.*

Sex goddesses.

 I don't know, in the end, what was in my control, and what was in hers.

—

Denise woke to her Scottish Highlands alarm. The sound of bagpipes cresting some emerald mounds into a fairytale sky. She snuggled deeper into her tartan bedspread, scuttling her toes like sand crabs into distant swells, savoring the moment. There are few mornings, after all, that one wakes to fulfill her destiny. She felt fat and warm.

She imagined all her married friends, who'd left their prefab homes on Thanksgiving night, painted on their yoga pants and drove in the unfathomable night to Hooksett, to the Target gleaming like an art installation in the coffin-still parking lot. When you are married, you go to Black Friday sales. When you are single, you sleep in, and wait for Cyber Monday.

Denise has rich kinks of dark hair. She isn't Jewish but her hair is. She's twenty-five pounds overweight but she doesn't lumber around, so she's not one of those fats that rankles. At a party, in a kitchen, you wouldn't feel stuck talking to her, over by the Camembert. If you saw her talking to a good-looking man, you wouldn't feel bad for the guy. But also, you would know he was not trying to sleep with her. If you were the man's wife, you wouldn't feel nervous, and you would continue sipping your Pinot Grigio with the sort of reckless summer night laissez-faire that's only available when your man is accounted for.

Denise's house is cozy and has excellent pillows. Both intricately decorative ones and long soft down ones for sleep. She lives in downtown Portsmouth, New Hampshire. Lots of old streetlamps, and the requisite chocolatier. Nothing about her house is homely. One time a rather vicious married friend said something about homely people wearing lots of scarves and necklaces and stuff, to jewel themselves up, to make themselves more interesting.

She does puzzles, expert ones with tons of pieces that go on to spell a Matisse. She seldom dines out. She doesn't need to; she cooks like a dream, poutines and crackling roast chickens and vertiginous grilled snappers with curling vines of thyme. Her place smells like a Williams -Sonoma magazine spread. She drinks a max of two glasses of wine. She has a nice computer with a princely screen that the cat, Princess Huega Peugeot, massages her spine against. The downstairs bathroom has red brocade wallpaper. If it were your life's goal to be cozy and well-fed every night of the week, and to take long, luxurious poos in a bathroom with pomegranate potpourri, then you would do well to live in Denise's home, forever.

Denise is not exactly single. Denise has a love, a warm and striking, red-headed and blue-eyed one, with the kind of jaw you could crack open a chestnut against. He's from Scotland, has 121K followers on Twitter. Which isn't a lot but it's not a little. His primary cause is mesothelioma and also, #DontbombSyria.

Jon Abercrombie!

When you hear that Denise has a love, and the love is Jon Abercrombie, you are going to put the pieces of the puzzle together, the cat and the pillows and the town of Portsmouth and you're going to say, Oh I get it.

But it isn't like that. Denise isn't just some homely fan with sticky underwear. This is not some sad tune about a fan girl worshipping posters of a hot movie star. Yes she masturbates to him riding a unicorn to a forest clearing where he ravishes her body, but. But this is an adventure tale. This is about Cupid's arrow pinging its target smack in the gonads. This is about getting what you deserve in life.

Denise works at the finest inn in Portsmouth. The Edmund Victoria. Mostly it exists for the rich parents of UNH students who come to visit their limber pothead children. Superior rooms start at $595 a night. The suites, $1200. Mismatched but expensive settees in the baroque lobby. Golden tassels hanging like the spangled nuts of kings from the drapery. The couches are the color of young girls, vicious little pinks, and the armchairs are the color of women, a lush but fatigued ruby.

Denise is the manager which, at a small luxury inn, means that she is the everything girl. She coordinates the Brazilian housekeepers. Answers the phones. Deals with every manifestation of shock that gasps from the other end of the line when she tells callers the price of a room. A funny yet predictable thing happens when you work in the service industry. You can't afford a $595 room, but you start to look down on other people who also can't. And you learn to hate the people who can, while also agreeing that they are better than you. Denise fell into this trap only on truly rotten days. Only on days when the distance between herself and her dream life felt like it stretched into infinitum. Like, for example, the very terrible day last month when the Viking Kings Meet & Greet at the Comic Con-X that was scheduled for THIS VERY DAY in Providence was almost canceled on account of a terrorist threat. Denise only heard about it because her friend Mary Sue is married to a Providence cop. Mary Sue treats Denise's love like it's fan girl obsession. Anyhow she told Denise that Jim told her that a threat had been logged for Comic Con-X. She knew Denise planned on going but she didn't know there was, like, a Plan.

Luckily, three days later, the terrorist was uncovered to be a thirteen- year-old dipshit who was pissed about not being picked as a volunteer for the Comic Con weekend. Something about his heroes letting him down. He had a Walmart-bought hunting rifle in his possession, plus a chart of the attack, or so Jim told Mary Sue who told Denise.

Denise was too old and removed to understand that angst. *Come talk to me*, Denise thought, *when you are thirty-five and the love of your life wears armor across his crotch, both literally and figuratively. Come talk to me when you are a virgin, and so is your cat, because you are untenably afraid you will be jealous if Princess Huega gets laid, before you do. Murder should exist at the discretion of virgins over thirty-five, not thirteen-year-old punks who've never suffered.*

Denise is a virgin, not because nobody has ever wanted to take it down. There are plenty of men, one would imagine. The world is full of men who will have sex with you. But Denise doesn't drink a lot, doesn't hang out in bars at the hours when people start pairing off. And face it, who goes on dates anymore? Only the truly beautiful, and exchange students.

The mission is Denise must lose her virginity to a movie star. This has always been the mission. Even the night in the Toyota with Thomas. Even then, Denise knew his thing wouldn't go into her thing. She might touch it, sure. Big whoop. Some sophomore's small-medium and the stench of ecstatic ball in her hands. The smell of someone who wants something badly but not badly enough that he'll wash up before he goes after it. She knew even then it would end before it started. That she wasn't giving it up for anything less than a movie star.

The movie star used to be Jonathan Brandis, and after that it was Kevin Costner, and after that it was Brad Pitt. But now those guys are either dead or married. Same difference. Anyway, they have grown up past her fantasies. They seem silly-sweet now and antiquated, like Fun Dip.

She's known about the Meet & Greet since early September. She's lost four pounds. She'd hoped to lose fifteen, but you know with these things. The nerves can make you hungrier. They can make you anxious at midnight. For a bit there she got into the habit of taking a sleeping pill around eight, so that she wouldn't be tempted to eat after dinner. She has a few doctors and they each prescribed her a different one.

But the sleeping pills only took the edge off the anxiety, and by ten she'd be wide awake and jazzed, walking around her house in her fuzzy socks and opening up the Make Love Not Porn window on her Mac and watching Love&Lasagna - her favorite real-life couple - go at it against the tormented corner of a velveteen couch. This week, Love&Lasagna were on a road trip across the country, and when they finally splurged on a hotel in Michigan, they really let loose. Lots of fervent Frenching and hard-driving intercourse. They were both originally from Mexico City, tan faces and slim, muscled buttocks. Denise wondered why they moved to the States.

She wondered if it was for Love's job, or Lasagna's. She was really interested in stuff like that. The minutiae of a relationship. Having never been in one, she always wondered how does it feel to be able to touch the nape of someone's neck while they're driving through a mountainous region, and not worry that they will recoil, or think you are weird. How does it feel to treat someone else's body as though it were an extension of your own.

–

Jon Abercrombie wakes up - *yargh* - stretches his arms like Christ the width of his hotel bed. Feels much-ballyhooed jawline. Has series of pimples, little bony horrors, on account of shaving and tiredness and gin and tonic before bed in lieu of a good hot shower, etc.

Outside his hotel he hears the Salvation Army bells toll. He runs a hand through his flowy and fiery hair. Often, he is hysterically aware of the things he does. As though a small army of his screamy fans are watching from the closet with the fold-out ironing board and the crummy pillows. He thinks of how silly things like running a hand through his mane could elicit a bunch of girls to tweet, My lady parts just went *boiiiiinnnnggg*.

Sometimes - like right this moment - to amuse himself, he strides all supreme-sex-god-like to the shower. He's nude of course, because sex gods sleep in the buff, naturally. He looks in the mirror at his form and clasps his hands at the nape of his neck, then fans the fingers down the sides, into the warm hard divots of his clavicle and out to the edges of his shoulders, which are sore from lateral raises plus raising the bar for his entire gender.

He turns on the shower. The water pressure is like what happens after you sneeze. The whole place is shitty, down to the towels that spread water, instead of absorbing it. If people think being a celebrity means luxurious accommodations every time you travel then they'd be dead wrong. The truth is some small cities, the best they can do is Marriott-level. The problem with America is that it's undone by its chains. It's like all the chains got together and agreed to be mediocre, to serve pancakes at midnight to compensate for bathrooms built for the blind. The bedspreads - Jon imagines God said to a jilted wife, "Here, design the linens your husband and his mistress will have to sleep in for the rest of their lives."

Look, Scotland wasn't a world-beater in the accommodations arena. But in Scotland Jon didn't expect anything. If he were still in Scotland, he would be fifteen pounds heavier and taken up with the harried older sister of one of his school chums. But America makes the mistake of telling you what it got you for Christmas; in frigging August it gives you the wink-wink. By the Epiphany you're out on the curb with the Douglas firs, holes in your socks and crabs in your pubes.

Pish. It doesn't bloody matter. For some people celebrity is the be-all. Even where he's at right now - a Starz period show is not exactly George Clooneyville - a lot of his friends back home eating beans from a can would bugger a hog to replace him. But for Jon this sort of "win" is not what he was aiming for. In fact, he'd been traveling down this path the way a med student might intentionally develop a perishing heroin addiction. Jon knows that celebrity is deadening. Of course, life itself is a scourge. We are nothing but disease disseminators. We spread virulence by having babies, by inoculating them against measles but spooning terrific doses of heresy and bigotry and moral dissolution into their gaping toothless maws.

Jesus Christ, says Jon Abercrombie to the ceiling, his arms supplicant, his beautiful body lit by nothing but Marriott gloom. Because he was used to doing it - because he had been doing it every morning for a number of years, he said – "Please God take me today, I cannot bear this world another day."

–

Two rough gents sit in a bar outside Glasgow. The pub is strung with colored lights. They look at their own faces reflected in the green glass behind the tall old bottles of liquor. They look older in the mirror than in reality, must be. One man has a beard to make up for his hollowed face and the other a blacked eye. It's a dreich day - two hours past lunch which is

59

the deadest time in the land and it's pouring like animals and there's no one on the streets and they've been in there since coffee. The bartender whose name is Fiona if there ever was one, does the thing girl bartenders in male places do best - acts like she can't hear or see nothing. Which tricks the gents at the bar into thinking it's true, that she only animates the moment they need her.

"Anither tae o' whiskys, love!"

Fiona nods, sets down the game on her phone, fulfills the request with sluggish efficiency. She wears all black against a bloodless face.

"Right Baltic in here," says the bearded one, hunching his shoulders and looking left to right, like everyone's a cheapskate but him. He says it louder so Fiona can hear: "Pumpin' cauld in 'ere!"

"Keeps the floors from howlin," says Fiona, absently, having already returned to Jelly Belly Pastel Crystals, or what have you.

On the telly overhead, a familiar face fills the screen, his locks of red hair whooshing out past the corners of the 27-incher.

"Aye thare he blows! Fuckin eejit. Fuckin pretty boy fucko." The bearded one downs his whisky.

The black-eyed one shrugs his shoulders. They are roommates the men, at that ripe point when the realization that they can't live without each other - fiscally and emotionally - collides with the bitter day-in-day-out hatred of one another.

"Aw whit nae, whit did ye dae that fur?"

"Nuthin," says Black-Eye.

"It's nae nuthin, whin ye shrug yer goddamned shoulders lik sae. Whit th' fuck - yer impressed by that simpering fucko, actin holier than us, lik' a bloody sassanack, a fuckin bonny laddie. Yer fuckin impressed, yer mum's fuckin impressed, th' hail toun is a bunch o' star-fuckin arseholes."

"Shut it," says Black-Eye. And Fiona comes round, sets down two drafts, because a female bartender needs to know how to wind her male customers down, keep them sated but not on the hard stuff. She steals a glance at the screen. Jon Abercrombie, not quite an old flame but they tumbled about six times. Girls like her could tell you a thing or two about who has a chance at stardom, by the way they are in bed. Let's say, Jon Abercrombie deserved his success. Let's keep it at that.

"I'll shaw ye whit tae shut. Fuck's sake, yer in loue wi' him, tae!"

Black-Eye looks right at his friend and enunciates clear as day: "Shut. Yer. Geggie." Then he looks down and says something else under his breath, right down into his mug of beer.

"Whit's that! Ho! I said whit's that ya said?"

Black-Eye lifts his fish-white face. On the telly Jon Abercrombie was shaking hands with Nicola Sturgeon. His dimples shone as he ran his hands through his fire-red hair. Nicola and the world blushed. You couldn't hide from celebrities these days. Not even in armpits in Crookston like this one, not even in your own toilet bowl; you tried to hide too much and you might poo your man's likeness into your own yellow water. Next to the bowl, by the way, is the wastebasket, and every month it was a forsaken battle between these two fellers, who would be the one to crouch down and empty the pile of scum. Whose slag had left bloody tampons in there that week, who had balled up a piece of shit paper and thrown it in the basket by accident. So, nobody emptied it, and they would each have to balance their Q-tips atop shards of toilet paper or slide a string of floss into an open slit in the refuse. Garbage Tetris.

"I said whit's that you said!"

"I said," says Black-Eye, "Mebbe he deserves it."

"Noo jist haud on!"

Fiona lets loose a grin.

"Whit's that ya mean, he deserves it? Deserves what? Deserves to prance aroond like a goddamned pony, lik' we'ur exportin a bunch o' bonny wee jimmies lik' we ..."

"He deserves it! I said!"

The bearded one turns to his own mug, chastened by his friend, the quiet one, who when he speaks he means it, you know the type. The single black eye, learn from it - means the other guy looked worse. "Yer aff yer heid," says the bearded one, quietly, having lost his verve.

"Why does he deserve it, then?" says Fiona.

"Thit man," says Black-Eye, pointing at the screen, "haes hisself the brokenest o' goosed hearts."

"Aw noo this I'd lik' tae hear!" says the bearded one. "Och gang oan then!"

"Rent, richt doon th' middle!"

"Zarrafact?"

"It is indeed."

"Well tell us then! Don't keep us mystified 'ere!" says the bearded one, looking at Fiona, like they are on the same team.

And so Black-Eye leans forward into his drink, as Scottish men do, and holds forth, as Irish men do, and enunciates, as Englishmen do, and exaggerates, as all men do, and tells the origin story of their fellow townsman.

You see, four score minus four score plus seven years ago, Jon Abercrombie was a youthful twat of twenty-eight, deliciously, frankly, untouchably, unicornally in love with a gorgeous Italian vessel of muliebrity.

Caterina!

She had to be seen to be believed, this lass. Even the scoundrels he rolled with didn't make a peep when they met her, didn't make any unseemly advances or grab their treacherous mounds. Nary a one whistled. The kind of gorgeous that is quasi beyond sexual desire.

Visiting her uncle who is the Principal of the University of Glasgow, is how she meets Jon. Dark coils of hair, everything about her rich and drenched. An angel. Blue-eyed and black-haired, they don't make them like that anymore. He's playing darts in a bar like this one, she's in there with her cousin and the rest is just. You know, eyes locking across a room and of course they would. The only two heavenly creatures in the town and they slammed together as magnets do. Jon at the time is a stage actor. He is going to give it up, it's too tawdry a profession, even the stage he says, for Caterina. He is going to become a scholar, or a lumberman, something noble. She calls him Jonny, his friends can't believe it. Jonny, they mimic, twinkling their jealous eyes up at him and he cuts them a stone look. Only she calls me that, he says. After her visit is over, she returns to Fiumana. She can't get involved with an actor! Her kin is university folk. For two months he courts her with gilded letters. He's depressed like you wouldn't believe. He's angry like someone who knows it isn't going to end well. Finally, she comes back to him. They move into a flat the size of a refrigerator in Glasgow for the run of his show. They are the couple everybody hates. True love all the time. Tongue kissing at the newspaperman. Hand-holding during tooth-brushing time. He proposes during a romantic weekend to the Cotswolds. Under a tree overgrown with good-looking moss. All of Britain quickened its pulse that day. It's a goddamned fairy tale, a terrific love story. And then …

"An then? An then whit?"

"An then," says Black-Eye - Fiona, too, is on the edge of her figurative seat - one night, Jonny's prepping to go on stage in Glasgow, Caterina is walking from their flat to go watch him. It's to be one of the last shows in his life. He's giving it up after this weekend, they are going to Fiumana so that he can meet the whole fam. And she's walking to watch her love, and she's carrying a red rose, and she's lost in her head is what the rags will say, because God forbid we blame our own drivers, and she's walking across a street and moonlight is twinkling and the world is right and you really can't ever turn your back in this life and *thwap*. She's hit by a gone-to-hell Astra and sails up like a football. And that's the long and short of it. She's buried in the Cotswolds, at the site of their engagement, at the loveliest swell of an emerald hill over a babbling brook the color of her eyes and they say that after that, Jon Abercrombie buried himself in the filthy show of it. Went right after the scum-heart of it. To die in the center.

"Bugger me," says the bearded one.

Fiona shakes her head, daubs some milky tears from her gothic lashes.

"Sae lea him th' bugger alone, ken? Ye dinnae blether aboot men wi' goosed hearts, if they're nae 'ere tae defend themselves."

Nobody says anything, for a good long time. The whisky comes out like something with a discernible soul. Fiona pours two on the house and one for herself. On the telly overhead, Jon Abercrombie is riding a black horse straight toward your nose. The hooves are loud and extreme, *clip clop, clip clop*. Jon's hair is blowing, his bare knees are sex, and his heart, you divine, is nowhere to be found.

—

The closest Denise has ever come to a relationship was on two occasions, both sad-making, in varying degrees.

The first was a hand job she performed while in college. After a date of Reubens and beers, a sophomore named Thomas drove her back to her dorm in the sprinkling snow and parallel-parked smoothly in a spot without a streetlamp. He stopped her midway, took her hand in his and licked the curved strait between thumb and index and then nodded like, You may proceed.

The other, was Joel. Joel. The name is still a burr.

Joel was the editor of the *Portsmouth Star-Herald*. Editors of small-town papers. When they're men. There's a certain ... Had they pictured themselves debonair international writers, dark scarves flung across square shoulders, penning essays from musty cafés in Paris and romancing failed and green-eyed Brazilian models? To cover up the desire they grew beards. They became so involved in their small-town paper and the lives of the fellow citizens they chronicled and feigned to love, that you could never accuse of them of having failed at life.

Denise met Joel at a dinner party, two Christmastimes ago. They were seated beside each other. The hostess, a divorcee named Jacqueline, was one of those dinner party throwers who firmly believed in seating spouses separately, and boy-girl-boy-girl formation all the way around a rectangular West Elm table. Denise knew hostesses who did this were just sad people who didn't love their husbands or didn't have one and wanted yours. Still. It rankled. Jacqui sat on the other side of Joel and the freezing thing was that she'd chosen Denise as the girl to his left because Jacqui was trying to land Joel. Joel was one of Portsmouth's Most Eligible. He had a

65

Harley and gave great e-mail. Did Denise know? That she was the type of single girl in her early thirties that another single girl in her early forties would not fear? If she did, then she braved it well.

In any case, Jacqui scared Joel with her intense gaze. She put her red-nailed hand on his thigh so many times the gesture lost its impact. She freaked him out right into a *tête-à-tête* with Denise that lasted from appetizers (a sweating plate of salumi and some courgettes stuffed with meat) through dessert (eclairs from down the street and a rhubarb pie baked by Jacqui's also-divorced mother).

Denise was pretty enchanted that night. Joel was smart and funny and very charming and thoughtful. She doesn't act like a virgin, or like someone with a cat. And she's more than her job. She's not merely the manager of an inn. She could run her own place, if someone threw some capital her way. They exchanged e-mails under the crisp awning of Jacqui's townhome. The streets were shining with rain. For a moment it seemed the evening wouldn't end. Denise actually went into her brain and rejiggered the promise. The movie star promise. Joel might not be a movie star, but he was a real man. An editor. A kind and well-dressed and well-traveled interesting man.

But then Joel looked down at his phone. Some buddies had texted, they were hanging at Fat Belly's down the road, catching the last half of the game.

"That sounds like fun," Denise had said.

Joel said, "Yeah, maybe I'll go meet them. Did you want to come?"

Did. It means something. Words mean something, even among the stupid but certainly among the editors. Did versus Do. What can you trust if you can't trust your own gut?

"No thanks," said Denise. They said goodbye with an awkward little embrace, and she walked home. She fed Princess Huega and drew herself a Lydia Lonelyhearts bath. She looked at her toes poking up through the suds. There was nothing wrong with her feet. If you saw them alone, you might think them the feet of a beautiful woman. She toweled off and got into some excellent new pajamas she'd bought online. She slippered her feet into a pair of sheep-fur clogs. She brewed a cup of Honey Vanilla Chamomile tea and took a nice sweet sip. "Life wasn't so bad, right Princess Huega?"

—

Tonight is the night. She can feel it in her bones. The coincidence is magical. This is the first year Providence has had a Comic Con offshoot and look, it's not like Denise wouldn't have traveled to a Meet & Greet in Boston, or even New York, but in very big cities Jon would likely have friends he knew, or people to show him around. It's in the smaller cities that celebrities can be caught off-guard. They have nothing better to do and will take a chance on something offbeat.

Denise spends her morning attending to her Fraser fir. First she makes a fire and Princess Huega helps set the mood by perching from the mantel and pawing at the hung Pottery Barn stockings. Feeling benevolent, Denise reaches into Huega's stocking and removes a packet of catnip, shaking it onto the parquet floor. Huega flings her soft body at the pile.

On Denise's four-poster bed, her special outfit is laid out, down to the underwear. The undies and the bra are white lace, by Kiki Di Montparnasse. They are sexy without being tawdry. On top of that she has a light grey cashmere sweater dress, a pair of dark Wolford tights, and a pair of exquisite mid-priced riding boots. She used a Deva Curl on her hair last night so the kinks are soft and look luxuriously fucked-upon. She purchased a special soap like a giant emerald, plus a new solid perfume from one of the specialty shops in town. Denise predicts she'll feel as close to beautiful as she ever has. For a long time, she has felt like total garbage. She buffers herself with all this cozy stuff, but inside it's a cold pile of rebar and scrap metal and used books and Container Store plastic tops missing their bottoms.

Joel's a big part of what's made her feel shitty in the past few years. It's rare for a woman in her early thirties to have that sort of night where the conversation just clicks, and there are so many smiles and laughs and you are just sitting next to some man, with gabardine trousers and a winter scarf, eating course after course. For the seven days after Joel left her for a bar, Denise watched her phone. She left her phone for ten minutes, then thirty, then one hour, and came back to it thinking, now he will have texted. But he never did. She couldn't contemplate why he wasn't getting in touch.

By the eighth day she was eating slices of yellow American cheese on the toilet. She had stopped performing as though an unseen beau were watching. She had stopped Googling to see if there'd been a murder on the streets last week. In fact, as the editor of the newspaper, it was quite clear that Joel was alive and well. The *Star-Herald* came out on schedule. The Holiday Edition shone in the sunlit snow inside her mailbox. A tattoo of Christmas lights adorned the rim of the front page. Denise vomited curds of processed cheese and bile, three times. She cleaned the toilet with fancy bleach after each gutting.

On the ninth day, she thought, perhaps we are on different schedules. Her stomach was clean of cheese. Her energy was high. Her wits, she believed, were dependable. So, she sent a text! And, NOTHING.

Every day she felt the nothing of it, like poison in her green smoothies, like an imbalance, like too much kale. And of course, in the way that happens, she saw him everywhere, from afar. In the popover café, in the card store, in the grocery store, and worst of all in the bookstore. He'd be at a table reading the papers from other cities, with a mug of coffee to stay, and people would walk over and he'd be holding court, and Denise would hide and watch from a corner and think, how silly of me, to think I was anything more than the best thing around for a few hours. And then a more terrible thought - Was he only being kind, was he just trying to give me a thrill, taking care of the lonely girl? A public service, a charity, the great small-town newspaperman Jimmy Stewarting her at the West Elm table, feigning exultation when she knew what Brillat Savarin was!

She never saw him with another woman, so even the theory that he'd met the love of his life at Fat Belly's that night, right after sending her that text, some amputee do-gooder with green eyes, even that couldn't be true. The truer truth was that she meant less than she thought, to anyone in the whole world.

But forget it all. It doesn't matter, because her clothes are laid out on the bed for the rest of her life. She's not delusional. She's steady as she goes.

Denise opens her computer and has a slice of American cheese folded around a pickle. She eats when she's not hungry and doesn't when she is. It's not a diet, it's a sort of life. On Facebook there are no Friend Requests, but there are two messages. One is from an acquaintance, a married woman named Clare who is inquiring whether she might be able to get her - Denise's - employee discount at the Edmund Victoria, so that she and her husband might spend a romantic New Year's Eve weekend.

The second message is the absolute worst thing that can happen to Denise. She brings a hand to her heart, as she believes it must have stopped beating. The next-to-worst thing is the clothes on the bed. They are small, woolen children. Their parents have just been killed in a plane crash. Someone will have to tell them. Their future, the picking of berries, the gifts wrapped in glossy paper, has just been withdrawn.

The event is canceled. Denise's life is over.

—

In Jon's room his cell phone rings. His publicist.

"Hi love," she says. Her name is Valentine. Pronounced Valenteen. She isn't French.

"Yeh," he says.

"I have news I think you'll like. The Meet & Greet is canceled. Another threat. This one legit. They already found one pipe bomb at the convention center."

"Feck."

"I thought you'd be pleased."

"So uh. onto New York then?"

"Well ...no. Portland, Maine is tomorrow. The DVD release."

Jon doesn't make any sound. It's the only power he has anymore. Except with publicists. With publicists, silence gets you nowhere.

"Okay love? So one more night? But the good news is, Providence is a great town. Big foodie town. Let me show you around. I went to school here."

Jon looks about the sad room. He has sad thoughts. He can't spend another night.

"No," he says. "Get me out of here. Get me to Portland."

"Oh, I tried, love! There are no flights, nothing is moving. A storm is coming! We'll have fun, I promise, let me ..."

Jon shakes his head violently; though she can't see it, he hopes she can feel it. It takes so long to get back to happy, and once you get there, it's only a matter of time again. And you begin to see the cycle of it. He knows because he lost his mum. Then his dad. Then his love. The fact that you survive each time is probably the worst of it. The inconsequence even, of tragedy. This is the most terrible room of all.

"No!" he screams. "Get me out of this room. Get me someplace else, anywhere else! Halfway there! I can't stay here. I hate this place!"

On the other end he can feel her believing he is irrational. They still want to fuck you, even when you are irrational. But she won't help him, unless he turns petty. The only way she can understand is if he embodies the stereotype of his kind. People don't want to be surprised, even positively. God help us everyone.

"Listen," he says quietly, as though every muscle in his body is not seizing in rage. "You gotta get me out of here, I can't sleep one more night on this goddamned bedspread. It's so ...cheap."

—

It begins to snow in New Hampshire. There is no better place in America to worship a snowy evening, than from inside the Edmund Victoria. Out there the first fritters are landing delicately on the linden trees and chestnut trees and magnolia trees that flank the walking path. Just inside the library, there are leather-bound books and hand-cut crystals on antique trunks and marble-topped tables. Everything is burgundy or hunter green or bronze. Even the old crusty parakeet, a terrible fuck named Steve, is green, and his cage is a rusting gold. Tonight, the smell of old people and old curtains is covered up by the balsam fir that's just been delivered, which Denise trimmed in a great deal of pain.

She looks out the window. The Joels won, didn't they? Denise's whole life is the smell inside a restaurant glass, that's been washed with dead eggs in an industrial and overstuffed dishwasher.

Bella, her young flippant employee, will be coming in soon, wearing her mauve snow boots. Denise looks down at her own carefully curated outfit. She was nuts, to buy it. The only real religion Denise believes in is that if you try too hard, it all falls down.

Just then she sees there's a new reservation that's come through Online Booking. The only reservation for tonight. Somebody must be stranded on account of the impending snowstorm. She clicks the link and there it is. Holy Moly there it is.

William Billiam IV.

Denise screams. It rings throughout the house, it vibrates across every scalloped edge. Her legs shake and her eyelids flutter. She feels in her abdomen the trickery and magic of every Amy Tan book she has ever read.

Just then the front door of the old inn twinkles, and in walks Bella with her hard water-stained boots and her lazy face. One time she told Denise there was a reason some people stayed single forever. That without them, what would companies like Chico's do.

Before Bella is all the way in, Denise trills, Go home! Don't need you tonight!

Huh?

Denise runs to the front door and tries to close the door on Bella's body and Bella goes, "Yo what the fuck?"

And Denise says, "Go HOME!" Only she isn't angry, she is hyper and smiling.

Bella keeps trying to come in. What is wrong with women who get everything they want all their lives? How could they possibly request more? Not today, Denise thinks.

Denise tugs Bella's handbag off her arm - it's small and has a chain and looks like dorm sex - and whips it across the mayonnaised and glittered lawn. It lands with a spineless thud in the street. Bella turns to look at it in disbelief and Denise seizes the opportunity to shut the door and lock it. She walks quickly, past the porcelain Christmas partridge and the coat hanger with her brand-new Barbour jacket and hyperventilates and shakes and laughs and Holy Jesus Shit Fuckers. Call off the end of the world.

Jon Abercrombie is coming to town!

–

He is in an UberBLACK car, lumbering through mushy snow on the road to Portsmouth. The driver is a woman who keeps looking in the rear-view at him.

For a long time before Caterina, Jon thought it was his duty to be kind to women. He thought the world was cruel to them and so all the good men must band together and care for the women. He couldn't count how many fat slags he'd kissed on New Year's Eve or how many cloudy mornings he'd spent eating Honey O's across from a poor sad bitch at a cheap pine table, pretending to be comfortable in the draft whistling forth from the doorway. The truth is, actually, he'd been at home doing those things. He figured, Sure, he deserved better. Someone hot and vibrant. But there were enough fucktwats who only wanted the hot and vibrant. Who would love the fat and brown?

Then came Caterina. All hell and love broke loose. In a way she was too much. He did not feel lucky, as a less handsome man might feel. Anyway, she was the acme and now he was broken. With all the women before her, if they died or left him, he'd have been fine. That was a good way to live. But Caterina was a world-ender. Her eyes. You had to throw up your hands.

"You look familiar," the driver says into the rear-view, which connects them via a reflective artery. Their glances travel to one another in a vacuum. Whoosh.

"Are you on TV?"

He shakes his head in a way he has perfected, that could mean yes or no. It's kind of a Stevie Wonder-slash-autistic sort of move.

The grief over Caterina has been a haunt for seven years. But lately it had been turning. The past few months, he could breathe without too much gin. He was surprised by the animation in him. He felt terrible of course, as we all do the moment we stop wanting the same fate as our loved ones, and begin to want the terrestrial joys again, to go to water parks, and twirl long noodles. Sometimes the exact swirls of her eye color escape him, and all he can remember is that they were a startling, preternatural blue.

"Yes or no?" says the driver. "I can't tell, from that move you just made with your head."

Jon cracks a smile. The first genuine smile he has smiled in a very long while. In the vacuum of the rear-view, the driver smiles back, and he feels his spirit growing, not quite as an erection does, but not exactly unlike one, either.

—

The absolute best room is the Donegal Suite. It has a gorgeous quilt and a view of the brook which looks otherworldly through the fancy Palladian window. The sham pillows on the bed are red velvet. Denise removes them every time a guest books it. Her favorite thing about it is the skylight. It slices a nice Parmesan hunk out of the ceiling and the Brillat moon is always floating up there, right in the window, like it's part of the rate.

Denise goes up there now, dreamily. She takes the red velvet pillows out of hiding and places them on the bed. She lies down then and looks up through the skylight at the flakes waving down. The snow tonight is a certain type. It's less saccharine than holiday snow. It's frank and heavy and feels like it comes from actual God, and not NBC.

What she imagines about lovemaking - if she had to describe it on a slip of paper and then look at it after to see how close she was, like Final Jeopardy - she would imagine it might feel like the way the power card plugs into your Mac, the way it's a magnet but also there's a very definitive insertion - the brilliant combo of the two modes of connection - so that you look down once it's in and say, "Oh! That's perfect, isn't it." And the little dot goes from orange to green, and *plink*, like that, you're on the other side. You can breathe out of the water.

Jon lets himself in the front door of the Edmund Victoria and the bell above the door tinkles like a cat. He stamps the snow off his boots. He does it for longer than most, because he was raised well. He looks around. The place is a giant doily. Oh bugger it was one of those places where they make your breakfast in front of your face and the eggs smell like rusted iron and you're supposed to sit there and ask questions about when the foundation was laid.

He walks past a porcelain bird and then a real bird, a demented green thing clucking solipsistically. There's a check-in stand but no attendant. He feels his hands reach almost immediately for his cell phone. That's what he's been reduced to lately - someone who calls someone else to fix a problem. And isn't he lucky, because that's what the human race aspires to - to be someone who does nothing. He stops himself. Tonight is a new day. This morning - just this morning in fact, as he'd started to say, "Please God take me today, I cannot bear this world another day," he didn't get past the "take." He sat down and turned on the telly, to see about a score instead.

"Hello!" he calls. He walks around to the foot of the emerald-carpeted stairs. What ghastly floral bedspread awaits him at the top, he thinks, smiling. "Hello!" he says, louder this time. He inhales deeply the smell. It reminds him of home. Baked, old things. He has a vision of his mother's broom, the way she smiled at him when he was a little boy. She was always in doorways, sweeping, and he was always in thrall to the simplest things.

He walks back to the counter and this time looks around it, lo! There's a woman there, flat to the ground. She's dressed to the nines and all made-up, so it's shocking to see her lying there, like an impeccable corpse. Jesus, he says. He drops to his knees and touches her neck, her heart. She feels warm but he can't feel her breath. She has hair like Caterina's, he notes with no small measure of excitement.

In the car on the way here the driver told him she was carrying the baby of a one-night stand. To her reflection in the rear-view mirror he gave a hearty "Hey ho! Congratulations!" He'd felt an abundant feeling, in the warm car moving through all that snow. He imagined everybody in New England was eating baked scrod tonight, with their wives and babies in high chairs, with snippings of fragrant pine dangling from the hearth and outside, a world of white. An hour later, after the driver had several times passed him a flask filled with warm whisky and he'd passed it back and they'd begun speaking frankly about life, she said that the bit about her pregnancy had only been half the truth. She said the full truth was that she was carrying the baby of the man who raped her. He thought she was fucking with him, but her eye contact remained steady in the rear-view. He didn't mind that she wasn't looking at the road. His life was not more important than this woman's truth. He felt the old familiar feelings creep back. He wanted to brush her hair.

Now he sees it's him who's lying on the ground, isn't it? Jesus. Again, and wildly he feels the fallen woman's neck but his own pulse is so eager he can't tell. He puts his mouth to her cheek. Please, he says, Please, darling wake up. He doesn't know why but it comes to him, as it did with a young

76

calf that, having been trampled by horses, was dying in the stables back home - it comes to mind to press his lips to hers, as he did with the calf. He kisses the woman who looks like a bloated version of his long-lost love.

Her eyes flutter open! Oh, thank Jesus!

They are not a swirled blue, but a kind and homely chestnut. They flutter and adjust and the woman screams, and so does Jon.

"*Ahhhhhhh!*"

—

He has not been with any woman since me. I know because I have watched him every moment. I have never taken my eyes from him. He beats them all away with a stick, then he goes home and cries and drinks, and he pleasures himself, to camera phone pictures of me.

When she heard the bell, and she knew it was *il mio* Jonny entering, she laid herself down on the floor. She pretended to be dead or fainted. I will say I admired it. It was not part of my plan.

He touched his mouth to hers. I didn't expect that he would begin with an act of tenderness. When he was a boy there was a calf that had been run over by the horses. It was dying in the stable and he touched his mouth to its mouth. It drew its last breath in his mouth. He did this now, with her.

And she "woke" up, this Dough White.

They go to sit on the couch by the fireplace of this inn. This part was also hard. The room was so ... tender, with the fire and the snow, and the way they were sitting facing one another, their knees touching.

On the couch he told her about me. This part I liked. He speaks of me like every woman wishes her man spoke of her. My hair was tendrils and coils. My eyes were running water. My heart was remarkable. I was a paragon, an angel.

Dutifully she listened. Oh, she is an excellent listener. The fat ones always are, and if you are a woman who wants to romance a widower, you must be. It's imperative in the beginning. You must act like she is more important than you.

In turn she told him about her newspaperman. She spoke of him as though he, too, were a long-lost love. Perhaps he might have been. I handled the newspaperman. I made sure he never called. I had just found her, this sad lonely girl with a desire to lose herself to a movie star. And then that week, she met a man! *Fanculo!*

I'd waited so long and had finally found a ripe one. I had to control things, so I did. I said to myself, the newspaperman will cheat on her one day, and a night with my Jonny is better than a lifetime with a small-town *manichino.*

But maybe know this: any time a man doesn't call, who you were sure was going to call, it maybe has nothing to do with you. You do not have free will, completely. There are things lurking under the ground, who decide sometimes.

As she spoke, my Jonny brushed a hair out of her eye. This was a gesture he has done with me. *Stronzo!*

He's only a man, I know. I kept telling myself. Down here, I have become Concupiscenza herself. It's been my charge. So I know. I understand. Sex is basement work.

He took her weak chin in his hand and brought her face to his. *Il primo bacio!* Seeing the man you love, doing that - I looked away. I let out a terrible whine. All inside me was churning and I began to sweat. The *stracchino* was whirling sour. Even when men love you, even on their way to you, they are breakers of guts.

Americans say, "You can't look away, it's like a car wreck." Indeed, I looked back. He'd brought her onto his lap, to straddle him. He'd removed the boots she'd bought for the occasion - the boots I'd willed her to buy, knowing how he likes riding boots. How all men like boots.

In the instant my own wreck was over, I saw myself as a collection of parts, a Furga doll with limbs in impossible directions, and I saw the people gaping. And the blood fascinated me, as it fascinated them. The theater of it. The shock. It makes you feel alive, even when you are just dead.

That is how I felt watching my Jonny with this American sow. I couldn't stop looking. More, I wanted more. *Che Dio me aiuti!*

He asked her which room was *theirs*. He carried her up the stairs, into the room she'd been saving for him. A woman of letters once said that no woman can stand to see another woman happier than she, and this is the truth. I saw this cow getting the thing she'd been wanting for, for so long, and if anybody deserved it, it was her, but still I hated her. I hated her for how her eyes shone. I hated her for the blood running through her veins.

On the bed he takes her and neither is worried about babies or disease. Do you understand? The kind of condomless fucking that predates worry. They fuck. It's terrible. They make love also. I don't know which is worse. Everyone will say making love is worse, but for me the fucking hurts in a more violent way. The fucking, for some reason, is harder to get out of your head. The dirty bits. There is something about limbs. The coarse hair on his legs, tooth-brushing the hilly fat at her thigh.

He makes love like a movie star, slow and generous and like the world is watching. She was enraptured and he was feeling what boys feel - the unremarkable physical delight. Men are like babies, who are predictable, who are up for three hours and then they need sleep, and everything they do is regimented and perfect for them, and you are only a servant of the intrinsic need. How I hated the man I love!

Some people can separate these things. They can say, here was a man experiencing an act of sex. Like eating a steak, he enjoyed it during its time. But not me. The steak might as well be his whole life, and it cancels out everything with me. I thought death would change me, but I am like a child still.

The actual hardest thing is the wetness. The wetness. The sheen. The glisten. Perhaps you have been cheated on. If you have, and you have gotten over it, because there are children or because it seems such a waste of a man and a love and a life, then fine, but imagine you had seen it. Imagine beyond imagining the worst, that you had actually seen the worst. And the worst is the wetness. Imagine your lover's pinkest parts, wet against someone who is not you.

They begin to build, the crescendo and the rhythm, you know how it goes. She plunges one of her feet between the crack of his celebrated rear, his neck arches back in approval. He opens his mouth and says, "Open your mouth," and she does and he spits into it, and he smiles. He is an animal. He is a *porco*! All celebrities are like this. Every hot man. Their noises, the *uhhhhh*s and breathing, and the grunting, the chaotic desire, there is nothing more cruel than to be on the outside of such a thing!

And then -

Oh *Dio*. No. You must be able to guess. What the worst thing would be.

HE COMES INSIDE OF HER. His body shudders and he moans the sound I hear in my dreams. To watch the man you love come inside of another woman. To watch his face fill with familiar gratification. My blood turns to liquid rage, but still I watch. I shudder, as well. I experience an orgasm of fury, the intensity of which causes me to double over and cry.

But it is part of the plan. All of life is a plan. There is no comfort in this, unless you are completely a *sempliciotto*.

Almost immediately, he falls asleep at her long sloppy breast and she holds his head there and I want to tear her eyelashes out. She strokes his flame-red hairs against her pale once-used flesh.

With grace she slips out from under his head and moves her large body down the stairs. There is a third beast at play, and it comes all from her. She knows this is the only way to keep him for herself. She knows that in the morning, he will fly, as birds do, as her cat would, with a door open to the white wound of a world she can only guess at.

So, she goes to fetch the drinks, hers and his, and his she fills with a crushed bounty of pills I have been willing her to collect. When he wakes, she will hand him the cup. She will whisper, Jonny, and he will squint his perfect eyes and he will drink because he will know, in some part of himself. In the part of him I don't hate. He will hear the name that only I have called him and he will drink. In her arms, he will fall out of this world. And my love will be on his way to me. I am disgusted. I am thrilled. I have waited so many years. I only hope I can forgive him, for not coming sooner, for not coming utterly on his own. I have planned and watched and died and hoped and now he will come. And my New England cow, I will not stop watching her. Slowly and fatly she will be baking my child and, when the time is right, I will fetch that down to me, too.

Solitude
By Mindy McGinnis

USA

There is something at the bottom of the lake.

I came here for quiet and have found exactly that, at first enjoying the utter silence of my isolation. There was no small joy in letting a cup of coffee grow cold in my hands as I sat on the deck, never hearing a car or the small vibrations of my cell, long dead. The white noise of life faded away, and once left with nothing I became keenly aware of the soundlessness, a pressure upon my ears.

I have walked the paths around the lake, the grass beneath my feet obscenely loud, each falling leaf that hit the ground as jarring as a record scratch. It was inexplicable, until I learned of the thing at the bottom.

A mother duck knew and went to it, her path crossing mine briefly as she led her babies to the water. They swam single file, heads dipping occasionally beneath the surface, shaking themselves as they came back up.

Until they reached the middle and never resurfaced. I stood on the bank, waiting. The ripples of their movements found the rocks at my feet, ebbed and flowed, until the tide they had created ceased entirely and I knew they were gone.

The second day, a fox followed, legs meant for land refusing to swim, the decision to sink already made. On the third an osprey plunged from above, diving for prey, never rising. His splash made a wave that reached the tips of my shoes, closer to the edge than they had been the day before.

That night I dreamed of creatures in the depths, not going to whatever waited for them, but returning. Raccoons trailing algae. A housecat with soaked fur, his tail reduced to exposed vertebrae. A moose with waterweed strung in its antlers. A girl, lonely, missing one slipper, her nightgown stuck to her knees. They all came to the deck, wide-eyed. Waiting.

Today I wore my coat and gathered rocks to fill my pockets. There is something at the bottom of the lake. And I go to meet it.

The Coal Mape
By Kurt Newton

USA

We were sitting around the dinner table when Poppa told the story of the coal mape. Momma told him right away to stop, but Poppa just smiled and said, "It's all right, Lottie, the kids are old enough to hear." Momma shook her head to let everyone know she disagreed, but she let Poppa speak.

"Working in the mines, there are times we see crazy things," Poppa said. "A lot of it is just shadows on the wall, or our brains getting drunk from not enough wholesome air. But sometimes, when the same thing is seen by more than one of us - it can't be no trick of the mind." Poppa glanced around the table to make sure he had our attention. Momma fidgeted with her napkin, her unease brewing. Poppa continued.

"It's been said that coal is the stone of living things. Millions of years of living things. Trees, grass, plants, animals. Even people. Now, I would imagine that sometimes in one of those stones - one of those clumps of coal we chip off and toss in the bin - there's a spirit of something trapped for more years than any of us can count. Maybe some kind of creature that graced this fine Earth back before people first walked out of the jungle. Back before dinosaurs even. Way back, after the war in Heaven, like the Bible says, when Michael fought the serpent and the serpent was cast out along with his dark angels. A creature that fell to Earth when it was more like a living Hell with its rivers of fire. A creature that didn't obey God's laws, and, instead of dying held still, its body turning to dust, but its spirit still alive, waiting patient for that day when someone would come along and release it from the Earth's grip.

"There's a name for something like that. A coal mape we call it. It's a name that's been whispered for as long as men have been digging holes in the ground and disturbing what's there. A coal mape appears like a swirl of black dust in a tunnel draft, but it moves about like no dust cloud should. It searches, drawing up close first to one man then another, until it finds what it's looking for."

Poppa stopped talking.

By now, Momma was crying and we didn't know why. She looked up, her face wet with tears, and we saw it - the darkness swirling in her eyes, a midnight black like oil on water.

"It's time, Lottie," said Poppa, and his eyes too were black as the belly of a summer storm cloud. Momma nodded. And between the two of them the coal mape surfaced, escaping briefly before entering all of us sitting around the dinner table. It raced into our lungs, then into our veins, swirling around until it found a place deeper still, and there it settled like bones at the bottom of a grave.

"Now, who wants dessert?" Momma said, like nothing was wrong, her eyes blue again.

"I do," said Poppa, his eyes, too, returning to their usual green.

The rest of us mimicked Poppa like a nest of magpies. "I do, I do...."

Momma brought dessert and we ate like thieves trying to feed a hunger that could never be satisfied.

Later, after the lights were out and I had drifted off to sleep in my bed, I had a dream so real it felt as if I were wide awake. In that dream I was standing motionless with my face tilted toward the sun, exulting in the sun's rays after such a long time spent in the dark.

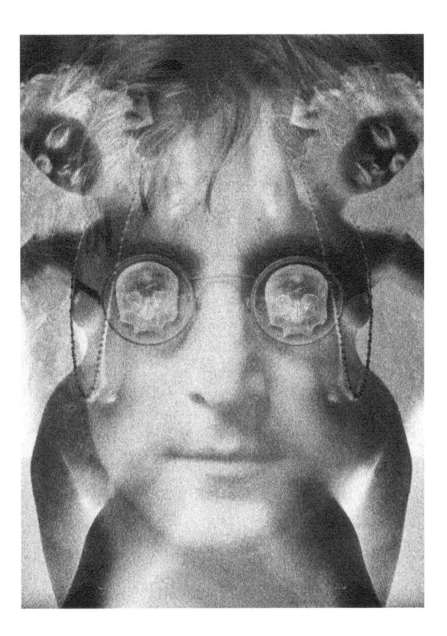

BUBS & JOHNS
By JL Schneider

USA

You're at the very edge of your territory in a run-down vinyl bar called The Memory Lane Lounge. You've just spent the day visiting a client, Lezel Meeks, whom you have to check on every couple of months. You don't like Lezel or his badly run store or his incessant talking. But times are hard, and you need his business. John Lennon's "Imagine" is playing on the juke box, and you're washing the taste of this rust bowl town out of your mouth with a couple scotches before going back to your motel room for the night.

At the end of the bar two men about your age but more worn in the face sit drinking boilermakers. They're whispering to each other and looking at you and snickering like children. The bartender, the only other person in the bar, has his nose buried in the sports pages.

The two men laugh louder. You know they're laughing at you, though you're sure you've never seen them before. Then you hear something clearly meant for your ears, something about your manhood, and you finally get up and walk over to them.

"Do I know you?" you ask.

They're unwashed and rheumy-eyed and fully cooked on a whiskey drunk. They burst out laughing.

"Know us!" the near one shouts.

You say, "If there's a problem …"

"Problem!" the other one screams between gulps of laughter.

They double over their drinks and pound the bar and laugh till they cough. You turn to leave. But the man nearest you finally calms down and holds up his hand, stopping you.

He says, "I guess you could say you know us." His voice carries an anger that seems to come all the way up from the cuffs of his pants. "Let me introduce ourselves. My name's Bubs. This is Johns."

The names are spoken with full authority on a razor line back to your earliest childhood.

"Who told you those names?" you ask.

"No one had to tell us our own names, Billy-boy. And we're the only three who know, aren't we?"

You stare at them, subtracting the years from their faces - they look like men just out of prison - and after a moment you begin to nod in recognition. No one, not even your stepmother, knew their real names.

"This is a dream," you say.

"That's what the imagination is, Billy-boy," Bubs says, "waking or sleeping."

Bubs, the older of the two - stockier, bolder when it came to adventure - pushes his face close to yours, forcing you to keep looking at him. Johns, the thin, quiet one, eyes you with a grin, his youthful shyness replaced by a quiet, bitter line at one corner of his mouth.

You say absently, as if they're not there, "I haven't thought about them..."

"Us!" Bubs yells. "And that ..." he points his finger at you like a gun "is exactly the point." Now Bubs' anger seems to come all the way up from Hell itself.

89

"Thirty years, Billy-boy. Thirty years without a word. But we never forgot you, did we, Johns?"

Johns downs his shot. "Nope."

You check the bartender still reading his paper. He hasn't moved or made any indication that there is anyone in the bar but you. Your impulse is to flee from these angry men. But ...you feel connected to them - although you are also repulsed by them, the way you would be repulsed by a dark, hidden part of your heart unwittingly revealed in a dream.

And you have to remember something, you tell yourself: No matter how real they appear - no matter if you've had two scotches or twenty - they must be now, as they were then, your *imaginary* friends.

"Have a seat," Bubs says. "Let me tell you where we been for the last thirty years, Billy-boy."

"People call me William now," you say without sitting down.

"Oh, do they? He wants to be called William now, Johns."

Johns looks at you with eyes leaking bile and whiskey, and says, "Aren't we the queen of the fucking court."

Bubs leans into you, his eyes narrowing.

"Where do you think we went when you stopped imagining us, Billy-boy?" He spits your childhood name at you like a piece of gristle. "Rio?"

Johns coughs up a laugh. He refills his shot glass from a pint bottle he draws from his back pocket, then silently stares at the tumbler, turning it around on the bar with two fingers.

"It ain't a pretty place where we been," Bubs continues. "It's a place of too much hope and no hope at all. Where everyone is alive yet dead. Alive with nothing but memories. Waiting. Constantly waiting to be imagined again."

Bubs looks away and stares straight ahead at a spot a thousand miles away. You then reach for your drink, and when the bartender comes to refill your glass you whisper to him, "Do you see them?" indicating the seats next to you.

The bartender glances toward Bubs and Johns and says, "See who?" pulling away the bottle before your glass is full. He's unfazed by the question, as if he's asked every night if imaginary people exist.

He goes back to his stool in the far corner of the bar, and you yell after him, "Can you at least turn off that fucking song!"

"I didn't play it," the bartender says, and snaps the paper open in front of his face.

You turn back to the men. "I don't care where you've ..."

"Old women," Bubs cuts you off. "Old, broken women in pigtails holding one end of a jump rope, waiting for someone to pick up the other end. Pathetic, middle-age men with slingshots in their back pockets, skimming stones over ponds, waiting for the sun to shine on their faces again. Fat, balding pirates looking to the horizon for ships that never come. Alive but dead, waiting, always waiting. Most of them just shells, millions of them, walking aimlessly around sandboxes remembering the joy they once had. They stumble around muttering to themselves, insane, their bodies curling up with age, just like yours, waiting to die."

Bubs' hands are shaking as he reaches for his shot glass, his eyes wide and glazed.

"That's where we been for the last thirty years." He drinks. "Now it's payback time."

"It doesn't sound very pleasant," you say, trying to be sympathetic, feeling more annoyed than responsible. Still, the ominous tone of Bubs' warning makes you order another scotch. "What do you mean, payback?"

"We been watching you, Billy-boy. We know all about you. So we're just going to hang around for the next, oh, let's say thirty years. We're gonna to be there for you. But it ain't gonna to be like the old days. This time we're in control, and for starters we're gonna remind you of every shortcoming you have."

"Shortcoming," Johns repeats, and the two of them chuckle.

Although there are some areas of your life you'd like to improve - like not having to come all the way out here to deal with Lezel Meeks, or not having to spend so much time on the road alone - you don't believe there's much you'd like to change. Things are pretty good, and you begin to wonder if this whole episode isn't merely the result of bad scotch.

"I don't think you have much of a case, gentlemen," you say confidently.

Bubs and Johns look at each other, as if deciding which one should speak.

"How's your wife?" Bubs finally asks.

"Fine," you respond.

"She doesn't mind that your pistol goes off quicker than a zit-faced teenager's?"

"Minuteman!" Johns shouts, and the two of them lean into each other and giggle.

Your palms begin to sweat. No matter how drunk you've gotten, this is a problem you have never confessed to anyone - in fact until now, you haven't fully acknowledged it to yourself. And suddenly you feel like a child caught in a lie, one you were sure would never be discovered, the fear of retribution making you tremble. Then the desperate attempt to cover it up.

"I'll just stop imagining you," you say.

They look at you, no trace of fear in their faces, Johns leaning around Bubs so you have a full view of both of them.

"Who could forget these pretty faces?" Johns smiles broadly, for the first time peeling his lips back to the gums. Several teeth are missing. "Too many sweets when I was a kid," he says.

Now you sit down. They've been watching you in your own bedroom, your imaginary friends spying on you while you were having sex, laughing. You shudder.

"How the hell did you find me?" you ask, resignation muffling your question to a whisper.

"You finally slipped up," Bubs says, now calm, the tone of a conqueror in his voice. "Just for a second. That's all it took."

"That's all it took," Johns pipes in, and he and Bubs toast each other.

"Remember when you were in Meeks' store this afternoon?" Bubs says.

"You were barely listening to him. But you heard enough. He said something about his imaginary friend from childhood, a pirate named Felix. He was trying to confess something to you, Billy-boy. He was trying to tell

93

you something from his heart. But, as usual, you looked at him like he was a moron. So he shut up.

"But that's all it took. Even if it wasn't a wholly conscious memory, you were transported back to your room on a lonely Saturday afternoon - you were there, and so were we, and it was real. And now we're free."

You spit out, "Asshole Meeks."

"Ahh," Bubs sighs. "You underestimate Lezel, my childhood friend. He may not run his business well. He may ramble on a bit. And he may be ugly as a stump. But he's got a good imagination. A lot of childhood left in that man. You could learn something from him. He keeps Felix alive in his heart. We *know* Felix - good guy, Spaniard, excellent swordplay. Still robust with life. One of the lucky ones."

You remember those lonely Saturday afternoons and the countless days after school when no one would play with you. Missing your mother. Your stepmother always busy with something else. Your father never home. The hours spent with Bubs and Johns, playing, talking, going on adventures. You try to stop thinking about them, fearing an increase in their power if you give them too much light in your mind. But in your heart, you know it's too late.

"We did have some good times," you say. Perhaps if you mollify them, they might reconsider. "Remember that time I let you win at Chutes & Ladders?"

Bubs brings one cold eye and an arched brow to bear on you.

"Childhood's over, Billy-boy. But what is it they say these days, Johns? It's never too late ..."

"...for a second childhood," Johns cackles to himself.

94

"Only this time," - Bubs' eye is like an auger - "it ain't gonna to be pretty. We got plans for you, Billy-boy. And all the time in the world."

For a long time, you sit without speaking. Bubs and Johns are humming along with "Imagine" and downing their whiskies. You wonder if they can read your heart, if they know how much you hate them now. How much you wish you'd never conjured them in the first place, that you had been a stronger child, that you could have endured the loneliness. You know them better than anyone on earth. They have cold hearts, forged by bitterness and abandonment - the same depth of abandonment that brought them into existence in the first place - and they will never leave you alone. And you know, finding that dark spot in your own heart that must be flowering in theirs, that you would probably do the same thing if you were them.

Your wife comes to mind. Does she hate you, too? What's it going to be like, now, knowing they'll be watching when you're with her? It was bad enough before. But now, even your fantasies won't help. Your fantasies ...

After a few minutes of looking around the dark bar, trying to pick just the right spot, you finally see them sitting in a booth next to the door. Red-headed twins, late 20s, peach skin, legs up to their necks. Almost as soon as they appear, Bubs and Johns see them too.

"Whoa!" Bubs says. Slowly he turns to you. "Well, well, well," he says, a smile of appreciation, almost admiration, spreading into his face. "You little rascal. So that's what you been thinking about while you're doing the missus. No wonder you been short-fusing her. I got to hand it to you, Billy-boy, you got a good imagination. But then again, you created us."

"Good imagination," is all Johns can manage, eyeing the girls.

"You see them?" you ask.

"Damn straight we see them," Bubs says.

"But you never saw them in that other place?"

"Johns and I are childhood fantasies, Billy-boy. Those girls are *adult* fantasies. More in this world than the other. But now that we're here too ..."

The girls look at you, lick their lips, and cant their bottoms toward you when they cross their legs.

"Just to show there's no hard feelings," you say, trying to mask your relief when you see how narrowly focused on the girls Bubs and Johns are. "I know you're pissed off, and I'm sorry. I guess there's nothing I can do to make up for what I did to you. I just thought you'd like a little present. I've never been able to do much with them, of course, except imagine. But maybe you guys ..."

Johns' open mouth is leaking spittle onto his bottom lip, and Bubs is rubbing his thin beard, their eyes glued on the women.

"That's mighty nice of you, Billy-boy," Bubs says.

"Yeah, thanks, Fuck-wad," Johns says. He's talking to you but staring at the women. "And you better keep them there, or there'll be hell to pay. We can only do it with ones from your head. So no fuck-ups. Now scram."

You take your motel room key out of your pocket. "Do you need this?"

"No," Bubs says. "We know how to get in. But ..." He turns to you, the black fierceness returning to his eyes. "...We know where you live. And when we're done with them, we'll be seeing you."

"Have fun," you say.

96

You pay the tab and leave, just a little jealous when you walk past the twins, who are ready and willing as only you know they can be. You drive back to the motel, pack your things, leave the key on the bureau, and get into your car. It's a five-hour drive home, the night is cool, and there's no one on the highway. You open the window and tune in a Lite-rock radio station. You think about Bubs and Johns in your motel room.

You imagine they're having a good time by now, each of them with one of the girls, grinning and swilling whiskey. You imagine the girls straddling them. On their backs, Bubs and Johns are reaching up for the perfect, bouncing breasts, the twins' long, strong legs expertly scissoring their tight rear ends onto your blissful imaginary friends like smooth-running pumps. You imagine Bubs and Johns almost delirious with pleasure, oblivious to everything except the women's inexhaustible energy and bottomless desire to please.

You imagine Bubs and Johns so enraptured, in fact, that they don't notice the subtle changes occurring in the wonders of flesh above them. It starts around the eyes. The doe-like innocence hardens. Their gazes sharpen, intent on the men below them. Their jaw bones thicken, the molars widen, and the incisors lengthen. Their cute noses sprout hard, distinctive ridges, then begin to elongate. Their perfectly trimmed triangles of pubic hair thicken and spread, and each woman constricts her silky grip until the man below her is locked within, unable to pull away even if he wanted to. The women begin exhaling gusts of foul air, accented by low growls coming from the backs of their throats. The lithe fingers of so much sexual expertise sprout claws.

Bubs and Johns are too engrossed in pleasure to notice any of this. Until it's too late. The huge jaws of the women part and dive for their arched throats. You imagine your imaginary friends opening their eyes to find themselves under assault by red-furred wolves whose lips drip blood. You imagine the men's screams of terror as the women, grinning with the first taste of their victims, dig claws into their eye sockets. The she-wolves continue attacking

97

in a frenzy, their snouts thrusting again and again, until the imaginary screams abruptly stop. And still it goes on, teeth shredding voice boxes, ripping jugulars, and closing on the cervical vertebrae to snap spinal cords like pencils.

You imagine the women pausing to lick their bloody lips, occasionally lapping the still bodies for more, sucking severed arteries like straws. They look at each other, their nakedness spattered with the red life of their prey, and they smile.

The wolf was your worst childhood nightmare - that pure, predatory beast. That ruthless killer without conscience whom your stepmother, looking somewhat wolf-like herself as she stood at the end of your bed in the dark, told you was always nearby if you weren't good. You recall the countless hours you spent in your bed at night, imagining the horror.

And now it's alive. The cool wind blows in through the car window, and "Imagine" starts to play on the radio. A wry smile comes to your mouth. You imagine the women rising off the lifeless bodies of the men, starting for the door. They have one thought, one intent, one goal - you. You've conjured them, and now, just like Bubs and Johns, they want more from you. In fact, they want *everything*.

You see their clawed fingers reaching for the doorknob. You're humming along with the song. Then, just as they're about to step into the night, you put them back under the bed where they belong.

Negroes Anonymous
By Gene Bryan Johnson

USA

Into The Twilight Zone and Black To The Future

1991: He's near the back of Bee Sharp's Jazz Club, standing at the bar, listening to a young trumpeter testifying about life he has not yet lived.

"Damn, he got everything in there. Fats Navarro, Clifford Brown, even a little Pops."

A skullcap and dashiki-wearing brother sits on the next bar stool, sipping Johnny Walker Red with one ice cube.

"Pops?"

"Yeah, Louis Armstrong."

"Louis Armstrong? P*ssst*. Why you even mention that coon-ass Uncle Tom?" Skullcap gulps the rest of his drink, turns to face the bar, and slams his glass down.

"Hit me one more time, Sweetheart!"

A few patrons turn their gazes from the bandstand to look at Skullcap who, bordering on drunken ostentation, shrugs with faux innocence and a sheepish grin.

 "What?"

The bartender puts her index finger to her lips. "S*hhhh*!"

Trumpet tones dance from the basement to the ceiling and back again, alternately solo-ing, duet-ing, trio-ing and quartet-ing with the piano, bass and drums, and devolving from post bop, to hard bop, to be bop, to traditional New Orleans and free jazz. The crowd, hypnotized into choreographed synchronicity, becomes the fifth member of the band, turning the club into a singular blob of quintet-ing sway. A candle-like flicker of muted lighting envelopes the stage and snakes mysteriously among the audience. Bartender Sharon refreshes Skullcap's drink with a flourish, but he is not satisfied.

"Put another ice cube in there, would you Baby?"

Bartender Sharon once again makes a show of raising a finger to her lips, using her other hand to add the requested cube. Skullcap mimics her motion - putting a finger to his own lips before snatching the glass from the bar.

Skullcap finishes the drink in one gulp as the trumpeter's dark suit, white shirt, lapels, and tie-width regress through the decades, from the '90s back to the '20s. The room spins at a leisurely pace as the musician's face dissolves into Freddie Hubbard, then a sullen Miles Davis, followed by a studious Lee Morgan, a balloon-cheeked Dizzy Gillespie, a demonstrative Fats Navarro, to a smiling Louis Armstrong. Bending, bopping, bowing, before the beat, beneath the beat, behind the beat, these men be blowing their black lives into the fabric of American experience. Skullcap slides on the stool but catches himself as the slowly revolving room accelerates into a whirlpool of shade and color.

A dark-skinned tuxedoed man, severely overdressed but, curiously, not calling any attention to himself, pulls up a stool and leans with his back to the bar while wiping a profusely sweating forehead with a face-obscuring handkerchief. He turns toward Skullcap.

"Youngblood blow so many notes ole Satchmo can't hear what he tryin' tuh say."

Skullcap's head lifts at the sound of the vaguely familiar voice. He turns around, does a double take and looks from left to right, hoping to make eye contact with someone - anyone - but everyone is focused on the bandstand. The ghost of Louis Armstrong is standing there, smiling that famous grin and wiping that famous forehead with that famous handkerchief.

Bartender Sharon extends the drink to Skullcap with one hand and wipes the bar with her other. Skullcap, from her point of view, is standing alone. "This is your fifth drink. You might want to slow down before I have to cut you off."

Skullcap takes the tumbler, raises it to his lips, but thinks better of it and stops short of drinking. He looks into the glass, then up at Armstrong. Then at the glass, then back at Armstrong whom, he is sure, has been dead for decades.

"Hey, Daddy, you look like you seen a ghost." Armstrong winks at Skullcap and starts singing. "Is I is, or is I ain't a ghost, Daddy? Drink that Johnnie Walker Red and make yourself a toast, yay-*essss*."

Skullcap downs the drink and winces. "Is this a dream?"

"Do you *think* this is a dream?"

"I don't understand."

"Do you *want* to understand?"

"Do I want to understand what?"

"I think you need another scotch."

"I do need another scotch, but I still ...who are you?"

"You don't know who I am?"

"I know who you are, but you're not ...I mean, what ...why are you here?"

"Why am I here?" Armstrong wipes his sweating face with the handkerchief. "Daddy, I'm here to remind you how you became *you.*"

Say It Loud

1968: Skullcap Dashiki and Armstrong's ghost, invisible to everyone but each other, are sitting on a park bench watching the cars that have turned Eastern Parkway from a tree-lined boulevard, designed a hundred years earlier for pleasurable riding in horse-pulled buggies, into an expressway for impatient automobile drivers seeking a quick route through the burgeoning borough of Brooklyn. A shiny black '63 Ford Galaxie stops at a red light, with James Brown's *Say It Loud (I'm Black and I'm Proud)* blasting from its down-rolled windows, Mom and Pop on the front seat, and Young Skull in the back.

"Isn't that...?"

"Yes sir-ree."

"That's Mom and Pop! And me! What the hell?"

Say It Loud! demands Mr. Brown.

"I'm black and I'm proud!" Pop joins in on the jubilant chorus, chanting at the top of his lungs and dancing in place to the beating drum, scratching guitar, percolating bass, and punctuating horns infecting the parkway's serenity with the tenacity of a newly arrived invasive species. On the south median, clusters of leisurely strolling Hasidim seem oblivious to the music, even as the animations of their trailing broods seem to be choreographed by the same funk gods who've got black- and brown-skinned neighbors on the north median beaming head-nodding smiles of solidarity in Pop's direction. The light turns green.

"Wait, they're leaving."

"Don't worry, Daddy. We goin' with 'em."

Armstrong and Skullcap vanish from the park bench and reappear on the back seat, invisibly flanking Young Skull, just as the car moves through the intersection. Pop grips the steering wheel with his left hand, elbow resting on the open windowsill and right arm draped over Mom's shoulders. He pulls her close, turns his head toward her and chants, full volume, into her ear.

"I'm black and I'm proud!"

Pop doesn't know it - he's not that self-aware - but he's been waiting his entire life to feel this. A man and his woman; car so clean you can eat off the hood; car note paid off; first-born son in the back.

Say it loud!

"I'm black and I'm proud!" Pop cannot resist proclaiming his newfound joy. Mom? Not feeling it so much.

"But he sounds so ..."

Mom tries to pull away, but Pop, peacocking for the same audience from which she wants to hide, enjoys restraining his wife. Young Skull, the impressionable pupil, raptly watches his father teaching him how to treat women.

Mom - mortified and horrified - tries to speak but words struggle to escape her barely opened lips.

"... he sounds so ...black."

"Yeah, black *and* proud."

Mom gets quieter, as if lowering her voice will protect her son from an awful truth.

"It's embarrassing, showing his color like that."

Her anxiety inspires Pop to chant even louder. "I'm black and I'm proud!" He turns around and guffaws at his son.

"Come on boy, *sing*!"

Young Skull laughs with his dad, drums his hand on the seatback and joins in on the next chorus. "I'm black and I'm proud!"

Mom's voice dips so low they can barely hear it above the music. "He sounds so ghetto. Just like a, a nigger on the street."

Father and son look at Mom, then at each other. *Who is this woman?* their raised eyebrows ask as Mr. Brown continues the revolution.

Say it loud!

"I'm black and I'm proud!"

Skullcap looks at Armstrong. "Can't believe I forgot the only time Mom ever said nigger."

"The only time you ever *heard* your mother say nigger. Maybe James Brown put her in touch with her inner Negro."

"Yeah, well. I do remember Pop singing *Say It Loud* though. He always liked James Brown, but *Say It Loud, I'm Black and I'm Proud?* That song changed him - like it was some kind a two and a half minute Emancipation Proclamation - a temporary reprieve, but still ...you know."

"Papa found a brand-new bag."

"Pop always talked about how James Brown and Ike Turner were *men*. In control of their bands and their women."

"Whipped them into shape, huh?"

"Unlike you."

"*Me?*"

"Yeah, you. Pop hated everything about you. He hated you singin' *Hello Dolly*, he hated you in the movies and hated you on television. He hated the way you always smilin' with whitey."

"Is that what he tole you?"

"Yep. Said it all the time."

"Maybe that's why I'm here. Cuz your Pop put me in your head. People even call me Pops just like you call your father Pop. That's what they call irony, Son."

"I don't think my father processed concepts like irony. He was a simple guy. I think the way you represented black folks made him feel ashamed."

"More ashamed than drug dealers, or murderers, or wife beaters and pimps?"

"I don't know. Maybe. Like I said, Pop was a simple dude. He just said you were a coon and always told me to stay black."

"Coon huh? Never heard *that* one before. Been called all kinds of nigger, monkey, Sambo, and midnight ooga-booga jungle bunny from when I was a little boy. And that's just from other black folks." Armstrong grabs Skullcap's shoulder - though Skull doesn't feel the pressure. "Lemme tell you suh-*mmm*. Ain't nothing blacker than what I accomplished with my horn cuz where I come from dey still fighting the Civil War - to this day. You know how many Negroes dem OATs kilt between assassinating Lincoln and murdering four little girls in Birmingham? Thas almost a hundred years and nobody know how many dead, less- un dem OATs keep a scorecard like the Nazis did."

"What's OATs?"

"OATs is Original American Terrorists, Son. My horn is me calling out the names of all the dead anonymous Negroes been kilt by OATs. And your father be calling *me* names. Humph. Maybe he jealous that I turned *my* survival into *our* art."

For the first time since Armstrong's ghost appeared, Skullcap takes time to think before speaking. "Yeah well, maybe jealousy and shame go together."

"Yeah well, maybe they do."

1963: Skullcap and Armstrong stroll back through a half-decade of Brooklyn-in-transition, walking beneath hundred-year-old trees and past the stoops of well-maintained limestone homes. They stop in front of Epiphany Lutheran, a majestic Gothic-style church and private school serving the middle class African-American and Caribbean-American families who can afford the tuition. The playground is filled with the sounds of recess cheer - black boys in blue blazers and black girls in plaid jumpers - playing tag and running aimlessly in circles of innocence.

"Recognize anybody?"

"Nah."

"Open your eyes, Brother. Right there."

"Where?"

"Right there, man. The happiest boy in the playground is you, Daddy."

"I went to private school?"

"Ain' dat you?"

Skullcap squints hard through the fence. "I'll be a motherfucker."

"Looks like you done forgot a whole lot about your childhood. You sure look like a happy boy to me."

They stand and watch the carefree children at play. Skullcap's face tightens as he struggles with long-buried memories. Armstrong watches Skullcap from his eye's corner.

Then it's dusk with weather as fine as Brooklyn gets – mid-seventies, light breeze, clear skies, and a full moon. Passersby can see through the picture window of a classic Bedford Stuyvesant brownstone as Mom, Pop, and Young Skull sit down for family dinner. A chandelier radiates a muted sepia glow, the table is meticulously set with napkins and forks to the left, knives and spoons to the right, and crystal water glasses lined up with the knives.

Young Skull leads the family in a solemn prayer of thanks. Fried chicken, mashed potatoes with gravy, and mustard greens from Mom's garden are passed around with a casualness that only comes from repetition. Pop offers his always-present hot sauce to Young Skull, who applies it with a perfect mimicry of his father's ritualized shake.

Armstrong and Skullcap are on the stoop surveying the subdued bustle of a neighborhood flowing from daytime into night. Skullcap points to a tall, light-skinned black man leaving a house across the street with a newspaper under his arm. The man looks both ways, not suspiciously, but matter-of-factly, and walks briskly down the block. He stops in front of The Corner Barbershop and waves before crossing the street.

"That's Mr. Morgan. He's a transit cop. Keeps his pistol folded up in that paper too. Just in case he needs it quick."

"That yo' barbershop?"

"Not really."

"What that mean, not really?"

"I stopped going there pretty young."

"How you gonna stop going to the barbershop? Who cut your hair?"

"My mother cut my hair to save money."

"Thas crazy right there."

"It's how they paid off the car and the mortgage and stayed out of debt. Mom always said it was about saving one dollar at a time."

"What did your father say?"

"Pop said Mom was stingy and uppity, but sometimes I thought that was his friends talking, cause you could tell he liked not owing the man any money."

"But the barbershop is where boys learn how to be men. That's where you learn how to walk, what to talk about, what to watch out for on dese streets."

"That's what they say. But Pop used to drop me off and come back three, four hours later. One day a man gettin' a shave got in a fight and got stabbed and the cops came before Pop got back. Never forgot Mom's face when she opened the door to me being brought home by the police." Skullcap stops and thinks for a minute. "I don't know where Pop disappeared to but they started fighting all the time after that."

Mr. Morgan comes back down the block carrying a paper bag and his folded up newspaper. "He even takes his pistol to the grocery store."

"I can understand that. Never know when you gonna need some heat."

"I think I had a crush on his daughter. What's her name."

"You tell me."

"Debra. Denise. Donna. That's it. Her name was Donna. I mean, tell you the truth, I pretty much had a crush on every girl who paid me any mind back then."

"A crush huh? What a wonderful world, all innocence and fairy-tales. Maaan, when I was that age I dropped out of school and ..."

"When did you drop out of school?"

"Fifth grade, Daddy. Drop out and hustlin' fulltime."

"Hustling?"

"You know. Well you would know if you had spent more time in the barbershop."

"Too late for that now."

"Yeah, I guess so. Hustlin' is a little bit of this and a little bit of that. Sell some newspapers, git some onions and tate-uhs outta one place garbage and sell 'em to another fo' some pennies. Run errands fo' duh hoes. Huh. When I was a boy it was unusual if I didn't see a knife fight every night."

"Damn. How old were you?"

"*Old?* I'm talking young, Daddy. Straight up young-un. Nighttime was where the money at. If I wanted to eat I had to stay up late, hustling for my bread. The eating kind and the spending kind."

Armstrong's gravelly voice fades into the whoosh of swaying trees and passing cars. Skullcap is spellbound by the storytelling until the sound of Mom's screaming shatters the reverie.

"You *what?*"

Skullcap and Armstrong peer through the window as Mom gets up from the dinner table.

"Are you out of your mind?"

"Calm down for a minute! Lemme explain."

"Explain? There is no explanation. That money is for next term's tuition and it's due right now!"

Mom is beside herself. She puts her hands to her head and paces in a circle. She tries to process but nothing makes sense. Young Skull crawls underneath the table. Mom runs from the dining room to the kitchen and back.

"Please. Tell me how you can take the money that I saved for our son's education."

"I didn't take it. I borrowed it. I mean, I lent it to Willie B..."

"Willie Bubs? You lent our money to Willie Bubs?"

"Willie Bubs and them gonna open up a ..."

"You lent our son's tuition to your lazy-ass, good-for-nothing friends? I'm scrimping and saving, and working overtime, and clipping coupons, and sacrificing so you can give my money away?"

"It's an investment!"

Mom throws her hands up. She somehow manages to whisper and yell at the same time. "I didn't ask you to contribute to the tuition because I knew you were against it. All I asked was for you to let me try to build a better life."

"Because my life is not good enough for my son?"

You should save *your* money to invest with your friends. I saved *our* money to pay off the house, and pay off the car, and pay for tuition because I want more for our son."

"That's the problem right there. You think more is white. More *ain't* white."

"What does that have to do with you stealing our money?"

Mom runs into the kitchen. Pop starts to follow but a frying pan flies through the air toward his head. Pop ducks as the pan crashes against the frame of the double-paned picture window, ricochets onto the table and bounces onto the floor where Young Skull remains cowering. Teary-eyed Mom comes back into the dining room panting with frustration and disbelief.

"Epiphany is all black. Black students and black teachers!"

"Training black children to be white!"

"You stole that money from us!"

"I invested in our future but you can't see it because you don't believe in me because I'm not white."

Pop is angry with his wife, but he is mostly angry at his life. He has been slighted, spat upon, rejected, insulted, beat down, handcuffed and ignored by white teachers in the New York City Public School system, white cops, white Italian mobsters who own the trucking company he drives for, and the white Jewish vendors on Belmont Ave who he has been buying from since childhood. He is angry for every time he has been made to feel like less than a man. And now he feels it from his own college-educated wife, in his own house.

He is most angry, most ashamed, and most worried, however, about losing the respect of the one person who should believe unconditionally in his manhood. At this point it's not clear if he's talking to his wife or muttering to himself.

"I'm not good enough for my son? Like he got to go to private school with them West Indian coconuts."

His parents seem to have forgotten that Young Skull is petrified beneath the table as they argue about his future.

"You don't want him to talk like me and my peoples cause you think my son gots to be better than me?"

Mom walks up to Pop and stands face to face with him. "What kind of man steals from his own son?"

Pop turns away, slams his fist onto the table, storms out of the house, and sprints to the Ford Galaxie. Skullcap and Armstrong watch him blow through a stop sign and turn the corner.

"Damn. I thought it was tough *not* havin' a father around."

"Funny."

"And you don't remember none a this?"

"I think I remember Mom throwing the frying pan, but I definitely do not remember going to private school, I'll tell you that much."

"Must be that skullcap you always wearin'."

"Why?"

"Maybe it's too tight."

"If you didn't play the trumpet you could have been a comedian instead of just a clown."

They sit quietly, watching night-time pedestrians and dwindling traffic. Skullcap breaks the silence.

"Later that night Pop ran through a red light and got busted."
"You remember?"

"That story is a family legend. They say he took the light and crashed into a patrol car with an open can of beer on the front seat."

"Damn!"

"Pop had a couple hundred bucks left over from the money he took from Mom's stash. The cops kept the cash and locked him up because they didn't believe his story."

"Unbelievable!"

"That's what they said."

"He could a been another anonymous Negro."

"Never got that money back neither. And Pop never forgave Mom."

"People never blame themselves for nothing."

"Nor for anything."

"He, he, he. That's pretty good, Daddy. I think you might be ready."

"You think I might be ready for *what?*"

"I think you might be ready to dig up the memories hiding in those nightmares you been having."

"How do you know about my nightmares?"

"Cause I'm in your head, Brother. We gone find out why you drink so much you can't hold down a job or keep a woman. That's why I'm here."

Where Were You When

Labor Day, September 2, 1963: Armstrong and Skullcap are sitting in the windowsill of Young Skull's room watching the child get ready for bed.

"You recognize any of this?"

"Not a damn thing."

"You need to try harder cuz it's waiting for you to stop being afraid."

"Afraid of what?"

"Afraid of your truth, Brother. I got tchoo here but now *you* got to do the work. Close your eyes, forget about me, and think about what's going on inside your seven-year-old head. It's time to remember what you spent your whole life forgetting."

Mom comes into the bedroom, kisses her son on the forehead and turns out the light. The nightlight comes on and she closes the door. Young Skull is excited. Tomorrow is the first day of second grade at his new school and though his eyelids are heavy he has trouble sleeping. He restlessly tosses as the nightlight flickers and the door partially opens. Did Mom come back in? He tries to open his eyes but the lids resist and he drifts, unaware of what it took for his mother to make tomorrow happen. She spent her remaining vacation time from work at the Board of Education headquarters, lobbying, begging, and threatening bureaucrats until they found a slot for her son, categorized as intellectually gifted by a standardized test, in one of the city's highest achieving (and whitest) public schools. His unshakeable faith in her commitment lulls him even as, downstairs in the living room, his parents argue.

"I am *not* sending him to a third-rate school, with outdated books and teachers who don't care and kids old enough for junior high school being held back and beating on the younger ones."

"You don't want him in a black school."

"He was in a black school until you decided they were the wrong kind of black."

"Them coconuts look down on me and my peoples cause dey ain't really black."

"Do you even know how ignorant you sound right now?"

The fighting has intensified over the last few months with Mom accusing Pop of recklessly driving while drunk and "stupidly crashing into the police" and Pop accusing Mom of deliberately leaving him "to rot in jail" instead of bailing him out. Fortunately, Young Skull has mastered the art of simultaneously listening, learning, tuning out, and forgetting; tonight he sleeps through the noise, fantasizing and dreaming about the *Romper Room*-like experience he anticipates for day one at his wonderful new school.

The only white children Young Skull knows are the super-nice television friends who lightened his preschool only-child isolation. Sure, ninety percent of the children lined up for Radio City's Christmas Spectacular were white, but their parents usually discouraged any child-to-child discourse. Just as many white kids learned about blacks from televised Tarzan movies, Young Skull's perceptions of whites came via the boob tube in the form of *Leave It To Beaver* and *Romper Room*. This new school, which he overheard his parents arguing about being public (whatever that meant) promises to be a perpetual play-date of sunny dispositions and generous inclusiveness.

Young Skull awakens to the usual household aroma of oatmeal, bacon, fresh baked bread, and coffee, but today is the first school day he's not wearing a uniform and Mom, who wants to make sure he represents the race as an upwardly mobile middle class American boy from a good family, has laid clothes out on his bedroom's settee. She is exceptionally talkative this morning.

"Finished all your breakfast and washed your plate?"

"Yes Ma'am."

"Pencils, notebook, ruler in your book bag?"

"Yes, Ma'am."

"Remember your pocket dictionary?"

"Yes, Ma'am."

"Lunchbox?"

"Mom, we checked everything already. Twice. Can we go now?"

He's glad stubborn Pop refuses to drive them to school this morning because public transportation is always a good excuse for adventure and fantasy. Usually this means a museum trip, the Floating Hospital Boat, or the Macy's Day Parade, but today is a special category that Mom and Pop keep calling "prepared for rest of his life," though they can't seem to agree on a pathway to the future.

Mom and Young Skull race down the block, reaching the corner just as the bus pulls up, hopping on board to the pleasant though bossy greetings of a uniformed and behatted driver.

"Step up. Please move to the back. Next stop, Atlantic Ave. Watch the closing doors."

Mr. Bus Driver looks out into his sideview mirror and into his rear-view mirror as his bus bustles with all manner of black folk jockeying for position. It's crowded but after a few stops they find seats near the center.

"Mommy, don't forget to tell me when to pull the cord so Mr. Bus Driver knows it's our turn to get off."

"I won't forget."

"Next stop, Eastern Parkway."

The bus passes St John's Place and the demographics begin a photochromic process that Mom is aware of, but Young Skull, on his knees looking out the window, is not.

"Eastern Parkway. Please exit from the back and watch your step."

Mr. Bus Driver picks up speed as the traffic thins, the windows becoming an impressionistic canvas of morning rush hour whoosh.

"We're going too fast, Mommy. I can't read the signs. Make sure you tell me when to pull the cord, okay?"

"Don't worry. I will."

Young Skull, hypnotized by streaks of colorful storefronts, scurrying pedestrians, and impatient automobile commuters, basks in the urban excitement until his wondering mind wanders back to overhearing one of his parent's heated conversations.

"Mommy, what's the difference between private school and public school?"

"What?"

"You and Pop were talking about me leaving private school to go to public school and I ..."

"Sit down then, and look it ..."

"I know. Look it up in my dictionary."

"Linden Boulevard."

Young Skull sits, pulls the pocket dictionary from his book bag and burrows while Mom unconsciously hums *We Shall Overcome* in the barely perceptible tone that signals anxiety to those who know her best. Her son, mindful of tension at home, suspects that her discomfort is Pop-related so, while leafing through his dictionary, he leans against his Mother to assuage her.

"Mommy, don't forget to tell me when to pull the cord so the bus driver knows."

"I won't forget. I promise."

"The dictionary says public means 'open to all members of the community.'"

"That's right."

"So why did Pop say you had to 'fight the system' to get me into a white public school?"

"Church Avenue."

The bus - excepting Mom, Young Skull, and one older uniformed black domestic sitting in the last row - is now filled with whites. Mom, looking

120

up to find many of them staring poisoned darts at her, avoids the negatives but does nod at the black woman and makes eye contact with an older white woman whose reassuring smile offers a bit of kindness. The relief is short-lived, however, as Mom gasps, jumps up and pulls the cord.

"*Whew.* Almost missed our stop."

"You promised I could pull the cord."

Mom sighs. "You can pull it next time."

"But you promised."

"Okay, but just once."

Young Skull looks into the rear-view mirror, zeroes in on Mr. Bus Driver's eyes, kneels on the seat, and pulls the cord with a child's defiant innocence. He holds Mr. Bus Driver's gaze and tugs the cord again and again until Mom grabs his arm and pulls him down into the seat.

"*Owww,* You're hurting me."

"I told you, only one pull."

Mr. Bus Driver glares into the rear-view mirror.

"Once is enough black there. That cord ain't no toy."

Mr. Bus Driver grins at his clever wordplay while some passengers chuckle and exchange glances. It occurs to Mom that, until now, she didn't see the driver as white - he was just a bus driver. Now, with a stare as hard as those of the other passengers, his eyes expose menace underneath the uniform. As they stand and make their way to the back door, he taps the brakes and throws them off balance. Then he stops too far from the curb when it's time for them to disembark, and they have to hurriedly jump down from the bus to the street rather than gently stepping down onto a raised sidewalk. The doors start closing and the bus starts pulling away almost before they hit the ground.

Mom and Young Skull walk in brisk silence until the sight of revolving red bubble lights and blue NYPD wooden barricades interrupts their escape from the bus ride. A woman breaks from the crowd of corralled demonstrators congregating near the school's entrance. Police officers, news reporters, and television cameras, as if on cue, turn away en masse as she approaches Mom and Young Skull with a welcoming smile. Mom breathes a sigh of relief until the woman spits at them - the saliva landing on the street but her words stinging with perfect accuracy.

"Stay with your own kind, niggers."

Mom's gentle handholding becomes a desperate clutch and she starts murmuring. "Yea, though I walk through the valley of the shadow of death ..."

Negroes, Niggers, moulies too, Jiggaboo, jiggaboo, jiggaboo-hoo. Go away now, cuz we don't want you! Negroes, Niggers, moulies too.

"...I will fear no evil, for thou art with me, thy rod and thy staff comfort me...."

"Jungle bunnies!"

"...Thou preparest a table before me in the presence of mine enemies..."

No, no, no, no, niggers, niggers, niggers, niggers ...

A white hand attached to a muscular white arm protruding from a whiter sleeveless t-shirt clutches at them. Mom wraps one arm around her son, squeezing so tight he cannot breathe. Gasping, he turns his head only to face a wall of bulging white pupil-less eyes protruding from snarling white faces. Flashes of white light explode through the whiteness. Mom's hand disintegrates into a white, powdery cloud. Young Skull reaches for her but she floats away. He runs down an endless white hall, through an open white door into a strange white bathroom where matte-white octopus-shaped dust-balls dance along glossy white moldings. He ducks behind a translucent white curtain, hides in a big white bathtub, crawls to the drain and dives headfirst, spiraling downward into a moldy-white cellar packed wall-to-wall with his rosy-cheeked *Romper Room* television friends whose glaring white teeth flash at him like a barrage of white lightning bolts. Young Skull, blinded by the whiteness, holds his hand up to shield his eyes but instead is struck by the contrast of his dark-chocolate brown skin. Time stops for a moment as he slowly inspects the dark side of his hand, drawing it closer and exploring every vein in each finger. Young Skull, astonished by his own dark-chocolate brown blackness, looks around the room and is released from the spell. For the first time in his life he feels different. Other. Alienated, isolated, and abandoned. He gasps for air as his friends morph from undulating white shadows into blood-red gargoyles and back again. They chant: *Spook! Brillo Head! Uga Booga Boo!* Cannonballs of molten white venom shoot out of their flaming eyes, their flaring nostrils, their sneering mouths.

November 22, 1963

Shortly after lunchtime, Mrs. S. calls her second-grade class to order. "Quiet down and take your seats please. I have an announcement."

Young Skull is sitting next to Robert H. who, since day one, has made no secret of his displeasure at the seating assignment.

"I hope we're not getting any more *n, n, n, N*egroes."

All the second-graders within earshot cackle in solidarity with Robert's wit, perpetuating the completely exposed yet invisible state in which Young Skull has been suspended since his first day in this wonderful new school. Mrs. S. raps her ruler on the blackboard. "Quiet down, children. I have some news to share with you. Bad news. Very disturbing news."

Mrs. S. takes a deep breath and sighs.

"Today the President of the United States was assassinated in Dallas, Texas. He died a little while ago. President John F. Kennedy is dead."

Hello Dolly

1991: It's last call at Bee Sharp's and the band has left the building. He is sitting at the far end of the bar, napkin tucked into his collar, eating fried chicken with a knife and fork while waiting for Sharon to close out the register and join him as he heads uptown to check out an after-hours jam session. Skullcap Dashiki is at the other end, half mumbling to himself and half trying to convince Sharon that, earlier, Louis Armstrong had been here.

"Come on Sweetheart. You had to see him. He was right there, wearin' a tuxedo and wipin' his forehead with a handkerchief." Then Skullcap projects his voice down the bar. "You saw him, right? He was standing next to you during the first set."

"Who?"

"Who? Louis Armstrong, that's who!"

"Louis Armstrong? You said you don't even like Louis Armstrong."

Skullcap shoots a vacillating look of recognition and dismissal in his direction before turning to Sharon. "Look at him. Eating fried chicken with a knife and fork. You know you ain' grown up eaten no chicken like that!"

She ignores him and puts his check on the bar. Skullcap takes his sweet ostentatious time looking at the check, taking out his wallet, counting and laying out some bills. He tries to stand but stumbles against the bar. Sharon puts a CD into the player on the shelf next to the bottles of booze. The voice of Louis Armstrong singing *Hello Dolly* fills the air. Skullcap Dashiki shakes his head in disgust and walks out into the night.

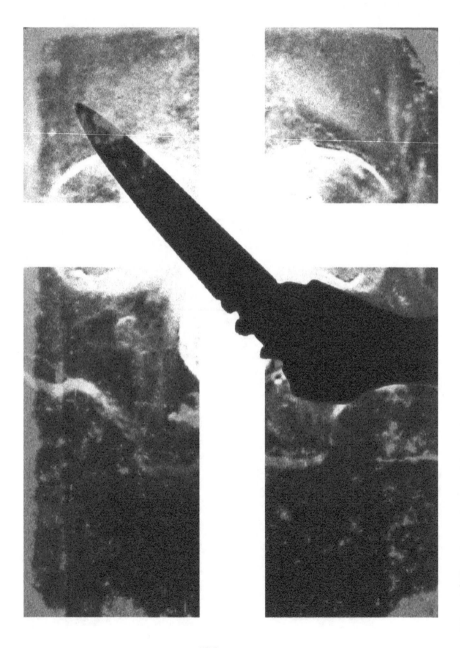

Holy Rollers
By Kevin McCarthy

Finland/USA

So, Timmy is just standing there in the doorway, smiling and brandishing a kitchen knife.

"Welcome, Pastor," he says. "Come in, come in." A voice inside of me is telling me, no, screaming at me to run, but after what Timmy said to me over the phone, I can't just abandon him now. Once we're inside, he leads me to the kitchen table. Using his free hand, he pulls back one of the chairs and, with a flourish of the knife, beckons me to sit.

Over the years, I've heard some pretty crazy stuff come out of Timmy's mouth, but his taking me hostage at knife-point is new. I don't know if I ever told you about the time a few years ago when I was driving the youth group down to the District Youth Convention in Rochester. Half the kids were asleep and the rest stared glazed-eyed out the windows. DC Talk droned through the blown-out speakers of the fifteen-passenger church van. Timmy was riding shotgun. About an hour outside the cities, just out of the blue, he leans over to me and is like, "I heard what you said. I'm not as stupid as you think."

The thing is, I hadn't said a word. Nobody in the van had said a mumbling word. And I certainly hadn't called him stupid. Not even in my head.

Anyway, there I find myself, sitting at Timmy's kitchen table. Not a single light is on in the entire house.

"When will your mom be home?" I ask.

"In three weeks."

"Three weeks? Where is she?"

"In San Francisco for work."

"Is it normal for her to leave you home alone for weeks on end?"

"I'm sixteen. I can take care of myself."

"Whatever happened to her boyfriend?"

"Which one?"

"I'm not sure of his name. The guy that works at One Stop Auto. He has a ponytail."

"Brian. He's old news. She dumped him over a year ago. Her latest boyfriend was named Phil."

"Oh. Well, where's Phil?"

"When Mom left, she gave him a week to move out." Timmy stops fumbling with the kitchen knife and makes eye contact with me. This is weird because he's probably never made eye contact before in the entire time that I've known him. He says, "Phil's gone, but I am not alone."

"Who else is here?"

"My friend, the Lieutenant."

"The Lieutenant? A Lieutenant in what army?"

"I invited you over so the two of you could finally meet," Timmy says, ignoring my question regarding the Lieutenant's allegiance. Timmy sets down the knife. "I have to warn you though, he doesn't like you very much."

"Wonderful. Is this Lieutenant one of your gamer friends?" I ask, figuring the guy is someone Timmy met online playing Dungeons and Dragons or something.

"No. The Lieutenant lives in this house. He's lived here since like the '60s." Timmy's finally starting to freak me out a little. Part of it is the way he says "*Lef*-tenant," pronouncing it like the British do.

About this time one of the bedroom doors sweeps open slowly, seemingly by itself. I watch as nothing comes out into the hallway and walks leisurely over towards the kitchen table. The floorboards creak under unseen weight. I think, if the Lieutenant is only Timmy's imaginary friend, then his imagination must be much heftier than my own. Whatever the Lieutenant is, it pulls back a chair and sits down directly across the table from me.

I try praying silently, but it's hard to formulate complete strands of thoughts when you can hear your heartbeat pounding in your temple.

Timmy interrupts my stuttering silent prayer: "The Lef-tenant has something he wants to say to you."

I glance at the knife and then at the empty chair. I am not so sure I want to hear the Lieutenant out. "Listen to me, Timmy. I came here to talk to you, not this guy, whoever he is."

Timmy doesn't respond. He doesn't even look up. I don't think he can hear what I am saying. He seems enamored of his reflection in the knife blade and has this look in his eyes that I can't quite gauge.

129

An idea comes to me, an idea that's either been planted in my brain by God or gleaned from the hundreds of episodes of *Cops* I've watched in my lifetime. I need to turn Timmy's attention away from the present situation and focus it on something else. Anything else.

"Remember last summer up at Lake Geneva Bible Camp when you told me the story about cutting the grass? About when that voice spoke to you, told you to tip over the lawnmower and throw your head into the rotating blade?"

"Yeah, I remember."

"You remember why you didn't obey that voice?"

"It would have hurt."

"Yes. No. Well ... true, it would have hurt, but what did we talk about after you told me the story? About the voice not having your best interest in mind?"

Timmy stares at me blankly.

"Do you trust that I have your best interest in mind?"

He opens his mouth and is about to speak, but then he hesitates. After a moment he says, "The Lef-tenant's right."

"About what?"

"You don't really care about me. It's your job to pretend you do."

"That's not true. I do care about you."

"You're just like my mom." Timmy picks up the knife and stabs its point about an inch and half deep into the soft wood of the, probably purchased from IKEA, table. "Both of you are liars."

Trying to talk Timmy down isn't working and I realize that I've thrown up in my mouth a little. I need a new plan. Nothing is coming to mind so I just wing it.

"I'm thirsty," I say, swallowing my vomit and clearing my throat. "May I please have a glass of water?"

"Sure. Stay here. I'll go get it." Timmy stands, yanks the knife out of the tabletop and takes it with him as he strides across the kitchen toward the refrigerator. He has left me alone at the table with the Lieutenant.

His back turned to me, Timmy says, "Sorry. My mom always says I am a terrible host. Do you want anything to eat?"

"Sure. What have you got?" Now is my chance.

"We have frozen burritos and . . ."

I make my move. I'm not sure if I get a piece of the Lieutenant, but I sure kick the stuffing out of his chair, launching it backward so it bounces off the wall. Before I can think of what to do next, Timmy charges me. Screaming like a banshee, he plunges the knife into the top of my shoulder. It hurts, but lucky for me the blade struck bone or something and he can't pull it out. I catch Timmy in a bear hug and we crash to the floor. Now, I am older than he is and quite a bit bigger. On top of that, I remember some of the jujitsu I picked up during Tuesday night Holy Roller sessions in the basement of the men's dorm at Bible College and eventually I am able to gain the upper hand.

131

"Get off me. You're not my friend - not like the Lef-tenant is," Timmy says, his face pressed against the floorboards.

"No, I won't let you go. The Lieutenant doesn't really care about you. Besides," I say, "I think I might have killed him." As we are having this conversation, I use my body weight to keep him pinned to the floor.

"Timmy, I have to put you to sleep now. But when you wake up, you and I are going to have a long talk about friendship and trust."

Then I do what any youth pastor in my situation would do to: a rear naked choke. I wrap my right arm around the front of Timmy's neck until his Adam's apple is cradled in the pit of my elbow, grab my left bicep with the opposite hand and gently squeeze, temporarily cutting off the blood flow to his brain, causing him to pass out.

After that, as I lie panting on the hardwood floor between an unconscious kid who sporadically attends my youth group and a broken kitchen table, I wonder if Timmy has a point. Would I still care about these kids if caring was no longer my job? Eventually I struggle to a sitting position, grasp the handle of the knife, and begin working the bloody blade out of my shoulder, which, now that the adrenaline has begun to wear off, hurts like the dickens. It is then that I hear footsteps scurrying down the hallway. The bedroom door slams shut. In all the commotion I've completely forgotten about the Lieutenant.

Now, I wish that at this point I had shouted something more befitting of my calling as a licensed minister of the Assemblies of God. Something confident, maybe containing a Bible verse. But that is not what I said. No; to my eternal shame, what came out of my mouth was neither eloquent nor spiritual. I yelled, "You better run, motherfucker."

A Brief Respite
By CL Dalkin

England

It was over. After seven long years, he'd done it. Seven years of mad, unhinged, up-and-down emotions. A rollercoaster, his sister had said.

He'd ended it the only way he knew how. By packing a rucksack and walking out. Everything else belonged to her anyway. Just the shirt on his back - light as a feather, mate. It felt good. Closed the front door - *click*! And he was off. Very satisfying.

Oh, all right, there had been a bit of a fight. She'd flown at him - screaming, pleading - and he was propelled backwards, over the arm of the sofa, taking her with him. It's okay - they had a soft landing. Oh, all right, her head did connect with the coffee table. Bit of a thump. Might give her a black eye. Maybe he should just call and check?

No. Way. Not going back there ever again. What about all the bruises she'd given him? Mental and literal? They just weren't suited. They had been, in the beginning, but some couples just bring out the worst in each other, don't they?

He'd left her peacefully sleeping it off, sprawled over the sofa in her patchwork jeans and pink hoodie. Oh, all right. Maybe not that peacefully. Snoring - noisy, rasping, laboured breathing. That'll be the whisky. And forty cigarettes a day. Always snored after the whisky, keeping him awake. Maybe now he'd get a full night's sleep!

What a relief. He'd soon be at his sister's - "Come round," she'd said, when he told her the news. They could have a take-away and a beer. Lovely. If only the rain wasn't so heavy. He was soaked through, right to the bone.

Speaking of which, he hoped she hadn't broken any? Of course not! People are always relaxed when they are drunk. Land like a sack of spuds and just stay where they are, limbs everywhere. Like a funny little straw-headed ragdoll. Nasty bruise on the side of her head though.

He shrugged off the feeling of - what was it? And noticed a figure on the other side of the road. Rain pelted his face, but he could see it was a woman in a pink hoodie, dirty blonde hair poking out. He felt a thump in his chest, wiped his face, and looked hard across the road. She was turning the corner.

He speeded up to the edge of the street. No one. You're going a bit nutty mate. Who would be out in this weather anyway? Not even the sun had bloody bothered to get its arse above the horizon. That's what it felt like, anyway. Nah, he was just feeling guilty, that's all. Her image must be burned on his retinas. Mate, you can't just shrug off a seven-year relationship.

Nearly there.

Bloody rain was getting harder. Battering the pavement - he heard it, along with the sound of running footsteps. *Clop! Clop! Clop! Clop!* Someone was up the road ahead of him, near his sister's house. He could hear the gate squeal and saw ... a flash of pink?

Not possible. He'd left her snoring. Dead drunk. Legless. She couldn't even walk, let alone skip along like a teenager. God, he hoped she hadn't been sick. He should have lain her on her side, like the paramedics once told him. Shit. Maybe he should have called for a doctor. Oh, thank God. His sister, smiling, waving through the front room window. She'd know what to do. Then he froze, his gaze drawn to the upstairs window. Another woman, also waving, looking down at him. Pink hoodie. Dirty blonde hair. Nasty bruise on her temple. Expressionless.

Fog
By Petra McQueen

England

The noise blunders into her dream. She cries out, hand fluttering at her chest. *Calm down*, she thinks, *it's only a car coming along the lane.* She drags back the covers and stands, feeling each stiff muscle, mouth thick with claggy breath. Opening the curtains, she sees a shiny vintage car. The noise, the sight of the car, familiar yet hazy, precipitates a slow dread. A locked memory shifts and threatens to break. She hugs her flannelette nightie close, telling herself that the unease is only the lingering remnants of the night - a dream in which the land shifted and changed in the wind: sea-corroded edges, swamped beaches, swallowed marsh and sand.

The car's rumble rattles her sash windows, thrums up through the floorboards. With a stutter, the engine ceases. Maggie breathes easier. She watches as a man gets out, dressed in khaki. A twitcher, no doubt, come for a holiday in the cottage next door. A fool, whoever he is, driving an old thing like that. He reaches into the back of the car, takes out a spade and a suitcase. A flash of scarlet darts out. It's a young boy in a woolly red jumper. With a thump of shock, Maggie steps from the window as though she's done something wrong. As she palms tights onto her legs and shrugs into her clothes, her throat feels thick with unshed tears. Lines come to her from a poem: *Four foot something / something every year of something.*

The words nag at her as she pads down the stairs. Which poem do they come from? Why are they so insistent? Unwilling to use the laptop her daughter foisted on her last Christmas, she lets the questions go and thinks of the day ahead. Today her granddaughter, Evie, is visiting. They'll stick cotton wool clouds on blue sugar paper.

After toast and marmalade, Maggie opens the back door. She tucks her chin against the cold and shuffles along the garden path toward the shed for her painting supplies. As a child, visiting the holiday cottage with her parents, she'd been afraid of the shadowy, dank yard and the rising distant dunes. For years after inheriting the place, Maggie never visited. But she hadn't ever got round to selling it, either - was reluctant, even, to think of the village. But now that her daughter and her family live close by, Maggie stays occasionally. Evie is worth anything.

She gathers straws and paints, paper and cotton wool. As she steps outside the shed, she is startled by the little boy bouncing a ball against her fence.

"Oh." She puts her hand to her heart.

The boy runs toward the dunes and flashes through trunks of silver birch. As he disappears from sight, a gust of wind blows back her hair, tugs at her skirts. She shades her eyes from sharp breeze and low sun. Above the filigree of black branches, a bank of thick white cloud is rolling in. Should she tell her neighbour to fetch the boy? Or go herself? But she's no age for wandering.

Evie rounds the corner and bursts in through the garden gate, curls bouncing. "There's a big fog coming. Big."

Her daughter comes to the fence. "Hi Mum, I better leave before it sets in." She gives a brief kiss and Maggie watches her go, relieved. Not that she doesn't love Amanda, but she holds a raft of unwritten rules about childcare Maggie doesn't understand. Why not give the child some chocolate as a treat?

Maggie steers Evie towards the house. She puts down paints and paper and hugs her granddaughter close. The cold is trapped in her curls. "Let's have a cup of tea."

"Can I go out, Granny? Can I?"

"I'll get my coat and bag."

When Maggie emerges from the cupboard under the stairs, Evie has disappeared. The front door is wide open. Maggie rushes out into a soft, wet wall of white. All is cloud and the damp smell of winter.

"Evie?"

Smudges move against the brume. Evie and the small red figure of the little boy. The poem plays again: *Four foot.* Still she can't remember the words. Evie shoots past the boy. "Come and get me!"

Maggie scrambles to lock the door, shouting over her shoulder, "Hold on!"

The roar of a car starting makes her jump. It semaphores, once more, the memory so carefully packed away. She knows it only as a well of dread she must not to peer into.

"Children! Be careful!"

They don't reply.

The car crawls towards her, headlamps on, light refracting against the wall of fog. Driving in this! Does the man have no sense? And leaving the boy alone to play in the fog! What kind of person does that?

She rushes ahead of the car. "Evie, where are you?" Close by is a blur of a tree, a bush, a garden gate. "Evie?" The car is behind her, engine thrumming, wheels crunching on grit. She feels it at her heels. An iron monster. "Evie! Please!"

"Granny, I'm here."

She bustles her away from the road. "You silly, silly girl!"

The car drives past slowly, rocking on uneven ground. Maggie wants to hammer on the windscreen but she mustn't scare Evie. She darts down, grasping Evie's shoulders.

"Where's the little boy?"

"You're hurting."

Over Evie's shoulder, she catches a blur of red in the distance. "Hello!"

Evie giggles. Maggie takes her small, warm hand and trots after the boy. Every time Maggie shouts "Hell*oo*!," Evie copies her in a high pitched echo. The boy doesn't turn. After a few minutes, Maggie gives up. She watches as the boy is swallowed by fog. He's too little to be on his own out here, in this unfamiliar world. But he's too far away to be any of her business.

She turns back to Evie. "Let's go home." But which way? She doesn't recognise a thing. Everything looks ancient and half-formed. A tree is a pagan god - twisted, lightning-struck, black branches reaching and fading into the white.

Maggie guesses the direction, takes Evie's hand and walks tentatively. It seems as though they are travelling under the only light in an opaque, dingy world. Maggie spots a stone lion leering at her through the vapour. The Everson's gatepost. Thank God. She knows where she is. Following the boy, they must've ended up on the dog-leg of Church Lane.

"Not long now."

It's not so murky here, and they can see the outlines of the houses set back from the road. It occurs to Maggie that the fog is not homogeneous. If it were possible to map it, you could walk the honeycomb, sidle cliffs of cloud and emerge in clear caverns. If you knew what you were doing, you needn't be lost at all.

They turn a corner. "Granny, look!" The black tower of the church rises out of a thin cloak of mist. Evie pulls Maggie's hand. "Let's go see."

Maggie shakes her head, "It's not the way."

"But I want to."

As though in a dream, Maggie lets Evie lead her to the church. She has the sensation of watching herself disappearing into thick mist. She is swallowed, erased, eradicated.

A noise starts: a *scrape*, *scrape*. Someone is digging a grave. No, how silly. Nobody has been buried in the churchyard for decades. And besides, the noise isn't coming from the graveyard, it's coming from opposite the church gates.

They turn right along Golgotha Road. As they walk towards the noise, the jelly-mould outline of the stationary vintage car comes into focus. She holds Evie's hand tight. Next to the car, her neighbour is digging. Why? What business does he have here?

They reach the man.

"What are you doing?" Evie asks.

"I'm putting in footings for a bench."

Maggie is about to berate him for leaving the little boy, when she sees the boy opposite, on the pavement at the church gates, bouncing a ball. He looks so small in the mist. *A four foot something / something every year of his life.*

141

"It's a memorial bench," says the man. "For my twin. Killed in a hit and run. Almost fifty years ago now."

Maggie catches her breath, feels the pressure of the fog bearing down on her, stirring secrets she's tried so long to forget.

"But I'm daft. I've forgotten the concrete." He picks up his shovel and walks to the car.

Maggie tugs Evie's hand, pulls at her to come away. But the little girl is firmly planted, anchoring Maggie to this place, this time. The man drives past and turns left down Church Lane, a lane which leads nowhere except round back to the church, back to Golgotha Road. Through the mist, she hears the car negotiating corners, turning left, left, back to the road.

"Oh God!"

"Granny?"

It was the same car she'd driven all those years ago. Drunk and stupid, so young, only just passed her test. As she'd thundered along, high on life and hope, she'd never thought there would be a little boy, a little boy in the mist. The poem comes sharp and clear. *A four-foot coffin / One for every year of his life.*

No! thinks Maggie. *No!* Things will be different this time.

"Stay here!" she says to Evie. She lifts the girl and places her under a tree, her back against the trunk. "Stay right here!" She steps out to cross the road. As she does so, a bank of thick fog streams up the street. The boy is lost in a shroud of white. The thrumming roar comes closer, closer. The sound is in each wisp, each tendril; it slides into particles, strums molecules, fills the cavities of her bones.

The boy bounces the ball.

Thwank, thwank, thwank.

She tries to shout. The fog is in her mouth, at the back of her throat. A wind rises, blows her hair, tugs at her skirt. It clears a cave in the fog. She is at one end, the boy at the other. Mist coils about them. *Thwank, thwank, thwank.*

Now is the time to run. Now.

Her legs are lead. The thrum is louder, louder.

Why doesn't she run?

The boy stumbles, ball skittering along the tarmac. He follows it, head down, almost dancing.

Out of the white, out of the fog, comes the car.

Now! *Now!*

Maggie speeds across the road.

"Granny! Wait!"

Evie runs too, after her granny, into the fog. Such a little girl. Only four years old.

The Tattibogle
By Kristin J. Cooper

Scotland

Based on an oral tale by the travelling Scottish storyteller, Stanley Robertson

When Sam stumbled upon the thing in the glen he screamed, and I laughed. But the thrill I felt at seeing my invincible older brother undone in a moment of pure fright ended as soon as I saw what he was staring at.

One minute we were racing each other through a copse of stunted pine trees, burning off the restless energy accumulated during the long drive, the next the sun was in my eyes as we burst into the open and stumbled down a steep slope. What lay before us must once have been farmland but was now a withered stretch of weeds. Parts of it were scorched black, as though someone had tried to set fire to it. And there at the edge of the long grass, tilted to one side and looking for all the world like it was trying to lurch its way up towards the sound of our voices, was a scarecrow.

It wore a suit that had once been black but now was mottled grey, bulging and humped as though something living inside it struggled to burst out. The worst thing was its head. The turnip was rotten, caved in on one side and oozing a stream of decay. The hat jammed over its matted straw hair cast a shadow over eye sockets that were nothing more than roughly gouged holes. It had a mouth of sorts - a hole framed by a pair of shrivelled lips that looked like dried worms twisted in a vicious sneer. It was a nightmare in broad daylight, and my brother had run straight into it.

Sam's limbs thrashed as he began crawling away from the thing. He quivered and twitched, gasping for breath. And so, although I was horrified, I let out another hysterical snort of laughter. His head snapped around.

I clamped my hands over my mouth but it was too late; he glared at me in a way that let me know there would be painful consequences. I was only nine but already I understood that according to Sam, the world belonged to him. He didn't believe in monsters under the bed, or in the closet. Sam believed *he* was the thing to be afraid of and was proud of it.

He scrambled to his feet and stumbled over to me.

"You think that's funny, Jack?" he snarled. "Well, why don't you come a little closer and see if you still feel like laughing?"

He grabbed me by the wrist and pulled. I struggled, trying to twist out of his grip, but he was too strong. He was twelve, after all.

"No Sam, please!" I begged. But his eyes were lit with determination and his fingers dug into my wrist. There was no escape.

"Come shake the scarecrow's hand, Jack," he said, dragging me closer.

Because that's what we thought it was, in the beginning. Just a plain, old scarecrow.

After two steps I was hit by the stench of the thing, and I began to whimper.

"Please Sammy. I'm sorry I laughed. I didn't mean to …"

"Shush Jack. I'll forgive you, once you shake old Scarecrow's hand. All you got to do is reach out …"

The hand jutting from the dirty sleeve was a rotten green. A dried black substance was caked in half-moons under the fingernails, and I knew if I reached out those fingers would move faster than lightning to grip harder than Sam ever could. My arm strained in its socket. My hand was too close.

"Sam! Jack! Where have you got to?" The sound of Mum's voice lifted the spell. Sam released me so suddenly I sat down with a thump.

"Not a word, okay?" he hissed. I nodded, not trusting myself to speak.

He started to walk past me, but suddenly whirled back to face the apparition.

"And as for you ..." he whispered between gritted teeth.

Sam launched himself at the scarecrow. I didn't see the pocketknife at first, the one he'd begged Dad for and finally got last birthday despite Mum's disapproval. Then I saw it in his hand, and something dark was dripping from its point.

There came a low moan like a night wind in a chimney. A flock of black birds burst from the trees behind us, setting my heart to hammering my ribs all over again. The scarecrow's severed hand lay on the ground for a moment before Sam kicked it into the trees and stalked away, teeth bared and knife clenched in his stained hand.

Mum was loading the last of the picnic gear into the car when I catapulted through the trees. She paused as she reached for the hatch door.

"Jack? What's wrong?" A hand grasped my shoulder.

"I just gave him a little scare, Ma," said Sam from behind me. His fingers tightened, and I hoped it wasn't the hand that had held the knife. The hand covered in dark stuff.

147

"Leave your brother alone, Sam." Dad's voice was stern but distracted as he walked back to the car, head bent over the AA road map in his hands. He'd been comparing it to the tourist information board in the car park while Mum cleared away the remnants of our lunch.

"It looks like it's no distance at all from here," he said, glancing up at Mum.

"Don't look at me." She shrugged as she opened the passenger door. "I was ten the last time I was here. I don't remember much."

She glanced uneasily toward the pine trees as she got into the car. "You okay now, Jack? Ready to go meet Aunty Morag?"

I nodded and climbed into the backseat where Sam waited. He smiled at me - not in a good way.

"Right," said Dad as he slid behind the wheel. "Let's find this Broon Farm."

—

It was the summer of 1985 and we were in Scotland because Aunty Morag had written to say she was not in the best of health and wanted to see her only living relatives before she made the final move from Broon Farm into a retirement home. She couldn't keep the farm going on her own and couldn't afford a farmhand. When we finally found the overgrown track leading to the dilapidated farmhouse that afternoon, it was clear the fields around it had been neglected for some time.

The sun stayed up long into the evening, lurking behind the hills in a sombre smudge. I'd never been a good sleeper. My mother blamed it on an active imagination. She said I got it from Dad, who was forever daydreaming about the next Big Opportunity. She said it like it wasn't such a good thing, which must be why she looked so scandalised when Dad started eyeing up the property, pound signs sprouting like crops before his bespectacled eyes.

"Not so good for farming anymore," he mused. "But residential property? We're not that far from the A96."

"I'm just thinking out loud," he said when he caught my mother's look. "You want to make sure the old girl is looked after, don't you?"

Aunty Morag was the ugliest woman I had ever seen, but that wouldn't have bothered me so much if I had detected a trace of warmth in her face, a hint of tenderness in her touch, or a genuine welcome in her smile. As she scuttled out the front door her muddy eyes shone with cold eagerness. Her long nails prodded and lingered over each of us in turn and her grin was that of a ghoul on an amusement park ghost train. She was utterly horrible. Even my father, a man who took everything in his stride, faltered as she clasped him about his waist.

"Here you are, at last," she simpered. "I've been waitin' an' waitin'. But you found it okay, that's the main thing. Come awa' inside."

Dad shot a look of bewilderment at my mother, but she just stood staring at the house.

"Mum?" I ventured, grabbing her hand. She didn't respond.

"Well," she said finally, looking at me with a brave smile that didn't quite reach her eyes. "This is certainly a lot different to how I remember it." She squeezed my hand.

Aunty Morag beckoned for us to follow Dad and Sam into the house.

We ate in a kitchen that had seen better days. The grey flagstones were stained; the curtains at the sagging casement windows were grimy and full of holes. Only the old oven seemed clean and maintained, roaring away in its arched stone alcove.

The meal was unappetising to say the least. Chunks of grey meat swam in a thin, greasy gruel, surrounded by blobs of disintegrating vegetables. It tasted gritty, somehow. The four of us ate in silence, pushing the food around our plates. Aunty Morag didn't seem to notice. She ate with gusto despite her few teeth, gravy dribbling down her chin. When she caught me staring she grinned, displaying gobbets of half-chewed food. I was convinced I was going to be sick.

Dessert was worse.

"Just coffee for me, please," Dad said quickly when he saw the curdled sludge that was, according to Aunty Morag, rice pudding being dished out.

"Ah, awa' wi' ye," said Aunty Morag. "Ye need some meat on those bones. Eat up, eat up!" And she cackled. She honestly did.

Sam stirred in his chair. He'd been quiet during dinner, but I suppose given the circumstances no one thought that too unusual.

"Can I ..."

"No, you can't," interjected Dad grumpily as the bowls were dumped in front of us.

Aunty Morag squeezed Mum's shoulder as she rounded the table.

"This was always your favourite, Katie, d'ye remember?"

Mum still looked kind of foggy. She shook her head.

"No, Aunty, I honestly don't. It's strange. I can't remember much about our visits here at all."

"Well, that's no' a surprise, considering a' that unpleasant business wi' your cousin George the last time ye stayed."

"What happened to George?" asked Sam.

"I ... I don't know," said Mum, confused. "I can't remember that either."

"It was a working farm back then, dear," said Aunty Morag. "Accidents happen on farms, especially to curious bairns who wander aboot in sheds full o' machinery an' sharp tools."

"Katie?" Dad sounded concerned. Mum had turned very pale.

"I'm sorry, Aunty," she said. "We're very tired from the drive today. Would you mind us getting an early night?"

"An excellent idea," said Dad, almost leaping from his chair. "We can talk tomorrow, can't we? Plenty of time."

Considering the kind of day it had been so far, I was not surprised to learn I had to share a room with Sam. We followed each other up the creaking staircase.

"Sorry aboot the lights, dear," apologised Aunty Morag as my Dad flicked at several unresponsive switches. "Some just need their bulbs replacin', but the wire's gone in most. Mebbe you could have a wee look at them tomorrow?" She patted Dad's arm and he tried not to flinch.

Our metal-framed beds squatted on bare wooden floorboards. A rocking chair sat in a corner next to a small table with a lamp perched on top, its weak light illuminating the mouldy wallpaper. A large window looked out on a huddle of oak trees and beyond to an overgrown field and mountains in the distance. I stared out at the unfamiliar view, absently picking at the curls of paint peeling from the window frame. Mum pulled the frayed curtains closed.

"I know it's hard for you to sleep when it's so light, but try to get some rest," she said, stroking my cheek.

"Okay, Mum."

She looked over at Sam, already in bed and flicking through his latest comic book.

"You okay, little man?" Sam frowned.

"So long as Toe Rag here doesn't keep me awake being a baby and crying all night."

"I'm not a baby!" I shouted. "I'm not the one who …"

"Enough!" said Mum abruptly, closing her eyes and rubbing her forehead with one hand. "It's been a long day, and I know Aunty Morag's house is a little … well, not what we're used to, but please try to get along. There'll be plenty for you to see and do tomorrow."

"Okay Mum," said Sam with a smug smile. "Good night."

"Jack?"

"Good night, Mum," I managed to say.

Sometimes I really hated my brother.

I couldn't sleep. Strange shadows hovered in the corners of the ceiling and the room smelled damp. And every time I closed my eyes I saw the thing with its dead hands reaching for me, the black holes in its head growing larger as its head swayed this way and that.

Sam was restless too. He tossed and turned, moaning in his sleep. Then I heard scratching, like sharp nails running down the other side of the bedroom door. Rhythmic, insistent … sly. Someone was muttering, eager and high-pitched.

Sam suddenly sat up. "Get *away* from me," he screamed.

The door creaked open and a shadow crept inside. I knew it was her before the dim light reluctantly gave up her features. Aunty Morag hovered between our beds, her eyes glittering.

"Dear wee bairns," she crooned. "I heard your restless dreams, an' these being unfamiliar beds in a strange house, I thought, mebbe a wee story will help ye to sleep?"

Sam recovered some of his composure. "No thanks, Aunty," he said, scorn evident in his voice. "Stories are for babies."

"I'd like to hear one, Aunty," I said. I looked straight at Sam. "I'd like to hear a story about a scarecrow."

I don't know why I said it; it was the last thing I wanted to hear. I could see that Sam's face was a thundercloud, so I guess that's the reaction I was after. But daft old Aunty Morag practically danced a jig on the spot.

"Ah loons, you'll no' be wanting a story aboot silly old scarecrows and their like; they're nae good for much in this part of the world." She giggled as she dragged the rocking chair closer. "The corbies are like vultures, ye ken," she said as she scrambled into the chair. "Tak ye eyes oot as soon as look at ye. No, ye want to scare the birds awa' from your crops 'round here, ye need a tattibogle."

153

Outside the wind picked up and rattled the windowpane.

"What's a ... a ..."

"Tattibogle? Well ... it's a special kind of scarecrow." Her voice dropped to a low whisper as her head jutted forward, weaving between us like a snake. "A scarecrow brought to life by the de'il himself."

Shadows crawled across the walls and pooled at Aunty Morag's feet. My body felt heavy, pinned to the bed. I couldn't lift my head from the pillow.

"There was once a farmer called Akey Broon, and he owned this very farm many, many years ago," she began. "I guess ye could say he was a distant relative. When he bought the farm, it was cattle most people raised, but a fearsome band o' cattle thieves plagued the district. The leader was a MacGregor, of course."

To my disgust, Aunty Morag spat a meaty wad of phlegm straight onto the floorboards. "He got his come-uppance in the end. Swung by his neck, along with the rest o' his band. But Akey - this farm is named for him even now, ye ken - he thought it was safer to plant crops. He didn't count on the corbies, mind; you've probably no' seen many on ye way here today, am I right?"

Sam and I both nodded. There weren't many birds at all, except for the ones I saw when ...

"That's because a tattibogle walked this land."

There was a long pause as these words chased each other around the room. I curled up into a ball under the covers, but couldn't resist peeking out at Sam.

He was full of contempt. "Oh yeah?" he said. "I think you're full of crap, lady."

Aunty Morag stared at Sam for a long moment while I held my breath. "D'ye want tae hear this story or no'?" Aunty Morag barked. Sam was silent.

"Now, where was I?" Her tone lightened.

"Oh aye. Akey Broon couldnae keep the corbies awa' from his crops. For every seed he sowed, two birds would fly doon tae fight over it, quick as he could tak a step. So Akey decided to visit the Warlock Stane at midnight, for he had heard that the dark spirits o' dead witches gathered at that place. And the night he went, old Akey called up none other than the spirit o' the great Warlock himself, Colin Massie."

Aunty Morag paused, still as a statue. I counted my heartbeats in the silence before she began to repeat the Warlock's words:

"This is the spell for the most powerful o' tattibogles, Akey Broon." Her voice had changed; it was deeper, filling the corners of the room.

"First ye must pull a turnip from the field, an' gouge oot sockets for its eyes an' mouth. Ye must cut the yellow eyes from a barn owl, stoned to death, an' cut the mouth from a child dead o' the smallpox. Place those in the turnip, and they will take root.

"Now dig out an eye from seven carcasses: a rabbit, a cow, a deer, a snake, a salmon, a badger, a wildcat, and sew them on as buttons for the jacket. Press the turnip onto a pole and add on the jacket, trousers an' boots, all stuffed with straw. Then ye must cut a pair o' hands from a corpse on the gibbet and pull oot its rotten heart to place inside the coat. To make it come alive, repeat the words o' this magic spell."

Despite myself, I leaned forward. So did Sam.

155

"A laird, a lord, a lily, a leaf, a piper, a drummer, a hummer, a thief."

Aunty Morag looked at me. I could see the cold light of her eyes.

"Say it with me, children."

I didn't want to, but she held me trapped in her gaze.

"A laird ... a lord . . ." I began, trembling. "A ... a ..."

She nodded encouragingly.

"... A lily, a leaf," I gasped.

She turned to Sam. He lifted his chin defiantly, determined to keep his composure.

"A piper," he said. "A drummer, a hummer, a thief."

She made us say it again, together this time. Then we stared at each other while around the room the shadows sighed.

"Sam? Is that you, honey?"

Mum's sleepy voice called from the far end of the hallway. Quick as a flash Aunty Morag pushed the rocking chair back into position and made for the door.

"Wait!" said Sam. "What happened next?"

"It came alive, o' course," she snapped. She was about to disappear through the door.

"What happened to Akey Broon?" I asked. She paused, then looked back over her shoulder.

"That's a tale for another night," she said. Then she was gone, and Mum's footsteps were outside the room.

"Sam? Jack? Are you awake?"

Mum's silhouette stood in the open doorway. Sam feigned sleep, but I couldn't lie still.

"It was just a bad dream, Mum," I whispered into the dark.

"Try and get some rest, kiddo," she said.

It was only her calm, reassuring presence that allowed me to drop off to sleep.

Much later, in the darkest part of the night, I woke, wondering what could have disturbed me. When my sight adjusted to the gloom I saw it sitting in the rocking chair, motionless but for the slow blink of lamp-like yellow eyes in its misshapen head. The tattibogle was looking at me.

I froze. *It's a dream, just a very bad dream*, I told myself while it sat there, watching me. After a long, long time it leaned forward, and the lips around the gaping hole of its mouth writhed into a sickening semblance of a smile.

I must have fainted from fear because the next thing I knew daylight was streaming in the window and Sam was smashing me in the face with his pillow. I pushed him off, looking wildly towards the empty rocking chair.

"Come on, Toe Rag," said Sam, back to his old annoying self. "Time for breakfast. Let's see if Aunty Morag's serving snails on toast with booger jam."

He launched himself off my bed and out the door. I followed more slowly, trying to decide if what I'd seen had really been a dream. I glanced toward the window - it was open, a soft breeze making the curtain billow. It had been closed when we went to bed. Then I saw it. A smear of mud stained the window ledge and on the floor beneath it lay three strands of dirty straw.

I didn't say anything. The bright morning sunshine dried up any words I had, and there wasn't a shadow in the world for a tattibogle to hide in. Thoughts of the night before disappeared completely after breakfast when Dad eased an ancient tractor out of the enormous barn behind the house. It threatened to shake itself to pieces as it wheezed into the light. Sam and I were both excited by the prospect of riding in it.

"You be careful in that thing," said Mum.

"Get in, boys," said Dad, grinning like a big kid himself. "Let's go see this farm."

It was a tight fit in the tractor's cab, but after some good-natured elbowing and squirming we settled ourselves in and were off to see the sights. There weren't many. Brown grass, nettles and wildflowers appeared over each horizon. A stream bordered by hogweed and the occasional willow tree snaked across our path. We trundled over an arched stone bridge. There were rabbits and a couple of highland cows that had strayed from a nearby field, but no sign of birds. Not even a crow.

There was, however, the sensation of being watched. The frown on Dad's face deepened. Our excited chatter petered out, and we were all silent when the tractor rumbled to a halt not far from a group of standing stones.

"That's strange," said Dad. "It just stopped." He tried the ignition a few times, but the engine didn't so much as cough. "We'll give it some time to cool down. Want to go look at the stones?"

158

There were five of them, one darker and taller than the rest. They were creepy, but I was curious. I darted in and out of their shadows, my hands tingling as I explored their rough surfaces with my fingers.

Sam hung back. He scowled, pacing back and forth in front of the tractor.

"Sam," called Dad, "What's wrong? Come and have a look."

But Sam just shook his head and turned his back to us, muttering. Something glinted in his hand, and I saw him run the pocketknife blade back and forth across the cracked surface of the tractor wheel.

The sense of being watched got stronger, and for a moment it was as if someone had turned down the colour on the whole world. Blackness edged my vision, and the stones appeared to rear up before us. Dad staggered away from them.

"Jack!" he called urgently, but I was staring at Sam. The pocketknife had slipped from his fingers and bounced under the tractor, and he was on his belly reaching for it, cheek pressed up against the wheel. Suddenly the tractor roared to life.

Dad stumbled toward Sam as I felt the breath leave my body. He looked as though he were moving in slow motion, shouting as the tractor lurched forward and Sam drew back, but not quickly enough. The back wheel rolled over his hand and stopped, pinning him in place. Sam began to scream. The blackness closed in and the world fell away.

—

Something was scratching at my cheek. A trembling, crooning sound brought me up from the darkness and, when my eyes cracked open, a dark and blurry shape hovered before me. After a moment of confusion, I realised it was Aunty Morag, singing to me and stroking my face with her long, dark nails. I tensed.

"Now then, now then, young Jack," she murmured.

I opened my mouth to protest, but not a sound came out.

"Dinna worry," she said. "Ye Mam and ye Da have taken Sam awa' to the hospital in Aberdeen, but you're safe with me, loon." She smiled, and all the dread of that awful moment by the standing stones came rushing back. I strained to speak, to ask the questions I needed answered.

"Cat got ye tongue?" Aunty Morag laughed, but it was not her high-pitched titter. It was a deep, throaty chuckle. "Or somethin' worse, I wonder?"

She leaned in close. "I ken how tae tak ye mind off things. How aboot I tell ye what happened to Akey Broon after he brought the tattibogle to life?"

I shook my head, tears starting in my eyes.

"Come now, Jack. I think ye like a good tale. Be brave now. Because things get much worse for Akey before they get better."

She pulled back a little, and I could see the night breeze playing in the curtain by the open window of my room in the farmhouse. It must have been late because outside the last glow of golden dusk was ebbing from the sky.

"Things improved for Akey," said Aunty Morag. "After the tattibogle came to life the corbies flew off into his neighbours' fields, and he harvested a plentiful crop that year. But the next season a blight appeared. Against that, the tattibogle had nae power. That didn't stop Akey blaming it, mind. One evening, drunk and full o' rage, he stormed into the ruined field wi' hisscythe and wi' one blow he severed its hand from its body. The tattibogle screamed."

I remembered the low moan that had risen up after Sam attacked the creature in the weeds and a sick horror came over me. How could she know what Sam - what we - had done? Why was she tormenting me with this story, especially now that Sam was ... but I didn't know *how* Sam was, and I still couldn't speak. It was like my throat was sealed with cement.

Her dark eyes watched me, a smug smile twisting the corners of her mouth. Outside the wind was picking up and sighing under the eaves.

"Poor Akey stumbled back from the wounded creature but, as he turned to flee, he tripped over the scythe, and accidentally cut off his *own* hand." Aunty Morag shook her head and tutted.

"There was nae means tae work his fields now. Filled with despair he resolved to finish the tattibogle for good. The next night he crept up behind it and, just as its head swivelled 'round tae stare at him, he swung the scythe wi' his remaining hand and cut the head clean off."

The wind grew more insistent. I thought of poor Sam lying in a hospital bed with his damaged hand and wished so much I was with him, with Mum and Dad. Anywhere but here. It was getting so dark.

"Poor Akey was found babbling an' half dead the next day. They carried him off tae the madhouse, and it wasn't long before he died there."

Aunty Morag grinned at me. "I lied about things getting better for Akey," she said. She turned her gaze to the gathering storm outside.

"Poor old tattibogle. He'd done everything Akey Broon had asked him tae, an' more. But he was a powerful creature now, wi' powerful friends. Colin Massie an' his witches didn't forget him, and soon put him tae rights. Colin even set one of his most powerful witches to watch over him, an' be his companion."

She looked at me then. "Ye were at the Warlock Stane today, Jack. Did ye sense my Master's presence, an' the spirits o' my sister witches?"

I closed my eyes and shook my head, not wanting to hear, not wanting to believe.

"O' course, the tattibogle can only stay alive if one of Akey's blood relatives remains on the farm, an' repeats the spell for bringing him tae life. But that doesn't mean he can't get his own back if they turn mean, like Akey did. That's only fair, isn't it?" Aunty Morag leaned in close.

"Sam will lose his hand, o' that I'm sure," she whispered. "But he's lucky. Your mother's cousin George, well ... he knocked the tattibogle's head off with a rock and pulled awa' his arms and legs. What a mess for me to clean up." She shook her head at the memory, turned, and spat on the floor.

"George came to a very sticky end in the threshing machine. It was so bad I didn't think the spell of forgetfulness I put on your mother would hold after all these years. I needn't ha' worried. My work is sound, and as strong as ever. I wonder if she'll even remember tae come back for ye? It's probably taken hold o' ye Dad and Sam by now."

A roll of thunder grumbled over the distant hills. Outside, I heard a dull thump against the wall.

"Ye see Jack, the tattibogle is used tae folk like your brother, always lashing out in fear an' anger. But he's never heard anyone laugh at him before. He liked the sound o' that." One long nail traced its way down my face and lingered over my trembling lips.

162

"I've already taken your voice. But for him tae use it, he needs one more thing." Her face loomed over me, blocking my view of the window, but I could still hear it scuttling up the wall.

"He just needs ye *tongue*," said Aunty Morag. Then she sighed with pleasure. "T'will be fine to have a Broon in the house again, ken."

That was more years ago than I care to remember now. My family never did come back. Aunty Morag's spells were, indeed, very strong. She's taught me many of them over years. The ones you don't have to say out loud, of course. One night a few years back she disappeared, and I didn't know she'd gone for good until I found the sixth standing stone, dark and gleaming beside its companions. And even though I often think of Sam, I'm not lonely. I have the tattibogle for company. When the sun sinks behind the mountains and the night winds rise up around the eaves, I can always hear him laughing in the dark.

The Haunted Still
By Ridge Carpenter

USA

"That's all well and good," Weathers said, "but what I'm after is a solid, American-spirited type of story. The pipe-smokers in the Old World have made enough of the bedsheets and terraces, and weeks away in cottages by the sea - those tales don't touch me anymore; they're stale, motionless, no bite to 'em. There's a substantial difference between those fine pipes and paneled drawing rooms where all the action takes place for the pipe-smokers, and the wood smoke and sawdust of the American wild, where one can still get lost and come to grips with the vital energies of the world."

He gesticulated as he spoke, gripping at the vital energies of the air with one hand and his glass of vital spirits (Black Maple Hill, no less) with the other. J.C. Weathers was in fine fettle tonight, working himself into a frenzy on the handling of the American supernatural. His own handling of the spirits tonight, we thought, seemed in good proportion; but we were happy to keep pace. The fire was blazing beautifully, the shooting had been fine that day, and nothing remained for the evening but dinner and whatever exotic tales we'd collected since our last outing.

"Surely one of us has savored such a story lately," he continued, warming to his topic with his free hand now upraised as if measuring grain. "There is still a lively and active spiritual life to this continent; they've not killed it off or sobered it into harmlessness. Not a hundred yards outside this cabin lie the feet of the Allegheny Mountains, beyond which are the vast plains of our young country's interior. We've had only a few tales from this wilderness, but each of them was as fresh and potent a draught as southern whiskey newly barreled. Stories of men carried off by the Wendigo in the icy wastes, of mines caved in by the vengeful souls of slain Indians - nowhere else can one find such savory and unique fare, but in the ample larder of the American territory." The measuring hand began bobbing up and down violently, weighing - and at the same time casting violently upon us - whatever substance he imagined to be in it.

"As it turns out, Weathers, I've just the story for you," Sullivan interjected, quelling the diatribe before it could rise to its loftiest linguistic altitude. He'd been listening with a more speculative and less jovial air than the rest of us, and he continued speaking after a long sip and a motion as if to ease his neck and shoulders. "It's one I heard from an uncle of mine, who used to ferret out moonshiners in the backwoods of these very mountains. It had

165

better wait, though - your dissertation is starting to resound with your appetite, dinner approaches, and it's too long a yarn to be sipped off with an aperitif, as it were."

When the plates were finally cleared, and the decanters and siphon had begun once more to make their rounds, Sullivan began his tale.

"The uncle I mentioned - Henry was his name - was one of those officers whose duty it was, not more than a decade ago in the days of Prohibition, to shut down any homemade stills that he could find among the trees. His was a decidedly rural 'beat,' and as such his work was usually along the lines of extended rambles through the woods, in different places every few weeks, including more social calls to get to know the locals - who weren't such a bad lot at heart, he told me. This last part was truly vital, as he learned much from these roughened individuals of the nature of their lives and, more importantly, of their own idiosyncratic spirits - homemade and otherwise. It was really on information from a neighbor or competitor that he usually exposed illicit doings; and so, it was best, Henry found, to keep an ear to the ground and a smile on his face during those walks through the backwoods. Of course, often there were obvious signs, as well - spilled barley, the smell of malt in the woods, or even outright intoxication on the part of a careless local toper.

"The problem with the moonshine trade, Henry said, was that one could never resist becoming one's own primary customer. Whatever implications this may have for our native spirits, Weathers, is a question for another evening; but for his part, and unlike some of his associates in the regulation of the trade, my uncle abstained entirely from its products. Even in days that followed our long national dry spell, he remained abstemious to a degree that might have seemed irrational to many of us. When pressed on the matter, he would make an illustrative example of the incendiary test of moonshine - a yellow flame indicating frequent contaminations in batches, and sometimes a red flame, which signified lead from a poorly constructed apparatus. But these he called insignificant in comparison to the flames that

166

were ignited in the *head* - those of recklessness and violence. He correlated the heady effects of the bottle with some of the other provincial foibles prevalent in the area - superstitions, wives' tales, magic charms. These things did no good for anyone, he said, and could lead only to harm when they became a habit, as they always did. Those habits and that of imbibing inevitably abetted one another; and to keep a 'level head' in a literal and figurative sense, he thought it best to avoid dousing his in irrational spirits - manmade ones, in particular. In practice, this meant listening politely to, but declining to partake in, the locals' fears of the forest - of going too far from the settled areas, say, or of being caught in the forest after twilight. The worst that the region had to offer came in the shape of wild animals, he thought, and these avoided humans as assiduously as he himself avoided intoxication.

"He spent comparatively little time in such ruminations, however. During the majority of his hours my uncle enjoyed that sensation so native to Americans of losing himself in the virgin forest - diluting the individual in a vast lake of the unknown and untamed, until the mingling of the modern man and the atavistic animal brought about by a catalyst of leaves and earth produced the headiest elixir in which men of his sort are given to partake. Often, the trees would stand far enough apart that the sun broke through to the forest's carpet of leaves and mast that, palette-like, hosted the calm colors of autumn emerging from late summer's robust shades, illuminating and stirring among them as if to bring out more elusive hues. Amid such lively lassitude, the real and serious reason for my uncle's presence in those deep woods sometimes began to seem almost trivial. But it was during a reverie of this kind, late one afternoon on the last day of October, that Henry spied a plume of smoke about four miles distant.

"The column of gray and black that spilled through the finely filtered tones of the landscape certainly didn't correspond to any home that he was aware of - in fact, it was far deeper into the forest than most illegal brewers cared to go, an area so remote that many thought it was populated only by the soul of the wild itself. But he knew he could reach it before the light failed, so he bent his steps toward it and quickened his pace.

"Almost as soon as he altered direction, he became conscious of a change in the woods around him. The music of the birds was suddenly lost, as was the chorus of small insects and the occasional stirrings of passing deer and rabbits. The only sounds remaining after a few minutes were an intrusive buzzing or humming, as of cicadas or the locusts he remembered from years before, and the exclamations of the occasional toad, sheltering amid muddy cairns nearby. Even these few noises faded, however, after another mile or so. By then the sky was streaked with deepening crimson, and he was engulfed in silence.

"The ground was even and easily traveled, and the black cloud remained in view against the darkening sky. Night was descending quickly, and the surrounding verdure lost its colors as the sun disappeared. The leaves, robbed of their vibrant vestments by the encroaching dusk, rattled underfoot like the hulls of insects, and the disrobed and shivering branches became black webs over the colorless vault of the sky.

"As the final, fragmented red of the sunset retreated below the hilltops, leaving only a deepening slate and making silhouettes of the forest, the silence became difficult to bear. The plume's fire could be seen clearly now - a low blaze that glowed at the base of the smoky black pillar, and it did not seem to flare or dance as would a welcoming flame on a hearth. This fire had the color and constancy of embers, of a hot brick-kiln, or of the dark red, poisonous flames from tainted whiskey. It burned in a small clearing below a still unlike any Henry had seen before or was to see again in the years to follow. This strange apparatus towered and twisted like a lightning-struck tree, and on it were visible none of the usual bright copper fittings or implements; rather all of it was black as pitch, and from its black and horn-like extremities it continually exhaled the dark smoke Henry had first spied from afar. As he gaped in astonishment, not a breath of wind stirred the trees surrounding the clearing.

168

"The thick smoke lacked any scent of wood or charcoal fuel, carrying instead a slippery, dense stench as of tar. It bore no heat, even so close to its source; in fact, it seemed to carry a chill deeper than that of the surrounding twilight. After a few moments, the fumes began to crowd the oxygen from Henry's lungs, and he backed away from the fire, gasping for air.

"In the midst of this reaction, he became aware of a watcher nearby. His observer leaned against a nearby birch tree, outlined against its silvery bark in the deepening gloom. This, my uncle knew immediately, was not one of the locals. The man was tall and gaunt, with wide shoulders like a ship's rigging stripped of sails, and hands as long and white as the desiccated branches of the tree behind him. He wore a dark, old-fashioned suit and a long coat - almost like the coat of a Quaker, Henry thought. At his neck was the stark white of a high collar, which was anchored in that expanse of black by the sharply angled face that rose above it. The man himself, however, in his gesture or circumstance, was nothing like a Quaker. His thin, pallid face tilted knowingly, as if about to chide and ridicule a careless child. His mouth appeared as a sardonically canted slash, and seemed about to speak, or perhaps to have just finished speaking. His eyes seemed deeper in his head than was possible and reflected none of the light that entered them.

"Aside from my uncle's ongoing gasps in reaction to the still's foul emissions, no sound disturbed the sepulchral stillness of the clearing. The tall man seemed not to move at all, and even the fire glowed steadily without flickering. My uncle managed to croak something vaguely in the form of a question regarding the ownership of the apparatus and its manufacturers; whereupon, in response, the tall man walked over to the still and placed his hand on it, directly on the pot above the fire. He leaned over it, into the intolerable film of smoke, and the hellish, steady glow of the fire colored his face as he tilted his head and looked at Henry. The indication, it seemed, was that *he* was the owner. He then raised his hand, gesturing to my uncle with an outstretched tree-limb palm. He indicated the monstrous convolutions of metal beneath him, and then made a sweeping gesture as if to share the blackened structure. My uncle looked on incredulously, his speech suppressed by the dreadful gravity of the man's intimations. He felt dizzy, possibly from the smoke, as well as completely lost among the towering trees and almost tangible stillness. He realized after a moment that he was being offered something - a bottle made of glass black and shiny as obsidian, that came toward him wrapped in the long fingers of the white hand. It was unstopped, and its vapors seemed to reach out to him, wreathing his nostrils in a scent at once intoxicating and terrifying; it smelled floral and promising, he later said, like a fine perfume on the wrist of an impossibly beautiful woman, and it seemed to expand in the air with a garden of unearthly savors and spices that were followed with a vague scent of moss, of ancient stones, and of rotting bark mingled, at the end, with the harsh, coppery tint of blood. The smell both sickened him and filled him with yearning, and he knew that a draft of it would be his undoing - that if he drank, he must drink forever. The tall man continued watching him - watching him intently now, prying at him with his gaze as with an instrument, as if attempting to remove a precious stone from its setting. After a moment he insistently pushed the bottle forward.

"Then the bottle was in my uncle's hands - though he had no memory of having accepted it from the stranger. The siren-song of scents that wafted from its uncorked opening stroked his nose with seductive fingers - fluttering touches of ripe fruits, ambergris, and sweet, perfumed flesh - but always, on the tail end, so to speak, there were those hints of damp, unfathomed depths, of decay, and of blood. The weight of the smoke pressed upon him, and he felt the bottle growing warm - or his hand growing cold. The tall man once more was leaning against the birch tree, his gaze fixed on my uncle, seemingly willing him to lift that bottle to his mouth. And Henry felt himself weakening, as if he'd carried a heavy weight for many miles. His hand, however, was *light*; it began to rise as if of its own will. Henry found himself parting his lips to receive the kiss of that black vessel - but then he caught sight of the stranger's eyes beginning to widen in triumph, and with a sudden, despairing shudder, he threw the bottle from him.

170

"The glass shattered against the still, spilling the bottle's contents into the fire. The scent of beauty vanished at once; only foulness remained. The fire hissed and steamed, throwing off its vile fossil smell mingled with the stench of corruption and frustrated evil. Henry glanced toward the tall man, and for a brief moment saw that angular face twisted with anger. Then the stranger vanished in smoke and darkness and my uncle lost first his view of the dark clearing and then his senses.

"Henry awoke the next morning in the clearing, cold and alone. The still and fire had vanished, and the music of birds in the trees greeted him. No sign remained of the previous night's events - not of the fire, the bottle, or the man. The birch tree, however, was split from root to crown, and splinters of it were flung far into the forest.

"Of course," Sullivan said in conclusion, "my uncle was always eager (but not quite able) to write off this strange event as a dream of some kind, the product of weariness or overwork. Clearly, though, he hadn't been feeling any stress or fatigue that day; and knowing him, it couldn't have had anything to do with any kind of bottled spirits - against which, of course, he became even more dead-set, the older he got. He may have indulged in a bit of credulous superstition, though, later in life. That late October day, he once told me, was the best day of temperance work he ever put in."

Yamanba
By Ridge Carpenter

USA

"Most men, when they've almost reached the final bell in their lives, consult their ledgers and fall into one of two categories," said our host. "They add up the years and find themselves rich with a life well lived, and experiences had, and can live off the dividends of those same quite independently for the rest of their existence; or, as is unfortunately the more common case, they discover a negative aggregation, a life that has drawn out their accounts, as it were. For some it is all they can do not to declare bankruptcy on the spot, give up the ghost, so to speak, to its creditors, and hope for another chance on the other side of the curtain. Others spend their remaining allotment on this plane in desperation to forget or repay those awful debts with oblivion, in tawdry entertainments, chemical stupor, or the opulent decorum of cultural indulgence.

"The debt, however, will be had, if the total is found wanting; and it is good to remember that no amount of forgetfulness will erase the stinging red of the past. I mention this, not in regret of my own life, but in explanation of the tale that will follow - to pass it on, for me, is to ease somewhat the strain it has put on an otherwise satisfying and rational existence. It was a very close approach to the unreal, to the profane and terrifying, which on its own very nearly wiped out my assets at the time, chief among them my sanity."

The speaker was our mentor, the great surgeon Col. Devon Dewey, one of the most influential teachers of the Royal College of Surgeons. He had remained largely silent that evening, unless consulted by one of us on a finer point in our discussions - the picture of reserved and confident mastery. Over the inevitable cigars, the discussion had turned to the supernatural, and after several tales from my colleagues on the influence of

173

the otherworldly, our host had manifested a desire to open the copious vaults of his thoughts to our eager ears.

"The time during which my accounts were so deeply unbalanced," our honored mentor began, "to perhaps stretch my metaphor a bit too far, was too long ago for many of you to remember - I would imagine most of you were born either during or soon after the second great war of our century. I, however, was already into middle age at the time - hardly fit for military service in the regular sense, but honored to lend my expertise to the efforts in the field. Ironically, most of the members of my regiment, almost all of them much younger than myself, had perished by the time of this tale - they died or were captured as we made our way from one theater to another in the war effort, cutting our way through the subcontinent of Asia after leaving the Mediterranean. In the absence of my countrymen I became informally attached to an American battalion in Malaysia and was with them still when we landed on the largest island of Japan after the two great bombs had silenced the voices of so many thousands. My new company was quickly assigned what turned out to be a rather distasteful task - investigating, assisting, and, if necessary, pacifying the numerous rural towns and villages of a mountainous province of the interior.

"The horrors of war, one finds out quickly, extend far beyond the battle lines: disease, starvation, crime, and madness prevail among the human wreckage of the war machine, as they did in the desolate world on which we had disembarked. As we ventured farther into the rocky wilderness, people's knowledge of the war and of the outside world became vague, and they seemed not to know or even care what the reason may have been for the disappearance of order, authority, and regularity - their lives had become simply a struggle for the resources to survive. This disconnection was not surprising, considering the lack of technological advancement in these rural areas. Electricity and plumbing disappeared as we ascended rocky footpaths through the hills, past stunted pines older than the United States, and shrines to gods forgotten before Columbus sailed. Cars and streetlights were replaced by wagons and lanterns, and grotesque stone effigies watched by the roadsides as if at the gates of the distant past - into which I frequently felt we were proceeding.

"Days passed like blood from a wound as we toiled through the cast-off human resources of a once-mighty military monster. Entire villages lay silent, from firebombing, starvation, or suicide. Some there were who clung to life, only to give it up with the approach of the victorious enemy - cliffs and rivers turned to abattoirs as we came in sight. These, however, were fortunate souls in some respects, compared to those remaining in the final sum: listless, weakened villagers squeezed to apathy by the action of two giant fists pressing against one another for half a decade, awaiting their destiny as spectators rather than conscious actors.

"The final town we came to had seemingly reached the height - or, I suppose, depths - of degradation. It comprised a scattering of wooden houses, the paper windows half-torn and flapping vaguely like warning hands, dominated by a hulking, half-collapsed watermill at the center athwart a filthy runnel, the corpse of a river. The fields all around were barren, and clearly had been so for a long time. Not a soul emerged to meet us, save a filthy child with its belly swollen from protein starvation and face marked by ill-healed sores.

"When the remainder of the occupants were convinced to come forth, they turned out to be, if anything, worse off than the child had been. The women were unkempt, clad in rags, their hair standing off of their heads like dusty wool rejected by a spinner. The men seemed spiritless, stooped as with a great weight, though not a member in the party appeared older than forty. Of children there were few, the lot being almost entirely composed of bedraggled and listless men and women who stood about, staring into space as if blind.

"At length, a spokesman was sent forward - seemingly the oldest citizen of the town, though he was hardly my age - and answered questions posed through our visibly disconcerted interpreter. The latter had been born in

175

Tokyo and raised in his adopted America and was dumbfounded at the existence of such persons in his homeland, of which his only memories were of tradition, decorum, and discipline. Seemingly as much to sooth himself as for the benefit of those of us listening to his interpretations, he prefaced the spokesman's initial answers with a reminder that these people had experienced a great famine and sickness, even beyond that brought on by the confusion of the war effort, of which they appeared to have only a dim recollection. After a pause, he then went on to relay the information that these compounded misfortunes had led the credulous townspeople to the unshakable conclusion that a curse had been laid upon them.

"When pressed as to the curse's supposed source the local spokesman halted, apparently fearful of mentioning whatever was at the root of the town's ills. He looked queasily around toward the silent surrounding peaks, and toward a strange sort of shrine at the foot of the upward path. Then, with apparent resignation, he spoke at some length, seemingly in a defensive way, and had to be halted frequently for clarification by our shocked interpreter. When our astonished and somewhat agitated colleague finally explained matters to us, our shock equaled his own.

"In the throes of famine, it was explained, the town had elected to rid itself of its most burdensome elements. The domestic and farm animals had been killed and eaten, after which even the last few invading rodents were trapped and consumed - and the villagers' attention had then shifted to the elderly. Time and hunger did away with any qualms among the community leaders, and those too old to work or forage were told they could no longer be fed and were forced to leave. Faced with threats of violence, the elders had fled in terror and confusion into the hills and forests and had doubtless perished there. It was at this point that the town's troubles deepened unfathomably. Since that time, we were told, the famine had worsened, the hillsides had dried up, rain had ceased to fall. The wild animals had long since abandoned the region, and various maladies had begun to plague the town's weaker individuals. Some of the banished elders had whispered darkly among themselves as they departed and made signs of

176

unambiguously malicious meaning before the rough-hewn statue by the path, which we all took a moment to examine as this was explained. It was a hideous, low figure of a woman who wore a broad and jagged grin beneath upturned, bulging eyes, was clothed in a robe that at one time had been painted red, and, as its dominant feature, sprouted a wild and tangled thicket of hair that reached entirely to its feet, where it twined around and appeared to grip the statue's inscribed base. Crowning the disordered thatch carved onto the head was what appeared to be another sizable mouth crowded with teeth more closely suited to the canine than to any kind of human figure. In expression the effigy was akin to some of the more ancient grotesqueries to be seen in Buddhist iconography, but it possessed also an entirely unique aesthetic of atavistic form - primarily in the crazed eyes and mouth - that was absent from and foreign to even the darkest representations in Asia's known religious and artistic movements.

"After failing to glean any identification or folklore on the statue from our native speaker - it was far too old, he said, for almost anyone who hadn't grown up in the region to know what it could be - we continued our questioning of the townsman. But while the man for the most part was cooperative, it soon became clear that there was one point on which he could not be induced to speak: that of the fate that had befallen the local children. He admitted that there were very few present, and that there had once been many others, but he vehemently denied they had been treated as the old ones had. They'd been the town's future, he said, not its past, so there was no motive for exiling them. I thought briefly of the horrors in some war-struck villages of Europe - of locked sheds and rubbish heaps strewn with small clothing and broken, blackened bones. Even these near-powerless creatures seemed capable of such atrocities after what I'd seen, and I made a note to explore this possibility at some more discreet hour.

"Having reached an investigative dead-end for the moment, my company began carrying out our various assignments. For my part, I established a makeshift clinic and began applying endless bandages and ointments, tonics, and nutriments; and hygiene was reinstated to some degree among the apathetic, listless villagers with the introduction of soap and water-purification procedures. These preliminaries occupied the greater part of the day, and twilight was approaching when we finally set up our own quarters in an empty barn and made preparations to turn in for the night. As we did so, we noticed that the townspeople displayed great care and even anxiety in accounting for the handful of remaining children, even though none of these had strayed far from home at all. The adults rushed to get themselves and their young ones indoors, and the lanterns lit. The sun had hardly set when the central square was empty, and the wind-swept mountain town seemed an abode of restless ghosts and forsaken even by crows and insects.

"The habit one falls into in the service is to sleep when the opportunity presents itself and wake easily. I had certainly done the first, and the second followed at some time after midnight. I came to feeling as though I'd been dropped into my bed, still hearing a vague echo of the sound that had called me into consciousness - a patter of swift, small feet outside, on the wooden slats of a porch or rooftop. Recalling the absence of animals - we'd seen none at all the previous day - I thought the muted disturbance merited investigation. Peering through a shredded window section, I could just make out the neighboring rooftops, black against a sky dark as the deepest obscurities of the ocean. A hint of movement, nothing more, from a neighboring roof caught my eye. A flag, possibly, or clothing left out to dry by some slovenly villager. Then the footsteps continued, accompanied by a soft noise like silk over wet stone, or a brush on paper - a dragging sibilance. Straining to get a better look, I leaned on an aged board that protested loudly in the still mountain air. The noises immediately stopped, and only a rustle among the stunted trees announced the departure of their unseen originator.

"I attempted to find out more the next day, by carefully describing the sounds I'd heard in the night through our interpreter to another of the village's relative elders, a young but prematurely bent and careworn mother whose child - a stunted boy of four or five - sat entirely still and inactive while she attended to some rudimentary morning tasks. When it became clear to her what I had heard and when, she displayed a previously unwonted alacrity in snatching up her son. Clutching the boy desperately, she asked me whence the sounds had come, and when I pointed out the house opposite and asked about any washing left out or hung from the roof, she became practically beside herself with a kind of imaginative, excited terror, and dashed inside that building. Realizing that it was her house the unknown visitor must have come to, I followed with more questions, but had to wait as she ran wildly about the inner rooms. Breathing quickly and staring as though her eyes would start from her bony head, she began closing all the windows of the house - a pathetic precaution given that these were constructed almost entirely of paper. She would answer none of my queries, nor would she agree to part with the child for the least moment to ease her labors. At length she fell into a sort of swoon on the matted floor and began speaking so incoherently that my colleague was able to pick out only a few recurring phrases. All he could tell me of their substance was that she referred to a female, though with various imperfections in verb and noun formation; and that she was deathly afraid of the sounds from the roof and of something that lived in the highest peaks of the hills surrounding the village. By then the slack-faced boy was sitting near his prostrate mother, idly scribbling with the stub of a pencil at a scrap of paper he'd picked up. It had been previously drawn upon, and it caught my eye - though all I could make of it, for the moment, was a rather naturalistic representation of a thorny bush. With another moment's puzzling I could make out something like a mouth among the branches; yet this signified little to me until a later date.

"I described my unusual encounter to our captain, along with the sounds of the previous night, and a party was assembled to search the higher reaches of the mountainside. The people of the village made no effort to join us but collected in a murmuring knot outside the unfortunate woman's house as we departed.

"The afternoon's search was initially unrewarding. Hardly a sign did we discover of any living agency; as before, not even birds or rodents seemed to have left any mark of their presence for months past. The sun shone down from directly overhead, making as clear as could be the desolation around us, and the only movements that greeted our search party were those of rocks that tumbled from beneath our feet and the slight stirrings of wind through the scrubby trees. The sky appeared so clear as to be empty and, if it were possible, airless. I say we sensed no *living* agency, however, because dubious relicts of life confronted us - shreds of weathered, tattered cloth that hung from thorns, or, more ominously, fragments of sun-bleached bone lying on the bare earth. A stick leaning against a boulder caught our notice in mid-afternoon, due to its rather artificial shape, and this was eventually identified as a rough-hewn cane, which reminded us of the grim fate of the town's missing elders. As for the banished people themselves, they had either moved on or perished in concealment.

"The true shock awaited us at the summit of one of the highest hills. We saw a sudden flutter of color among the bushes, and, unaccustomed to such vibrancy in the absence of birds and flowers, followed it as one would a beacon.

"Deep within a thicket, we came upon a strip of cloth much brighter than the faded remnants we'd earlier found; it had been torn recently from some garment by the bushes. This scrap bore, in addition to its bright dyes, a dirty, rusty tinge that boded ill for its former wearer. Following an improvised path that in places had to be hacked through the brambles, we eventually arrived at a sizable clearing. Our ears rang in the surrounding stillness, and the mountain air suddenly seemed unusually close and warm. Standing at the center of this opening was a thatched-roof hut that was practically falling in from great age and weathering. The walls were of dusty, desiccated split branches, and bore no adornments save a signboard or cartouche above the door. The faded ideograms in the main defied our native-born companion; through the mists of age and style he could make out only a supplication that concluded on the general lines of "We dare not

180

forget." Our repeated calls brought forth no occupants, though the silence was weighted with a feeling, shared by all of us, that we were being watched. Finally, our captain touched the sleeve of another man, gravely inclined his head toward the hut, and together they moved aside the matting over the door.

"The interior of the shack was unfurnished but for a shrine or alcove on the far wall. This was cluttered with diverse objects, odd relics of sinister and doubtful outline, which obviously had been much handled in their long histories. Though many were entirely incomprehensible in their shape or function, a few presented an unmistakable aspect of *teeth*, smooth from age and abrasion. I judged them to be first-growth molars, and definitely not from a sole individual. A few other bones littered the area - these were mostly so cracked and defiled that one could as little tell what had once possessed them as what had so abused and scattered them; it surely had not been the work of scavengers, of which we'd still seen none. A group of pathetic, flimsy things that may have been folded paper fans and toys rested among the other relics in frozen, dusty poses that gave the impression of eternity. This unsettling collection, combined with all else we'd discovered that day, provoked much speculation among us, as did the dominant man-made object amid the assortment - a sort of outsized ornamental comb made of what appeared to be heavily oxidized iron. This artifact was the only thing that seemed as if it might have been handled at all recently, and it had in its rusty tines a single hair that was fully as long as our tallest man was tall.

"What was this place? As yet we had no explanation - but we were more than happy to leave it and head back down from the hills.

"We attempted a reassuring tone with the villagers, who peppered us with anxious questions upon our return. Our report of the thicket and its clearing provoked unease among them, and a few of them turned pale at our description of the enigmatically decorated dwelling at its heart. But nothing could have prepared us for their reaction to our accounting of its contents

- which was the abrupt collapse of two of the disheveled women present. By this point, we considered ourselves entirely justified in demanding some answers from the terrified rustics, and after much interrogation we finally obtained what might have passed for an explanation were it not entirely more mystifying than the original mystery had been.

"There was, it turned out, a superstition among the townspeople of a malignant presence or spirit lurking among the rocky wastes. It was thought to have returned among them in recent years as a result of the elders' curse, though it had been present in the mountains since times long before their most distant inherited memory. Prior to the war, and during the town's more prosperous days, the thing had served as a sort of bogey to frighten children who were unruly or inclined to wander.

"Over the course of this narrative, haltingly delivered by two or three of the elders, the eyes of the assembled townspeople rolled continuously toward the grotesque idol by the side of the path, and I found myself studying it again with as much disgust as curiosity. The weathered pigments remaining on the statue's robe were reminiscent of the rusted hues with which a soldier becomes familiar - but these colors brightened near the face and the horribly tusked mouth. It appeared the image had at some point been touched up so that the red showed thicker and newer near the hands and head and about the feet, where the obscene hair curled and grasped in a twisted mass of graven strands. I resumed listening in time to hear a summary dismissal of the "fairy tale" from our captain, after which we excused the frightened townspeople and went about our various duties for the remainder of the day. Not long after nightfall I fell asleep in our makeshift barracks, and dreamt of combs, of paper fans, and of teeth.

"The climax of the entire adventure, and the nearest approach I have yet made to the unexplained and the unnatural, occurred later that night. I awoke when the witching hour had come and nearly gone, and at the sound of swift, padding feet outside the barn, I immediately awakened our interpreter and the captain. Motioning for silence, the latter led the way outside, and the three of us crouched behind a disused well to observe the rooftops. The town was silent, and the still air wrapped the scene as does a parting curtain on the expectant stage. The night sky was radiant through scattered, racing clouds that lent white backbones to the silhouettes of the surrounding buildings.

"The nearest of these, scene of the previous night's disturbance, again claimed my attention. Under the shadowed edge of the roof's eave I saw a ragged, crouching shape drawing itself along the very contour of the architecture, clinging like a limpet to the underside of the hanging roof and moving with great stealth. My fellows observed this as well, and we were debating whether to call out to it when the shape surged, with a projection of spidery limbs, beneath the projecting roof and through a gap that would have seemed too small to pass a child. No sooner had that flash of trailing tatters vanished through the recess than a shriek resounded from within - and it was unmistakably that of the little boy who lived there. We dashed madly for the door and burst through it just in time to see the terrified mother falling as she ran toward a torn window through which a small, struggling shape thickly wrapped in some weedy, black mess was being drawn. The flimsy architecture of the house aided our pursuit, and we crashed through the wall in a stride and immediately sprinted after a crackling shake in the bushes ahead of us. As we climbed the hill above the town, the moon came leering out from the clouds overhead and illuminated, as vaguely as it had on the rooftop, a shambling mass of limbs, cloth, and vine-like hair sweeping with inhuman speed through the thickets. We heard the little boy shriek again - but this desperate cry was cut short before it was completed, and we never heard it again.

"Our steps, guided by a presentiment of the creature's destination, brought us swiftly to the hateful clearing, which was washed in moonlight and slashed chaotically with the maniac scribblings of thorny shadows. Hesitating only momentarily at the thicket's edge, we ran to the filthy hovel into which only moments before the horrible light steps had vanished - only to be thrown back almost bodily by a screech that, for an instant,

183

nearly stopped our very hearts. This exclamation only vaguely resembled a human sound, so broken with age and coarsened with fury had it become over the untold centuries its earthly existence had occupied. The brief but terrifying silence that followed was broken when a ragged, gasping mass passed swiftly between the captain and myself like a clot of rotting weeds down the rapids of a stream. Then it was gone, and the deathly silence returned to the desolation of the empty thicket.

"After what we had seen and heard, we held no expectations for life remaining in the hut - and to our sorrow, when we went inside we found that our pessimism had been justified. As soon as we'd given the meager remains as decent a burial as we could, we turned our steps back toward civilization.

"The town's evacuation was more than necessary on far saner grounds than what we had seen, and our terrified captain had no intentions either of remaining in the area or attempting an explanation to his own superiors of what had truly happened. Many of the villagers, permanently trapped, it would seem, in the apathetic fog brought on by the curse, refused to leave. I imagine they sooner or later perished of any number of causes - but I pray they died without seeing what I myself had seen. Of the captain, the interpreter, and myself, none of us ever spoke on record of that night's horrors. For my part, as soon as I was away from there, I required the only sick leave I've ever taken in a vain attempt to efface from my mind the vision of those hands, so like thorned branches, clutching that poor child as the creature to which they were appended fled from us into the darkness and up the side of the hill. An old crone it could have been or been once - as wrinkled and blasted as the tatters she wore and wreathed in a seething mass of hair that writhed like a living thing."

185

Moss Man
By Scott Loring Sanders

USA

"I never seen him directly," said Bubba, the proprietor of the Lonely Tavern, where I sat drinking a can of Pabst after my third day in town. Bubba also ran the gas station/convenience store which sold not only gas and snacks, but every plastic Jersey Devil trinket and keychain imaginable. And I'm not talking about hockey team souvenirs. I'm talking about various replicas of the beast who had supposedly haunted the area for the last two centuries. Distorted face, elongated fangs, little T-Rex arms with bent wrists, veiny batwings protruding from its back. That's the Jersey Devil I mean.

Bubba didn't look like he should've been named Bubba at all. Tall and thin with white hair, sixty-ish, and a pair of over-sized glasses, he looked more like a Kenneth or Stuart. He stood behind the lacquered bar, sipping on a draft while I sat on a stool next to Katherine, the owner of the adjoining Lonely Tavern Lodge where I'd been residing. The pair had become my companions each evening after I'd been out talking to people, driving around the desolate swamps and bogs trying to gather info from the locals (or Pineys, as they preferred) who, more often than not, weren't overly excited to speak with me.

"The whole thing's bullshit," said Katherine, whose rough voice could be attributed - at least in part - to cigarettes, one of which currently wobbled between her lips. Apparently, Chris Christie's state-wide smoking ban in restaurants and bars didn't apply here. A hard woman, this one was. I'd smelled liquor on her breath that first morning when I'd strolled into the lobby to get a room. "But bullshit or not," she said, "the Jersey Devil's the only reason me and Bubba can scratch two dimes together, so I'm thankful to have him around. Tourists eat it up."

186

She finished her beer, and Bubba grabbed the empty glass without being asked. He angled it beneath the tap, expertly drawing a head that bulged over the rim like a white, foamy muffin-top. That exact ritual had probably been repeated tens of thousands of times. Hell, I'd witnessed nearly a dozen refills within the past two hours, with no money exchanged. Yet Katherine was as steady and even-keeled as the sturdiest ship.

"You've probably heard fifteen variations already," said Bubba. "Everybody's got their own version, but I've lived here all my life and my story's been passed down all the way back from my great-great-granddaddy."

"Okay, I'll bite," I said. I opened my pad and flipped through the notes for my article. My boss had sent me south to the sweltering, bug-infested Pine Barrens to inquire about the mutilated carcasses that had been showing up lately. Possum, deer, even a bobcat, their bones snapped and twisted, their pelts peeled back from their bodies. It was impossible not to discuss the Devil when such things occurred, and if I could spin it, I would. As my boss had told me, "The Jersey Devil sells copy. Period."

I lifted my empty, gave it a little shake in Bubba's direction. He pulled a fresh one from the cooler. I clicked my pen, dated a clean page. "Go ahead, lay it on me."

"Well, in the late 1700s," said Bubba, "a woman named Mrs. Leeds birthed her thirteenth baby. But it wasn't normal. Instead, it was some sort of hideous monster. A winged creature with hooves and a tail. Some say the head of a goat. The doctor, he bolts, not even bothering to cut the cord. Mr. Leeds, he follows the doctor right out the door. Not to bring him back, mind you, but to run off and hang himself in the closest tree.

"Mrs. Leeds, left to her own devices, rummages through the doctor's bag, finds scissors, and snips the cord herself. The thing - her own offspring - is hissing and spitting, angry and mean, but Mrs. Leeds was angrier and meaner. She picked it up at the base of its tail, holding it upside down like a caught chicken, and tromps a half mile to Miller's Bog. She drops the thing in the muck, leaving it there to drown. But of course, it didn't drown, and it's been flying around ever since, feasting mainly on animals, but the occasional person goes missing too."

I sipped on my Pabst, amused at Bubba's earnestness. "And you've never seen him?"

"Not straight away. Though on two occasions, right at dusk, I've glimpsed a strange shadow scoot over me. Kind of like the way you every-once-in-awhile see a hawk's shadow, you know, gliding over the ground? And each encounter shot a chill up my back. Left me feeling cold. On that second occasion, that very same night after I'd seen it," he said, looking directly at Katherine as if her nod of affirmation would give the story validity, "that Simpson girl went missing. Snatched right out of her house. Never found her. You remember that?"

Katherine extinguished her cigarette into a plastic Budweiser ashtray, immediately lit another. "Yeah, I remember, but no goddamned devil stole her. That girl was sixteen, had met a blackjack dealer in AC. Ran off after that fella got her a fake ID. They say she's been working in one of Trump's casinos ever since."

Bubba's face reddened. "More people around here believe in it than not." He glanced at me as he pushed his glasses up the bridge of his nose. "Old Katherine's just grown bitter."

Katherine exhaled, letting some of the smoke snake back through her nose in a French inhale. "You really want a good story," she said, "then you ought to find the Moss Man. Now that's a fella to write about."

Bubba immediately shook his head, scowling at Katherine.

188

But it was too late; my ears were perked. "Moss Man?"

"Don't go bothering Bill," muttered Bubba. "He's an old Piney who don't like to be disturbed. Lives way out in the thick of the Barrens."

My scalp tingled - journalist instinct. I had to talk with him, no doubt about it.

"Tell me more," I said, looking directly at Katherine. Then to Bubba, "And put her drinks on my tab."

Bubba rubbed the bar-top with a rag, pushing circles into the wood though there was nothing to clean. Through clenched teeth, he grumbled something inaudible. And then, much clearer, "Whatever you do, don't bring up his family."

I didn't squeeze much more out of Katherine, as Bubba grew increasingly irritated and eventually cut her off. But I did learn that the Moss Man lived alone, making money by gathering what the Pine Barrens offered. I also got a rough set of directions. Emphasis on rough. Things like "Turn at the bridge, go five miles to green dumpster. Make a left by a giant sycamore."

Using Katherine's final marker - a rusted No Hunting sign nailed to a tree at a sharp bend - I veered onto a lane that was hardly wide enough for my little Jetta to fit through. Moss Man's driveway: two bare patches, knee-high weeds Mohawking the middle. My car jostled over the bumps and runnels, and I felt sure the guts of my transmission would rip out. The morning was hot, and with my window down, chirping frogs superseded everything. There must've been millions of them, singing eerie springtime love songs. In a different setting, it might have been pleasant and peaceful. At the lane's end, dense trees gave way to a clearing. An old shack with warped boards faded to gray sat in the opening. A stone chimney, somewhat askew, poked from a tin roof muddied to rusty orange. Despite the heat, a trace of smoke trickled out. A 1960s pickup - tailgate gone, fender dented, pocks of rust on the passenger door - sat in front.

I parked behind the truck, the chirrup of frogs even more intense after I killed the engine. The yard, or what I'm calling a yard, consisted of low-lying weeds clinging to a soft, sandy soil. Parallel lines were scratched into the dirt, and it took a second to realize the entire grounds had recently been raked.

"Bill?" I called with unease. A quiet had overtaken the place. As soon as I yelled, every little frog shut the hell up as if I'd rudely broken etiquette. I beckoned again, waiting for a vicious dog to bust from the barn, but got no reply, not even from the frogs.

Three swaybacked steps led to the front porch, which housed a rocking chair. Then I noticed the flowers. Not standard geraniums or pansies. I'm talking exotic flowers. Whites, pinks, purples - blooms popping out all over. They were part of the house, clinging and growing straight from the porch railings instead of in pots, some of the root systems wrapping around the support posts like snakes encircling a staff.

Because of the flowers, the place had a charming, Hansel-and-Gretel-ish feel, which, after contemplating that comparison for a moment, I wasn't overly comfortable with. I was literally in the middle of nowhere. In the Jersey Devil's stomping grounds, which, up until then, was a notion I'd only found amusing. The way Bubba and the other Pineys believed in him so devoutly was what I would've attributed to - only a few days before - ignorance, naiveté, or blind faith. But now I wasn't so sure. The isolation, the forest's darkness, the silence, it all gave a bit more credence to believing some infamous creature lurked in the swamps.

The porch-boards sighed as I climbed. The two windows bookending the door were blocked by a combination of shades and thick curtains. As I went to knock, someone spoke. I wheeled around to find a man at the bottom of the steps, eyeing me in a not-so-friendly manner.

"Bill?"

"I'm Bill," said the man, "but that's not what I asked. I said, 'Who're you?' And what's the whys of you trespassing?"

He was thin, his long-sleeved flannel and jeans so loose they looked borrowed. His beard, thick and a silvery gray, matched the house's facing boards. Katherine had said he was mid-seventies, and upon first glance, that seemed right. But when I looked deeper he had one of those faces, hidden beneath his beard, that could've been plus-or-minus fifteen years of seventy. Part of that agelessness was his eyes. They were a piercing blue, nearly robin's egg, which I'd never seen before. Maybe on a Siberian Husky, but not on a man.

"My name's Dave Hamilton," I said, nervously extending my hand. "How're you? I'm with *The Star-Ledger*. Up in Newark. Would it be okay if I asked you a couple questions?"

Bill licked his lips. "To question one, I'm fine. And to question two, it would be okay except you've already done it."

I tilted my head. "I'm sorry?"

"Can you ask me a couple of questions. You already did, and I've answered them. So, are we done? Can I go ahead and shoot you now?"

My mouth opened but nothing came out. He moved a hand behind him, letting it rest near the small of his back. "I'm only messing with you, pal," he said, letting out a deep laugh. "Don't get a lot of visitors. Which is the way I like it. But you caught me on a good day. What do you want to know?"

191

I forced a laugh, then retracted my hand since he didn't seem interested in shaking it. "I'm doing a story on the Jersey Devil. There's been reports of mutilated animals. Somebody suggested I talk to you."

"*Um-hmm*. And who's this somebody?"

"Katherine? From the Lonely Tavern?"

Bill nodded. "That's a woman who'll make you curse the son-of-a-bitch who invented liquor. Got a bite like a copperhead."

I laughed again, this time more naturally. "She does seem to know how to toss them back."

"Good enough girl though, at least when she was young. And tough as a pine knot. Same as her daddy."

"Yeah, that's what I gathered. Anyway, she said you might have a theory about those animals. And maybe the Jersey Devil."

"I got work to do, but if you want to come along, I don't mind jawing. But those dead animals? That's the work of coyotes," he said, pronouncing it ki-oats. "Not any devil. Been seeing them more and more lately. They're mean, tough little SOBs." He pulled a sleeve of sunflower seeds from his pocket and poured a few into his mouth. "They'd give Katherine a good run for her money, that's for damn sure."

I flipped open my pad and scratched some notes. Bill worked the seeds like a plug of chaw, spitting out the shells.

"Is that all you got to wear?" he said, eyeing my Timberlands.

"My boots? Yeah, that's all I've got. Why?"

He shook his head, spit a few more shells. "Those things wouldn't last ten minutes where we're going."

I examined my boots, less than a week old. "What do you mean? I paid over a hundred bucks for these things. Bought them just for this trip."

"Come on," he said as he walked off.

In the barn's dark shadows, he removed a pair of hip waders hanging from a sixteen-penny nail. "Take off your hundred-dollar boots and put on these rubbers. Got 'em for ten dollars back in 1975. Impressed?" He didn't look at me with derision exactly; it was more like bemusement. Before I could answer, he pointed toward a hay bale. "Sit down there, slide 'em on, and we'll go. I'll get the barrow."

I took a seat, but to my surprise the hay bale wasn't a hay bale at all. I sank several inches, and when I used my hands to brace myself, the material was soft and spongy. As my eyes adjusted to the dark, vague images of rectangular moss bales appeared, each secured with twine. There must have been a hundred of them, the aroma rich and earthy.

I exchanged my Timberlands for the waders. Behind me, a wheel squeak was followed by Bill saying, "You ready?"

"Sure. We going to collect moss?"

The night before, Katherine had informed me that Bill made his living by selling sphagnum moss to local nurseries and flower shops. And I'd been fascinated by that.

Bill took another shot of sunflower seeds. "Boy, they sure grow 'em sharp up there at *The Star - Ledger*, don't they?"

I reddened, feeling a bit foolish.

193

"I'm just busting your chops, there, pal. You want a story about the Jersey Devil, well, thought I'd show you where he lives. Might as well get a little work done while I'm at it, right? You're working, I'm working."

Bill stepped out of the barn shadow, pushing the wheelbarrow into the morning light. It was the biggest one I'd ever seen, twice as deep as any The Home Depot carried.

"That seems like a good tool to bring along," I said, trying to joke, motioning toward the pitchfork resting in the wheelbarrow's cavity. "Kind of apropos considering we're going devil hunting."

The old man didn't laugh or even smile. "Use it to loosen the moss."

I sidled up, my pad and pencil at the ready. "Before we start, can I get your full name?" I said, scratching the date into the upper right corner.

He spat a glob of shells. "You best put away your little book and pencil. I never yet seen a man who could push a barrow with one hand. Damn near impossible."

He started toward the forest where several faint trails wiggled through the trees in different directions. I pocketed my pad, grabbed the handles, and hefted the giant wheelbarrow before hustling after him. But he'd already vanished. As quietly as fog dissipating over a river.

The sunshine dimmed once we got into the thick of it. I followed, navigating the wheelbarrow along the narrow path, the pitchfork tines clanging against the worn metal tub. Bill didn't look back or bother talking, and I had to give it to him, the old guy could motor. He hopped over downed trees like a deer, bobbed and weaved through low branches like a graceful boxer.

The deeper we went, the more anxious I became. The tall pines stood in formation, sentry-like, the forest floor a carpet of dead needles and creeping moss. And it was so quiet. As Bill trudged on, I noticed a squelch beneath my feet. With every step, it got worse, the wheelbarrow harder to push as the tire slurped in the bogginess. I immediately appreciated the waders.

A mile in, Bill stopped, waiting for me. As I schlepped toward him, an annoying whine rang in my ears. Then a mosquito drilled my arm, followed by several more. Bill seemed amused when I tried to smack them. He pulled a handful of moss from the ground. "Rub this on you."

I slapped at my forearm again. "You got any bug spray? Some OFF! or something?"

"Yeah, I sure do," he said. "Right here next to my hairspray and tampons. Just give me a minute to rummage through my purse."

I smacked again. "You're a real funny guy, Bill. Let me tell you, a real funny guy."

"Take the goddamned moss already."

I grabbed the clump and rubbed it over my exposed areas. It smelled like dirt but, I have to admit, immediately did the trick.

Bill winked. "You can leave that stuff here," he said, indicating the wheelbarrow and pitchfork. "We're going off-road for a few."

The ground became even soupier. Like slogging through fresh concrete. Yet Bill moved deftly, slicing through briar thickets and copses of trees. At one point I stepped on a plant that emitted an awful odor.

"Skunk cabbage," he said. "You ought to avoid that."

"You might've warned me beforehand," I said, plugging my nose.

"A jackass learns to plow a row by doing, not by being told."

We reached the edge of a murky pond, the water stagnant and black. The sky had gone overcast, a soaring red-tailed hawk offering the only contrast. The water was so dark that the mirrored bird zipped across the surface, only dissipating when the image collided with the tops of a few snapped trees poking through the water, their branches gnarled and twisted. I imagined strange tree-people lurking below, trying to fight their way to the top. The eeriness had returned, and if Bill had decided to run off right then, I'd have been screwed. Even in the thick humidity, a chill ran up my arms.

"So, what's this place?"

Bill looked out over the pond, two hundred yards across and surrounded by the green heads of pines. He seemed to be in deep reflection. "His home," he said.

"His home? What do you mean? Whose home?"

Bill didn't reply.

"You mean the Jersey Devil lives near this pond?"

"In it."

"In it? How does he live in it? I thought he was some sort of flying winged creature."

"He might have wings, can't say for sure, but this is where he lives ... far as I'm concerned."

"You've seen him here before? In this pond?" With the others I'd interviewed, the mood had been light, mainly because I thought the whole thing was a lark. Some urban legend people took a little too seriously. But with Bill it was different. He was so damn grave all of the sudden.

"It's been nearly fifty years." he said, soft and monotone, "... but this is the place."

I forced a faint chuckle, attempting to put myself at ease. "Care to expound?"

"Care to what?"

"Expound. Explain. As in, tell me what happened?"

Bill cupped his bearded chin, eyeing the dark, placid water as if trying to see beneath the surface. As if searching for something he'd lost. "Nope." He then headed back into the forest. The hawk had vanished.

I fumbled with my iPhone and snapped some pictures. Then I jogged to catch up, asking myself what in the hell I was doing out there.

Back at the wheelbarrow, Bill had shut off. I asked a few questions but he wouldn't say a word. Instead, he shoved that fork into the ground, pulling up moss, meticulously working his fingers through it, dropping some into the wheelbarrow while discarding other pieces. It all looked the same to me, grayish-brown blobs, but he saw things I didn't.

Once it was full, I pushed the load. Along the way, I'd seen more of those same exotic flowers clinging to various tree trunks. I asked about them as we neared the barn, and finally Bill answered. It was as if being back on his own land snapped him out of his funk.

"Those aren't just flowers," he said. "They're orchids."

197

"Same as the ones on your porch, right?"

"Yep. They say money don't grow on trees, but I beg to differ."

"How's that?" I said, relieved to have him talking again.

"Besides all the moss, the nurseries buy up the orchids I collect. There's money to be made just about anywhere, long as you know where to look."

I dumped the moss in a corner of the barn. I anticipated being sore in the morning. My arms were fatigued, my calves taut. Scratches crossed my hands while mosquito welts bubbled my neck and forearms. Yet Bill appeared unscathed. I removed the waders and laced my boots.

I met him on the porch where he casually rocked, assuming we'd go inside to wash up, but he made no such offering. "Well, thanks for your help," he said instead, chewing on sunflower seeds. "I've pushed that barrow upwards of ten thousand times I'd say. Nice to have a morning off."

"No problem," I said, probing the muscles near my elbow. "You think I could use your bathroom? Maybe wash my hands and take a leak before I head back?"

"Nope. I'd rather you not." He shifted in his chair.

The tightly drawn shades covering the two front windows made me want to see inside that house. Badly. I wanted to understand how he lived. "Come on, Bill. I've really got to go. Need to rinse this mud off, too."

Bill started rocking again. "There's a wash bucket around the corner if you need it. And the world's your bathroom. Can't take a piss in your own yard then your yard ain't worth a piss."

He wasn't going to budge, and for some reason, a part of me started to believe maybe there was some truth to this Jersey Devil stuff. It went against all my innate logic and reason, but whatever secrets he was holding onto, I had no doubt they were in that house.

"Listen, you mind if I come back tomorrow?"

"You don't want to be here tomorrow. There's a gulley-washer coming."

There wasn't one cloud in the sky, which struck me as odd because back at the pond things had been overcast. I was sure of it. I'd also watched the forecast on the local news that morning. "They're not calling for rain anytime in the next five days."

"I don't know who they is," said Bill, "but they is wrong. It's gonna be a frog choker."

"The weatherman said otherwise."

"Weatherman?" scoffed Bill. "You don't need a weatherman to know which way the wind blows."

I laughed. "If I use that in my article, should I quote you or Dylan?"

Bill looked at me blankly, his eyes saying he'd never met a bigger fool. "Me or who?"

"Never mind. Forget it," I said. "Would it be all right if I come by again, next time the weather's nice?"

Bill spat a mishmash of shells over the railing. "I suppose that'd be fine. Don't know what good it'll do, but I'll be here."

When I got back to the lodge a half-hour later, a distant boom of thunder rolled across the sky, a stack of cauliflower clouds building on the horizon.

A day and a half after Bill's correctly predicted deluge, I approached his porch again. But this time I came with a different attitude, mainly because of what I'd learned from Katherine and Bubba. We'd had a few drinks when Katherine opened up about some unimaginable things concerning Bill. It was horrific, and as much as I didn't want to ask him about it, the journalist in me said I had to.

He sat in the rocking chair when I arrived, my waders bunched at his feet as if expecting me. The orchids around the columns had turned their little faces to the early sunshine. "Morning, Bill. How you doing today?"

"Fair to midland," he said, sipping coffee.

"It's a pretty morning. Was wondering if we might talk?"

"That'd be fine, but I got work to do."

"Don't suppose you've got an extra cup?" I said, wanting more than anything to get a look inside that house, to perhaps dispel the rumors I'd heard.

Bill hoisted himself slowly out of the chair. His body, despite easily out-working mine the other day, was thin and frail. His back was permanently hunched, albeit slightly, as if leaning into a stiff wind. The veins on his hands poked through like green worms; his throat dewlaps drooped loosely. Whatever mirage I'd seen that first day had vanished. Bill no longer seemed ageless. Now, he just looked old.

He turned the doorknob, with me right behind. But before he even cracked it, he said, "Cream and sugar? Or black?"

"I can pour it myself. Just tell me where you keep the cups."

"You put on your rubbers," he said, careful not to push the door open. "I'll be back in a minute."

"I really don't mind getting it."

"Cream and sugar? Or black?"

"Black."

"Good, cause I don't have any cream and sugar." That spark in his eyes had returned.

The rest of the day found Bill in excellent humor. His disposition hadn't shifted or changed the way it had after he'd shown me the pond. It wasn't until we were finished, after I'd pushed three wheelbarrow loads, that I decided to mention his family. Except I was nervous and found any excuse to avoid the topic.

"Those orchids are beautiful," I said as I removed the waders. "You think maybe tomorrow we could go out and find one for me to take home? I'm heading back north in the afternoon."

"I can just pot you up one of these right quick. No charge. I got milk cartons I use."

I saw the milk cartons as my chance to finally get in the house. When I'd mentioned to Katherine and Bubba about how Bill hadn't wanted me inside that day, they'd both nodded. Katherine had said, "One time a nursery guy sliced his hand wide open on his tailgate while loading Bill's moss bales. Bleeding bad. He wanted to run water over it in the kitchen, but Bill found a rag, wrapped the man's hand, then sent him on his way."

"Yeah, he was the same way with me," I'd said.

Katherine had paused to blow a stream of smoke upward. "Some say he's captured the Devil. Has him chained up in the cellar. Don't necessarily believe it myself, but that's what some swear by."

"Sure, I'd love a potted plant," I said. "If you don't mind."

"Cartons are in the barn, against the back wall. Go grab one and pick out whichever orchid you want."

I hesitated. "On second thought, I want to choose my very own. From the wild."

"Ah, I get it. Got yourself a lady back home?"

"Well, not so much anymore." I hesitated again. "I'm in the middle of a divorce, actually."

Bill nodded. "Relationships can be tricky."

And just like that, without even trying, what I'd wanted to ask was right there in front of me. "You ever been married, Bill?"

"Never did have much luck with marriage," he said. "Married three different times."

Now here it was. I didn't know there'd been three wives. Katherine had only mentioned the one, and a couple of kids, too. "So you're familiar with divorce too, huh?"

"Nope, not divorce. My first wife, when I was still quite young, she was murdered."

"What?"

"Yep. They never caught the guy. And my second wife, a few years later, well, she died from eating poisonous mushrooms."

"Man, I don't know what to say."

Bill rocked in his chair, solemnly. "That's all right. Not much you can say. And my third wife, well, she died from being beaten over the head with a baseball bat."

"Goddamn, Bill. I'm..." But I didn't finish. An apology would've been pointless.

Bill nodded as he stopped rocking. "Yeah, the last one, with the baseball bat, that happened because the stubborn old thing refused to eat the poisonous mushrooms." And then he let out a laugh that echoed off the surrounding pine trunks. I paused before joining him.

When we finally calmed, he said, "I'll see you tomorrow, there, pal."

—

Going to the lodge, I reflected on what Katherine had told me the night before. About what had really happened to Bill's wife, understanding why he'd been so pensive while showing me the pond that day.

"Happened in the early '60s," Katherine had said. "I was in second grade. We'd had a rough winter. Most people lost power for weeks because of an ice storm. But word still got around. And I knew it was true for sure when I went to school, because Bill's little girl, Sophie, didn't show up. Teacher informed our class, but I refused to buy it. It took another month of seeing Sophie's empty desk before I finally wrapped my head around it. If there'd been a funeral, then maybe I'd have believed sooner. But you couldn't have a funeral without a body.

"From all accounts, Bill was a good husband to Caroline. Good father, too. Sophie was eight and her little brother, whose name I don't even remember, was six."

"Lawrence," said Bubba, drinking from his glass of draft. "His name was Lawrence."

"Right, Lawrence," said Katherine. "Bill had taken the kids and Caroline ice skating, some pond in the middle of the Barrens. They'd been skating when Sophie strayed toward an area where a moving creek filtered in. Caroline went after Sophie, pulling Lawrence along, while Bill was out in the middle, making figure eights or some such. Next thing Bill knows, there's a horrible pop, some screams, and by the time he gets halfway to them, all three have gone under. Swallowed up. Sucked down. My daddy told me Bill plunged right into that hole. Dove head-first, but they were gone. Said Bill nearly died too, and, I imagine, probably would've preferred if he had. Ever since, he's lived out at that place all alone, never quite the same. And who could blame him? Just crawled up inside himself and shut the world out."

"Damn," I said.

"Yeah, damn. Of course, there's other theories out there, too."

"Such as?"

"You do the math," said Katherine. "No bodies ever recovered. Bill turning all sorts of secretive. Not too hard to figure that rumors would get started. But the cops never pursued it, far as I know."

That final morning, as I walked toward Bill's porch, he sat in his rocking chair as usual. As I mounted the three steps, I said, "Hey old man, how's it going?"

He didn't reply, and it took a second to realize he was napping. I spoke again, louder, and then I knew. I nudged the curved bottom rail of the rocking chair with my Timberland, moving it forward and back.

"Goddammit, Bill," I said. I didn't want to touch him. I'd held a dead dog once when I was a boy, after it got run over by my neighbor, and it messed with my head for months.

I had never checked a pulse, nor did I have any idea how to actually do it, but when I grabbed Bill's wrist, his skin was cold. Or not cold exactly, but certainly not warm like it was supposed to be. His eyes were closed, his mouth slightly ajar as if whistling.

I reached for my phone, ready to call 911 when I noticed something, partially hidden by the chair. It was an orchid, standing about knee-high, and potted in a plastic milk carton cut in half, the base packed tightly with fresh moss. The flowers were open, white with flecks of purple spotting the petals. I stared at the orchid, then at the closed front door. And that's when I put the phone back in my pocket. After all, at this point, what was the rush?

Was I expecting to find some chained beast inside, foaming at the mouth and utterly hideous? Some vicious winged creature whose mother had attempted to murder it? Or maybe Bill's own family, old now, imprisoned for fifty years? Of course not. But I'd be lying if I said I hadn't thought about such things.

The door opened to the living room: a couple of floral-patterned upholstered chairs, a crocheted granny-squared afghan draped over a loveseat, an enormous console television. But I was immediately drawn to a bookshelf filled not with books but record albums. In front of the bookshelf was a phonograph with one stray album cover sitting next to it, noticeable because it was the only thing out of place. A young Bob Dylan stared back at me. I picked it up, fanning myself, and chuckled, "You sly son of a bitch."

The kitchen was as neat and orderly as the living room: white refrigerator that reminded me of my grandmother's, shaped like a rounded bullet. Breadbox and toaster on the counter. Pots and pans hanging from hooks above a woodstove. But the kitchen table was what caused my stomach to drop, what prickled my skin as if I were racked with fever.

A pair of children sat at the table, a girl and a smaller boy, empty plates in front of them. And behind the children, a woman stood dressed only in an apron, hunched over as if about to pick up one of the plates. But they weren't real, living people. Instead they were replicas, frozen in time, completely fashioned out of dried moss. The woman had an hourglass shape to her, even faint humps for breasts. Though the face had no distinct features per se, somehow, she was almost attractive. Maybe it was the prominent cheekbones, or perhaps the shoulder-length blonde hair, made from what appeared to be bleached moss. At each end of the table were unoccupied chairs though each spot had a complete place setting, as if the entire family was about to sit down to breakfast.

An immediate thought came to mind. Of those people in Nagasaki who'd been obliterated by the bomb, their white silhouettes smeared on blackened walls as they'd walked down the street. Their shadows the only reminders of lives completely evaporated.

There was an eeriness to that image which I now equated to the moss family, yet it was touching and beautiful, too. A family frozen in time.

I wanted to touch them but somehow it felt wrong. Felt like a direct violation of Bill and his privacy. I decided it was time to call 911 but then hesitated. What would Bill want me to do? Would he want the whole community to know he'd kept a moss family in his house as some sort of homage? Did I want people going around talking about Bill as if he was a deranged, troubled freak? Because I knew damn well people would create all sorts of stories, make up rumors - just as they had before - many of them depraved and perverted. Bill deserved better.

So, one-by-one, I picked up the family and carried each one out the front door, where Bill watched silently from his rocking chair. I paused momentarily with each passing to let him say his final goodbyes, and then I took first little Sophie, then Lawrence, and finally Caroline to the edge of the woods, where I carefully dismantled them, unknotting the twine that held their bodies together, as well as the underlying pine limbs that had acted as the framework. Stick figures, in the most literal sense. I kept looking over my shoulder as I worked. What if somebody caught me? What if somebody witnessed me tearing the family apart? What would they do? What would I do?

I dispersed the moss and limbs into the woods, destroying the evidence. No one in a million years would be any the wiser to the love and compassion Bill had had for his family. No one would know how badly he had missed them. And I believe that's the way he wanted it.

Back at the house, I washed my hands in the sink, dried off, then walked down the hall, compelled to see the rest of the home. There were two bedrooms, the back one obviously Bill's, while the other had two small single beds, one with a pink bedspread, the other red. A stuffed bear and a Raggedy Ann lay on the pink bed, and in the corner of the room were several toys. A yellow metal Tonka trunk, a hula-hoop, a miniature Radio Flyer.

As I was about to exit, the faintest little something on Lawrence's bed caught my eye. It was tightly made, the bedspread folded back just beneath the single pillow. And it was there that I now focused. Two or three strands of moss, barely noticeable, stood out in contrast to the white pillowcase. Like fine hairs left by someone who'd been sleeping.

I stepped over to Sophie's bed, where I observed something similar. A few more wisps on the pink covers. I didn't bother to check Bill's bed but imagined the same on Caroline's side. And probably, if I'd examined the living room, I might've found more moss on the chairs and loveseat, where the family perhaps once gathered to watch Bonanza or The Dick Van Dyke Show but were now stuck with American Idol or, God forbid, Jersey Shore. Those little strands of moss scattered about were like fibers at a crime scene, painting the full picture of Bill's lonely existence.

I stepped outside, grabbed the milk carton, and sat on the top stair. I angled my body so I was more-or-less facing Bill. Between thumb and finger, as if examining expensive fabric, I gently caressed the petals of the orchid. Then I pulled out my phone and dialed.

My heart pounded when the other end started ringing. Bill's corpse watched me intently, as if listening. Or at least hoping I was smart enough to say the right thing.

A Nearly Perfect Five by Seven
By Rebecca Ring

USA

The squeal of the backhoe teeth on stone always gave him shivers. He'd hit a rock again. Second time this morning, and the damn thing wouldn't budge. Horace Underwood climbed out of the cab and walked to the front, knelt by the almost finished grave. He'd planned on being done by ten so he could eat the other half of his peanut butter and jelly sandwich. The thought of it created a gnawing in his stomach. And to make things worse, a yellow bus was pulling up the long cemetery drive, which meant invaders of the miniature kind - always a distraction. There was nothing for it; he was going to have to drive the backhoe around and try to get at the rock from the other side.

The October morning had lost its chill. Briefly blinded by the sun, Horace stood up, pulled off his jacket, and watched the school bus give birth to its swarm of little vermin. He shook his head. Couldn't they see he was working here?

Fifteen minutes later, Horace had managed to get his bucket around the boulder and was rocking it back and forth like a baby in a cradle. "It's a-comin'. It's a-comin'," he said over and over to himself. It was a monster. He was no longer a young man, but the power of the backhoe made him feel like Atlas or Sisyphus, or one of those ancient gods who moved mountains. Every time he finished preparing a gravesite, he felt a sense of achievement and pride. He sometimes watched from his truck - always parked at a discreet distance - as the coffin descended from its regal support frame into the waiting hole he had made for it. At these moments of great emotion, with family members slumping to the ground or wailing as their loved ones disappeared into the earth, Horace became emotional too, because he had made the hole with his own hands.

"Mister?"

Horace, startled into releasing the backhoe's joystick, watched the bucket drop the boulder it had finally snared. "Damn!" he said. "Dammit all to hell!" Then just as quickly, he put his hand over his mouth and looked around. A child's voice. He'd heard it. But where was the child?

Off in the trees he could see small groups of children led by overeager adults as they traipsed through the cemetery. But they were far away now, having wandered in the opposite direction from the bus. He saw them every year around this time - carrying clipboards and little magnifying glasses, kicking at dry leaves. They were often crouched down in front of headstones, inspecting them with their hand lenses, scribbling busily on their clipboards while the adults herded and shouted directions.

Once, a young teacher with pencil-straight brown hair had stopped him while he was whacking weeds around a monument to ask for directions to some city founder's grave. She'd been offended when he said he didn't know. Horace hardly ever read the headstones; he just dug the holes and kept things tidy. Only occasionally - when he noticed a stone whose birth and death dates were less than ten years apart - would he give a closer look. Something about a person dying that young set Horace's heart thumping, made him need to read the epitaph, always hoping there'd be a reasonable explanation. That was the day he'd finally found the nerve to ask, "Why do you bring these kids to the cemetery every year?"

The teacher had pushed up her glasses and, in an effusive, bubbly voice, told him what a great place it was for her fourth graders to learn about local history and geology.

"Geology?" Horace had asked numbly.

"Rocks and minerals. You know, what tombstones are made of. Metamorphic, sedimentary, igneous."

Horace didn't see anyone today who looked like that teacher.

"Mister?"

This time Horace looked down, out of the left side of the backhoe's cab. She was about nine years old, he figured. Pale and blonde, very pretty, standing alone and staring up at him with big, gray eyes and a hesitant smile.

"Hey, Missy," he said. "You'd better get back with your teacher and the rest of your class. Can't you see I'm working here?"

"Will you play with me?" she asked.

He pointed. "Your teacher's right there. Your friends…"

She shook her head, the blonde pigtails whipping back and forth across her face in a blur. "They're boring. I choose you."

"I don't have time for nonsense," he muttered and shifted the backhoe into gear, aimed his bucket for the boulder again. As he managed to get a purchase on it, he peeked out from the corner of one eye. She was still standing there, watching him. The backhoe belched a puff of black smoke. Its teeth sank into the dirt. He tried not to look at her.

Then he heard a scream and his head swiveled around. It was one of the school kids, surrounded by a gaggle of friends, jumping up and down on a fresh grave. The one Horace had filled in just yesterday. He killed the engine and clambered out of the cab, almost falling, and ran toward them. "Hey! You! Get offa there!" he yelled. Where was their teacher? The kids galloped away, shrieking and looking over their shoulders at Horace, who waddled more than ran. He stopped and clutched his chest, his breath coming in short, wheezy bursts. He wasn't up to this anymore.

The red bandana he used to wipe his forehead came away dirty and greasy. He looked at it briefly, stuffed it in the back pocket of his denim overalls, and stumbled wearily back to the gravesite.

The little girl was gone. Good, he thought. One less urchin to give him grief. Probably all part of some prank, her and that other group of kids who had given their teacher the slip just to see if they could get a rise out of the gravedigger. Nope. Not today. He had to finish up this hole by noon.

As Horace grunted his way up to the well-worn seat of his backhoe - noticing as he climbed how once again that nemesis boulder had fallen back out of the bucket - a light rustling from behind made him turn. And she was there again, the little girl, this time swinging her legs from side to side atop a nearby marble headstone. The swish of her black-stockinged legs against the sandiness of the unpolished rock made a sound like leaves skittering in the wind. Like a big cricket, Horace thought. That was when it dawned on him that she wasn't dressed like the others. The other kids all wore white shirts and beige pants, some kind of school uniform, but she had on a lollipop-pink dress and patterned black tights with holes in them. Her shiny, red, patent leather shoes were scuffed, and one buckle was undone. Horace pointed his finger at her, trying to think of something to say. She jumped off the headstone and hid behind it. One eye peeked out, teasing.

"Come on outta there, Missy," he finally said. "You need to get over with your teacher and friends." He waved and nodded toward them. "Look, they're gettin' on the bus. Time to go back to school. They'll be lookin' for you."

She turned and sprinted away from him, away from the bus. Instinctively Horace slid down from the backhoe and started after her. As he ran, he felt a tightness crawl across his chest and realized he could never catch her. He turned and lurched back toward the school bus. Only two kids left, and when he finally reached them, the prematurely graying teacher was climbing the steps. The driver swung the handle just as Horace's fist intercepted the closing bivalve door.

"Hey!" he cried. "You forgot a kid! There's still another kid in the cemetery!"

The teacher's face grew wide with alarm.

"That ... little girl over there," he said. He lifted a shaking finger in the direction he'd come from. "The one running away."

Her eyes skipped across the cemetery. "I don't see anyone," she said, and then with her gaze fastened on Horace, she called into the bus, "Evelyn! Can you count the kids again? Make sure everyone has their buddy?" Stepping into the sunlight, she shaded her eyes. "What did she look like?"

"Pigtails..." Horace was still out of breath. "Stockings. Black. Pink dress. Blonde."

The teacher shook her head. "No. We don't have anyone like that."

The woman who must have been Evelyn poked her head out the window. "All accounted for, Janet."

"I'm sorry," the teacher said to Horace. "You're mistaken. She's not one of ours." She gave him a pinched, suspicious look and hurried back onto the bus.

Horace stared out across the cemetery and wiped the sweat from his eyes with his bandana. "Goddamn kids," he mumbled to himself. He started back toward the unfinished grave. "Should be a barbed wire fence around this place."

Finally, after ten more minutes of scraping and rocking, the heavy boulder seemed to leap into his bucket from the underground vault where it had re-nestled itself. "Ha!" he shouted triumphantly. Before it could get away again, he slammed the joystick that raised the boom. The backhoe arm hoisted the boulder with a dusty shudder and sat poised to deposit it onto the ground above. Horace, glowing with pride, glanced into the nearly perfect five by seven hole from which it had come.

Beneath the crumbling dry clay something seemed to shimmer, something shiny and red. He slid from the cab for a closer look. Was it a shoe? Only the toe of it. Had the girl -? In the next instant, he was scrambling into the grave. Breathless, gasping, he clawed madly at the dirt with his bare hands. As he struggled, his ears filled with the rasp of his own breath and the thunder of his own straining heart, so he didn't hear the whoosh and grind of the hydraulics or the gradual, rusty release of the backhoe arm slowly returning its burden to the hole. As he pulled out the little red shoe and realized it was the only thing in there, a shadow fell across him. He looked up to see the boulder blocking the sun as it closed in.

—

The morning light glinted off the backhoe window, but the sunbeam that hit Horace Underwood smack between the eyes went right through him, illuminating the tombstone behind him. His face was placid and unsquinting in the sun's glare as he stood graveside. He looked down. A breeze fluttered the red bandana hanging from the back pocket of the denim overalls on the body pinned beneath the boulder - his body. And next to the hand that would forever be reaching out was the red shoe. His heart gave a slight murmur of regret, but it felt lighter in a way too, less braced - as it had recently seemed - for imminent explosion.

Funny, in all these years he'd never given a moment's thought to the likelihood he would someday end up in a grave - had certainly never imagined digging his own. The boulder sure had been a large one. *Metamorphic, sedimentary, or igneous?* he wondered. Horace had never

215

left a grave in such a muddle. The hole would have to be filled in. He wondered if, in his present condition, he would still be able to operate the backhoe.

While he stared into the hole, two little feet appeared at the edge of the grave next to his - one encased in a scuffed red shoe, the other with a dirty toe sticking out of a black stocking. A small hand slipped into and merged with his.

"Silly shoe, always falling off," she said.

He looked down into her gray eyes. Her grin was wide and toothless.

"You see, I chose you. Now ... tag or hopscotch?"

Palette
By Barry Charman

England

The conditions were challenging, but Suzette didn't mind. Exhilaration had a price, easily paid. Ever since she'd first glimpsed the field, driving past all those months ago, all she'd been able to think of was painting it. She set up on a small ridge so she could see the field fully as it extended into the distance. A river of golden wheat, glowing like a sea beneath a sun. The wind blew colours her way. The view seemed to change by the moment. Down at the far end of the field an old black mill, hunched like a wounded animal, was the only thing that seemed to stay in place. At least, until she noticed the figure. *A man*, she thought, *some local?* He was just standing there, unmoving. She continued to paint, greys now whirling into black - such a sky - but his fixed presence began to distract her. She almost thought of going down to talk to him, when she suddenly realized it must be a scarecrow. Of course. Some farmer must have added it after she'd first scouted the field. It was annoying, but she could overlook it.

Suzette just concentrated on the painting. She wanted to capture the rush of life. The breath against the inert. The resistance, the mutual hatred of all things. Later, when she was packing up for the day, she spared a glance for the figure, but as her eyes scanned the field, she realised it was no longer there. She gripped her easel, more troubled by this than she could explain. Back at the hotel, she sat on her bed and called her sister. They talked about the landscapes she was developing. The therapeutic nature of art.

"It's been such a terrible year," Jane said.

But Suzette blocked it out. She visualized the accident and painted over the parts she didn't like. She tried to explain this, but Jane wasn't happy.

"You have to face what happened." She talked on, but Suzette began to block her out too.

The next day Suzette took her canvas, her easel, her paints, and went back to the spot she'd found. The calm sky was maddening, but she could ignore it. There was no figure. Except, as she set up the painting, she realised she had painted him into the landscape, which she hadn't remembered doing. His appearance on her canvas was abrupt and improper. It seemed an intrusion in the composition. She raised her brush, intending to paint across him, but it was a watercolor; any attempt to paint over him would end badly. This thought made her pause so long, she almost forgot what she was doing.

She tried to push past it by returning her attention to the sky. In the painting the sky was a howling, churning animal. The strokes were thick, aggressive. Had it really been like that?

Suzette paused again. She shook herself and focused. She went back to the crops, adding more to what she'd painted yesterday. She made them bow and break. She wanted them to suffer, to know the inevitable pressure of existence.

She blinked. Turning away from the canvas, she stared at the field. She felt her heart beating. She remembered how he would put his palm to her chest, *oh, the poor little thing.* He'd smile, then. Wicked smile. Beautiful smile. Then he would rest against her, his steady heart calling to hers to slow down. That beat and echo of love. That moment. So solid. The weight of it all, so brutally worthless over time.

She realized that no matter what she painted, she could not capture the simple, raw horror of the world. No more than she could make any sense of it. Her eyes were blurry, but in the field she saw the figure of a man, waving. Stepping back, she rubbed her face and glanced at the canvas. There was nothing in the landscape but the howl of life. She saw now that no man could exist in such a climate. The violence in the painting made her unsteady and she turned quickly away. Uncertain, she slowly raised her arm, and waved back. The man brought his pale hands up, pressed together, and rested his head against them.

Sleep, he was saying. *Sleep*.

But she'd slept at the wheel. She never wanted to sleep again. She must have been tired; the next thing she knew she was kneeling, her legs folded neatly beneath her. The easel loomed beside her, but she didn't look up at it. She didn't look at the field either. Wherever he was, he was not. The thought should have maddened her. Should have made her want to paint over the bleak white canvas he'd left behind. Instead she looked down, at her paint-streaked palms. Blacks. Greys. Reds. His eyes had been turquoise. His lips the palest pink. Where were these? She thought that coming here, attempting another painting after all these years, would be the challenge - but the real challenge was in trying to paint something that was not the landscape of a butchered heart. It was in trying not to find madness in her palette. She smiled. It was the softest feeling on her face, like a light brush mark against her own canvas. Like the fingers that once brushed her so. She found she felt less tired than before. Somehow, it was enough to sit and watch as the sky turned pink. This morning, she would have called it bruised, and she would have thanked it for being honest.

But that was this morning. Before her, below, the crops waved. So she waved back.

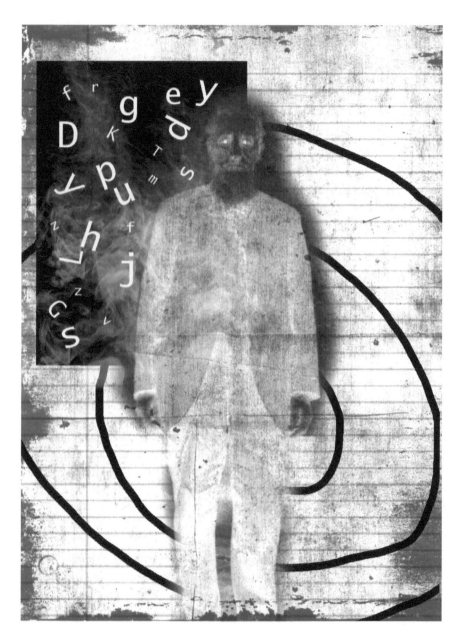

221

Tongues
By Emma Murtagh

Ireland

Maria turned wearily in her chair and looked out across the River Corrib from the office window. It was too dark to see the bridge and archway and Claddagh Quay, reaching out to where the river met the ocean, but the streetlights on the walkway between the canal and river threw columns of light on the water that glimmered gold and white on its inky, restless surface, like flickering spectres standing watchfully in line.

Her desk was in the corner of the small office, facing toward the open door that framed the corridor, which was dark and quiet without the daytime commotion of clients and other office workers banging their way through the fire doors and setting off the sensor light with its obnoxious ping. Maria was glad. The text she was working on was dense and unforgiving. It was almost impossible to concentrate on such a difficult translation in the hum of the office during business hours. She liked working late at night when there wasn't another soul in the old converted mill that perched upon the river like the herons did along its banks.

With a burst of resolve, Maria got to work. She was deep in yet another ludicrously long and complicated sentence when she began to feel a distinct sensation. It arose before she was aware of it, like an insect crawling on skin for a while before the tickle is felt. She began to feel an unpleasant tingle, starting first at the back of her skull and spreading so intensely it demanded action: She was being watched.

Her eyes snapped towards the corridor and the silent figure that stood stock still in its shadows. "*Joder, que susto!*" Maria cursed as she got to her feet, her heart thumping.

It was a man. An older, slight man, dressed in a dark suit. She was relieved it was not someone more threatening - but something still felt wrong. In her panic, it took her a while to realise what was niggling at her as she stared, frozen with shock, at the man in the doorway. The lights. Of course. Perhaps the sensor was broken. But she hadn't heard him open the door either.

She cleared her throat and - after such an unmerciful jolt - found it hard to put some words together in English.

"I'm sorry. You scared me," she said, attempting a smile.

He said nothing but walked towards her. Instinctively, she tried to back away but there was nowhere to go other than out the window. Subtly, she palmed her phone and unlocked it, opening her boyfriend Eoin's contact. Her thumb hovered over the call button.

"I'm sorry, we are closed." Her voice sounded weak.

Still silent, he moved into the light. There was something slightly off about his face. His pale blue eyes were too big for his withered skull and they peered up at her in the most peculiar way. He took a leaflet from her desk and held it up, pointing at the word "translation."

"Yes. We do translations ..." Maria felt a rush of guilt as she considered that he might be deaf or otherwise impaired. He was old and could be confused. She should help him. Feeling heartless, she tried to relax, despite her gut insisting otherwise.

The man fumbled in his pocket, taking out a rectangle of paper and unfolding it carefully. His huge eyes were bright as he extended it to her in a pale, trembling hand.

Warily, Maria took it from him, expecting to find some kind of plea for help. She knew immediately that the ornate script on the yellowing page was not in one of her languages. She scanned the words looking for a clue to its origin. It was in the Latin alphabet but other than that it was indiscernible.

"I don't recognise this language," she told him, still trying to read it, "Can you ... yu ... ya ..." She cleared her throat. The letters on the page were contorting in front of her eyes, becoming increasingly meaningless.

"I ... eh ... *eeehhh* ..."

Her trembling hand went to her mouth as if she could scoop the strange, strangled noises back into her throat. Her eyes wide, she met the old man's gaze. He was smiling now as he walked around the desk toward her. Maria backed into the corner helplessly. She tried to speak again and, failing that, tried to scream but only produced whimpers.

The old man, rounding the desk, watched as she sank to the floor with her hands held above her in surrender. He crouched down and looked at her closely. Still smiling, he reached a hand toward her face; Maria flinched as his index figure came to rest on her lips, quietening her strangled gasps.

"*Shhh*," he said. Maria shuddered. Removing his hand from her mouth, he gently unfurled her fingers from the crumpled page and took it from her.

"Thank you," he said. He stood and she heard him plod from the room, laughing wheezingly. The sound faded to silence in the dark corridor.

FIVE DAYS LATER

"Mr. Canavan, we've done every possible test. Physically, she is perfectly normal and healthy. It has to be psychological."

Eoin slouched in his chair, exhausted.

"What kind of psychological event makes you forget not one, but four languages? She can't even recognise letters. She keeps trying to draw, but all she can muster are scribbles. I don't ..."

His voice caught and he bit back tears as the doctor shook her head sympathetically. At a table nearby, Maria hunched over a lined notepad, her eyes wide and desperate, trying to recreate the image of the man in the doorway. She needed them to see it. But she could only manage a vague rectangle and a deep, dark spiral.

Left of Heaven
By Dessa

USA

Matthias sleeps on his back. Tonight, he has one arm flung out, one bent across his chest, like an archer painted on a cave wall. I lay down beside him, my head on his pillow. This close, I can hear the ringing in his ears that my nearness induces. His breath clouds when it hits mine. I wait until I'm sure he's out, then leave for the night.

Back at camp, I play cards again with Misha, win more than I lose. She never gives much contest; drowned girls are over-tender, better fit for pictures than for poker. But she loses gracefully - lovely, blue, and luminescent as a television set. At my urging, she deals one more hand, dampening the deck.

Everyone here falls into one of a few categories, sorted, more or less, by the circumstances in which they left the Earth. As a rule, those who died by violence aren't much for conversation. Their faculties are occupied in suppressing their hysteria. The suicides, meanwhile, amuse themselves with constant banter. They're generally funny and smart, but self-absorbed - a clique of slender know-it-alls deciding how to hold their cigarettes. The lay-overs, who are here to settle a last bit of unfinished business, come and go too quickly to learn too much about. I stay up with whoever's up and out late. I'm not in a position to be too choosy about my company.

Misha loses one more time then knocks against the table top to say good night. It's late already, so I don't try to make her stay. I walk the long way home, by the water. It's dark, but I know the route. The midnight barge goes past, piled high with sleeping children. It's headed west to Nightmare Island where it will dock until morning. There are still several hours before Mathias wakes up and my next shift begins.

227

I sing one of his songs while walking. The words are not romantic, something about a bear cub, but the melody is nice: sad for the verses and happy in the refrain. When I get close enough to see the shape of my house in the darkness, I switch to humming. My parents will almost certainly be asleep already. They stay curled so close they hardly need a bed for two.

My father died in Babylon, foolishly, beneath his own plowshare. Overrun - as he tells it with a wink - by the premonition of my mother's love. The joke's wrung out, but she blushes every time he makes it. She died in New York City in a famous factory fire. She leapt from the ninth story and - my father's quick to add - straight into his waiting, broken arms. Their affair here went undetected for a long time. But they got careless after I was born, or maybe the secret just got too large to keep. A neighbor discovered and reported their tryst, though they managed to hide me for another whole year.

My parents' mutual affection was deviant, enough to have them both expelled. Here love is not a reciprocal arrangement. Love is for export only, to be sent and spent on Earth - that's fundamental to the nature of a ghost. But I'm told that even at my parents' trial, they held hands. They refused to answer questions, their intertwining fingers revealing an inclination to haunt only each other. Finally, the councilors brought in a living dog, at great expense and greater risk, to assist in the investigation. And they emptied the entire colony of every living ghost. Let off his leash, the beast found me immediately: in the bottom drawer of my mother's vanity, asleep and lightly drugged with a thumbnail dosing of valerian from my father's garden.

There were angry meetings, votes, another public hearing. Almost everyone agreed that my parents were past redemption - but what should be done with *me*? There was no one else to take me. So, the three of us were sent to the camp's farthest margin, exactly one inch shy of exile. And I grew up as the only native, the only ghost that had never lived or died. The council made it very clear that I wouldn't receive any special consideration. I was expected to conduct myself like any other citizen. So when I came of age, having no natural tie to a particular place or person in the living world, I had the unusual task of choosing my own haunt.

I followed a few men around, each for a few days. I didn't see much of a difference among them, so without too much deliberation I picked Matthias in Stockholm. Now, with so much feeling for him, it's strange to think he meant so little to me at the beginning. In the seven years I've been following Matthias, he's grown a beard, learned to work a table saw, moved north, and then farther north to Luleå. The local accent is muddy, so thick that it felt like learning Swedish all over again just to be able to follow his conversations at the grocery. He can cook now, but he never did fill out. When he takes off his shirt to step into the shower, he is slender to a degree that arouses all my sympathy. I sit on the bathroom sink, a hole in the steam. I like to hear him sing.

The sun stays up for days during midsummer in Luleå. Sometimes he does too - the locals call it sun-sickness, a sort of mild mania from the constant light. On those yellow nights, I sit beside him on his doorstep while he rolls his cigarettes, sometimes draw circles with my finger in the smoke. We watch the sun pretend to set, then rebound before touching the horizon, like a skater who doesn't land between her jumps. By the time the first hour of darkness arrives, he has blue rings beneath his eyes. I think maybe it's a preview of how he will look when he gets old.

Matthias is clumsy, particularly when he's tired. He'll sometimes clip the doorframe of his bedroom with his shoulder and then spin off of it with a hurt expression, as if the floor plan had shifted deliberately to sabotage him. He's dropped almost everything in the kitchen, but, in his defense, he catches most of it before it hits the floor. Once I saw him catch a falling pot of stew; the bit of it that had gone airborne landed right back in the pot, like a tower collapsing. After checking his shirtfront, still spotless, he

229

laughed out loud at himself. I had never thought of that - laughing alone - and it was such a nice a habit that I started doing it too.

I know him so well now that it's easy to forget that he doesn't know me at all. But we're very similar, I think. So maybe in knowing his own mind, he knows part of mine too. Sometimes, just for fun, when his phone rings, I pretend it's me who's calling and I fill in the other side of his conversation.

"Hej, how are you?"

I'm fine.

"Where are you?"

Sitting beside you.

"What are you up to?"

Sitting beside you.

Just recently he started doing push-ups in the morning. At first, I thought maybe there was a problem - that he was struggling to get up - but it's only an exercise. Now I do them alongside him on the braided rug, and we are up to thirty every day.

When there is a girl over, I know I should be slamming doors. Sometimes I do. But other times I just pace the ceiling in the kitchen and leave them at it. Girls are not over very often, though, so mostly it's just us. I stack the coins on his dresser or walk behind him to watch the short hairs stand against his collar. On the rare occasion that he's photographed, out drinking with his friends from work, I loop my arm around his sharp shoulders to blur the shot. When he leaves the table to smoke outside, I cup my hands around his drink to keep it cold until he returns.

When he can't fall sleep, Matthias watches old cowboy movies in bed. He has a TV on his dresser and a remote that he keeps under his pillow. If I lean the back of my head against the screen, it feels like we're looking right at one another, like his eyes are fixed on mine. I bother him when he's in bed sometimes, hoping he'll turn on a movie for a while. But I don't bother him while he's driving or when he's at work on the big machines.

When we're together, I'm careful with him. But on these long walks, I let myself imagine that there might be an accident at the shop. And I imagine him following me, his heel slipping into each footprint as soon as I lift my toe out of it. I entertain the possibility that he might die in violence, or on purpose, or with a great deal left to do - so that he would come here where he could haunt me back. It can't hurt just to imagine. But just a little bit, it does.

A Ghost of a Smell
By John Reaves

USA

Holly took Steven's dinner out of the microwave and set it in front of him. She sat down across the table, determined to get his attention before he opened his laptop and pulled up a financial newsletter to read as he ate.

"Steven," she said, "I had lunch with Mom today." He looked up at her, squinting.

"Let me guess. She wanted to borrow more money."

She started to protest that her mother had borrowed from them only once, well, twice really, but she didn't want to be distracted.

"She met with Uncle Mike's attorney. He showed her the will."

"And?"

"He left me his house."

"That old rat's nest? It'll probably be condemned."

"It's not that bad. Besides, he also left me $50,000 to fix it up." Steven pushed his plate forward and stood up.

"Let's think about this legacy," he said. "What kinds of strings are attached? Do you have to keep the damned thing, or can we unload it the second we get the deed? Fifty thousand won't be nearly enough to make it marketable, by the way."

"I don't know."

"Why you? He had other nieces and nephews."

"I have no idea."

"Maybe we ought to just refuse it, let the house go back into the estate. Then someone else would have to deal with fixing it up and selling it. You'd get your share of it instead of the whole thing, but we'd avoid all the hassle." He sat down again and picked up his fork. "There's no sense talking about this now," he said. "We don't have enough information to make a decision. It seems like you could have gotten some details out of your mother, but you didn't, so never mind. I'll call the attorney tomorrow."

Dismissed, Holly went upstairs and looked for a picture of her Uncle Mike. She found one in a closet. She looked at it a long time, speculating about her mother's bachelor brother, what his life must have been like, why in the world he would leave his house to her. He was a big man, and in the picture, he was wearing a thick woolen coat that made him look even bigger. His hair was long, thin on top, tied in a queue in the back. He had a pipe in his mouth. She realized she had seldom seen him without a pipe or cigar. The truth was, she didn't know him very well. He was always at family gatherings, talking, taking pictures, handing out small gifts of money to the kids, but it had been decades since she'd had more than a five-minute conversation with him. In her early years the family often celebrated birthdays and holidays at his house, which had been his parents' home, but those visits became less and less frequent as she grew up. Mike was not a good housekeeper, and he smoked all over the house. The house had a musty, forbidding smell. His sisters started taking turns inviting the family to their houses for special occasions.

So, she felt like an intruder the next day when she got the key from the attorney and went over to have a look. The neighborhood, she noticed, was getting better - yards were mowed, shrubs trimmed, houses and picket

234

fences newly painted. A house near her uncle's, an 1890s mansion that she remembered as a dilapidated rooming house, had apparently been restored as a single-family home with a pool house in the back. She began to think her uncle's house ("My house," she corrected herself) might be worth more than Steven thought.

But she had to admit it was an eyesore, all the more noticeable because the houses on each side of it had been recently remodeled. On the front porch was an old glider with a pillowed cover she could smell from the street. *That'll be the first thing to go*, she thought. Inside, the smell was almost too much to bear. She went from room to room, raising the windows that could be raised, sticking her head out each time to suck in fresh air like a swimmer between dives. By the time she had finished, the smell had abated somewhat, enough that she could have a look around without gagging.

Apparently, her uncle had occupied the living room, kitchen, and one bedroom. The other rooms were coated with thick dust, as if no air had stirred inside them for ages, probably since Holly's grandmother died more than twenty years before. The rooms he used were dusty now as well but with a thinner, less stable coating. Ashtrays filled with cigar stubs and pipe ashes were everywhere. The rugs and upholstery were covered with dog hair and dotted with burn holes.

"This will all have to go," she said aloud. As if to confirm her opinion, a stench like rotting cabbage seemed to rise from nowhere and assail her nostrils. She reminded herself to bring a mask the next time she came over.

She began to look at the pictures propped up on the mantel and hung on the walls. There were a few paintings, possibly valuable, she thought, but mostly there were framed photographs of family and scenes from her uncle's travels. Her cousins, her mother, her aunts, her grandparents were all well represented, but where, she wondered, were pictures of her? She was in the group photos, but there were no individual pictures of her. She went through all the rooms again, specifically looking for a single photograph of herself. There were none. *How odd*, she thought. *Didn't Uncle Mike like me?*

She stopped in the living room, looking for ...what? She noticed a large indentation in the couch, evidence that her uncle's sheepdog had slept there often. She wondered what had happened to the dog. He must have died first. And then it occurred to her that Uncle Mike had died in this house. She shivered, but she also was intrigued. Where, exactly, did he die? Probably in the bed. She went into the bedroom, looking for clues - what kind of clues, she had no idea. She supposed she could ask someone, but who? Would her mom know? Her aunts? She wasn't sure who found the body or how long he had been dead when someone found him. She decided she didn't want to ask; she would figure it out.

A cross breeze blew through the house, and for once she could breathe almost freely. A different smell was wafted on the breeze, an almost pleasant smell. It was sort of like a cake in the oven, maybe a cake just starting to burn. It seemed to be coming from the living room. She followed the smell and found herself standing in front of an enormous leather recliner. A piece of crocheted cloth, something like a shawl, hung over one arm of the chair. On a table within reach of the chair were a lamp and some books and magazines, plus the inevitable ashtray, a couple of pipes, and a pouch of tobacco, which she picked up, opened, and sniffed. It was this smell that had brought her here, the smell of this particular tobacco burning. It was one of several brands Mike smoked, the only one she had found the least bit pleasant.

"He died here," she said with conviction. "Right here. I know it." She surprised herself by starting to cry.

Then her cell phone jingled.

"Where are you?" Steven asked. "I made a point of getting home by 7:00 so we could eat together, and you're not here. As far as I can tell, you haven't been here. There's nothing cooked. What's going on?"

"I'm at Uncle Mike's house," she said. "I just wanted to see it again, maybe figure out why he wanted me to have it. I lost track of the time."

"Well, you may be over there a lot in the next few weeks. Turns out we can sell it, but the only way we can get the fifty thou is to put it into the house. It's in a dedicated fund. We'll have to spend our own money on repairs and then get reimbursed up to fifty. Be sure you keep a receipt for every nickel. I don't want any of my money going down that toilet."

"Aren't you going to oversee the repairs? You know I'm not very comfortable with that sort of thing."

"You know I can't do that. I'm tied up till next summer. You'll be fine. Just check with me before you do anything expensive."

"I wish you'd at least help me with it."

"Cannot do. You can do this. Besides, it wasn't my uncle who died and left us a white elephant."

"Okay, I'll see you in about an hour. I've got to close this place up before I can leave. Do you want me to pick up some take-out?"

"No, I've got to go back to the office for an hour or so. I'll see you when I get home."

During the following week, Holly developed a routine. She would rush home from work, change, and leave Steven a note suggesting something he could warm up for dinner. Then she would go to Uncle Mike's house, stopping on the way to pick up a sandwich, and work for as long as she could stand it, sometimes until 9:00 or later. Her goal was to rid the house of its smell. She pulled down the curtains in the rooms that Mike had occupied, washed them, and put them back up. She swept and mopped and vacuumed, sprayed air freshener by the gallon, but she did not move any of Mike's personal belongings. She did her best to leave things the way he had left them, to just clean around them. Moving them seemed wrong somehow, arrogant, insensitive. But by the end of the week, when the smell had dissipated but was still very noticeably present, she decided it was time to take decisive action. The culprit, she believed, was the pipes and ashtrays. She wondered briefly if some of the pipes might not be collectors' items, but how could she know, whom could she ask? She imagined taking a boxful of smelly used pipes into an antique shop and asking what they were worth. Surely nobody collects used pipes, she told herself. So she doubled a black garbage bag and started through the house, tossing in pipes and tobacco and ashtrays. The ashtrays could be cleaned, she supposed, but what would she do with them? Goodwill? Probably not, and she didn't know anyone who smoked. So she tossed them into the bag and dragged them to the curb.

When she got back in the house, the smell was stronger than before, much stronger - as strong, in fact, as it had been a week before when she first opened the door. She started to clean the surfaces where the pipes and ashtrays had been, but the smell overwhelmed the lemon-scented cleaner and almost choked her. It seemed to spin around her like a whirlwind, but the curtains were motionless, the leaves on the trees outside the windows perfectly still. It was tobacco smoke and stale beer, spoiled bean dip, belched broccoli, rancid grease, rotten onions, a hint of spoiled fish. It was flame orange and angry, angry at her. She felt her face pucker like a gargoyle's; her eyes teared up. She fled without even closing the windows.

Later she tried to tell herself she had imagined the whole experience. She was tired, stressed, had been spending too much time alone. Smells can't be felt on the skin, they don't have color, they don't get angry. They don't attack. But below her interior voice of reason was another voice - smaller, more primitive, more insistent. It said, *But it did. It attacked me.*

The next day after work she went back just to close the windows. She noticed her hand shaking a little as she fumbled with the lock. She half expected a family of squatters to have climbed in through the open windows and set up housekeeping, and of course, she feared another attack. Inside, though, the house definitely did smell better. She walked through the living room, peeked into the bedroom, then entered the kitchen, sniffing the corners like a drug dog. The house was nowhere near as antiseptically odor free as the suburban home where she and Steven lived, but it was bearable, almost ready to be shown to a potential buyer. She began to feel elated, as if she had fought hard against a formidable foe and won. She began to imagine what the old house might look like after it was renovated. The kitchen was really too small. There was a small porch on one corner that could be closed in to add extra space, and beside the door to the porch was another door she had hardly noticed before. A closet? A butler's pantry? She wasn't sure. She tried the door and found it locked. Wait, somewhere she had seen a ring of keys. Where would Uncle Mike keep keys he didn't use every day? After a fruitless search of the kitchen, she found the keys on a hook above the mantel in the living room and tried them one by one until the bolt slipped and she could push the door open.

She found a deep, narrow room, perhaps five feet by twelve, without shelves or furniture. A single, small window that reminded her of the slots she had seen in the walls of castles allowed in just enough light to let her know the room was empty. She had started to close the door when she noticed things hanging on the walls. Her fingertips and the dim light told her these were picture frames, but she couldn't make out the pictures. Carefully she took one down and stepped out into the kitchen where the light was better.

It was a picture of a tiny baby, no more than a week old. Just a baby. She couldn't tell if it was a boy or a girl. She turned the frame over to see if there was some identification on the back, but there was none.

Then she saw a string dangling from a naked light bulb near the ceiling. She pulled it, and suddenly she could see that both walls were covered with pictures. She replaced the picture she had taken down and began to look at the others one by one. Next was another baby, or perhaps the same baby a few weeks older. And the next and the next, each one a little older, until she found a picture she recognized, one she had seen among her mother's photos. This child was a little girl, maybe eighteen months old. She wore a stiff white dress, and a ribbon pinned to her tight sausage curls was slightly askew. One eye was almost closed, as if she were trying to wink at the camera.

"My God," she said aloud. "That's me." And a moment later, after looking at half a dozen more, she said, "Sweet Baby Jesus, they're *all* me."

She moved along the left wall and then back along the opposite wall, dazedly reliving moments from her life, some momentous, some trivial. There were graduations from kindergarten, fifth grade, and high school, birthday parties, Christmas mornings. In most of the pictures she was alone, but in a few she was with her mother or cousins or friends. Near the end was a picture of her and Steven dressed up for their senior prom. In the last picture of all, taken two years after the prom, she was feeding Steven wedding cake.

It's as if my whole life flashed before my eyes, she thought. *All but the past twelve years of it anyway. Does that mean I'm about to die?*

She shivered and turned quickly toward the door, half expecting to see her uncle staring down at her, his huge frame blocking her escape. He was not there, or at least she could not see him, but she caught a whiff of that cake-in-the oven smell of his pipe tobacco, an aroma that grew so strong she was convinced he was standing just outside the door, puffing away.

What will I do if he touches me? she wondered. *What if he puts his arm around my shoulders and pulls me to him?*

She didn't stay around to find out.

"Was Uncle Mike some kind of pervert?" she asked her mother at lunch the next day.

"No, he was not," her mother said. "What gave you that idea?"

"I found some pictures."

"Pornography?"

"No. Just pictures. Of me. They cover two walls of the butler's pantry, or whatever that room was. It's like a shrine, and I'm the goddess," she said. "It's creeping me out. I'm not sure I want to go back over there."

"My brother was a sweet, good man," her mother said. "I've always believed he would have been a wonderful husband and father if he could have mustered the courage to ask a girl for a date, but he could not do it. It was just too much for him, too scary. He simply could not handle rejection. I tried to fix him up with my friends. It was always a disaster."

"But why me? If he had some love/hate thing going on with women, why didn't he fill his little gallery with pictures of movie stars or something?"

"Because he loved you more than anybody else on this planet. He told me once, when he had had about three gin and tonics too many, that he considered you the daughter he never had. I guess because he was always close to me, and your father was out of the picture…"

"But we never were particularly close."

"Actually, you were, when you were little. You used to crawl all over him, and he would pull you around the yard in your little wagon or push you on the swing."

"I don't remember that. Well, maybe a little. But for the past twenty-five years or so, I've hardly spoken to him, outside of normal niece-uncle chitchat at family gatherings. What happened?

"You rejected him. You were too little to know what you were doing, but you pulled away and insulted him."

"How?"

"You told him he smelled bad."

"I *did?* I can't believe I was that rude."

"You were a little kid, maybe four or five, possibly three. You were an imperious little tyrant at times, and you blurted out just about anything that crossed your mind."

"I *was?* Then how did I turn into such a dishrag?"

"That's a whole different conversation we can have some other time. Right now, I want you to know that you really hurt your Uncle Mike, damned near killed him, but I don't want you to start beating yourself up about it. You were a little kid. You did what little kids do."

"What, exactly, did I say to him? Were you there?"

"I was. He grabbed you as you ran by and set you down on the arm of his chair, just like he'd done a thousand times before, but when he put his arm

242

around you, you sat up really straight and stiff and said, 'No. No. No. Won't sit here. You smell like Prissy's poopy box.' It was kind of funny, but Mike didn't laugh. I could tell you'd hit a nerve. He left a few minutes later, and he came over less often after that. He stopped picking at you the way he had before. He was friendly to you. He loved kids. And he even tried to clean up after that, washed his clothes more often and took more showers, but it was hopeless. He couldn't stop smoking. And he always was flatulent, poor boy. Our daddy called him Whistle Britches."

Holly laughed, but her eyes were burning. Their food came and for a few minutes, they concentrated on eating. They commented on the food, the weather, the number of dogs you see downtown these days. Then Holly blurted out something she had promised herself she wouldn't tell anybody.

"He's still there, Mom. I think he's still there."

"Who's still where?" he mother asked. "What are you talking about?"

"Uncle Mike. I think he's still in that house. I can smell him."

Holly's mother almost choked on her beet salad. She laid her fork down and fumbled in her purse for Kleenex. She dabbed at her eyes.

"You're making this up," she said at last. "I always said you should be a novelist." She started to laugh again but then stopped abruptly. "You're not laughing. My God, you're serious, aren't you?"

"Never mind," Holly said. "I shouldn't have said anything. I'm sure it's just my imagination anyway, but I swear I can feel his presence. And when he doesn't like something, like I start moving his stuff, the smell gets overpowering."

243

"So that's how you communicate with him?" She tried to imitate Holly's voice. "Are you comfortable in the afterlife, Uncle Mike? Fart once for yes, fart twice for no."

"Mom, please. This is your little brother we're talking about." Holly's mother abruptly stopped laughing.

"You don't have to remind me," she said. "I don't believe in ghosts, but if I did, if I believed for a second that Mike was still in that house and that I might be able to go over there and be with him and know that he's okay, I'd be on my way over there right now. But I don't believe it. He's gone forever, sweetie. It's your house now. And soon the smell will be gone and you'll forget it was ever there."

In the parking lot, before they parted ways, Holly's mother hesitated, then spoke softly. "I read a book about ghosts once," she said. "A couple of books, actually. The books said that when a person's spirit stays behind, it's because they have unfinished business in this world. If they can somehow finish it, or you can finish it for them, they'll go on to the next world. I don't know why I'm telling you this."

"It's okay, Mom. It's probably just my imagination. Remember my imaginary friend?"

"Of course, I do, honey. By the way, Mike had one too. That's something you and he have in common." She quickly corrected herself: "Something you *had* in common. He's gone, baby. Let him go. Try to enjoy the house."

When Holly arrived at Uncle Mike's house that evening, Steven's Lexus was in the driveway. She found Steven in the narrow side yard. At first she thought he was doing push-ups, but then she realized he was trying to look under the house without getting his suit dirty. When he jumped to his feet, she noticed that his tie was tucked into his shirt so that it wouldn't touch the ground.

244

"Come on," she said. "I'll give you the grand tour."

She took him around to the front entrance and pointed out the wide stone steps, the curved wrap-around porch with sturdy posts, almost pillars, supporting it.

"I haven't noticed any sagging," she said. "Of course, I'll have to get an engineer to look at it at some point. Now look at this door. It's got to be original, but it's still in great shape. It may need refinishing, but it would be a crime to replace it."

Inside she pointed out the abundance of varnished wood, darkened with age - the baseboards, chair rails, a curving staircase. She pulled open heavy pocket doors, four inches thick, with one finger, showing him how, after all these years, they were still perfectly balanced on their rollers. She told him about her idea to use the porch and the butler's pantry to enlarge the kitchen and make it sunnier.

After a few minutes, he interrupted her in midsentence. "Okay, okay, so what have you actually done?" he asked. "You've been over here every afternoon and every night for two weeks, and what do you have to show for it?"

"Not much, I'm afraid," she said. "I've gotten really familiar with it. I've cleaned up a lot - thrown away a bunch of moldy, smelly stuff - washed the curtains - I know that doesn't sound like much."

"Well, you're right about that. It doesn't sound like much at all. Here's some free advice. Hire a cleaning service. They'll have this place cleaned up in an afternoon. Call a general contractor. Get an estimate, not to make this anybody's dream house, just to make it presentable. The idea is to spend $50,000 and then dump it. I'm afraid you've gotten distracted. Focus never was your long suit."

"I told you this is not my kind of thing. I wanted you to help."

"Okay, so now I'm helping. Hire professionals, and then start coming home after work and paying some attention to your husband. I haven't had a home-cooked meal in two weeks."

After Steven left, Holly realized the smell was back. Her eyes were burning; she felt like she might throw up. She was certain Steven had noticed it. No wonder he thought she hadn't accomplished anything. Funny he hadn't mentioned it, though. It was not something anyone could ignore. This time it was mostly cabbage - sour, rotten cabbage - or maybe it was the smell of a flatulent old man who loved sauerkraut and wieners and ate a lot of it.

In the days that followed, she tried to stay away from the house. She came home from work, had a meal ready at 7:00. More often than not, she gave up and ate alone at 8:00 and then nuked Steven's dinner for him whenever he showed up. But she couldn't stop thinking about the house. She called a cleaning service and made an appointment, then called back a few hours later and canceled. She just couldn't do that to Uncle Mike. If he really was still there, he'd be upset by all the noise and activity, by the presence of strangers, especially strange women, in his personal space. She told herself she would work on the house herself for an hour after work each day, then go home and still have time to cook, but it seemed that something always drew her in, needed more attention than she had anticipated, and she found herself staying longer and longer. One day she was still cooking when Steven got home, and she tried feebly to explain that she had run by Uncle Mike's house and gotten more involved than she had intended. She felt like a little girl trying to explain how her jeans got muddy and her lunch got lost. Then one day he got home at 7:00 and she was still at Uncle Mike's. He didn't say much, but it was clear that he was furious. The next day when she arrived at Uncle Mike's house, there was a "For Sale" sign in the front yard.

"There's been some kind of mistake," she told the woman at the realtor's office. "My house is not for sale."

"I'm sorry. Do you want to buy a house or sell one? I can have an agent call you."

"No. I already own this house, and one of your agents has put a sign in the yard. You're advertising the wrong house."

"What's the address?"

"1400 Mabry Street."

"It's for sale, all right. The owner is Steven Bradley. I can have Ms. Wilkins call you."

"Don't bother. Just tell her to come get her sign. She'll find it under the front porch. I may have damaged it a little when I pulled it up."

That night she got home before Steven did. She nuked his supper and then excused herself, saying she felt bad. She didn't tell him she was angry. What was the point? The next day, instead of going to work, she packed her clothes and toiletries, a couple of paintings, several boxes of books, and a few of her favorite dishes. She ferried all of that across town in three loads, but then she remembered the house plants. Steven would let them all die. She stuffed as many as she could into her little SUV, leaving the ones that were too big for her to handle by herself.

She had intended to finish by 5:00, take a shower, and cook a simple supper for her and Steven. She would tell him calmly why she was leaving and then make a graceful exit. But by the time she had lugged the last plant up onto the porch she was exhausted. She decided to lie down on the couch for a few minutes before she went home. When she awoke, it was dark, and her phone was jingling.

"I see you've been busy," Steven said. "Stay where you are. I'll be right there."

She met him on the porch, hoping to talk outside, but he insisted on coming in.

"Everyone knows everyone's business in these old neighborhoods," he said. "The houses are so close together. You're always looking in someone's window."

Inside it seemed that he had brought the smell with him. It was back in force. Holly wanted to open the windows, but she knew what Steven would say. The smell swirled around her, almost as intense as it had been the day she tossed out the pipes and ashtrays. If Steven noticed, he didn't mention it.

Once he was out of earshot of the neighbors, he let her have it. He said she had lost her goddamned mind, that he was giving her one chance to come back home, and if she didn't leave this house right now and promise never to even drive through this neighborhood again, he was having her committed. She tried very hard not to cry, but the smell was stinging her eyes and assaulting her nostrils. She lost control. She slipped back into her usual response to Steven's anger. She sobbed. She groveled. She made excuses.

"So it's settled, then," he said. "Let's ride together. We can pick up your car in the morning."

She gathered up her purse, her sunglasses, her keys - and then she stopped. She set everything down and stood up very straight.

"I'm not going home with you, Steven," she said. "Not tonight. Maybe not ever. I can't explain it, not even to myself. I've got to stay here. I've got to finish what I've started. I want you to go home now and leave me here."

248

She walked to the car with him and tried to give him a kiss on the cheek, but he pushed her away. She watched the Lexus pull away and felt nothing, just empty, drained of all emotion.

She watched television for a while, some cop show whose plot she didn't try to follow. She was hungry, but she didn't have any food in the house and didn't feel like going anywhere. She tried to stop replaying the scene with Steven, but she could not. She hated herself for breaking down, letting him see her cry. It was the smell, she decided. It was so intense, so awful. Like Steven's anger. *But I stood up to him*, she thought. *I didn't let him bully me. Why? What happened?* In her mind she recreated that moment, and it felt good. She remembered standing up straight and pulling in a deep breath.

Yes, she thought, *a deep breath*. There had been no smell at that moment - and none since.

When, exactly, had the smell gone away? And why was it so intense in the first place? What had Uncle Mike been trying to communicate? The smell started when Steven entered the house and got more intense as his voice grew louder and more vicious. Maybe Uncle Mike just hated conflict. Or maybe he had gotten used to her, had forgiven her for throwing out his stuff, but resented having a virtual stranger invade his space.

Or maybe he didn't like Steven. The thought had never occurred to her before, and she pondered it. She tried to recall occasions when the two of them had interacted. Very few examples came to mind. Instead she remembered a couple of times when Uncle Mike broke off a conversation with her when Steven entered the room.

The smell went away, she decided, when she stood up straight, at the moment she grew a backbone, so to speak.

So now it all made sense to her, but she couldn't be sure her memory hadn't rearranged things a little. She'd always had an overactive imagination. She knew she sometimes remembered things that weren't quite true.

Sometime after midnight she went to bed in the downstairs bedroom, the one Uncle Mike had slept in. She couldn't sleep. At about 1:00 she started feeling sorry for herself and having second thoughts. She even thought about calling Steven and asking if she could still come home. By 2:00 she was up and pacing, becoming more and more agitated, and by 3:00 she had curled up exhausted and depressed in the big chair in the living room, unwilling to return to the lumpy - and lonely - bed.

She awoke to bright sunlight streaming in through the east windows. She closed her eyes and snuggled into the chair, feeling warm and secure, reluctant to get up and face the day. After a few delicious moments she tried to stretch, but her arms were restricted by a kind of cocoon. Another moment passed before her sleep-fogged brain realized it was a blanket. She untucked it and laid it aside, thinking she must have felt cold during the night and gotten up and found it, but after a second, she rejected that idea. She never sleepwalked, never failed to remember any sleepless night-time moments, not even trips to the bathroom. And the blanket had been under her on both sides. She could not have done that herself. *He tucked me in*, she thought. *Oh my God, he tucked me in.*

"Thank you, Uncle Mike," she said aloud.

The room filled with that cake-in- the-oven smell of burning pipe tobacco.

She called the library where she worked and told them she would not be in that day. Then she called her mother and said, "Meet me at Panera."

She told her mother about the "For Sale" sign in the yard, about the conversation with the woman at the real estate office, about moving out,

250

and about the confrontation with Steven. She did not tell her about the chair or the blanket.

"So now you're living with your imaginary friend," her mother said. "So, how's he doing?"

"I thought my imaginary friend was a girl."

"The first one was. The new one is a middle-aged man who communicates by farting."

"That's not funny, Mom," Holly said. "Besides, I think Uncle Mike will be leaving soon. I think he may have concluded his unfinished business."

"Well, if he's still there when you get back, give him my love."

She said she would, but when she arrived at her house, she didn't have any sense of his presence. The house was odorless, or as nearly odorless as old houses ever get. She thought she caught a whiff of the pipe smoke, just the faintest whiff, but she wasn't sure.

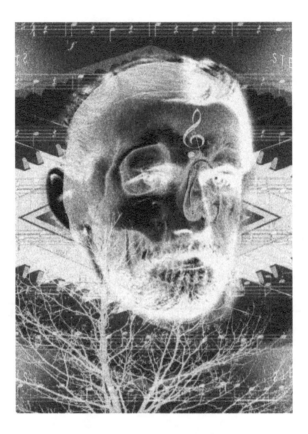

A Well-Urned Talent
By J.P. Egry

USA

Tuesday, after the Saturday Funeral:

I told him I refused to wear lipstick until he returned home. I didn't know then he'd come home in a jar.

Well, not a jar, exactly. A grand-piano-shaped urn with a G clef handle on its lid. Not that I need a handle. I don't plan to open it any time soon. It's not a large container. Amazing how little room a person's ashes need, how quickly we can be reduced to nothing.

I sit here at his seven-foot concert Steinway staring at that urn, then moving it. First to the left of the music desk, then to the right. Which place would he have wanted it? It doesn't matter. He can never play again. I decide on the right - the melodic end of the keyboard. Where he would want to be most is sitting right here at this keyboard playing scales and Bach and Chopin and jazz.

That's correct. Bernard was a jazz pianist and composer - had recorded many pieces of his own music and had other compositions ready to go for several more recordings. But now his new creations will be forever silent - heard only in our imaginations.

After the accident they told me he'd never walk again (correct about that) but that his hands were undamaged and he'd be playing beautifully again in no time. Boy, were they wrong. First, the paralysis set in. Then the pneumonia. When he told me melodies constantly ran in his mind like water from a faucet, but he couldn't write them down, I went home and cried. Then there was the virus - one of those deadly hospital things that appear out of the atmosphere, and one for which there is no cure. No known medications touch the devilish organisms. So, we waited to see who won - the patient or the virus. I can tell you now that the patient never wins that game.

So here we are. Me in a stupor, him at forty-seven reduced to ashes in a jar. That's what he wanted - cremation. Now, he's as close as I can get him to the greatest passion of his life, his music. I came only a distant second.

I know it's my imagination running wild, but I swear I can feel the heat from his body on this chair cushion where he sat for so many years. I revel in the mystic warmth and pained memories radiating through every nerve and muscle of my body.

Staring at the silent black and whites in front of me, I suddenly remember how he loved black and white milkshakes. Silly how the mind works. And how in high school someone took a picture of his jazz band, and when that picture fell out of an old yearbook, I put it up with all the other photos of him at the piano. Then he laid it face down and told me not to put it there again. Why? Because in the photo he was wearing white socks with black pants and shoes. Such an embarrassment.

But he'd like this urn - an ebony Steinway replica, complete with white and black keys and a white G clef perched on top. He admired three-dimensional art pieces like this. Oh, and this urn has a battery-operated recording inside. If one were to lift that lid with the clef handle (they'd better not), it would trip a switch. There's a second switch on the side, and either one will cause one of Bernard's own compositions to play - the one he wrote for me way back when we'd been dating for over three years - "Waltz for Betty."

I absentmindedly caress the G clef as if it is the top of Bernard's head. A surge, almost electric, prickles my fingers, and I jerk my hand back. What was that? Did I imagine it? I gingerly reach out again and place my fingers on the tiny keys of the urn. Nothing. Just my mind running wild. Or maybe static electricity - the house is very dry. Which reminds me, I must get the humidifier running here by the grand piano.

I check the pendulum clock on the wall, and I'm suddenly aware of the steadiness of time ticking on, working its way to eternity and eventually leaving behind all of us who are forever rushing to try to get ahead. Time is the turtle to my hare. But even from this experience will I ever learn to be a turtle and accidentally win through perseverance? Not likely. The actual

254

time finally registers. Betty Anne, you've been sitting here for two hours. Time to do something.

Do something. But what? My seat feels warmer again. Probably from the hot flashes that have been keeping me periodically entertained. I drop my head on my left forearm, which rests across the piano desk, and as I lift my right arm to settle it beside the other, the side of my hand brushes the urn. Another small jolt of electric-like heat.

O...kay. Not my imagination this time. What kind of batteries are in that music box anyway?

A chill hits my shoulders and escapes through my toes. I shudder. I want to leave - run to the kitchen for tea or aspirin or perhaps a stiff swig of rum or whatever liquor might be left dozing in the pantry. But I can't. I feel glued to the cushion. In an attempt to push away, I drop my hands and hit the keyboard. A beautiful diminished chord sounds. I look at my fingers and sure enough, they are positioned exactly over a D diminished chord, sounding like one I've heard so many times in the midst of Bernard's compositions.

Even though I've had basic music instruction, usually I cannot identify specific chords, nor could I ever begin to play by ear. I need a black spot on a music staff for every note I play on an instrument. It's a totally mechanical process for me - no inborn intuitive talent for improvisation. Now here I am playing a D diminished chord and, in addition, recognizing what it is. How can this be?

All the sorrow in my tired mind and body vanishes and is replaced by energetic curiosity and curious energy. What if I try playing something? What will happen?

I used to play a couple of ditties from memory, so I tentatively begin my old standby, "Turkey in the Straw." I close my eyes. My fingers feel light as air,

255

and I suddenly hear a familiar melody - but not the one I expected. Can that be? Can it be me playing "Brahms' Lullaby?" I certainly know the song well, but I've never been able to play it before, even with the music in front of me. I stop and clasp my hands to keep them from shaking.

From the music cabinet behind me, I grab the book of Brahms' compositions and plop it on the piano desk. With frantic fingers I thumb through until I come to the lullaby. I return my fingers to the keyboard and begin once more. Five minutes later I've finished the piece with no mistakes, never having looked at the music score. Stunned, I sit staring at Bernard, unable to respond to what has just happened.

—

Ten minutes later I rise and wobble to the kitchen. Now a glass of wine is a must. I pour a snifter full and, sipping at the merlot, I pull a stool up to the island counter and sift through random possibilities of why I can suddenly play. None makes any sense at all. Did I have a growth spurt of creative brain cells? Of course not. Did I have this innate ability all along? Did I just suppress it into my subconscious until the right moment came to release it? I doubt that very much.

Could it possibly be that Bernard's ghost was hovering over me telling me what to do? There was that warm feeling that came through me as I sat there. *Now you're really crazy, Elizabeth Anne.*

The last sip of wine reminds me just how tired I am. A little afternoon nap will be welcome. I shut off the phone and flop on the too - large and too - empty king-size bed.

One after another, fleeting visions trip across my dreamscape, none sticking around for long, each one pushing the one before it into oblivion: faces from my childhood - the grandmothers I knew only from their photos; college friends; a long hotel hallway where I can't find my room; my feet that won't move in the dark alleyway when footsteps behind me are coming closer and getting louder. And then, clear as if he were standing in front of me, Bernard's wonderful face - his kind, brown eyes, his salt-and-pepper beard, his smile with one large dimple to the side - all exactly as he was a year ago when he was healthy.

He attempts to speak, but I hear nothing. I step back. "I'm not dressed right," I say. "I can't go dressed like this." I look down at my ripped jeans and naked torso. He stretches his arms toward me and turns his hands palms up, then down, back and forth several times.

I watch his lips and try to read what he's saying because I cannot hear his voice. "Help me," his lips say, his eyes plead. "My hands don't work."

I back up, tripping over Bongo, our long-deceased cat.

—

With a jolt, I wake up covered in sweat. Not just Bernard, but the cat? What the...? I throw off the quilt and sit quivering on the edge of the bed. My new jeans are in perfect shape, and I'm completely dressed.

I turn on the phone and listen to the dial tone. I want to call someone to tell them, but who would listen? Most of my friends think I'm crazy enough as it is. I drop my head into my hands. The live cat, Flutie, rubs against my leg and meows, her large yellow eyes staring at me. Then she hisses and raises her back. I think I hear a whisper. "Tell no one." I whip my head around, checking every part of the room. Nothing here. All is silent except for Flutie's purr. The hair on her back has settled in place. I place the phone back on its cradle.

Stumbling down the hall and into the living room, I try to avoid the piano. "It's suppertime," I mumble, but I'm strangely not hungry even though, except for the bran muffin at breakfast, I've eaten nothing. From the corner of my eye I can see that the light around the piano is darker now, the southern sun on its way to the horizon having left the picture window. Yet I clearly see the urn, almost as if the sun's rays were still upon it. Strange. But nothing about today has been normal.

I can't control the attraction pulling at me. My feet move reluctantly toward the piano. Flutie follows me and flops on her side next to the pedals. I step around her and ease my haunches onto the cushioned chair. As I lift my hands toward the keys, they tremble, and I force them back to my lap. I can't. I just can't!

Tears overflow my eyes and drop to my chest as I gaze toward Bernard, caged in that container. The G clef on the ceramic piano comes into focus, looming larger in my mind than its actual size. Drying my eyes with the back of my hand, I wipe the tears on my jeans and trip the outer switch to start the music.

Bernard's rendition of his beautiful song, "If You Could," taken from his recording, fills the room. Flutie rolls at my feet and softly mews as if attempting to sing along. I smile in spite of myself. Now Bernard is singing the words. I'd forgotten that he also sang on this particular recording. "If you could, would you be my love for all time . . ." Shivers parade up and down my spine. How I miss that voice. "... would you be gentle with my fumbling ways," he croons. Feeling peaceful for the first time in months, I relax into my own reverie.
But wait. Something isn't right. What I hear jolts my mind, and my heart thumps loudly against my ribs. These words are wrong! *Yes, you can, you can be my hands for all time -*

The music stops, although the batteries can't be dead already. Then his voice repeats the words - not singing, but speech. After that, the room is silent. Except for Flutie. She rubs back and forth against my legs and mrr*owws* in decibels I've not heard from her before.

"Don't worry, Flutie. He can't speak to us. The voice is all in my mind." The cat rises up on her hind feet for me to scratch the top of her head. I reach down. "Oh, but you heard it, too, didn't you?" She puts her ears back as I rub between them. Her eyes close, and she starts to purr.

I am numb. Yet still I tremble. I've never believed in ghosts, but we are not alone here. "Bernard?" I whisper. "Bernard, are you here? Are you here with us?"

Something gently brushes the top of my head. Though I do not attempt to move, my shoulders are being forced toward the keyboard, and my hands, like puppet's hands on a string, are rising over the keys.

Betty, you can. You can play. No mistaking that voice now. Bernard is here. He is in my head. Somehow he has entered my body and my brain is filled with scores of notes forcing their way toward my fingers.

The recording begins again and I am playing along with it - with all the melody, all the chords, all the exact interpretation that Bernard would have done in his elegant jazz style.

I am exhilarated with the feeling of freedom - a feeling of competence and capability that I've never experienced before. I try another tune, not one of Bernard's but "You Look Good to Me," a difficult Oscar Peterson jazz composition. I breeze right through it.
My trepidation subsides and is replaced with confidence and pure joy. I can't wait to share this new-found talent, even if it's not technically my own. I must call my friend, Charlotte. She is a psychologist who has delved into the supernatural and paranormal. Maybe she'll help me understand what is happening.

Heat rushes into my face. I must be overexcited. Flutie leaps into my lap and howls, her mouth close to mine. Then I hear it again. Bernard's voice, more stern now.

Betty, tell no one. No one. Or it will be gone.

"What, Bernard? Why?" I say aloud. "I want to play now. It's wonderful."

Play. But play for me. Take my place. I need your hands. No one must know I'm playing.

My head feels as if it's about to burst from the urgency in his voice. *Betty, it's all I have left. You must do this for me. Just enjoy the spotlight and other people's surprise at your ability.*

His voice rings so clear, and so complete in my head. It must be real. So I don't call Charlotte. I don't call anyone. The phone rings several times, but I don't answer it. I just sit there at the Steinway with the urn turned off, and I play.

I play into the late evening, digging into the keys with as many songs as I can remember, even though, now silent, Bernard is likely doing the remembering. At eleven, Flutie paws at my leg with her right forefoot. I remember she hasn't eaten. Still entranced, I float to the kitchen and empty a can of seafood medley into her dish.

Exhausted, I brush my teeth and flop into bed without undressing. I hope I don't dream.

Wednesday:

I wake up starved, my stomach telling me I've eaten nothing since breakfast yesterday, and I see the sun streaming through the window onto the sleeping tiger at my feet. Though I recall a vague dream of a gleaming black piano being lowered into a deep grave of bright red soil, I must have slept well, because I feel refreshed.

260

I shower long and hard, scrubbing off the weekend residue of physical and mental debris, and slip into new tan denims and a red shirt. After checking the answering machine, I decide not to return any of the well-meaning calls of friends and relatives who want to know how I am doing. How do they expect I'm doing after my husband's early death?

If only they knew! But they can never know, so I won't talk with them. Not today.

In the living room, I take a wide path around the piano to avoid looking at it. From the kitchen counter, I grab a paperback novel - the one I started while Bernard was in the hospital - and open it on the table next to my freshly made coffee. After feeding Flutie, I make myself a hearty breakfast of granola with blueberries, coffee, and orange juice. And I read. Great escape, reading. Whole new worlds apart from one's own to wander through.

Bernard's voice is not in my head. All is clear. Perhaps I slept all through yesterday and, in my exhaustion, dreamed the whole crazy thing. Yet I have mixed feelings about that. Part of me wants it to be real.

Since our friends insisted on a gathering here this coming weekend "to help me out," after breakfast I decide to clean the basement family room. The downstairs is a terrible mess. For months, throughout Bernard's rehabilitation and later his sickness, I tossed things everywhere - books on tabletops, piles of papers surrounding the computer, laundry baskets of unfolded clothes and linens, plants dying of thirst by the French doors.

Cobwebs float down from ceiling beams. Clumps of dust and cat hair chase each other around the floor whenever I move. Evidence of Flutie's indigestion problems are scattered around the room. So, I vacuum rugs, mop tile floors, wipe down walls, and vigorously dust every inch of the place including the hallway, the laundry room, and the bathroom.

261

I fold the clean laundry and stash the remaining clothes to be laundered in the washer. Most are Bernard's anyway and will be given away. The top of the file cabinet behind Bernard's electric keyboard is stacked with staff paper of his original compositions yet to be filed in the drawers beneath. Exhausted, I cannot sort them, and I sit on the bench between the keyboard and the file cabinet. I'm more tired than I thought. I'll need a nap.

Without thinking, I switch on the piano power and run my hands over the keys. Perhaps I'll try just a scale or two. I'm startled with the realization that my playing is just that - a scale or two. Nothing else I try works. So yesterday was in my imagination, after all. It's not surprising, given how much I want Bernard back with all my heart and mind and soul, never mind the transferred talent. Just him. Alive. Here. Now. I flick off the switch and drape the keyboard with its cover.

—

After a nap and a snack of sliced apples, sweet pickles, and cheese, I try to resist but I cannot. I carry my cup of tea and set it next to Bernard's urn on the Steinway - always a no-no in case it spills into the piano, but today I don't much care. I sit on that blasted flowery cushion, and I'll be damned if I don't hear the command of his voice. *Play, Betty. Play now.* The voice hesitates. *Please.*

In response, an uncontrolled high-pitched screech leaves my throat. Flutie comes running from her bowl in the kitchen, leaps onto my lap, and yowls loudly. I run my hand along the raised ridge of fur on her back. "Sorry, little cat. Did I scare you, or did you hear that voice, too?" She settles her haunches into my thighs. As she calms, my whole body shudders.

Even though I don't believe in ghosts and have never seen one, I admit a bit of me has always wished that if they exist, I could encounter one. At that thought, a charge of energy, almost shocking, rips through me, and my hands reach toward the ivories. I hear the beautiful jazz rendition of

262

"Dream Dancing" in a style similar to Dave McKenna's, so much like the way Bernard used to play it.

"So it is. It must be Bernard," I murmur to Flutie, who is now washing her paws. "But why? What does he want from me?"

From an imperative that I have no power to resist, I sit there and play all day. I don't eat, I don't answer the phone, I don't go to the bathroom. When, at seven o'clock, my fingers finally take a rest, I jerk them away from the keys and curl them into fists in my lap - a lap Flutie has left long ago. She is crying for her supper in the kitchen.

I feed Flutie, grab a can of sardines and an orange for me, and brew a large pot of tea. I plan to drink the whole thing - likely with a little (or a lot) of Bacardi rum mixed in. What the devil am I going to do? He said not to tell anyone. So, then, what?

After a few too many gulps of my hot, spiked tea, I rise unsteadily from the kitchen chair that was Bernard's. I stumble in and stare at the stylized urn. It can't stay there. I can't do this, Bernard, you have to go.

I lift him, still well-contained, lock him in my arms, and tread downstairs to the family room where I set him on the back of the electric keyboard. "There, that's better," I tell him. "You'll have to stay here, Bernard. I have to sleep."

Without looking back, I start to leave, but I am drawn - no, compelled - to return to the covered keyboard sitting in partial darkness. When I drop onto the bench, the cover falls to the floor. With determination, my hands land on the plastic keys. Arpeggios and jazz riffs ram through my mind and out my fingertips. I can't stop them. I try to pull away, but they keep coming with an anger I've never felt before. Now I am afraid. This seems too much like the occult. Film clips of *The Exorcist* and *The Shining* flash past my unfocused eyes.

Then all is quiet - so quiet that I think I can almost hear the plants on the windowsill growing. I slump, my arms flopping at my sides. I look around the room. Nothing moves. Flutie is upstairs. Now I hear her crying at the door, wanting to come down.

A whisper. I think that's what it is, anyway. Then again. *I'm sorry* ... It trails off.

"Bernard?" I whisper, too, not knowing why. "Bernard, is that you?"

A warm breath passes across the back of my neck. *Sorrrrrrry.*

I leave Bernard on the keyboard and race up the stairs to Flutie, who welcomes me by poking her nose into my leg. I grab her into my arms and hold her tight against my chest. Her warm purr calms me, and I sit in my recliner, keeping her head close to my cheek.

Thursday:

Still in the recliner, I wake to Flutie meowing in my face. "Good morning, kitty." I scratch her head and then rub my eyes, gradually realizing where we are. "Wow. We slept here all night? Both of us must have been exhausted."

Morning sun radiates through the air, a spotlight on dust particles that dance in slow dips and swirls before they ease toward the floor. I feel rested. I shower and feed us both. I am ravenous, and I am half-finished with my meal before I realize that I'm eating Bernard's favorite - scrambled eggs with shredded cheese, onion, and bacon bits - something I've never cared for that much. I'm a granola, berries, yogurt person.

Uneasiness seeps into my bones, and I feel unnerved again. Thursday is the day when Bernard played with the trio at the Backyard Jazz Café. Someone

264

else will be taking his place tonight. They hired random substitutes for him while he was ill, and now one of them will be permanent. I hate it! No one can take Bernard's place.

Yet I know I have to go tonight. No one would expect me to be there now, but, except for last week, I haven't missed a Thursday night there in two years. Even while Bernard was sick, he wanted me to go to keep track of what was happening and report back to him. A force deep inside compelling me to go tonight cannot be denied.

I do not go near the piano all day. I leave the urn downstairs. At five I start to become undone. How should I dress? I'm in mourning - does it have to be black anymore? What would people expect? Bernard would want me to wear something classy and neat - maybe bright colors. So what's appropriate? Oh, who cares!

I select a cream-colored gauze poet's blouse over a fitted just-below-the-knee lavender skirt, lavender beads and black flats. I don't really care what people will think. The love of my life would have liked this.

When I open the front door to leave, a sudden impulse turns me back. I need the bag. The huge black pocketbook I used when Bernard wanted someplace to put the music sheets he carried. I scour the closet for the bag, empty the contents of my small lavender purse into it, and clatter down the stairs with it over my arm.

I grab the piano urn and set it deep at the bottom of the bag. Bernard would want to go. I think I hear a whispered *yesss*, as I lower it. Wait a minute. Are you crazy, Betty?

At this point, I'm not sure, but I suspect I'm hallucinating wildly. Wishing that Bernard were alive so much that I'm hearing his voice. But the playing - how could I have played like that? Could that have been a dream, too - a

265

dream so real that it imprinted its own reality in my mind? Likely, that's it. Perhaps. Maybe.

But what if ...

—

I don't remember driving to the Jazz Café, nor finding a seat at the bar.

"Hi, Betty, how are you?" says Jen, the bartender. "I never expected to see you."

"I never expected to be here, but for some reason I couldn't stay away." I set the black bag between my feet on the bar footrest, squeezing it tightly between my ankles to keep it in place.

"What can I get you? You look exhausted. Are you okay?"

"Hmm ... what? Oh, yes, thanks. I'm managing ... considering."

"I understand. It's just that the dark circles around your eyes ..." She stops. "Sorry. Would you like your usual?"

I nod. "Sure. That's fine."

A moment later Jen sets a ginger lemon drop martini on a napkin in front of me. I finger the corner of the blue napkin with "The Backyard" in cursive-style black lettering, and in small script underneath, "featuring jazz by Bernard and the Boys." They haven't changed the napkins yet - probably want to use up the old ones.

I gulp at the martini, hoping for courage to actually look at the band. Another swallow and I gaze toward the group, trying to see the piano player. The brilliant street lights shine through the window behind them. I raise my hand to shield my eyes from the glare.

No! It can't be, can it? But yes. It sure is. They've hired egotistical Bruce, the rival pianist Bernard disliked the most - brash Bruce always trying to horn in wherever Bernard played - always asking club owners to hire him instead, telling them how versatile and polished he is.

The keyboard looks short from here - maybe sixty-six keys rather than eighty-eight. Apparently he doesn't play any long runs. But I listen. Doesn't sound too bad - not as good as Bernard, but with Joe on bass and Mike on drums, the solid rhythm section hasn't changed.

I chug down half of my drink and feel my adrenaline pumping up. I'm angry, really pissed. How could they do this?

Bully Bruce is in the middle of a solo chorus of "Here's That Rainy Day," pounding the devil out of the keys, showing off his prowess. Hah! That's a wrong chord. Even I can tell that. There's another. I cringe. Mr. Great isn't so perfect.

The bag between my feet seems to vibrate - probably I'm shaking in annoyance. I finish my drink without taking a breath and ask Jen for another.

She leans her elbows on the bar in front of me. "Are you sure?"

"Yeah." I hesitate. "I'm sure."

"Gotcha."

The voice in my head is back. *Betty. Betty.*

I cover my ears and rub the sides of my head. "Go away. You're not here."

But it continues. *Betty, play. You have to play.*

Even if it really could be Bernard, this is crazy. Why would I play? Here? With the guys? They'd think I was nuts. Maybe I am. "Stop it! Just stop it," I whisper through my teeth.

Jen sets the second lemon drop on a clean napkin and slides the dish of bar nuts toward me. "Here. At least nibble on something. Sure I can't get you a sandwich or some soup?"

I gag at the thought of food. "No, thanks, really. I wouldn't be able to eat it."

Bruce is attempting a jazz riff on Bill Evans' "Israel." He's murdering it. I can't stand it. Why did I come? That's a question I can't answer. I was compelled. Bernard made me do it. That's silly. I sip my drink, grab a handful of nuts.

I want to be home, but there's no way I can leave. I stay here on this bar stool through the first set, the second set. During their break before the last set, Mike and Joe approach, ask Jen for a beer and a soda.

"How ya doin', Betty?" Joe says. "Surprised to see you here."

"I'm fine," I lie. "I'm doing okay. Hard to stay home on a Thursday after all the years of being here."

Mike sips his soda and nods. "I guess it'd be hard for me, too."

I look away and see Bruce chatting up a solitary young girl at the end of the bar. I force the tears back that are nearly brimming over my lower eyelids. "But it's hard to be here, also."

Bernard's voice is clear now. *Play, Betty, play for me. I need your hands.*

I suddenly blurt out, "Joe, could I sit in - I mean - try to play a couple tunes?"

Joe's eyes widen. He stammers. "I ... I didn't know you played piano."

I hesitated. "You're right. I never could play anything worth a damn. Well, I never did much. But Bernard taught me a few things. I'd just like to try something, in his memory."

"Ah ... sure." He looks perplexed - doesn't know what else to say. "I'll have you come up when we go back to start this last set. Looks like Bruce is occupied anyway."

Bruce has his forehead practically touching the long curls around the girl's ear - probably he's feeding her a bunch of bull about how he could be the best thing that ever happened to her.

"Good," I say to Joe. "I'll try not to sound too bad."

When the guys finish their drinks, I grab my bag and follow them to the bandstand. Bruce doesn't even notice. He has his arm around the girl, his fingers kneading her bare upper arm beside her ample bosom. I place Bernard on the floor right next to the keyboard. Just like yesterday at home, I feel trance-like, and my hands lift to the keys on their own as a warm electric charge runs through them. I am no longer Betty. I am Bernard. I feel his mind in mine, his blood in my blood, his heart beating in my heart. I hear the notes, but they're not from me.

As if in retort to Bruce's earlier renditions, I hear "Rainy Day" and then "Israel" exactly as Bernard had performed them here the final time before he died. Bruce stops nibbling the girl's shoulder and stares at me. I hope I've unnerved him. I can feel delight from Bernard envelop my whole being. Having finished the two tunes without a hitch, without a missed note, with all of Bernard's emotion, I stand, ready to return to the bar.

"No, wait," Joe says. "How did you do that? I can't imagine ... sit down. Do a few more."

"But I don't ..." I begin. Something pushes my shoulder, forcing me onto the seat.

Bernard's voice is in my head again. *Sit, Betty. Sit. Keep playing*! He's more demanding this time. His agitation ripples through my bones. So I sit. I play. One tune after another - Mike and Joe encouraging me on after each tune.

Bruce has moved closer to our end of the bar, with a glare that could cut through me. Too bad. Now I'm having fun. I've never had a taste of talent like this before. When we finish the last tune, Mike says, "Play a few more," but Bruce rushes over to shut down his amplifier. He pulls all the plugs and yanks the piano away, zipping it into its carrying case.

When I turn to thank Joe and Mike, Bruce whisks the bench from under me almost before I'm fully standing.

"Our pleasure," Joe says. "You were amazing. I don't understand how you play exactly like Bernard."

Pulling at the hem of my poet's blouse, I mumble, "I didn't think I could, either." I look directly at Joe. "But I wanted to try - to give him a little tribute - a remembrance." Now I'm sweating, an anxiety attacks imminent. "I guess it's because I've heard him practice so many hours every day." I pick up the bag and cradle it against my chest. "Got to go. Thanks so much, guys."

Mike slides his drumsticks into their case. "Come on down again, Betty. You're always welcome, if it isn't too much for you."

I down the last of my now-warm ginger lemon drop, slap a twenty on the bar for Jen, and hurry out.

—

For the next few weeks, at Bernard's constant and persistent command, I practice at home on the Steinway or the electric in the basement, always remembering to carry the urn with me. Once, after I'd left it in the basement the night before, I sat at the Steinway in the early morning sun. Forgetting that I was alone, I raised my hands to the keys. The A-flat scale I attempted was ragged and uneven, my fingers occasionally hitting the wrong notes and feeling like wooden dowels.

So now I know. I am possessed. Bedeviled. I cannot play on my own. Meanwhile, Bernard is unrelenting. I've not missed a Thursday night at the Backyard in three months. But his voice keeps warning me not to tell anyone. I need to tell Joe and Mike. This isn't right.

Last week, they pulled me aside - away from Bruce - to beg me to take the job full time. They're fed up with his ego, his less than acceptable performance, and his antics with the customers. But, how can I? What if I forget to bring the urn? What if it breaks, or I lose it? Then where will I be? Where will the guys be - left without a piano player. Worst of all, I'll have to confess that I can't play a note by myself. No one will believe me. They'll put me in the loony bin!

Bernard gets more obnoxious every day - demanding, insistent, and angry if I don't spend the time he requires. I can hardly eat or sleep. He's gaining kinetic powers, too. Pencils and saucers have flown across the room in his tantrums, a vase almost hitting Flutie in the head yesterday.

He was never like that in real life - no raging - always considerate in spite of his obsession with music. I've become afraid. The more I play, the more his negative powers seem to grow. I want to stop, but he won't let me. Even Flutie is racing around the house in a frenzy, often hiding where I can't find her. Continuing this way will kill me, or at least drive me insane.

I sit for days in the porch rocker far away from that urn, hoping for the sun to purify me, to put up a screen around me preventing the demons from entering. Finally, early one Thursday morning, I know what I must do. Bernard has to go. But I can't let him know, or even let him sense my plan ahead of time. I must bury the urn somewhere - somewhere far away. Where and how is the question. What if people ask about it, ask where it is? By now, they know that I keep it on the piano.

So, what then? If not bury it, then empty it. That's it. No one would ever know it was empty. I could scatter his ashes someplace that he's always loved - into the ocean from a cruise ship; on his favorite beach, perhaps Myrtle, or better yet Assateague Beach at Chincoteague not far from his family's summer house. What would happen music-wise then? Would the crabs start fiddling, the seagulls squawk Bernard's tunes? Stop it, Elizabeth Anne! Now you're just being ridiculous. Yet I do know now that some seemingly impossible things are very possible.

What if I sprinkled him in the fields of his grandfather's old farm in the country? That could be troublesome - other people own that property now. Then it comes to me - the perfect place - the grounds of Tanglewood Music Center in the Berkshires where there is constant music all summer long.

Eagerly, I search the storage shed for the old metal lock box where Bernard kept his grandfather's eclectic collection of items from the World War II era. There I find a pocket watch, a ring made of scrap tank material with Bernard's initials engraved on it, an 8x10 painting of a St. Bernard dog that Bernard's great-grandmother painted (I wonder if he was named after that dog), and various cuff links, tie clasps, political lapel pins, and newspaper obituary clippings of deceased family members.

I pull all the items out and toss them in the largest plastic zipper bag I can find. My hands are shaking as I realize I must handle that urn again and lower it into the metal box. It's essential that Bernard think that I'm taking him to the Backyard Café. The black bag I take on Thursday nights still sits under the Steinway below the urn.

As I approach, I feel tingling in my hands, my feet, and at the back of my neck, so I grab the piano urn, drop it into the metal box, flop the lid closed, latching it as fast as possible, and zip the box into the black bag. The tingling diminishes. I doubt Bernard can overpower me now.

Lifting the ring of keys from its hook by the door, I lock the house and race to my Honda Civic, shove the bag into the trunk, and slam the hatch closed. It's an hour and a half drive to Tanglewood. I tune the radio to NPR, turn up the volume, and listen to Otto Klemperer conducting Beethoven's Fifth. It seems appropriate for what I am about to do - a great send-off for Bernard.

I drive up Route 183 and park in the huge lot in front of the main gate. I look at my watch. Two hours before they open. I pace up and down the side path underneath the towering pines, then I go back to the car and try to doze, but I cannot. I really don't want to be near that car trunk for too long.

So I pace again, sit on a flat boulder, pace some more. As soon as the ticket booth opens, I buy a lawn ticket. I don't even check who's performing or what building they'll be in. I don't care because I'm not staying.

I look back at the Honda. Well, this is it. I have to do it. The button on the key fob seems to push itself and lift the automatic trunk lid. Without looking at it, and without saying a word, I haul the black bag out. It seems heavier than usual when I carry it back to stand in the line forming at the gate. No wonder. The metal box has added considerable weight.

At last the gate opens. We file in. I show the attendant my ticket, and I'm finally on the grounds. People spread out, checking out the kiosks with t-shirts and CDs. Some head for the cafeteria or the bathroom, others to the gift shop full of music books, recordings, clothing, beach towels - a myriad of music memorabilia. I sigh with sadness. Bernard and I loved to browse there during intermission and after the concerts had ended. No more.

Definitely not now.

With Bernard in the metal box in the black bag, I head for the smaller performance area where students give recitals. Surrounded by a large expanse of ancient evergreens and backed against an intricate shrubbery maze, it is deserted. Everyone is at the opposite end of the lawn. Nearly two feet in diameter, the outstretched arm of a nearby pine grows parallel to the ground - a perfect spot to sit. I rest there and glance in all directions. No one in sight.

Excellent.

Moving fast, I unzip the bag, pull out the box, unlatch it, and lift the blasted piano urn up and out.

Okay, Bernard, here is your final resting place. Perhaps you can aggravate, or should I say, inspire, the students here as you have me the past few weeks. I have loved you as I have no one before or since, but now we must say goodbye.

My heart begins to pound, tears well in my eyes and spill onto my cheeks. I can barely swallow.

Nevertheless, I lift the G-clef cover and begin to pour the gray, powdery remains of Bernard along the pathway that circles the old theater. The ceramic piano warms in my hands until it is almost too hot to handle.

"Bernard, I'm sorry," I whimper. "You must rest, and I must go on - until the day I can join you. Thank you for all you've given me."

With the ashes nearly gone and the breeze gently wafting the remaining particles into the grass, I turn the urn completely upside down and give it a final shake. I should have brought some kind of brush. A tiny gray spot remains in each of the two front corners of the little piano. No matter. Bernard is at home in music land where he ought to be. Be at peace, my love.

Replacing the lid, I stuff the urn into the box and into the black bag. With hurried steps, I head for the less busy exit by the bathrooms, and for the security of my car. Barely breathing, I sit for a long time before heading home.

—

It has now been several months since I left Bernard at Tanglewood. I have not returned to the Backyard Café. I sold the electric piano to a young man in a rock band. I have not touched the concert grand where the empty urn now sits. But today the sun is pouring through the window onto the closed mahogany lid. The rich wood gleams in the light, and for the first time, I'm drawn to raise the cover over the keys.

I sit on the flowered chair pad. Flutie hops into my lap and brushes my newly glossed lips with her nose. The empty urn is in its place to my right. I have had it permanently sealed. Both sadness and relief envelop me as I realize Bernard is gone forever. Without thinking, I fondle the G-clef top as if petting the cat. Tentatively I touch a couple of keys, then a few more. Hmm. Not so bad.

How about a scale? I try a B-flat major scale, four octaves - smooth, very smooth.

Rapid and perfect.

Too perfect for my ability. I shudder.

Then it begins - the first eight bars of the "Brahms' Lullaby."

A Rational Explanation
By Ailsa Thom

Scotland

I've never believed in ghosts. I've always had faith in science - which is a bit of a prerequisite when it comes to working as a lab technician in the forensics department at the university. But it was a combination of these two things which led me to become a presenter for *Ghost Gumshoes* on the telly. My co-presenter is Colin, someone who wholeheartedly believes in ghosts. It was, the producers said, the perfect combination. The woman of science and the man of imagination - turning previous formats on their head, reinventing the genre, they said.

It had been a mutual friend, Andy - Colin's agent - who suggested that I become a consultant on the show.

"A consultant what?" I'd asked.

A consultant who could help explain paranormal activity through science, he'd said. I'd be perfect for it. I was ready to say no, until I realised that the fee he quoted me for just one show would pay the mortgage for several months.

Having looked at my screen test, the director thought that I had some kind of chemistry with Colin, and he offered me a contract as co-presenter for the series. It was a more prominent profile than I'd envisaged, but my boss agreed to my taking unpaid leave from the lab for a few months.

You've probably seen the program. Each week, Colin starts with a "piece - to - camera" (I've learned the jargon) about some sighting of a ghostly presence in a picturesque setting. Sometimes we show a blurry image in a photograph. Sometimes, there's a punter telling the story of the time a picture flew off the wall, or something brushed against their leg when they were the only person in the room. Or the story about the lady in old-fashioned clothes who smiled but didn't say a word. Colin then shares some of the information that the researchers have given us - the history of the building, who used to live there, any unfortunate happenings like a death or murder - that kind of thing. We then cut to the live results of the lie detector test which we put all the punters through. I'm not allowed to say that of course they will pass the test - they do actually believe what they saw was real, after all. The lie detector can't pick up on foolishness.

Colin then asks me about the architecture of the house, and I use this time to explain the likely causes for their experiences - ventilation drafts, changes in ambient temperature, distortions within the camera itself, and so on - and then he asks me about the tests and experiments I will be running this week.

These are tests which usually involve setting up a series of infrared cameras, some thermal imaging equipment, and very sensitive microphones which can pick up even the slightest of noises. Colin gets really excited at this part as it also means that we take the decision to stay in the "haunted house" overnight. I mean, we do it every week, and it's even written into our contracts, but from the way he reacts, you'd think that this was news to him each time. And he's not even acting. Colin is a believer. Believes in ghosts, spirits, fairies, demons, poltergeists, witches, and werewolves. OK, I've never actually asked him about the werewolves, but it wouldn't surprise me if he did. Colin believes whatever nonsense he is told, and can scream, shriek, and hyperventilate like a Victorian heroine. The fact that he's 6'3" with a rugby player's physique apparently makes it all the more believable television.

But I believe the science. There's always a rational explanation for things - even if we can't work out what it is at the time. Although we have good equipment, it's not state-of-the-art - not on this cable channel. And while I believe the science, I'm not so blinkered that I don't take arcane things ·

like ley lines and electromagnetic fields into consideration. Just because we can't see them, it doesn't mean that they don't influence the outcome - they are still part of the science.

Take that last episode we filmed. We were in the most haunted castle in Ireland. (No one seemed to remember that the second episode of the series had been in another castle, also reputed to be the most haunted in Ireland.) This one was all rickety turrets and crow-inhabited battlements. Local lore had it that, hundreds of years ago, two sisters had been in love with the same man. Cad that he was, he dallied with them both in a very obvious manner. Soon the sisters began to hate each other, but the object of their affection only seemed to revel in this. Eventually the sisters' father put his foot down and demanded that the choice be made. The suitor said that he would do so at the ball on the following Friday. However, no one knows which sister he would have chosen, as when the ball was in full swing, the younger one fell down the grand staircase to the ballroom below and broke her neck. No one could prove that the surviving sister had anything to do with this, but people began to say that she was a witch. Her father used his money and influence to get her away on the next boat to America, and she was never heard of again. History doesn't say what became of the suitor.

The staircase was blocked off with thick tapestries and no longer used. The family eventually sold the castle and, over the years, other owners lost their wealth and grew too impoverished to maintain it. Now it is a ruin of a place. Not so ruined that the roof has fallen in but decayed and diminished inside. The floors are cracked, mold speckles the walls, and little trees have taken root in the stone work. Local youths had long dared each other to take a walk down what had come to be known as "the haunted staircase," but when one of them fell down it and broke his back, the Council bricked it up, and handed the owners a notice of demolition.

I was never sure if we had actual permission to film inside, but as most of our work takes place after dark, it is probable that no one knew. In his piece- to-camera, Colin made a lot of the fact that this was the anniversary of that very first ball, when the sister had been killed and the "curse" began, over three centuries before.

He was feeling really spooked, he said to me later in bed at the hotel as we took a nap before the evening filming started. No one knew that we were sleeping together, as we'd mutually agreed that it was probably unprofessional. I laughed and reminded him that a few bumps in the night meant for better viewing figures, and that if we did a good episode this time, perhaps it would be picked up by one of the larger networks. I had already decided that I didn't want to go back to working in the lab.

We returned to the castle about 9 p.m. to find that workmen had already knocked down the Council's wall at the top of the staircase. There was a lot of brick dust in the air which I knew would make for weird images and luminosities on camera. With this, and the full moon shining through the windows, I felt that my job tonight would be all too easy. The tech guys had already set up the cameras and infrared lights, and we were warned to watch out for the cables. Colin had to do his piece-to-camera eight times as he was so nervy he kept forgetting the script. In the end, the director decided that this authenticity would actually add to the atmosphere.

As the lighting guys were setting up the next shot, Colin and I took a wander through the empty, decaying rooms.

"Imagine living here," he said as he flashed the torch around the walls of a bedroom. "I mean, when it was in its glory. When I was lord of the castle," and he bowed to me, "and you were my lady." I did a mock curtsey and giggled as he slipped his arms around me, pulling me close.

"I like your perfume," he murmured. "Gardenias? Very old-fashioned of you."

I kissed him to stop his nervous chatter. I wasn't wearing any perfume.

"Hey, stop messing with my hair!" he complained. "Continuity will have a fit."

"I'm not touching your hair," I replied, rolling my eyes. "I know not to touch the hair!"

"You did so. And you just did it again. Look, stop it!"

I took a step back from him and squeezed my hands where they had been all along - on each side of his waist.

Colin swore. "Let's get out of here. There was definitely someone touching my hair." He shivered dramatically. "I can feel a presence."

"It was probably a cobweb, or something falling from the ceiling," I said, following him. "Or maybe the ghost fancies you! Hey, hands off, ghost, he's mine, all mine!" And I cackled a laugh as I waved the torch around the room.

Colin jogged quickly back to the hubbub of the cameras and attached himself to the side of the director.

I did my own piece-to-camera, and didn't fail to mention Colin's experience, reassuring both him and the audience that there was a scientific explanation.

Colin then had to walk down the grand staircase, speaking to the camera that was being lowered on the jib in front of him. I could see that he was petrified - more scared than I'd ever seen him before. What a waste of energy; I'd tease him about it later. But the audience would love that tremble in his voice and the way his eyes gleamed as wide black pools in the moonlight.

This part of the filming over, the crew went to set up in the ballroom below. We were to spend the night in there and record any sounds or movement in the room. On camera, it would look like it was just Colin and me, but in reality, the whole crew would be there, just out of eye-line of the cameras.

Somehow, I found myself alone. Everyone had gone downstairs, and for a few minutes there was peace and quiet. I actually quite like being in these old places, looking at the craftsmanship and architecture, and picturing them as busy, lived-in homes. I may be a scientist, but I'm not without imagination.

I could hear my name being called and decided that by using the grand staircase I could show Colin that there was nothing to be scared of. As I walked toward it, the scent of something floral caught me unawares - gardenias perhaps, after all. But of course, in reality it would just be some chemical reaction, perhaps an emanation from the damp, old wallpaper. As I began descending the stairs it felt like something tapped my shoulder, but I must have just caught my foot in a cable someone had forgotten to remove, because I found myself falling down the stairs, the world tipping and tumbling in disorientating explosions of light and color. I slammed down onto the marble floor of the ballroom, hurting, the breath knocked out of me.

I possibly passed out for a moment, hallucinated even, as blue flashes throbbed in front of my eyes and a cacophony of noises swam around me. Then the light stopped flashing and grew whiter and brighter. One of the arc lights, I imagined. But when I opened my eyes, there was nothing there. I mean nothing at all. The silent ballroom was empty of people and equipment, lit only by the full moon. The director must have had a last-minute change of plan and set up in another room.

Cautiously I got to my feet, but nothing seemed to be broken. Right at the moment I needed a cup of tea with a shot of brandy, and a reassuring hug from Colin.

I hurried from room to room, using the moonlight to find my way. I even climbed to the battlements, shouting Colin's name as I went, but the castle was completely empty. There was no evidence of the crew having even been there. Perplexed, I wandered along the corridors wondering what to do next, and when I came to the top of the grand staircase again, I paused. That floral scent was particularly strong here. Then I saw the moon shining onto a bunch of drooping flowers tied to the bannister - pink roses, my favorite. I was sure that they hadn't been there earlier. As I leaned in to smell them, I saw a small card amongst the faded blooms. By moonlight, I read the message:

Miss you forever. I know you'll be a happy ghost - I will wait for your sign. All my love, Colin.xx

Like I said, I always have faith in the science. There is a rational explanation for this, and I know that, in time, I will work out just what it is.

Wilbur
By Rebecca Emanuelsen

USA

At night, after Mama has already tucked her in and switched off the light, Helena climbs out of bed and makes her way to the chimney stack that runs through her bedroom. She presses her hands to the rough brick and slides them up and down, side to side. This has become her bedtime ritual - feeling for hot spots in the chimney. It's warm but doesn't burn her - safe, then. She tiptoes back to bed and draws her blankets tight around her, imagining she is a caterpillar safe in her cocoon. Mama and Papa's muffled voices drift from down the hall. Helena fights to keep her eyes open, but the sound of her parents talking lulls her to sleep.

She starts awake to a scraping noise in the attic above her bedroom. The room is completely dark, the light from the hallway gone. She wrings her blanket in her hands and sucks in a breath, feeling her heart pound in her chest and hands and ears. She had hoped the noise wouldn't come tonight.

Another long scrape, heavy furniture against attic floorboards. Helena turns and pushes her face to the wall. She draws her blankets up over her head, tucks the covers behind her back and under her feet. The air beneath the blankets becomes hot, muggy with exhalations.

Upstairs, a steady rhythm begins against the floor. *Bmp-ump, bmp-ump*, like the house's heart is beating in the attic.

After half a minute, it stops.

Helena strains to hear. She relaxes as the silence stretches on, unfurling her legs from the tight ball she's curled into.

But then a new noise comes: *bm-bm-bm-bm-bm*, louder, closer with each repetition - something bumping down a set of stairs. Helena pictures the door to the attic across from her room - locked tight, Papa reassured her last time. The noises have come on and off for weeks now, usually staying upstairs but occasionally ending with the door across the hall swinging open. The creaking of its hinges sounds again, but this time Helena hears something else - something rolling right outside her door - and her breath stutters, caught up in her throat. *Thunk* against her door, and she screams.

Papa arrives quickly, throwing open the door, flipping on the light, grabbing Helena up from her bed. He shushes her, and she clings to him. Over his shoulder, she can see the set of stairs across the hall, the attic door open, and she stares into the darkness, watching for movement.

"You're getting too heavy for this," Papa mumbles, patting her hair.

Mama walks into view and huffs. "Not again." She closes the door leading upstairs. "I thought you said you locked it."

"I did," Papa says.

"You clearly didn't, Christopher."

"It was locked. The house is old - things shift around."

"Locks don't shift."

The two eye one another as though an argument is on its way, but then Papa sighs.

"I'll look into it in the morning."

Mama and Papa let Helena sleep in their bed for the night, nestled warm between them. The mattress shifts when Papa gets out of bed in the morning. It's still dark, so Helena tries to go back to sleep, but Mama's snoring keeps her awake. She rolls off the edge of the bed, shivering when her feet hit the floor. The fire in the furnace will have died down overnight, as it always does.

She makes it to the top of the staircase in the dark, allowing her memory to guide her. She feels her way down the stairs, light from the kitchen helping guide her way. The door to the basement is open, and Helena can hear clanging below. She calls, "Papa?"

He pokes his head around the corner. "What are you doing up?" he asks.

"Can I come down?" Helena doesn't often enter the basement - Mama says it's too dirty because of the coal furnace, which burns hot to the touch.

He twists his mouth this way and that, as he always does when considering something likely to upset Mama - things like sneaking Helena candy in the evening or putting pennies on the railroad tracks by the house so that Helena can collect the shiny pieces of copper after a train has flattened them. Papa gives in to Helena's request this time, as he often does. "Be careful." He disappears, and Helena creeps down the stairs.

Just around the corner is the furnace, cast-iron and monstrous. It takes up a quarter of the entire basement. The little door on it is open, a wood fire already burning inside atop a rocky bed of orange-speckled coals.

"The coal is just starting to catch," Papa says, a shovel in hand. Its metal blade goes *shuck-shoo* when he plunges it into the enormous pile of coal and lifts it out again. He tosses the coal into the furnace.

"You know how to make coal burn well?" Papa asks.

"You put it on fire," Helena answers, and Papa laughs.

"There's a little more to it than that," he says. He leans down to snatch up kindling from one of the wooden crates where it's stored. "You can't add too much coal at once or it'll smother out." He tosses twigs and a few dried corncobs in. The cornhusks, still attached to the cobs, ignite and vanish in seconds. After a minute, Papa adds another small shovelful of coal.

Helena has watched the coal being delivered before, heard the rumble and clatter of the rocks traveling down the chute and landing in a pile in the basement, sometimes avalanching until it's more of a vast black lake than a pile at all. But she hasn't watched Papa stoke the fire to warm the house in the morning until today. She rakes her eyes over the stove, checking for cracks in its metal surface where embers might jump out.

"How would you like to shovel some coal?" Papa asks. Helena tucks her hands up into the armholes of her nightgown and shakes her head hard, and he laughs again.

A water pipe rattles nearby, and Papa pauses, a guilty look on his face.

"Sounds like your mother's up," he says. "You'd best run along."

—

Helena washes her face and dresses for school. Her parents are already at the table when she comes downstairs for breakfast. The phone rings just after she's taken her place, three trills before Mama answers.

Helena uses the side of her fork to slice her egg yolk in two, dragging her toast through the yellow center as it spills across the plate. It's the way Papa eats his eggs too - mopping up the liquid mess while leaving the whites behind - but he's already finished his meal and is tamping tobacco down into the end of his pipe.

"Of course you can stay, Francine," Mama says into the receiver. "When are you coming up?"

Helena draws in a long breath and widens her eyes at Papa. His own expression becomes solemn. His teeth click against his pipe. He glances sidelong at Mama, patting his pockets for a book of matches, but Mama's facing the wall, scribbling a note on the pad of paper they keep beside the phone.

"Tomorrow? Sure, sure. Christopher can pick you up at the station."

A flame jumps to life as Papa strikes a match. It fizzles out before he can light his pipe though, so he discards it on his plate.

The receiver lands heavily against its rest when Mama hangs up. Papa takes his pipe out of his mouth when she turns around, as though he's about to ask a question, but he stays silent when he sees her expression.

"Poor Francine," she says.

"What's she coming up for?" Papa asks.

Mama takes her seat at the table, shaking out her napkin and tucking it onto her lap. "Settling some things with the bank."

"About the house?" Papa asks.

"I imagine. I'm sure she could use a break from our mother too."

"She won't be able to talk to anyone at the bank until Monday, you know."

Mama frowns. "What's wrong with a weekend visit from my sister?"

A hint of anxiety is evident in the tensing of his jaw, but Papa's verbal response is conciliatory. "Nothing. It'll be nice to see her. It's been months since we were last down to visit."

Mama eyes Papa a moment longer before she is content enough to carry on. "She's bringing the baby. She'll need your room, Helena - you'll have to sleep with us."

"Okay," Helena says, smiling as she crunches her bacon.

Papa closes his lips around the bit of his pipe and lights another match, but it fizzles out too, and he throws it and the entire book of matches onto his plate. "Must be a bad batch," he says, and sets his pipe on the table.

"That's been happening a lot," Mama says. "Maybe it's time to switch brands."

Mama cuts her egg up like a little pie, eating it slice by slice. "Anyway, what we talked about earlier - you've got time before Helena needs to be at school," she says, teeth scraping against the tines of her fork.

"Hm?"

Mama offers only a pointed look in return.

Helena chews her last bit of bacon, sensing a conspiracy.

"Right," Papa says, standing. "Let's go upstairs, Helena."

Helena hunkers down in her chair, making herself as small as possible. "Why do we need to go upstairs?"

"Your mother wants me to give you a tour."

"Why?"

"Up you get, my dear," Papa says, hoisting Helena from her chair, hands icy beneath her armpits. He sets her down, takes her hand, tugs until she follows. They walk upstairs, turn toward her room - and the attic. Helena digs her heels into the floor.

"Come on, Hel. I don't want to have to carry you."

"Why are you doing this to me?"

"I'm not doing anything to you," Papa says. "You're hearing branches scraping the roof and wind rattling the shutters and building monsters from it."

"I am not!"

"Helena," Papa says, clasping her shoulders. "You can't keep waking us up at night. We'll go upstairs and see that all's well - and then I'll give you a ride to school so you don't have to walk in the cold."

Grumbling, Helena follows Papa up the narrow attic staircase, dragging her feet over the edge of each step. In the attic, Papa has to stoop, bent over like a giant. A lightbulb hangs from the ceiling, a pull - chain dangling beside it, but Papa simply pushes aside the curtains of the two windows to let light in, illuminating specks of dust in the air. Helena stays close to him, whipping her head around in case something jumps out of a corner. There's a trunk near the stairs. A few boxes are piled in one corner, pieces of disassembled wooden furniture in another.

"You see?" Papa says. "Just old things."

"Can I go now?"

"Yes," Papa says, and Helena is already halfway down the stairs as he calls, "Get your coat on and give your mother a kiss."

—

Papa fixes the lock on the door to the attic that evening, tightening screws, allowing Helena to yank on the knob as hard as possible to ensure a fast hold. The night passes in relative silence - a bit of scraping in the attic (branches on the roof, she tells herself) but no locked doors swinging open, no alarming thunks against her bedroom door.

Before school, Helena moves the things she'll need during Aunt Francine's visit into Mama and Papa's room. She piles outfits in her arms, but the pile is precarious, and she loses two pairs of socks as she moves them. She finds one pair in the hall, and the other she spots just under the edge of her bed.

When she crouches down to grab them, she is distracted by the other things she sees beneath the bed: a dusty peppermint, a drawing she did of Mama wearing her blue coat. But most intriguing is a ball in the back corner, which Helena crawls underneath the bed to retrieve, ignoring the rest of the items.

Emerging back into the light, she sees that the ball is green, paint chipped to reveal wood underneath. She turns it around in her hands, trying to remember where she's seen it before.

"Where did you find that?" Mama asks, walking into the room with a dust rag to clean up before Aunt Francine arrives.

"It was under my bed."

"That's odd," Mama says, stepping forward, taking the ball from her. "We don't own a croquet set."

Helena leans away when Mama offers it back, and says, "I don't want it."

"Maybe it belongs to one of your friends." Mama drops it into the toy chest. "Ask around at school today."

Helena doesn't need to ask around at school though, because now she knows where she's seen the ball before - it belonged to Wilbur.

—

Although Wilbur had lived only two towns over with his parents, Aunt Francine and Uncle Edwin, Helena never knew him very well - family get-togethers were irregular. Aunt Francine was Mama's sister, and though they always ended their visits with promises to call to catch up soon, neither ever followed through.

The last time Helena saw Wilbur was last summer, just after his father, Uncle Edwin, had returned home from shooting Nazis. Aunt Francine threw a party in celebration. In the middle of a game of tag among the children - most of them neighbors, because the family was small - Wilbur had pulled Helena aside.

"Isn't this dumb?" he said. "Let's do something else."

"I don't know ..."

With a slowly spreading smile, Wilbur said, "I could get my croquet set out." He always seemed to have many more toys than she did.

Helena didn't quite trust his smile, but she had always wanted to play croquet, imagining the mallets as flamingos, the balls tiny, spiny hedgehogs. "Well, all right," she said.

The shed was at the very back of the property, its thin side slats splintered with age. Wilbur fiddled with the lock. "You'll have to help me carry the box," he said. "It's heavy." He hefted the door open, gesturing for Helena to enter.

It was dim inside, and Helena squinted to find a box large enough for a croquet set. But then there was a sudden rush of air, ruffling her skirt. She jumped as the door slammed behind her.

"Too easy!" Wilbur said from outside, laughing.

Helena tightened her hands into fists, annoyed at having been duped.

A minute passed. Wilbur said, "It must be scary in there. Just say, 'Wilbur is smarter than me,' and I'll let you out."

Helena didn't say a word. Wilbur had done things like this on other visits - jumping out from behind corners in an attempt to elicit a shriek, dropping worms into her shoes - but after the first time or two, she'd learned to act unaffected. Eventually, he'd get bored.

"C'mon," Wilbur said. "Say it and I'll let you out."

After another minute, he said, "Fine! Stay in there all day then," and stormed off.

Helena didn't like being trapped in the dark, but her eyes adjusted, and enough light filtered in between the wooden slats for her to see a few things. She found a dusty stool and took a seat, prepared for a long internment. She tapped her feet and practiced counting to twenty, then noticed a large spider spinning its web over the metal blades of a lawnmower.

Then there was the sound of Uncle Edwin shouting. He soon arrived and flung the door open, and Helena saw Wilbur cradling his ears nearby, his expression pained.

"Thank you," Helena said to her uncle. He nodded curtly, left the door open, and marched back toward the porch, several hundred feet away, where most of the adults were gathered.

Helena dusted off her bottom, then found a stick on the ground just outside the shed and spun it in the spider's web, gathering up the spider itself. She took it outside so that it wouldn't be diced to bits the next time the grass was cut.

After he recovered from having his ears boxed, Wilbur dragged a heavy trunk out of the shed and showed Helena the proper way to arrange the wickets for a game of croquet. They pushed them into the ground, earth giving way to the metal stakes, and Wilbur, only slightly sore over his punishment, demonstrated how to knock a ball with a mallet to send it through a wicket. When Helena's turn came, she chose the green ball, but was too distracted by pretending to be in Wonderland to do well at all. Afraid of harming her flamingo's beak or hedgehog's back, she barely tapped the ball each time her turn came around.

Wilbur was in a better mood after his easy win. They played together the rest of the day, catching toads in the yard and playing tag with the other children.

It was only shortly after that, six months ago, that Mama received the hysterical call from Aunt Francine. Her tinny voice had been so loud that, even from the kitchen table, Helena had deciphered the scrambled message: *fire, ash, death.* The house had burnt down, and Edwin and Wilbur had gone with it. Only Aunt Francine made it out, along with the baby she carried in her belly. She'd stayed in Helena's room for a week after the fire, sobbing, despondent. There had been a funeral service, but Helena was dropped at a neighbor's house beforehand.

A few days later, Aunt Francine went south to stay with Grandma. Before leaving, she'd asked Papa to store a few belongings in the attic. It had been the things untouched by the fire - the shoes and coats that had been in the mudroom, far from where the fire started, and the items from the shed, croquet set included.

–

Despite the nipping wind, Helena is slow on her walk home from school, stopping to peer in the windows of the small downtown, jealous of a fine pair of gloves at one shop, her mouth watering at the sight of rock candy at another. She pulls herself away eventually, drags her feet through the

295

muddy layer of snow coating the road home. Her nose is so cold that it doesn't feel like it exists at all by the time she arrives. She eases the door open and shut, careful not to let the screen clap.

Chatter drifts from the kitchen - Mama and Aunt Francine. Helena slips off her shoes and leaves them by the door to sneak upstairs. A crib has been set up in her room - she wonders whether it is the same one she slept in as a baby. A suitcase rests by the head of the bed.

The green ball is still in the toy chest, nestled between a scraggly teddy bear and a wooden duck. Some part of her had expected the ball to disappear during the day - back into the attic, maybe.

She wonders what it was like, to burn up inside the house. She thinks of the time she accidently touched Mama's curling iron, and the time she plucked a hair from her head and held it to the stove burner out of curiosity. It had released a pungent odor as it curled up and turned black.

According to the firemen, it had been a cigarette that killed Wilbur and Uncle Edwin. An untamped cigarette, knocked from ashtray to floor. For a moment, Helena sees flames engulfing her home, setting her bed ablaze as she slumbers.

Because she won't be able to check it again tonight, she slides her hands against the chimney stack. It does not burn her.

In the kitchen, Mama presses a kiss to Helena's forehead. "You took your time getting home," she says.

Aunt Francine sits at the table, a bundle in the crook of one arm. Although her eyes are ringed red from crying, she looks better than last time, hair swept back into a bun, dress tidy. If her nose were more hooked, her hair a bit darker, she'd look quite like Mama.

"Hello," Helena says to Aunt Francine, hesitating at her mother's side.

"Hello, dear," her aunt says. "It's been a while since you last saw your cousin." She switches the arm in which she holds her bundle, and Helena sees that it's baby Edith, her ruddy face peeking out from the blanket.

"She got fat," Helena says. Mama and Papa had taken her to Grandma's house to visit Aunt Francine and the baby right after the baby's birth. Edith had been tiny then, more fragile-looking.

"Babies are supposed to be fat," Mama says.

"Can I hold her?" Helena asks.

Anxiety flits over Mama's face, but Aunt Francine is quick to agree.

"Just sit down and use both arms. Make sure you support her head," she says, setting the swaddled baby into Helena's arms. Edith's upper lip curls out, and when Helena leans in to examine her, the baby widens her eyes and sticks her tongue between her lips. Helena returns the gesture.

"She isn't bald anymore," Helena says, curling a finger in the baby's downy hair.

"Mm-hm," Aunt Francine mumbles, digging through her purse. She pulls out a shiny cigarette case. She already has a cigarette in her mouth halfway through the question, "Mind if I smoke?" and she's struck a match against its book before Mama can answer. As she raises the lit match, it goes out as if snuffed, a thin trail of smoke dancing from the blackened tip.

"Shoot," she says.

Another match. The flame flickers, disappears before she's able to light the cigarette. "Goddamn it."

297

"Francine!" Mama says.

"Must be a draft. I'm going to the living room."

Mama stays in the kitchen and adjusts Helena's arms around the infant, drawing Helena's own attention back to the baby. "Don't repeat what your aunt said." When another curse word drifts from the living room, Mama adds, "Or that either."

Helena shakes her head, then watches Edith, who watches her back. She bounces her lightly, pats her on the back. The baby wriggles and lifts a skeptical eyebrow.

—

"Can I play with the baby?" Helena asks the next morning.

"I don't see why not." They've had a late breakfast - Mama doesn't like to get out of bed early on the weekend - and Helena is looking for ways to put off practicing writing her letters for school. Aunt Francine sets Edith on her back on the carpet of the living room and takes a seat on the couch, flipping through a crisp issue of *Life*.

Helena sits down beside the baby. She rests her hands lightly on Edith's feet, encircling them, and the baby kicks them around as if riding a bicycle. When Helena dangles a rattle over Edith, shaking it lightly, Edith reaches up and grabs Helena's pinky, latching on for several minutes. When she gets fussy, Aunt Francine nurses her upstairs, and when she returns afterward, Edith scrunches up her face and spits up on her mother's blouse.

Papa drives into town after lunch, returning with a new box of matches. Mama turns on the radio and works a crossword in the newspaper, and Aunt Francine runs Edith upstairs for a nap. Helena sits on the floor at the coffee table and works on forming each angle and curve of the alphabet.

The radio plays a swing song, quick and catchy, and Helena nods her head to the beat.

When Aunt Francine returns, she sits with Papa on the couch, and they strike one match after another, flames puffing out of existence before they can light his pipe or her cigarette. Finally, Papa strikes three matches at once and manages to press them to his tobacco before they go out. He uses the same technique to light a cigarette for Aunt Francine.

"I don't know what's wrong with the air here," Aunt Francine says, relaxing into her seat as she exhales a lungful of smoke. "Too damp, maybe."

Helena doesn't like the smell of Aunt Francine's cigarettes - too bitter, unlike the homey scent of Papa's pipe.

"Feels dry to me," Mama says.

The song on the radio ends, and the announcer's big, booming voice comes on, but then there is a tremendous *whomp* from upstairs. The movement in the room is immediate: Helena drops her pencil. Mama throws the newspaper aside, tossing it halfway across the room as though in a fit, and stumbles up out of her chair. Aunt Francine starts and accidentally breaks her cigarette in half between two fingers, and Papa struggles to get up from the deep cushions of the couch. Mama is the first to the stairs, followed closely by the other adults. Helena feels her pulse hammering as the adults rush upstairs, and then she's running upstairs too because being closer to the noise is better than being all alone far away from it.

The attic door is open, the lock busted. The trunk that had been next to the stairs in the attic is in the hall now, flipped on its side with its clasps broken. A coat and a pair of shoes spill from its mouth. Mama and Papa relax when they see it there.

"Thank God," Mama says, looking down at the trunk, her hand on her chest. "I thought the crib had collapsed."

"I can't believe the baby didn't wake up from the noise," Papa says, patting Helena on the head.

"Oh," Aunt Francine says, and she kneels down. "Oh, oh." She reaches for a shoe, not much larger than Helena's own, and turns it over in her hands. Then the sobbing starts. Mama kneels down next to her, and Papa, his pipe still in his mouth, steps over the items and quietly goes up into the attic. "My baby," Aunt Francine says.

Mama tries to calm her, but Aunt Francine scrabbles through the items in a hysteria, pulls the trunk further open. The handle of a croquet mallet falls out.

Helena backs away into her bedroom and closes the door behind her as her aunt breaks down. In the crib, Edith is awake but apparently unfazed by the noise. She glances at Helena, opens her toothless mouth, makes a little noise. Helena fits her arm between two of the wooden bars and tickles her cheek. The sound of Aunt Francine's crying grows distant.

Helena snatches a glance of the green croquet ball from the corner of her eye.

The door opens, and Papa looks around the edge of it. "Oh, just you?"

"I think Mama took Aunt Francine downstairs."

"Ah." Papa opens the door more fully and leans against the doorframe. "Well, nothing's out of sorts upstairs, but something pushed that trunk down. Maybe it's raccoons you've been hearing in the attic."

"It was Wilbur."

"Where did you get that idea?" Papa asks.

"The things in that trunk belonged to him."

"So?"

Helena clasps one of the crib bars tight. "I found a croquet ball under my bed."

With a wave of his hand, Papa dismisses her evidence.

"And he's been snuffing out the matches!"

Edith fusses.

"Ghosts aren't real," Papa says.

"He's doing it because he's angry he burned to death."

"Don't ever say anything like that again," Papa says, not yelling like Mama would, but lowering his voice and letting each word fall like an anvil.

Helena trembles with the injustice of Papa's response. Edith lets out an unhappy noise.

"Go downstairs," Papa says. "And don't speak a word of this."

—

"I think you'd better take her to see the doctor," Mama whispers to Papa in the kitchen. "I already called. He said he can see her at six."

Aunt Francine has been on the couch since Mama brought her downstairs. She cried for a long time before Mama managed to make her stop. Helena

301

watches Aunt Francine from the bottom of the staircase, perched between kitchen and living room. Her aunt has been staring at the wall, an unlit cigarette dangling from her mouth, for over an hour.

"She seems fine now," Papa says.

"Fine?" Mama asks. "Do you think you'd be fine if you had just been reminded that you were responsible for the death of your spouse and child?"

Helena, feeling sick to her stomach, throws a worried look toward her parents.

Mama's cheeks color when she realizes Helena's overheard, but she doesn't otherwise respond. Instead, she lowers her voice and says to Papa, "She needs something for her nerves."

"All right," Papa says. "I'll drive her over, but what about Edith?"

"Francine brought Pet milk - it's here somewhere. I'll find it."

Aunt Francine acts like a machine when Mama tells her she's going to the doctor. She gets up and slides her cigarette back into her case without saying anything. She puts her shoes on and buttons up her coat methodically.

It's snowing out, light, powdery.

"Be careful driving," Mama says.

"We'll be back in a while," Papa says, giving Mama a kiss. "Take care of your mother and cousin," he tells Helena, and she nods solemnly.

—

Edith's cries are piercing. It's the first time Helena has heard a baby cry up close, and the volume is impressive.

Mama digs through Aunt Francine's suitcase. "It's got to be in here," she says. "She told me she'd bring a can or two in case we went out."

"Maybe she's not hungry," Helena says. "Maybe she pooped."
"She hasn't," Mama says, dumping the contents of the suitcase out on the bed. A dress, a sweater, hose - nothing but clothing and a comb. "Damn it," Mama says, then realizes what she's said and adds, "Don't repeat that."

Helena sticks her fingers in her ears. "Can't you feed her something else?" she asks, hearing her own voice as though underwater.

Mama shakes her head, goes to the crib, and picks the baby up, shushing and cooing.

"Maybe she put it in the pantry," Helena suggests, unplugging her ears as the baby calms, hiccoughing instead of screeching.

Mama perks up at this. "Go check," she says.

Helena runs down to the kitchen and opens the pantry but sees nothing out of the ordinary. She throws open the refrigerator, then each cabinet, but returns to her room empty-handed.

"No luck?" Mama asks.

"No."

The look of disappointment on Mama's face tugs at Helena. She tries to think up other solutions. "We could go to the store."

"You know we can't do that, Helena. Your father took the car."

303

"We could walk?"

"Don't be ridiculous," Mama says. "It's a mile and a half away, and it's snowing. We're not dragging an infant through that."

"Oh."

Mama sets Edith, now quiet, back into the crib. She drums her fingernails lightly on it, thinking.

"Georgia's son must be a toddler by now, but maybe she's kept something around," she says.

"Mrs. Bates?"

Nodding, Mama says, "Come on. Let's go down before we wake her."

In the kitchen, Mama calls Mrs. Bates. "You do? Oh, that's wonderful."

"Listen, Helena," she says after she's hung up, already pulling on her coat. "I'm going to run over to Mrs. Bates' and pick up some milk. You know where she lives - just down the road - so I'll only be gone a few minutes. Can you be good while I'm away?"

What if Edith wakes up?"

"She'll probably stay asleep. If you hear her crying, just shake her rattle or sing to her. Don't try to take her out of her crib."

"All right," Helena says, skeptically drawing out the words.

"Good. Now promise me you won't answer the door if anyone knocks."

"I promise."

Helena goes to the living room after Mama leaves and considers practicing her letters.

But the burnt-out matches in the ashtray remind her of her earlier conversation with Papa, when he'd as much as called her a liar.

—

Helena stands at the bottom of the attic stairs, tightening her hand around the box of matches. She is determined to prove to herself, if not Papa, that Wilbur is in the house. She calls his name and trembles while awaiting an answer.

None comes. *Wilbur wasn't so bad*, she tells herself, putting her foot up onto the first step.

After the first step, Helena realizes that she's growing more frightened by the second, so she grabs her skirt and charges up the stairs before she can think better of it. The attic is musty and pitch black, and she almost hyperventilates as she jumps around, feeling blindly for the light's pull-chain. When she finally finds the chain, the filament flickers to life, glowing orange-red. Helena turns in a circle, searching wildly for a sign of her cousin, but finds none.

"Wilbur?" she whispers, but nothing happens.

"Wilbur," she says again, and opens the box in her hand. She grabs a wooden match, hand shaking. "If you're here, put this match out." She slides the red tip along the striker, but it doesn't light at all. She drags it across again, faster, and a flame shoots from the tip and almost instantly goes out. Her breathing accelerates as she stares at the blackened tip. She sets it back inside the box.

Trying not to let her fear show, she picks out three matches at once, struggling to hold them all with the ease with which Papa had held them.

She places the tips against the striker, pressing firmly. With a flick, they ignite, but before she has an opportunity to call out to Wilbur, the flames lick her fingers.

She drops the matches automatically, sticking her finger and thumb into her mouth to soothe them. She immediately realizes the danger of having dropped the matches. One is burnt out. Another is still lit, burning against the floor. She leans over and blows at the tiny flame until it disappears. She searches for the third match but doesn't find it for several minutes - not until the smoke begins to rise from between the loose floorboards.

She drops the box of matches. Her voice lodges in her throat. She sees a flicker of light beneath the floor, thinks that this feeling in her stomach is the feeling of her body turning to ash.

She turns and bolts. Down the stairs, down the hall - then she turns back.

"Edith!" she shouts, as if to rouse the baby to action. Her socks slip against the floor as she reaches her bedroom, but she manages not to fall. She bursts into the room, thinking of how to get Edith out of the tall crib. But when she reaches the crib, she sees that there is no baby inside, no one for her to take out of the house.

"Edith!" she calls.

Not in the crib, not under the crib, not under the bed. Frantic, she flings open her closet and pulls dresses down. She cries as she scrabbles through the toy chest, looking for the baby tucked away somewhere. Upstairs, there is an enormous rushing sound, like dozens of matches being struck at once.

The smoke has been getting thicker, but now Helena can hear the fire eating at the house above her. She coughs as she throws Aunt Francine's clothes off the bed and checks for Edith under the covers.

"Helena!"

The voice is Mama's, angry.

Helena runs from the room, gasping at the sight of the attic stairs engulfed in flames, choking on the smoke. She hears Mama yelling her name again, but this time the pitch is higher, frightened. Helena reaches the staircase and sees Mama on her way up, still in her coat.

"Come down here!"

"I can't find Edith," Helena cries, almost turning back.

Mama says, "She's on the porch," and, with a fearful glance toward the end of the hall, she hoists Helena into her arms.

—

Helena watches her house burn from the neighbor's window. Smoke billows into the sky, blotting out the stars. When the roof collapses, the fire explodes upward. The fire truck comes, but Mama pulls Helena away from the window before she can see them extinguish the blaze.

"What were you doing?" she says, but only kisses Helena on the forehead, pulls her in close.

Helena looks at Edith, asleep on an armchair, bundled up in one of the neighbor's shirts. After taking Helena from the burning house, Mama had set her down outside and scooped up Edith from the porch. Mama smacked Helena then, screaming at her for putting the baby outside, for leaving her in the cold.

"It's the middle of winter," she yelled. "She could have died."

Guédé
By Rachel Wyman

USA

Months before I met Sugar, I bought a roll of easel paper, pinned a six-foot piece to my closet door and made a huge drawing of a gap-toothed man in a top hat and sunglasses smoking a blunt. He wasn't supposed to be a man, but a spirit in the Vodou pantheon called Guédé.

I was learning about Guédé, Vodou, and all matters of spirit in a Haitian dance class that I chanced upon soon after moving to Brooklyn. I didn't notice for a long time, but my mind was changing.

I surprised myself, drawing Guédé. When I stepped back and decided the larger-than-life sketch was finished, I hardly recognized my involvement in its creation. I examined Guédé's staring face and thought, *I did that?* Then, *why did I do that?* At the time I decided it was spontaneous creativity, but I see I was beginning a very slow, monumental transformation. I think of that drawing as a catalyst, an invocation that caught the attention of some force I didn't know I needed.

I've always liked to put my finger on turning points. Identify the Why. Find a dangling thread and follow it back to its source, admiring how it connects everything along the way. I love being able to say, *Oh yes, that was the moment. The thing that brought me here. Made me this way*. It makes a story, and stories neutralize every good, bad, and sad thing. They let you realize it's all there to be what you need.

In my story, the usual transitions and rites of passage shrink in comparison to that drawing. Losing my virginity, moving away from home, getting a degree. Those signifiers of change don't seem so significant to me. When I think of pivotal moments, odd memories stick out. Years before I drew

Guédé, for instance, I remember telling my parents that I wanted to quit riding horses. I'm certain that act precipitated the end of my childhood.

I was eight years old when I started, with skinny legs and arms. I took lessons with a lady who lived in a trailer surrounded by wheat fields thirty miles out of town. She was bighearted, had stray dogs, cats, and guinea hens roaming on her land, and often brought up The Lord. I didn't know anything about The Lord, but miles away from town, sounds, and other people, I started to feel something I didn't know. A feeling like being nothing and everything. So comfortable in the air and land around me I would forget thoughts, identity and body. Evaporate in the sun and slip back into being the no body I vaguely knew I had been.

I remember many summer days in scorched dirt paddocks. Sweet animal smell, star thistle growing rampant. Creaking saddle leather, the sound boots and hooves make kicking up clods of dry dirt. Then, my favorite, riding bareback after a lesson. Feeling the sweat and heat of another being, so close that the body boundaries softened, sometimes disappeared completely. I couldn't be sure which of us was an extension of the other animal, baptized in a fine layer of dust.

The changes must have started before I actually quit, around when I turned fourteen. My interest in boys had probably grown enough to sicken me with the desperate want for a desirable body. Surely, I was already getting pubic hair, breasts. But as far as I remember, it was the act of telling my parents I was done with riding that brought on puberty to sex and possess me. The walls of my body, once so insubstantial, still halfway in ether and imagination, hardened and held me. Some unfulfilled instinct left me ill at ease and hungry, constantly dissatisfied.

Part of me believes that it all could have been prevented, that I did myself in. My declaration was an incantation, a conjuring that worked on me until I unwittingly summoned a new force with my drawing, a long way from wheat and horses. The root took hold in Brooklyn, where Guédé planted the seed. When I finally met him, Sugar germinated it, grew it till it filled me up.

—

I liked D the moment I saw her. She must have been six months pregnant when I walked into her class for the first time, but still dancing hard, *going in* as I would hear Brooklyn people say. I panted and puffed in the sticky June heat, thinking incredulously that I needed to start a training regimen if I wanted to keep up once D's baby was born. Aside from her perfectly round belly, she was long and lanky with high cheekbones, large dark eyes and biscuity brown skin. She kept her head shaved and habitually wore purple sweatpants with one leg rolled up to expose a slender shin. As she explained in the first class, the dances she taught were mostly connected to Vodou, and she was serious about dispelling misconceptions and ignorance.

"People be like 'Vooo*doooo*!'" she'd say, wiggling her fingers by her face and widening her eyes. "But Vodou isn't about sticking shit in dolls. It's a beautiful system. It's about getting deeper into your soul, deeper into the natural world. Serious stuff."

I admired D's dancing, her long elegant limbs. But I marveled at her way of casually infusing class with information - for the body, brain, and whatever was in-between. I was a few months into my transplanted life, and New York was constantly reminding me that I was naive and uncultured. So, I was surprised at how comfortably her teachings sat with me, even while being completely foreign. I began to meet the major Vodou spirits, and through D, they showed me new ways of moving. Their dances embodied principles and personalities.

I immediately fell in love with a dance called Yanvalou, for the serpent spirit Damballa and his wife Ayida, the rainbow. D explained that together Damballa and Ayida encircle the world without beginning or end, and Yanvalou's continuous spinal undulations symbolize timelessness and infinite presence. She demonstrated this with supernatural fluidity, sine waves traveling through her spine, shoulders and neck. Where one undulation rippled through her back and disappeared, another was already gathering underfoot, traveling up through her legs to resurface.

I couldn't imagine a body doing anything more beautiful and learning to move this way felt supremely important. I undulated in my room, in the shower, in front of the mirror in the living room while my roommate was at work. I stood on trains and buses, trying to feel every subtle weight shift in my pelvis and spine as we slowed, sped up, rocked. Each time I practiced, my body found the undulation faster. After a while the movement became reflexive and thinking about it seemed disruptive, so I surrendered thoughts to sensation.

In the last week before D went on maternity leave, Guédé appeared to end class in a brief, clamorous finale. The drummers started up with a rhythm so driving and staccato it was nearly frantic, and D took the last five minutes to lead us in a procession around the room. Her steps were light and fast, her pelvis loose. The dance had a sly personality, at least the way D did it. At one point she stopped to respond to a break in the drum rhythm. Rooting her left foot, she swept her right leg up and out to plant herself in the slightest of squats. Then, the punchline, she slowly lifted her pelvis in a suggestive grind and abruptly let it drop. It was sexual without being sexy, with D's execution so frank and humorous that it never became coy. She introduced the dance as Banda, and the spirit behind Banda as Papa Guédé.

"My personal favorite. He's death, rebirth and regeneration. He sees the really big picture, so he can't take our emotional hang-ups seriously. Especially when it comes to sex. He's just pure creating energy, without the social expectations. He tears apart all the romance and sentimental stuff we put on it."

I watched D absent-mindedly rub her pregnant belly. "For Guédé it's like, 'Y'all got here somehow so don't even pretend.' Sex is creating power, and that's everything. When we do this little ..." she marked the pelvic drop "...

we're not just flaunting our stuff. We're asking for fertility. Maybe you want to make new life with your body. Or maybe you want to make art with your soul. Either way, we ask Guédé for those blessings."

She gave a small smirk, put her hands on her hips and said dryly, "Can't nobody run home tonight and put me on blast for hoochie-coochie dancing. Guédé is deep."

Interlude I

Growing up in a rural area, I didn't see hordes of people every day; I saw stretches of uninhabited land. The vastness of open fields dwarfed the already small slice of humanity I was familiar with. I looked at myself and the people around me as random, unimportant figures passing in and out of a permanent landscape. The land had lasting value, but whoever and whatever we were was inconsequential.

In the city, people are everywhere and everything. The city tells people that humans and their doings carry the world's meaning. And because there are so many people and endless possibilities for different interactions, encounters feel significant. Destiny seems to guide every path.

–

Sugar and I could have intersected early in my new New York life. My first year in the city, I would only venture into Manhattan to visit a particular dance studio I liked, and Sugar owned a small store across the street. By day it was a somewhat inscrutable boutique proffering an array of vintage clothing and rare vinyl. In the evenings, when he wasn't toiling away on his own projects, he hosted happenings and workshops for artist friends.

Of course, I knew nothing of those gatherings on the evenings I emerged sweaty and exultant from class to sway back toward the subway, open and receptive to whatever twilight spirits would have me. On how many occasions had I unknowingly heard his voice from across the street,

313

mingled with other voices as an event broke up? How often had his deep, sweet laugh rolled over me and receded like a wave as I walked obliviously in the opposite direction? And how many times had our paths run parallel, had we not quite merged on the road?

Sometimes I'd mournfully wonder why we couldn't have met sooner, why Fate didn't guide me across the street one single time. Why I had to wait so long. But I always concluded it was supposed to happen this way. Otherwise, I would not have recognized his place in my life.

–

When adolescence hit and reorganized my priorities, I wasn't interested in boozing or blazing. My mind was already altered by the charms of the opposite sex, and what I craved was sticky, sweet body contact. A childhood friend became my first serious boyfriend, the summer I was sixteen. We took every opportunity to be alone and stole the time that wasn't ours by lying to our parents and sneaking out of school assemblies. He seemed to get a thrill from lying and sneaking, but I hated it. For the next two years I was constantly anxious we would be discovered - on the living room couch, in his truck in empty parking lots, on playgrounds after dark. Even so, my worrying mind never gained leverage over my body. Sex seemed more urgent than any possible consequence.

Miraculously, I maintained my grades and was accepted to a college I loved, across the country. I had an instinct I needed to get out of town. My boyfriend stayed in the area and stopped speaking to me, wounded that I chose to break us up. As I packed and prepared to leave home, it occurred to me for the first time that I was lucky. I had floated along fairly thoughtlessly, and by some good fortune I wasn't pregnant, married, or stuck in town. Refocused and free of my own compulsive urges, I realized how easily obsession takes over.

For that reason, I was wary of romance when I left home. I saw how much living and learning I had to catch up on and perceived no room for anything but growing into something better than what I had been.

The idea of spiritual satisfaction was easy in good times, but I was drawn to quick sources of sweetness and comfort when I was unhappy. I was easily swayed by a look of love and any sign of a tender heart. My second winter in New York, I was underemployed and depressed, desperately trying to find shape in the ridiculous mud-pie life I was slopping together. Along with dancing and whispering prayers for clarity, sex was medicine for my malaise.

I wanted reassuring touch and intimacy, the distraction of another body. But I was often torn between lust and repulsion, finding that so many men were clumsy and predictable. The same seduction, the same touch. I could see the wheels turning, calculating where to put hands and lips. Pawing and squeezing, no finesse. I'd get bored, yet I was always curious and ever hopeful that something interesting would happen. I counted on my mating mechanisms to kick in and force satisfaction out of the event.

It was like drifting on a gentle current, bodies passing easily without a snag of joy or anguish to grab onto. By February, I needed grounding, a different kind of physical expression. Something that lingered. I found an art supply store and bought easel paper, then I went home and drew Guédé. Lying in bed that night, I examined him staring back at me from the closet door until my eyelids got heavy and I turned off the light.

Interlude II

As a kid, I was both deeply unsettled and fascinated by ghost stories and anything supernatural. I wanted constant reassurance that the spooky thoughts I came up with were trapped in my mind and couldn't enter the physical world. I was afraid just thinking of something made it real.

I couldn't help but think those thoughts, though. My imagination spun images and stories against my will, pulled material from such unknown depths of mind that I believed I'd invented something out of thin air. Or that something had come to me from outside myself. Images, scenes. A revelation, a flash of insight, a spirit. Tucked into my bed in the dark, I understood logically that thinking of a ghost did not mean it was in the room with me. But my body didn't understand logic and its fear told me I couldn't be certain.

Almost every night I ran down the hall to my parents' room, trying to escape the solitude of my mind with its shapeshifting thoughts and dreams. Seeking the solid comfort of real bodies, warm and breathing.

—

I thought I would die of relief when D started teaching again in the middle of March. Her first class back was salvation and rebirth. We did a series of agricultural dances to encourage the advent of spring - a Kombit Suite, D called it. In her earthy voice she sang, "*bonswa Kouzin, bonswa Kouzine oh*" - greeting Zaka, patron spirit of farmers, vendors, and all hardworking, salt-of-the-earth people. I was ecstatic, sweat disguising my tears of joy. Lost memories of square dancing in high school gym class resurfaced in a sentimental light. I thought of all the boys at my school who wore Carhartts and camo, kept hunting rifles in their pickups and spoke with an unplaceable accent that might only be classified as "rural."

The days slowly became longer. It rained a lot and got warmer; the smell of damp earth and new foliage refreshed some part of me that had become brittle. I felt better to be taking class with D again, but I still didn't know what I was doing with myself and all of the time invested in dancing. Believing that serious dancers are in serious companies, I went to auditions under a cloud of obligation and dread. I found most of them unpleasant and a few depressing. So many bodies crammed together, identified only by numbers pinned on spandex leotards. I always felt a heaviness in the air.

The concept of energy was still new to me as a recent transplant, so I didn't understand what I was sensing. Back home, I had never felt the emanations of so many people. Their desires, fears, failures, ambitions, intentions, visions, nightmares, passions, wounds, mistakes, neuroses, schemes, delusions, grudges, and hope-against-hopes. Constant projections mingling in different combinations, blessing the air of New York one day and making it heavy with mourning the next. I was learning to handle other people's energy in daily life, but it was poisonously concentrated at auditions.

Finally, I stopped looking at dance company notices. I decided I didn't need validation as a dancer so much as the freedom to keep exploring what was speaking to me. In my favorite self-indulgent fantasy, kind patrons supported me as a full-time student and practitioner of Vodou dance. But I knew I needed to pay a fair price for spiritual enlightenment and self-actualization. I thought the price involved working a lot, being resourceful and living below the poverty line. I found work babysitting. I stuck to a strict budget. And I focused all thoughts and energy on Vodou, cutting off every romantic prospect I had entertained during mid-winter loneliness.

I had casually dated more that winter than ever before in my life, although I tried to avoid the intimacy of sex. I decided never to sleep in an unfamiliar bed, and the prospect of my roommate's silent judgment made me reluctant to bring too many different men to our apartment. After Guédé appeared like another presence in my bedroom, though, I became bolder and brought more of my dates home. I was curious about their reactions.

In the intimate act of creation, I never considered the possibility that anyone would enter my sacred space and see Guédé. But it was a prominently displayed piece, and a life-size figure in a top hat and sunglasses demanded some explanation for the uninformed. I tried to articulate Guédé as best as I understood him. In return I received raised eyebrows, smirks, sage nods, and uncomfortable silence. Most moved on quickly to seduction, while others asked questions. I wondered if the men who probed further were curious about Guédé himself, or in what my

317

interest in Guédé revealed about me. I shrugged when one guy asked why I wanted him watching me each night. I had never thought about it like that and had no answer.

Everyone reacted to Guédé, and most reactions fit somewhere between Mild Interest and Mild Disapproval. But it was Sugar who stood in front of the drawing and declared, "It's me."

—

I imagine the memories and information we accumulate as little streams that flow into an ocean of knowledge. If our minds were designed differently, maybe we'd see their boundaries and sources clearly. We'd know exactly when some piece of information entered us and where it came from. As it is, everything runs together. I'm forgetful. It seems so long ago, and so many memories have come to crowd this one that I think it must be warped. Clear, chilly day. The end of April, maybe. White shirt, buttoned all the way up, a felt hat tipped on his head. Dark. Wide cheekbones. Ethnically ambiguous eyes, like mine. A subtle exchange of gazes, one of those minute subconscious interactions between animals.

—

He liked to tell me he was a genuine love child, a product of his parents' first passion. They were eighteen, still growing up even as they raised him. There was a lot of love between them, he told me. Many evenings he found them dancing to records in the living room. George Benson, Marvin Gaye. They were romantic.

"They separated for a while," he said. When I asked why, he was silent for a long time.

"They didn't know how to handle practical problems," he offered finally. "But they got back together eventually. They loved each other too much."

"They're still together now?"

"Yes, to this day. My mother is dead, but yes, even so. I was on the phone with my father yesterday. He said, 'I dreamed about your mom again last night. She was right there.' He dreams about her all the time. I don't dream as much, but I think about her."

"You were close with her?"

"Very. She was the one who always called me Sugar. Even when I was bad."

Aside from that, he asked many questions and spoke little about his life. This endeared him to me, since I liked receiving other people's words silently and sympathetically, without interruption. I had learned that other people would handle the talking if I asked a few questions and shut up. His immunity to magic silence forced me to tell him things. The things became stories as I spoke, and I listened to my own narrative with some wonder.

He turned every query back on me, opened me up while maintaining his mystery. I always went away feeling that he had stared straight in as I shamelessly revealed myself. He saw me and it felt nice. I sensed the danger of intoxication lurking in that feeling, threatening the equilibrium I had finally regained.

—

"What keeps you from doing what you want?" he asked.

"Self-doubt and fear. Questioning the value of what I want to do."

"That's honest." He smiled. I smiled back and shrugged.

"What is it you want to do?" he asked. I was going to say I didn't know yet, but some other words came.

319

"I want to understand what I can. But also find some peace with not understanding."

"You're looking for spiritual enlightenment?"

"Maybe. I didn't know I was looking for that."

"Do you think your dancing fits in there somewhere?"

"It's everything."

"Tell me."

"I don't know how to explain."

"You do. Relax. Your brow is all furrowed."

"I'm going to get wrinkles. It's furrowed in every photograph since birth." He laughed. I rubbed my brow and took a breath.

I said, "I read so many ghost stories as a kid but they scared the shit out of me. I hated to think anything like that could be real. Things I couldn't see in the physical world ... the idea was too spooky. I always loved dancing because it felt so solid." I stopped, trying to find the thread.

"And?" he prompted after a while.

"Now the more I dance, the less solid it feels." He waited for more, realized I was done.

"Now I don't follow."

"I don't know how to say it. It started feeling beyond my body."

"Transcendent?"

"Maybe. I told you I've been learning about Vodou?"

"Yes ..."

"That stuff is all about invisible things. Everything that I would usually say isn't real, period. But the dances are so beautiful that it all seems beautiful. The different spirits, the symbolism. The ideas. It makes me unsure about everything."

"What do you mean 'everything?'"

"Just ... everything. What is or isn't real. There's so much out of sight. Unknowns. Not just specific questions I'll never fully answer, 'What's the meaning of life' or whatever. Questions that I'll never know are out there at all. It makes me uncomfortable. But maybe that's good."

"Why?"

"Everyone says life is uncertainty, and that's hard to live with. I want to learn how to live."

He looked into my face with an indecipherable expression. After a long silence he said, "Do you know what you are?"

"A hillbilly in the city," I offered. He ignored my joke.

"Authentic."

"What does that mean?"

"You're open. Maybe even too open. You don't hide."

"Not from you." I gave him a shy smile, but he didn't respond. His expression remained unreadable and where before he felt so close and warm, he was suddenly remote. Then his face softened slightly.

"You need boundaries in this city," he said.

Interlude III

Vodou speaks of spirit possession as horsemanship. In ceremony, a person becomes *chwal* - the horse for an arriving spirit to mount and ride. The human body is necessary for spiritual contact, allowing "divine horsemen" to join the physical world and mingle with the living. But to enter the body, the horseman must displace its steed's consciousness. While everyone else enjoys the visitor's company, the horse wakes up with no memory of divine communion. Just a tired body and other people's tales of what happened.

—

"When's your birthday?" he asked.

"December twelfth."

"Our Lady of Guadalupe."

"How did you know?"

"I grew up in New York. I know everybody's special days. What do you know about it, country bun'kin?"

"There's a big Catholic Hispanic population in my town."

"I thought it was all rednecks where you're from.

322

"Yeah, and folks who came up from Mexico. And California." With some difficulty, I formed the letters 'b - l - o - o - d' with my fingers. "I think a California transplant taught me that."

"Country gangster. I like you. Or maybe it's because we're both fire signs."

"When's your birthday?"

"I'm a Leo."

"You won't tell?"

"It was last Tuesday. Don't suck your teeth at me, I don't celebrate birthdays."

"You could have said something. I wouldn't have made a big deal out of it. How old are you?" I realized I had no idea. I looked closely at his face. More than twenty, less than eighty.

"How old are *you*?" he asked.

"Twenty-five. And . . ." I counted on my fingers, "eight months." He pulled his driver's license from his wallet and showed it to me. I did a quick calculation. He had just turned forty-eight.

"I can't believe it."

"That freaks you out?" he asked.

"A little. You look good."

"Black don't crack."

"It don't. I won't look that good in twenty-three years."

"That makes me sound old."

"A number is just a number."

"That's true. You still like me?" The question surprised me, especially its hint of vulnerability.

"Why wouldn't I?" I wondered. He nodded. We sat in silence for a while.

"I never had birthday parties when I was little. I'm not in the habit of celebrating."

"Not even with family?"

"I don't remember when I was really young. My parents split by the time I was eight or nine and I went with my mom, so we kept it minimal. Sometimes she would make a cake. Or my aunt would. Women always pay better attention to stuff like that." He smiled, looking lost. Then his face lit up.

"I forgot all about this till now," he continued. "I had this girlfriend in high school. I hadn't said anything to her about my birthday coming up, but I guess she knew. Must have been ... I think my seventeenth. We had planned to go out, just have a regular date and go to a movie or something. But when we were almost to the train she said she had forgotten something and we needed to go back to her house. I was like, 'What! We have to go all the way back!' Really annoyed. Turned out she had planned this surprise party, gotten all our friends in on it. We walked in and everybody was there, she had made a cake and everything. Man, they really got me ... I had no idea. It was the only surprise party I ever had." He shook his head, grinning.

"She must have cared for you a lot," I said.

"Yeah. We were a little serious."

I tried to imagine the girl who planned his only surprise party, who lovingly baked his cake and delighted in his look of astonishment when the lights came on and everyone jumped out. I felt a pang of jealousy. When Sugar was seventeen and running around New York with his sweetheart, I was still six years away from even existing. I couldn't decide if the thought made me feel better or worse.

Sugar always saw me home after we'd been out, but he never tried to come inside. He'd deliver me to my doorstep and plant a chaste kiss my mouth, the way my father used to kiss me before picking up his briefcase and heading out the door. I had a feeling he would never ask to come in. The choice would have to be unambiguously mine.

"My roommate is away," I told him under the streetlight. The air outside was finally cooling, drying my sweat. A jagged white band of salt had formed across the front of the leotard I'd worn to class and sported on our date. He noticed and lightly touched my ribs.

"Okay."

"Do you have to leave right away?" He checked his watch.

"No. I don't have to leave." He looked at me and waited, making no moves. I was uncomfortable asking for what I wanted, unsure what to expect from him.

"Will you come in," I finally asked, "and spend some more time with me?"

"Yeah. Let's see your nest."

I led him in. As I showed him the living room and kitchen full of my roommate's furniture, decorations, and cooking equipment, I realized that there was nothing of mine in the common space. My bedroom contained my few possessions, and they rarely spilled out of that boundary.

"Nice," he said as I opened the door to my room. He put his hands on his heart and crossed the threshold with a look of reverence. He gazed around and I watched, trying to see myself as he saw me. The plants on the windowsill, the dreamcatcher I'd brought from home hanging by the bed. The mattress dressed in old pink sheets, pillows bunched up to make a nest and a few books stacked nearby. My bureau with its piles and scatterings of earrings and necklaces, half-used bottles of scented oil and lotions, wheat pennies, and plastic hair ornaments. All of it sitting in dust.

He looked at the small shrine I had recently constructed in a corner on the floor, my attempt at honoring the spirits I was beginning to know and love, along with my better-known creators. I had amassed and carefully arranged pictures of my parents and grandparents, candles, seashells, heart-shaped jewelry and trinkets, crosses, beads, and anything else that struck me as a nice offering. I thought suddenly of my childhood home and how my mother would pick up any shiny thing off the sidewalk - a piece of glass or wire or wayward bracelet charm. How those things would find their way to the kitchen windowsill or living room mantelpiece, along with rocks and shells from beach vacations, feathers found out in the countryside. Once, playing in a dark corner of the basement, I had come across an artful scattering of shells on an abandoned shelf. Everywhere I turned were little arrangements, artefacts of life.

Finally, Sugar examined my closet door. He stared into Guédé's face for a moment, then turned back to the bureau and grazed his fingers over a dusty pair of snake earrings from the dollar store.

"Nice." He turned to me with a small smile. "I see you, country bun'kin."

Interlude IV

Being possessed fascinates me. I like the idea of coalescence, merging the small self into a bigger whole. How sweet to transform the ego, to crack that hard, little nut that guards its boundaries so carefully. To expand into something beyond the body or to be swallowed up by it, who can tell the difference?

I have read all kinds of accounts of Vodou ceremonies and what happens when spirits ride. There are things about it that frighten and attract me at the same time. The loss of control, for instance. When you are possessed you are literally out of your mind, and someone else is there.

Sometimes a spirit will punish a practitioner who has done wrong. I read an ethnologist's recollection in which Damballa mounted a man who had failed to properly serve him. Ridden by the snake spirit, the man effortlessly climbed a huge tree. When he was up beyond all reach of the congregation, Damballa departed, leaving him to figure out his own way down.

–

When he brought his face close to mine, my heart jumped and my whole body burned. He radiated heat and smelled like earth, cloves, and something oily. I felt a little dizzy, and the silence around my head made my breath loud.

"You're open." He murmured. Our lips hardly touched as he breathed into me. An image of large, soft nostrils overpowered my mind, my first riding lesson suddenly resurfacing. Horses greet by breathing into each other's noses, I thought hazily. I was burning up. I sighed and he inhaled my exhalation. I floated to the bed, took off my shorts and lay down in my leotard, incapacitated by blood that felt too viscous in my veins. He shut the door behind him and removed his hat and several long, beaded necklaces. He put these items down carefully in a pile, then stripped naked and shut my lamp off.

I watched him approach. From down on the bed, his darkened figure reminded me of the way shadows stretch long in evening sun. He eased onto me with his full weight, covering me like a blanket. Silky and leonine, heavy. He took my head and kissed my lips and cheeks. Then he was beside me, shucking off my damp leotard. I opened up for him. Time and movement slowed and became dense, like honey had replaced sand in the hourglass. I was being consumed by my own fire. I wondered when I would disintegrate, and would Sugar disappear too, or just find himself covered in soot?

Before either of us spontaneously combusted, he disentangled and pulled me to his side.

"That's enough for now," he told me. My face was hot and there were tears on my cheeks. I stared at him.

"I have to get back to the store," he explained. "And get ready for an event tomorrow." His mind was moving to the next thing; he gave me a small squeeze then got up and went into the bathroom. I heard the faucet running. I tried to reconstruct what had just happened but the replay was already scratched and skipping. I was sweating again, my body agitated.

"It's me." He had come back in, was standing naked in front of Guédé. I sat up.

"With the teeth and everything," he continued. He mimicked the drawing's expression, pointing a finger at his own face and another at Guédé's. It was true; they shared a sly, gap-toothed grin. I remembered the warmth I felt, watching his broad face take shape. The pleasure I took in making his mouth just so.

"Who is this?" he asked.

"A Vodou spirit." I replied. He smiled and pulled his pants on.

"Wouldn't it make more sense to stay here and get some sleep, and go to the store in the morning?" I asked. He shook his head, putting on his shirt.

"No, love. I really need to work on a few things."

He untangled the beaded necklaces and put them on one at a time, then tucked them under the shirt. I reached for him and he came to the side of the bed. I wrapped my arms around his waist, noticed his body was cool. He'd siphoned his fire into me. I looked up into his face and we contemplated each other. Then he patted his pockets and came up with a small bottle.

"I have a solution," he told me, uncapping the bottle and taking out a dainty brush. He gracefully smudged a line of amber liquid on his palm and with ceremonial gravity, swept his hand over my pillow. It was earth, oil, and cloves.

"So that I can be here," he said. I wondered if it was a gesture of care or pity. He put on his hat and I walked him to the door. Then I came back and lay down with the pillow.

Logic told me a man is just a man, but my body could not be sure that I hadn't been hexed.

—

Riding my bike in an unfamiliar neighborhood one day, I got caught in a summer thunderstorm. When the rain let up to a drizzle, I decided I would walk the rest of the way home. Coming up a quiet side street, I saw Sugar's familiar figure approaching from the opposite direction across the street. A young girl was beside him, wearing his felt hat. When he caught sight of me, he took her hand and crossed to meet me.

"This is Benita," he said, watching me carefully. A beautiful little girl, with Sugar's eyes. She pushed the oversized hat up her forehead.

"Pleased to meet you," I said, and we shook hands. "Your daughter?" I asked him. He looked down at her, and I followed his gaze. Benita smiled and nodded shyly.

"Her mom asked me to take her to a doctor's appointment. I'll call you later." He gave me a hug and a chaste kiss, and we all waved goodbye.

—

"Are you married?"

"No."

"Are you sure?"

"I promise."

"Were you ever married? To anyone?"

"No. Her mom and I weren't together like that."

"Why didn't you tell me you had a daughter earlier on?"

"What would you have done?"

"I don't know. But at least I would have understood."

"Understood what?

"You. The situation I was getting into."

"I didn't know how to tell you. I'm sorry. Running into you like that was a relief."

We were both silent. Then I said, "It's hard now."

"What's hard?"

"I'm attached to you and I don't know if that's okay. Are you attached to me?"

"You chose me."

"What does that mean?"

"You chose me. I'm here for what you need."

"Never mind. Talk to you later."

"Wait, hold on. I am attached to you," he said quietly. "But don't ask me to tell you that. Ask me to show you."

"Most people don't care for everyone they sleep with. The body can lie," I said.

"So can the mouth."

"I can't care for someone who's not open. It's too scary."

"Why?"

"Wouldn't you want to know who a person is and what they've got going in life? So you could make your own decision about it? I don't want to be sitting in the dark." He didn't respond. We were silent for a long time.

Finally, he said, "We're like soil and seed."

"What does that mean?"

"We're connected. And we're helping each other."

"How am I helping you?"

"You share a kind of ... innocence with me. An openness."

"And what are you sharing with me?" I asked.

"The opposite," he said.

—

My apartment was on the ground floor and it sweltered in the heat of summer. Even with the windows open, no breeze blew in. I came home from a long day of babysitting, sighing into the stuffy air. I had been neglecting D's class while I worked more to make rent, and my whole being was drained. I also felt slightly unhinged. I hadn't seen Sugar in two weeks, despite prayers for a chance encounter, a word from him. Any divine or magical intervention would do - some tangible sign of connection. I carried his presence constantly, but I ached with the uncertainty of whether I stayed within him.

I went to the kitchen and stared at the refrigerator's bleak contents. A carton of almond milk, an ancient jar of olives. I went to the couch and sat listening to fragments of street conversation, the rhythm of traffic. When the light changed I'd hear cars idling, lining up down the block. Sometimes a strange melody formed from many songs projected out of open windows. Other times there would be just one, which went flat and eerie driving away.

Abruptly overcome by fatigue, I went to my room to lie down. Late afternoon light angled in and I let it roast me, too lackadaisical to pull the curtains. Kids from the day-care next door were playing outside. I listened to their voices; they shouted at each other like grown people. Then the voices faded as a teacher ushered them inside.

I groped for my phone on the mattress, thinking I would set an alarm in case I accidentally fell asleep. But I felt a form and realized Sugar had come in to lie down by me. My voice was gone, but he knew I was overjoyed. I closed my eyes and felt him shift onto me. I could barely breathe, my body magnificently heavy with his.

"That feels good." The words were hard to get out. He said nothing, but he crushed me, emanating love and warmth.

The sound of my own heavy breathing opened my eyes. I was alone, flat on my back in the oppressive heat of a sunbeam that had moved only slightly since I lay down. The feeling of the dream lingered, his presence so strong I almost believed that if I called out he would answer, emerge through the open door.

I found my phone and called, but he didn't pick up. I rolled to my side and closed my eyes. When my phone rang and roused me, the light through the window had gone from yellow to red.

"Hi there. Sorry I missed you."

"I just called to say you were in my dream." My voice was thick with sleep.

"A good dream?"

"Yeah. It seemed so real."

"What happened in it?"

"Nothing. But you felt close."

"I am close."

I glanced involuntarily at Guédé, staring and grinning from the closet door.

"I miss you," he said.

"Then why don't you reach out?"

"I am reaching out. I've been juggling all of my obligations."

"I'm not trying to be an obligation."

"I know, and I appreciate that. I'm going to come see you soon."

—

I flew home in December to spend the holidays with my parents. It felt good to watch the city shrink away beneath the airplane, its looming buildings, volatile energy, and life-and-death decisions quickly reduced to memory.

Getting home from the airport was an hour's drive through mostly empty countryside. My parents and I talked about life in the city and I elaborated on things I had told them over the phone: dancing, Vodou, the New York hustle, and searching for direction. It was hard to summarize daily life with all its moving pieces and mystical occurrences waiting to unfold at any moment. They told me they missed me, but that they were proud of me. I was overwhelmed with gratitude. Their love was like a buoy, and I hadn't noticed how weary I was.

I was jetlagged and fell asleep before dinner. When I woke up it was a little after six in the morning, still dark outside. I tiptoed down the hall past pieces of my mother's artwork that had hung for years in the same places. I knew every dusty corner, every creak, every smell of the house as if it were part of myself. Downstairs, I put on my running shoes and slipped out. It took ten minutes to reach the city limits, and I didn't encounter a single car, human, or animal.

The stars were bright and sharp in the cold air; the eastern horizon was turning blue. I ran along a path heading towards the reservoir in the wheat fields beyond town. The fields were bare and tilled in preparation for warmer weather, when they would turn green and finally yellow-gold. I ran farther out, came to a long, steep incline and ran halfway before I had to stop, winded. As my breath quieted, I became aware of deep silence; I heard nothing but my heartbeat. A pinprick of fear tingled in my spine. I had forgotten what absolute solitude felt like.

I took a moment to reason with myself, to ask why I was spooked if I was indeed by myself. Was it actual uncertainty as to whether I was alone? I saw nobody, no roaming farmer or coyote, yet my body was increasingly uneasy. I felt a strong urge to flee, so I began running again. I reached the top of the hill where the levy and trail joined - a beautiful view overlooking the reservoir, but I didn't slow down. I followed the path as it took me down, up, alongside farmers' fields and into groves of trees with naked, contorted branches. Still no other sign of life, yet I was neither looking for another presence nor running away from one that I knew about.

My lungs burned and my muscles began to fatigue. I had a sudden vision of myself as a bird might see me, a tiny figure moving almost imperceptibly through endless space. I slowed to a walk, my sweat instantly cooling. Against the chill, I felt the heat and push of blood defining the borders of my body, speaking my liveness. Still alone. I was calm again. I looked up and saw stars, the horizon's new pink and purple light.

—

"Are you coming back?" he asked.

"After the holidays."

"Will I see you?"

"You know the answer to that."

"It's nice to hear it."

"I can't distance myself from you."

"Because you chose me."

"Maybe. Did you choose me?"

"I let myself be chosen. By you."

"I hate when you say that," I said.

"Why? It's a statement about your agency. Your power." I sighed in reply.

"I see you," he said.

"I know." I paused. "I hope our lives are always entangled."

"They will be. Who's in your room?" I glanced around my childhood bedroom, confused. Then I thought of Guédé, grinning into an empty room in Brooklyn.

The in-between and undefined is hard for me, and from what I've seen in the city it's hard for most people. I see the way we try to embrace mystery. We explore religion and spirituality, learn about planetary positions and meditation practices. But always with a purpose. To justify good or bad behavior, or to explain why so-and-so doesn't love us, or even to find a reason for keeping on, a story that makes sense enough that we continue struggling along the path to see what's next.

I struggled for a long time, searching for a narrative with Sugar. I desired clarity and began to write with the hope of finding it. A friend suggested that I'd never finish the writing until I reached some kind of conclusion with him in life. I thought she was right - I needed a resolution to understand the story.

Somehow, it's not so. If anything, I'm beginning to believe that no real story ever has a resolution. There is always more string behind the loose end, and even when the whole thing comes unraveled there are still the remnants of what was, and what could be next. The last page comes, the curtain falls, but stories continue as long as life continues, and even death can't end them. A spirit clings, revealing itself in gestures, memories with no origin, lessons learned, and words exchanged. Consciously or unconsciously, something keeps unfolding. It leaves its imprints.

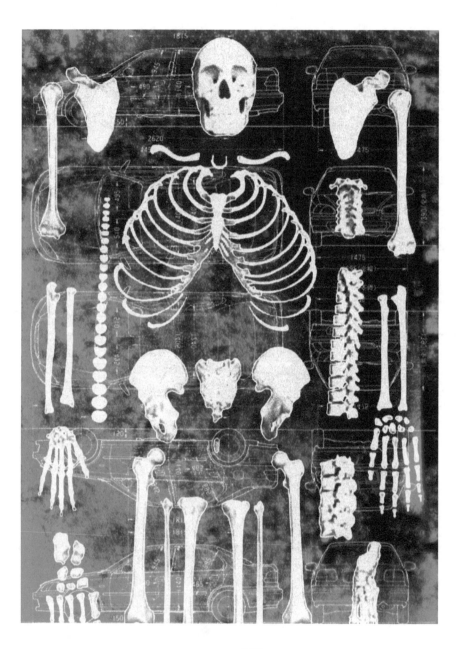

338

Hindsight
By Carie Juettner

USA

It's Sunday morning, and I'm in the center lane of Mopac, driving with one hand and digging in my purse for lip balm with the other, thinking about how there's no such thing as rush hour in Austin anymore, just a steady stream of hours and cars, when a silver Civic just like mine pulls in front of me.

It's not often I see a twin of my eleven-year-old hybrid anymore. When I first bought it, they were everywhere. I remember once, a few weeks after I got the car, trying desperately to unlock it in the parking lot of HEB and cursing my fob for breaking. It wasn't until I was fumbling with the key in the lock that I saw the baby seat in the back and realized it wasn't mine. My car was one row over, flashing its lights in exasperation.

But here is a long-lost sibling traveling the same road as me.

I gaze at the butt of the beat-up Civic and wonder what its story is. It has a dent in its rear bumper similar to the one my own hybrid sports from that ill-placed pole in the parking lot of that old bar on South First. Mario's? Marco's? I was so mad the night I backed into that pole. My friend Sally accused me of being drunk, but I wasn't the tiniest bit tipsy. I was just a bad driver, which at the moment seemed worse. I went back a few months later and saw the sign they'd put up in the parking lot. It read, "There's a pole behind you." It made me feel better to know that I wasn't alone.

Maria's. The bar was called Maria's.

I speed up a little, wanting to get a better look at my car's twin. The closer I get to its back bumper, the more the dent looks familiar. I shiver and turn

339

off the air conditioner. Maybe the driver used to go to Maria's too. That would be a pretty big coincidence. Then again, enough people hit that pole to warrant a sign. At this range, I can see more of the car. It's the same year as mine. It has the same dorky antenna and faux spoiler. And the same deep scratch down the center of the trunk.

What the hell? The Maria's pole, maybe, but there's no way the lady who owns this car got that scratch the same way I did. Only I am clumsy enough to accidentally key my own car while juggling an armload of books. But it's there. It's definitely there.

I reach to turn the AC down, but it's already off. I drag my teeth over my bottom lip and feel how chapped it is. I reach into my purse again and this time find my peppermint lip balm. I flip the lid with my thumb and apply a thick layer. While I'm putting on a second coat, I notice the driver of the car ahead of me bring her hand to her mouth as if she's doing the same. I drop the lip balm and take my foot off the gas. As my car slows and the distance between my Civic and its sister grows, I take deep breaths and try calm my suddenly racing heart.

I put on my blinker and move into the left lane. As I do, I look into the rear-view mirror and realize the car behind me is changing lanes at the same moment. Shit! I wave an apology, but she's waving too, so it must be okay. Then I see it. The car behind mine is another silver Civic.

I realize it's been too long since I looked out the front window. I snap my eyes forward and see that the car in front of me has also changed lanes. The driver looks tense. She's playing with her ponytail, wrapping her fingers around and around her long hair, then letting it go. Over and over again. I let go of my own hair and grip the wheel with both hands. The driver ahead of me does the same. I slow down and look back, trying to get a glimpse of the driver behind me, but she's turned around. My sweaty palms slip on the steering wheel and I turn the AC up full blast, which makes the purple graduation tassel hanging from my rear-view mirror dance.

340

The center lane is wide open. I move into it without signaling.

The other two Civics move in unison.

I swerve to the right lane, realize there's a car there and jerk the wheel back to center.

My shadows do the same.

I step on the gas, trying to get around the dented car in front of me, but I can't. She anticipates my every move, speeding up and zigzagging between lanes. One peek in the mirror tells me there are three of us playing this game. Soon we're doing 80 mph on a crowded highway, and I want to stop, but I don't know how. I stare into the rear-view mirror, willing the driver behind me to look at me, but she won't stop staring into her own mirror, her own graduation tassel swaying in the breeze. I tear my eyes away just as the semi-truck, two cars ahead, slams on its brakes. I scream and move my foot off the gas and lift my hand to press the horn to warn the driver in front of me to *stop stop stop* before it's too late, but all I hear is the sound of a horn blasting behind me before everything goes black.

Kitsune
By Stuart Riding

Scotland

You find yourself in a wood surrounded by bracken and undergrowth, the moonlight dappled between leafless branches. You are thereby mildly inconvenienced - pausing for a moment - but you soon untangle yourself and start moving. Moving on all fours.

On all four paws.

Fast. You are fleet-footed.

You pause again to look down at your fur ... dirty dark-auburn moonlit brown. You look back around at your off-white tail.

You think: Fox.

Again! Yes. We are going for a little walk, you think. Escaping a dim memory of vague, intangible threat you take yourself down to the beach. The moon's still out. It is low tide.

"So let's get this straight, you've been having these ..."

"Visions."

"Dreams."

"Well, the one last night was sort of a dream, yes. It was a vision I had whilst asleep, so, if you want to get technical about it ..."

"And always at the end of the dream you've been ... what ... waking up?"

"Dying."

"But it's never you - you're never 'you' in the dreams?"

"Visions. No, well, yes, I am me - but I know I'm not exactly myself. Like in other regular dreams; talking, walking, trying to get somewhere, playing football, etcetera ..."

You'd been hoping for a dog. You like dogs. Thinking about dogs last thing at night, head angled to your favoured left side on the pillow, but you never ended up as one. Foxes were surely the next best thing. Sleek and fast. You were beginning to enjoy it.

But then you glimpse a flicker, a memory that you fail to grasp hold of ...

You put it out of your mind without much difficulty. That's why you were down at the shore anyway. Darting fast along the river into the estuary, deep into the salt-marsh. Natural instincts take over for a while: running, skulking, hunting. You begin searching for crabs.

You dive paws - first into moon - shaped reflections in rock - pools. Lunge, bite, crack!

Mmm ... Spongy, hairy crabs.

"And ... how do you know this?"

"Well, it's usually obvious. For example, early this morning I was a fox. And the other day, in my dad's new 'movie' room - he's converted the spare room and filled it with old DVDs and VHS tapes - I was in the middle of *Das Boot* and the next thing I remember I was some kind of migratory sea-bird, a slender-billed curlew I think, judging by the length and curvature of my beak . . ."

"Oh. I see."

"Plus, we - that's myself and the rest of the flock - ended up in Egypt. And then we, almost, made it right over the Mediterranean."

"But, how did you know where you were?"

"I could see the pyramids."

Your appetite temporarily sated, growing more confident - forgetting recollections of "last time" altogether - you infiltrate the tip, stalk the graveyard and saunter down the high-street in the quarter-light of dawn. Instinct takes over and you go back to searching for food.

Proper food. From bins. No more of this seafood crap.

But your sense of direction is terrible, generally. You often get lost in new, unfamiliar environments even with a map. The fox has no map.

You try to make your way back to the carpark next to the beach, but you take a wrong turn and end up crossing some fields. You try to find the shoreline again to get your bearings and end up in more fields.

That's when you hear the pack of dogs.

"What do you mean, almost?"

"I remember the flock being - we were shot at - over an island. Maybe one of the Balearics. Or Minorca. Mallorca? One of those. It was terrible, losing folk left, right, and centre. Then they got me - sharp pain and then … falling. Falling and falling."

"And then - let me guess - you woke up?"

"That came secondary to the dying, yes."

"And the fox?"

"I've been doing some reading around that, actually. Research."

"Cunning."

"Did you know the Japanese believe foxes have magical shape-shifting powers and some of these Japanese foxes are thought to have three, six, or as many as nine tails? Get this: They have been known to possess humans! The greater the number of tails, the greater the powers of the all-seeing, omniscient fox."

"OK ... so, how many did you - I mean this Japanese fox - have?"

"One. Just one."

The sound of howling is getting closer.

You run for your life - you didn't see this coming at all - except ... except for those dim recollections of ... something both terrible and mysterious, uprooting you briefly to some distant recess of your inherited memory, then returning you, fleeing desperately into the present.

Now the memory is clearer.

Being pulled at, splayed and torn limb from limb by a pack of hunting dogs kept hungry for days, their overlords behind them: "The Unspeakable in Pursuit of the Inedible." You are the inedible.

"What if I'm possessed by a shape-shifting fox demon?"

"Unlikely. I think I know what's going here. I think you've got empathepsy."

"Shut up ... What do you mean?"

"Yeah, you had an empathetic attack. You've empathised so much with these poor creatures, you've actually become them for a little while."

"Shut up."

"Well, that's what you would have, were you not making it all up. Telling porkies. You'll probably be a pig next."

You wake up dirty and disoriented on the floor next to your bed, half-wrapped in your bedsheets. Arms and legs splayed out on every direction, your limbs and joints aching, the clammy smell of blood lingering in your nostrils, an acrid taste on your tongue and recriminatory accusations crossing swords in your mind.

You could never have saved that fox, you think. *It's not your fault.*

It's not your fault.

348

Compression: A Very Short Story
By Robert Perchan

South Korea/USA

I ran into H. at the Closerie. It was early in the afternoon. A gray winter day. He had his notebook and three sharpened pencils in front of him on the table. But he was staring off into space. He was not writing. He looked stumped. He had gotten a few words down. Maybe a whole line. But no more than that. He looked stumped. He had on that hat he sometimes wore when he wrote. But it looked a little bit too big for him today. It kept slipping down over his eyes and he had to push it back up again in order to stare off into space properly.

H. was a big man but he did not look quite so big today. Maybe he was having problems at home, I wondered. He was famous for having problems at home. No, he wasn't having problems at home. Wife's fine. So is the baby. It's this shirt. And these damn trousers. Too loose.

Good for the circulation, I said. Blood flow. Free flow of thoughts. Ideas. Impressions.

No, he said. Opposite. I got this iceberg inside me. Iceberg in my heart.

Maybe you should see a doctor, I said.

A doctor, he said. He looked down at the line in his notebook. If it was a whole line. No, he said. No. Tried that. It's this iceberg. This iceberg in my heart. Everything feels so compressed.

Go fishing then. Get out of Paris. Get out of town.

No, he said. No. Tried that too. It's this damn compression. It just comes over me. I'm fine one minute and sitting here writing and one word leads to another word and then boom - I get so damn compressed. It comes out of nowhere. Done. Finished. Look at me. Look at this hat. It's two sizes too big. And this shirt. And these trousers. Don't even look at my shoes. Don't look under the table. I used to have the biggest feet in Paris. If I get up and take two steps I'll walk right out of them. He moaned. He groaned. It all started, he said, with that six-word story business. I bet everybody I could best them. Write a whole story in only six words. Better story than anything they could come up with in only six words. And won. Hands down.

Sure, I said. I remember. I was here. *A clean, well-shaven place it wasn't.* I remember that.

No, he said. That wasn't it.

I tried again. But I couldn't remember well. We had all been drinking that afternoon. *Mendicant hits lottery. Farewell to alms.*

No, he said. That wasn't it either. Something about shoes. Baby shoes. Look at my feet. I could probably fit into them now. I get so compressed.

That's where it all started, I said. With those little six worders?

And then it spread, he said. To the real stories. About that summer up in Michigan. Compression everywhere. Can't escape it. I get so compressed.

It happens to everyone, I said. Sooner or later. Look at me. Ever seen anyone so compressed?

H. stared. Squinted and stared. Like he didn't even recognize me. Like he was trying to make out something that wasn't really there.

No, he said. Not like this. It's in my stories now. Look. Here. This one about Nick and his old man. The doctor. The pregnant squaw. Uncle George. The Indian father in the bunk overhead. It's gone. I can't see it anymore.

Indian Camp, I said.

That's it. Indian Camp.

He slid his notebook across the table. I looked down at the line. The handwritten words: *Boy goes. Blood flows. Father crows.*

That's compressed, I said. That's compression.

Full blown, he said. The worst kind. Can't shake it.

You need to decompress. You've erased your best ever story so far. Compressed it till it's nothing but six words.

Cut. I cut and cut. Can't help myself. And this damn iceberg in my heart. Compression. Twenty-nine pages down to seven pages down to less than a single line.

You've got to cut out all this cutting out, I said. Decompress.

Decompress, H. said. I can't. It's gone. I just can't see it anymore. He was staring off into space again. Almost like he had never really seen me at all.

Waiter, I said, and I raised two fingers. Absinthe. Deux. Your under the counter stuff. One for the gentleman in the too-big hat and too-loose shoes.

And one for the empty chair he's talking to.

The Salish Sea Zombie
By A.J. Rutgers

Canada

Cal-my-Ish-met-al squatted at low tide on the beach of the Salish Sea, and
with his hands he leveled a patch of sand. All night he had sheltered from
the rain under the train trestle with a small fire. He now watched as the
Canadian Coast Guard hovercraft dragged the young whale into
Semiahmoo Bay. The humpback had died on the beach, strangled in an
entanglement of fishing lines and nets.

The whale had beached himself on the Canadian side of the bay, where he succumbed to the inevitable. Many people from the seaside town of White Rock came to the beach to try to rescue him, but it was too late for Y'bo'm.

All day men, women, and children gathered by the carcass. The elders from the Semiahmoo Nation burned sage and performed a drum circle. Children placed flowers on Y'bo'm's head. Wasps swirled over his flesh. But Cal-my-Ish-met-al kept his distance, waiting for the proper time. He had more important work to do.

Samples of blubber were cut from Y'bo'm before they towed him into the bay. There they slipped the rope from their craft and let the cetacean drift to the ocean floor. Y'bo'm's body remained enshrouded in fishing lines and nets, and the rope trailed his carcass to the bottom.

Cal-my-Ish-met-al knew he had to act. He would have only one chance when the tide slacked and turned to flood. He sat by the cold June waters of the sea and from the back of his sandy altar he dredged a small canal down to the water. There the flooding tide would start to fill it and surround his magic and carry it to Y'bo'm.

Murmuring an incantation, he took his moose-hide satchel and shook it. Inside the beaded bag were ancient bones that had been handed down to him from his grandfather. Cal-my-Ish-met-al scattered them over his temporary altar. He lit some sage and leaned into the smoke, giving himself a smudge bath as he pulled the tendrils of smoke onto his chiseled face.

He had only seen this sign once before, when his grandfather told him to commit it to memory.

"If these bones ever show this pattern near the death of a whale," his grandfather had said, "then you must crush them, and burn them into a fire of sage and seagrasses and return them to the sea, close to the carcass of the whale, with the next flood and ebb."

Cal-my-Ish-met-al studied the divination, praying he has misread it. But the longer he sat on his haunches and stared at the sculpture on the sand, the more certain he was there had been no mistake. From his belt he slipped the hatchet he had used to cut the wood for his fire. Then on his altar he placed the large, flat rock he had carried with him from the train tracks. With the blunt end of the hatchet he began crushing the ancient bones. The sage smoke and his sadness for the loss of his lifelong talisman combined to flood his eyes with tears. He began to chant.

At dawn Cal-my-Ish-met-al sat on a polished driftwood log high on the beach. He stared at the flat Salish Sea and the flat grey sky and the flat sandy beach and wondered, *what have I unleashed?*

Part 2

Donny Holmstead sat in the back of the Grady White and fired another steely into the grey waters of Bute Inlet. It cut into the light chop with a zing and a bloop that you could hear over the hum of the trolling outboard motors. He glanced at Nick, the fishing lodge owner, who was sipping a whiskey soda.

"I'll take another if you're pouring," he said, as he reached down into the white plastic bucket on the floor of the boat and picked up another ball bearing. In his left hand he held a slingshot that extended over his wrist. Stretching the rubber band back behind his ear, he punted another steely high into the air. He followed its arc with his outstretched arm as it fell from the sky.

"Hold up your glass," said Nick, hoisting a bottle out of the built-in cooler under the bench seat.

Donny reached back and Nick poured, slopping some onto Donny's fingers. Donny set the glass down and licked his fingers clean, paying special attention to the three Stanley Cup rings on the gnarled digits of his right hand.

"Spillin' booze is bad fishing luck," he said with a grin.

"You get those three with the Canadiens?" asked Joe, the lead guide.

Donny stared at his rings and replied, "Yeah, these three with Montreal. These other two" - he gestured with the hand that held the slingshot - "were with Detroit."

"Seal," yelled Darrel, the boat's pilot. He pointed off the port side where a black, bulbous head bobbed some fifty feet from the boat. Donny took dead aim with the weapon and let it fly. The ball bearing thumped into the skull of the seal; blood spurted up like a clam spouting water on a beach. The seal sank below the water.

"He shoots! He scores!" Cheered the men.

The two women that Donny had brought with him both took another sip of their Smirnoff coolers and stared at each other.

"That's one who won't steal anymore salmon," said Nick. Seals were notorious for clamping onto hooked fish.

"Hey Joe, you play hockey?" asked Donny of the fishing guide. Joe was balancing on the gunwale of the craft. His arm was looped around a wire stay while his eyes scanned the four fishing rod tips looking for any sign of action.

"Just some pickup in the off season."

"Well, never play with a damn ring on. Once I went to glove a slap shot and that puck crumpled my wedding ring into my finger. They had to cut that

355

mangled band off my swollen finger with the skate sharpener at the rink. I finished the third period though, with a goal. Never worn a ring playing again. And I've been married three times." He winked at the two beauties as they curled up in the cushioned seats at the aft of the boat.

"Look, look," said Joe, pointing to one of the rods that started flattening from its hard bend. "We're getting some action. Once it goes slack I'll grab it, set the hook, and then hand it to you, Mr. Holmstead."

"Screw that," said Donny. "This ain't my first rodeo. I can set my own hook."

"No problem," said Joe backing away, his hands in the air, still smiling. He knew how to handle legends like Donny Holmstead.

Then the back port - side rod slacked straight. Donny lunged at it and wrestled the rod from the holder, jerking it back hard and reeling as fast as he could. He pulled again but it was obvious nothing was there. He had missed the hit. Now the starboard rod went slack and Darrel yelled from the flying bridge.

"Fish on!"

Joe grabbed the rod and jerked it hard once, reeled three times fast, then jerked the rod again. The line started to sing and the rod bent down hard.

"Got him," said Joe, as he adjusted the tension on the reel. "Here you go Donny."

Donny began working the fish as Darrel brought the boat to a stop. The three men - Nick, Joe, and Darrel - jerked up the other rods to dislodge them from their down-riggers and started reeling them in. They were well rehearsed. Donny kept working his fish.

"Feels like a big one."

The three experienced fishermen said nothing.

In the wake a silver fish rolled on its side and drifted to the boat.

"It's a beauty!" yelled Joe. Donny moved to the gunwale to get a look. "Keep your tip up. She's gonna run."

Donny lifted the rod as the salmon, spooked by the hull of the boat, jolted back to life and surged back into the depths. The reel screamed. Donny held the rod high, the tip pulsating in the afternoon sun, spray slinging off the line.

"Whoo*wee*!" he shouted.

The line slowed and Donny began wrestling his prize back to the boat. Darrel bumped the throttle to edge the Grady White around so the line was playing out from the side. Everyone focused on the water.

"There it is," one of the girls squealed. Just as she spoke, the fish jumped and danced on its tail, its head thrashing and the orange lure dangling near its jaw.

"Bet she's twenty pounds," said Nick.

"Twenty-five," said Darrel as he lit another smoke.

Donny grunted as he hauled back up on the rod. He was beginning to sweat.

The salmon now bobbed to the surface, it's snout poking above the water. The exhausted creature came to the side of the boat.

Joe shoved a net deep into the water. As the net came up the fish jumped again and did a headstand. Normally Joe would have backed off and let the prize dive deep under the boat, but since this was the first fish for Donny, he lunged deep and scooped the salmon into the net. A moment later, the fish hit the deck flopping.

Everyone cheered and shook Donny's hand.

"Congratulations. Nice fish."

"Pour me a drink," said Donny, lifting his baseball cap to wipe a hand over his bald dome, with its rim of scraggy blond hair.

Hoisting glasses, everyone toasted their success - all of them except Darrel, who studied his watch and surveyed the waters of Bute Inlet.

"We should be heading back."

"Back? Hell no. The fish are just starting to hit," said Donny.

"Well, you do have your presentation to do for the King Drug's staff back at the lodge," said Nick.

"Oh that. I'm not worried. They paid me already. So they can wait. Besides all I gotta do is jump on one of Vigor-fit's exercise machines. They just want me to wow the store managers with my celebrity. Let's keep fishing. We can be late. What's our daily limit?"

"Two," said Joe.

"All right, let's get one more. Then you boys can take me out again tomorrow."

"Okay, your call," said Nick. "But we can't take you out tomorrow. The Grady's booked. You'll be fishing with one of the guides in the Boston Whalers. It's a different experience; you're closer to the elements."

"Who's your best guide?"

"Depends what you want," said Joe, as he took a small wooden bat and thumped the salmon hard on the forehead. The Chinook jerked and flopped in the net, a small wound spilling blood onto the white anti-slip deck.

"Let's get a photo," said Joe. He handed the prize to Donny, who held it across his chest. The two women came to stand on either side of him, and Nick snapped some pictures.

"Both of the guides who could take you are pretty good," Joe continued. "But it's their personalities that you want to pay attention to. You'll be out on the water with them for twelve hours." He grabbed the salmon back from Donny and slipped it into the cold saltwater catch hold.

"There's Pacific Willy, who's a tree hugger type. Very meticulous, well organized, quiet guy who communes with nature. He has a real feel for where the fish are. Treats his catch with reverence. Then there's Shoeless Sean. Never seen anything like him. Goes barefoot year-round. He's a crazy bastard. Takes chances but gets fish. Has a quirk though - he hates mud sharks. So, if he catches one, he takes 'em and flips his trolling motor up and feeds it into the prop. Chews them into bloody bits and pieces, pretty crude."

"I'll take him," said Donny. "I like crazy."

With the rods set, the Grady White settled back into trolling. Donny and Nick poured more whiskey. Joe grabbed a bucket, leaned over the edge of the boat, and filled it with salt water. He sloshed the water onto the deck to wash the stringy fish blood down the floor drain. The smell of fish, motor

359

exhaust, and blood filled the cockpit. The Grady turned into the sun and trolled back towards Sonora Island.

Part 3

Down on the silted bottom of Semiahmoo Bay lay Y'bo'm. Strewn along either side of him were round, algae-matted crab traps, torn from their marker buoys by storms, their ropes now twisted around Y'bo'm's black, barnacle-encrusted corpse. Inside the traps lay pale, dead crabs. In a cruel twist of fate, each trap also held a few live red crabs that had crawled in to feed on the dead ones. Once they realized their error, they poked the tips of their claws through the netting and clung to Y'bo'm, pulling at his flesh in a vain attempt to escape.

As the rising full moon penetrated the murk, a stirring began. The crabs dug harder into the whale. Y'bo'm's black skin began to shimmer and change color. The barnacles on his back started to glow, and the dead crabs awoke in new eerie white shells. Y'bo'm began to move. His mighty tail shook and the towrope lashed the bottom of the bay like a sea serpent, kicking up plumes of mud. His large eyes flickered and, glowing red, opened.

The great creature twisted and tensed. Then, rising from the bottom, Y'bo'm thrashed his tail and pulled his pectoral fins to his body. Up he rose, and with one great convulsion broke through the surface. He was glowing white. The crab traps clung to him draining muddy water, and the white nylon lines and mesh trailed him like jewelry. He crested out of the sea and broached on his side - water, shrimp, and mussels spewing from his blowholes. He was moving. He had become Y'bo'm K'ic'd. He was possessed.

Out into the Salish Sea he surged, awakening to his new consciousness. He broached the surface and rediscovered his strength.

Into the Strait of Juan de Fuca plunged Y'bo'm K'ic'd. He bashed the rusted hulls of freighters that plied coal from Roberts Bank to the power plants of China. North he moved - up the Strait of Georgia - his mind beginning to focus on one all-consuming thought.

Revenge.

Revenge on those who had starved him. Revenge on those who had cut short his youthful life. Revenge on those who had robbed him of his soul. It was on these evil creatures that he would wreak his vengeance. The twirlers of lures, the twisters of hooked herrings, the dispersers of nylon mesh, these he would destroy.

Y'bo'm K'ic'd was in a rage. North he swam to the Discovery Islands. North to the Johnston Pass. North to the fishing grounds of Bute Inlet. Pity all those in his path, for Y'bo'm K'ic'd was unleashed.

Part 4

Donny stood on the dock in his red, full-body Mustang floatation suit, the zipper pulled up to his waist. His barrel chest prevented the jacket from cinching all the way up. For warmth he wore his new Tyee sweatshirt. The fishing lodge had given it to him because his salmon tipped the magical thirty-pound mark. That was rigged. They had shoved some fishing weights down the Chinook's throat before they weighed it. Nick wanted a photo for his celebrity wall.

Behind Stuart Island, the sky was glowing with the rising sun. In another hour it would crest the island's mountaintops and bathe the fishing lodge in warmth. Donny stared at the flotilla of Boston whalers that were skimming across the inlet. They were coming to gather the sport fishermen - the staff of King Drugs - who were congregating on the dock. The lodge supplied them with coolers and thermos bags full of lunches and snacks.

Cookies, chocolate bars, apples and oranges - but no bananas, as the guides considered them bad luck.

Donny stood alone, avoiding eye contact with anyone, not wishing to talk. He was hungover. Instead, he stared at the overlapping orange and purple starfish. They were cemented on the rocky ocean floor, almost fluorescent in the tidal stream. Around them carpets of seagrass blossomed and swirled like anemones. Now flowing south, though later with the changing tides they would turn north. Donny searched the faces of the incoming guides, trying to guess which one was Shoeless Sean. He picked him out right away: the cocky young kid who came in a bit faster than anyone else. He was standing in the back of his Boston Whaler.

"Mornin' Mr. Holmstead. Welcome aboard."

Donny went to load his cooler and thermos bag, but Sean interrupted him.

"You just step on board sir," he said. "Let the attendant hand me those. No use in us losing our lunch and beverages to the salt chuck when we have such fine-looking attendants to help." He winked at the cute blonde who had secured his stern line. She was now holding the bow tight to the dock so Donny could board. Donny had no problem with that; he was feeling a bit unsteady on his feet anyway.

Donny lowered his frame into the vinyl fishing chair and faced his young guide. Sean kept his banter going with the attendant as she handed him the thermos bag and cooler. As soon as the cargo was secure Sean unhitched the stern line from the dock cleat and nodded to the blonde, who then pushed off the bow. Once they were clear, he gunned it. The wake of the boat jostled the other Boston Whalers at the dock and everyone yelled at the young punk. Sean laughed and swiped back his greasy, long hair as he booted it south.

"I see ya already got yourself a big one," he yelled over the roar of the motor, gesturing at Donny's sweatshirt.

"Yeah, just barely," replied Donny. The wind in the speeding boat flapped the hood of his survival jacket over the back of his head. In the damp morning air Donny wished he had stayed in bed with his lovelies rather than being out here in the cold.

"Wanna coffee?"

"You got any whiskey for it?"

"I'm sure the lodge packed some for you," said Sean, as he throttled back on the motor to rummage through the insulated bag.

A few minutes later they were skimming over the rippled waters of the Yuculta Rapids, each sipping a "Poor Man's Irish." Donny began to cheer up.

"Where're we heading?"

"Well the tide's pretty slack at the moment. So, we're going to poke our nose into Hole in the Wall. With luck there are some Chinook feeding on the schools of herring trapped in the whirlpools. We can't stay long in there; once the tide turns that place is as crazy as any whitewater river in the world. Only worse, because them whirlpools suck down deadheads that will puncture any boat. This little Whaler wouldn't stand a chance. We'd get sucked right down 'em, never to be seen again."

"Sounds exciting."

"Sure is," said Sean, as he put on the sunglasses that were dangling around his neck. "And magnificent!"

The Whaler throttled back at the entrance to the pass.

"We'll prep our bait here, in calm waters. I see a few guys have beat us here."

Donny twisted around in his chair. To the west he could make out twelve or so fishing skiffs circling in the passageway.

From the side gunwales Sean pulled out two rods. They were already rigged with musket-ball-sized weights and hooks. He settled the rods into the holders and pulled enough line out so the weights rolled around at his bare feet. Reaching behind him he pulled out a small cutting board and from his vest pocket he produced a file. This was all part of the show.

"Ya gotta have sharp hooks. Salmon don't see very well and they'll graze up on your bait a few times before they hit. So when they do, you wanna make sure your hooks bite." He grinned at Donny and filed the hooks on each line with short rapid strokes. Then he opened the bait well beside him and plunged his hand into the cold water. Trapping a herring in his lightly clenched fist, he placed the fish on the cutting board. Pinching it hard in the spine behind its head, he continued talking.

"We'll just put one hook in for the time being. Later when we're trolling I'll use cut bait and then we'll use two hooks. But for now, I want this little fella swimming in distress. That's what attracts the salmon."

Soon he had both rods baited. Balancing the cutting board and bait on his lap, he throttled up his motor and entered Hole in the Wall.

The passageway was awe-inspiring, narrowing at first then widening. On the north side were the cliffs of Sonora Island and on the south the rising mountains of Maurelle Island. The waters were churning. Slow, giant, twisting whirlpools moved between the beds of kelp. Gulls and eagles screamed from the cliffs and seals lay on the rocks.

Sean maneuvered his boat into the current of one of the whirlpools. They joined a carousel of other boats circling the eddy.

"Okay," he said. "Grab that rod and I'll throw the bait in."

Donny did as he was instructed. Sean dropped the musket ball in the water and then lobed the squirming herring overboard. Peering over the side, he made sure the bait had the right action.

"All right, pull the line out about twenty-five pulls."

Donny pulled, the reel clicked. The musket ball swept down into the vortex, pulling its wounded cargo with it.

"Do the same to the other one." said Sean. He now focused on the other boats. The mangle of fishing lines converged into the center of the whirlpool.

"Don't they ever get tangled?"

"Sometimes, but if they do I'll cut 'em loose, and we'll bugger off and troll up the other side of Stuart in the sun. For now, we'll fish here."

Round and round the whirlpool they went. Donny began to feel sick.

"Ya know what," he said. "That sunshine is sounding pretty good. How about we pull up lines and head there?"

"You're the boss," Sean said, and he steered the boat out of the current and started winding in a line. Donny worked the other. When the bait appeared, Sean grabbed the line and swung it hard, whipping it around his fingers. With a clean jerk the herring flipped into the water.

"One for the fishing gods."

They fired up and headed for the calm waters.

—

The afternoon sun was beating down. Donny had removed his survival suit and Tyee sweatshirt. His burly white chest was turning pink in the first rays of a delayed summer. The two fishermen were puttering down the coastline with two rods bent over the side. Each was nursing a cold can of beer.

Donny lifted an eyebrow as a seal surfaced behind them.

"You got any slingshots?"

Sean beamed. "I got two," he said. He pulled out a tarnished bucket. "Not everyone is into busting seals."

Donny loaded and thwacked one off.

"Missed."

"I bet you'd like gull kiting," said Sean.

"What's that?"

"We used to do it on the seiners. We'd bait herring and hook gulls. Then as they flew away we'd tow 'em with the line like a kite. You could reel them in or let them fly high. When you got bored you'd jerk the hook out. It would pull their guts out and kill 'em. But who cared. It was funny."

Donny laughed and took a pull on his beer.

"So, tell me Sean, what's the biggest salmon you ever caught?"

"Forty-five pounder. Last fall. It was close to where we are. Had a lady on board - Carol-Anne something. Well, we fought that fish for over two hours. She was great. Bet she sweated off ten pounds in that fight."

"Wow, I'd sure like to catch something like that. Wonder what the biggest one ever caught was."

"Oh, it was a ninety-three pounder up in Alaska on a rod and reel. Commercial guys have gotten bigger - around a hundred and twenty pounds. Couldn't imagine catching somethin' like that. It'd be awesome."

"Well there doesn't seem to be anything here."

"Don't sweat it," said Sean. "The tide is turning. They'll ride in with the schools of bait on the flood. I'll turn on the radio and see if there's any chatter from the other guys." He reached down and turned on the small marine-band radio bolted under his seat. Some garbled voices cackled to life. Sean listened for a few moments, his ear tuning to the speech. Donny couldn't understand a goddamn thing they were saying.

"Jesus. Everyone's still talkin' about it."

"What?"

"Ah, strange shit. Started last night in the Gulf islands. A long-line fisherman had all his lines stripped clean from his boat. I mean every single one. That stuff is like piano wire. Whatever he snagged it on, it ripped it clean off his gear. Then farther north a seiner had his nets shredded. Never heard of such a thing. And this morning the talk was a big commercial trawler got his nets demolished."

"What do ya think it is?"

"Don't know. Submarines maybe. The Americans are always prowling these waters. Maybe a flotilla of them on exercise. They won't bug us though. They'd travel up Discovery passage for Johnston Strait."

"That's good," said Donny. "Want another beer?"

"Ooh!" cried Sean, stiffening in his seat as the starboard rod suddenly went slack. "We got a hit."

Donny dropped his can and snagged the rod. The foam from the beer spewed out on the bottom of the boat, mixing with the bilge water. He jerked hard, reeled and then jerked hard again.

"Nothing."

"No, no. Keep reeling. Fast."

Donny started turning hard, and after a few seconds he felt it. He jerked the rod again and it took off. The line streamed out of the reel.

"Jesus Christ!" yelled Sean. "Have you got a seal?"

The line slowed and Donny started the rhythm - pulling up and reeling down.

Five, ten minutes he pulled and reeled. Then off the stern something rolled and flashed silver in the water.

"There she is. It's a giant," said Sean as a silver tail flopped for a second on the crest of the wake.

The game was on. Sean reeled in the other rod and stowed it.

Donny's reel was chattering out more line. Ten minutes later he was still reeling.

"I don't think he knows he's hooked," said Sean.

"I'd just like to see him. Make sure it's not a seal."

"Oh, it's not a seal. I saw it. It's a fish all right. Maybe a halibut, but they're pretty rare in these parts."

An hour they fought and wrestled, reeling in, only to have the line play out again. Donny's chest dripped streams of sweat. Then the line went slack.

"I think I lost him."

"No keep reeling. He's turned towards us," said Sean, revving the engine to get tension back in the line. Then through the churn it appeared. It was a salmon. A big one. The biggest one Sean had ever seen. His voice blasted with excitement.

"Holy Cow. It's a monster. And you've snagged him in the side. That's why he's so hard. You can't turn him." Sean leaned into Donny and grabbed his knee, his hand vibrating. "This is gonna take a lotta skill. Ya can't bully him. You'll have to play him out."

Two hours later they were still working the rod. The fish had towed them back towards the entrance to Hole in the Wall. They were no longer in the sunshine; the mountains of Maurelle Island now cast them in shade. It would not be dark for many hours here in the North Country in mid-June, but in the mountain shadows a chill crept back into the air. Donny didn't feel it. He just kept reeling.

Sean looked nervously at the passage entrance and feathered the prop to keep the line taut. He didn't dare try to drag the catch too hard. He prayed it would tire. They couldn't go back into Hole in the Wall, not with the tide running. White water gushed from the pass. Where they had baited the hooks that morning, the water now boiled in six-foot chops that held no rhythm, just chaos.

Come on fish, he thought. *Give up.*

As if by command, Donny suddenly found it easier to pull the rod up.

"I think we're winning." He announced.

Sean grabbed his net. "I hope he fits."

Donny grinned back at him.

The fish surfaced, its nose and fin breaking the chop. The hook was lodged in the flesh just in front of its dorsal fin. Donny gently lifted and reeled down. The fish gyrated and squirmed away from the boat, running on the surface and looking like it was going up a river. Sean throttled the motor and pulled him back. They were getting close.

He glanced at the pass; logs from the spring runoff were shooting into the bay. Then from the froth something gushed. Something was thrashing through the foam. Y'bo'm K'ic'd had arrived.

Part 5

The rain pattered on the trailer roof like metal brushes on a snare-drum. Farther back on the other side of the kitchen large droplets spilled from the cedar boughs and plunked onto the tarp that patched the roof above the bedroom, providing the tempo bass.

In the living room Cal-my-Ish-met-al sat in meditation. Beside him crackled a cedar fire in his scavenged cast-iron stove. Surrounding him

370

were shelves of mason jars full of herbs, minerals, and dried animal parts. In the windows hung dream catchers. And from a place of honor on the wall glared a wooden mask with two eagle feathers drooping over hollowed black eye holes. The mask was trimmed at the top with horse's tail hair that cascaded down and framed it in grey and black. At the bottom a red-painted mouth screamed out.

Through the din of the November rain, Cal-my-Ish-met-al heard a metallic rap on the aluminum door. He rose, his knees cracking. He had aged in the six months since he had sacrificed his talisman.

He opened the door and before him stood a man in bare feet. He wore a red coat that was slick from the rain, the long sleeves pulled down past his hands. From below a drenched baseball cap a voice asked, "You the shaman?"

Cal-my-Ish-met-al closed his drooping eyelids and nodded. Stepping back, he allowed the man in.

"I will make some tea," he said. And he turned to his kitchen.

The man stepped up into the musky trailer and seated himself on the worn couch. He did not remove his hat or jacket.

Cal-my-Ish-met-al plugged in the kettle and threw two teabags into his teapot.

"Why do you seek me?"

"I'm told you know about incantations and evil beings."

Cal-my-Ish-met-al took a jar from his shelf and grabbed a twist of the dried abdomens of yellow jackets. He tossed them into the teapot. He knew it would be a long night.

"I have some knowledge."

"Then let me tell you a tale," said the man.

Shuffling in his kitchen, Cal-my-Ish-met-al assembled mugs, honey, and milk on a tray. Finally, he poured the boiling water into the teapot, placed it on the tray, and carried it to the coffee table. Bending down he grabbed some split wood and poked the pieces into the stove. His grey hair fell over his brow as he stirred the embers. By then, the stranger was already deep into his story.

"We had that Chinook right up against the boat, half in the net, and water sloshing everywhere. Then something thumped us from behind. We turned and the beast was upon us." He paused while Cal-my-Ish-met-al settled himself into a stuffed chair.

"I tell ya I never seen anything like it. It was white, with red eyes, and all over it was a veil of debris: hooks, metal, and crab traps. It was fearsome."

Cal-my-Ish-met-al poured some tea, the aroma wafting through the room.

"The handle of the net that salmon was in somehow got twisted into the gunwales. We were stuck with a huge chinook thrashing in the water beside us. But now we had to face that beast. We gunned the motor, but it was faster, rising up on the stern of the boat. So, we pivoted the motor up outta the water, the propeller slicing at the monster like a weed whacker. Chunks of flesh or something flying into the air."

Cal-my-Ish-met-al blew on his tea, and a wasp abdomen spun on the surface. He took a sip. The man continued.

"That devil slipped back into the water, then raged at us again. He broached out and towered above us, pivoting in the air. I tell ya I saw his blowholes. I stared right down his mouth. Right down his baleen. It was like a venetian blind of razor blades. I just started punching. That was the last thing I remember."

"What do you want of me?"

"I came to in the hospital in Campbell River. I told them my story but no one believed me. They said we were swallowed by a whirlpool. Knocked silly by deadheads. But I know what I saw." He bent his head. "I was the only one to survive. You have to tell me if such a thing could exist."

Cal-my-Ish-met-al took another sip of his tea. "I know of your demon," he said. "They call him Y'bo'm K'ic'd. He is not evil. But he was too young. It was my mistake."

"*Your* mistake?"

"Yes. It was I who summoned back his soul. I did not learn until later that the young ones are not suited for this task. It was my error."

"Then you understand him."

"Yes, I suppose I do. More than any other human being."

"Then you can help me hunt him."

"Hunt him? Why would you want to hunt him?"

"So, I can kill him," he said, reaching for his tea, the sleeves on his coat sliding back and exposing his hands. On his left, just a thumb and pinky finger remained. On his right, a metal hook.

"And gut him. And get my rings back," said Donny.

God Appears to the Fisherman
By Matthew Stephen Sirois

USA

He slid open the plate glass door, glancing toward the Band-Aid he'd stuck at eye-level to remind his wife the door is shut and please don't attempt to walk through it again. He strolled down to the water, the bite of morning on his bare arms, dew wetting his feet. He thought about plane crashes, house fires that start at night, and death by chronic illness. He lit a cigarette. This was how Bob began his days.

The lake lay flat and still, the yawning entrance to a mirror dimension. Every waterfront home, each individual tree, every cloud, bird, rock, and bug in Bob's universe was met by its inverted double on the other side. The island, not a football field's length from where Bob smoked, appeared to be suspended in null space - its own, tiny planet - with a tall tree and eagle's nest on its North Pole and a tall tree and eagle's nest on its South. His cigarette had only half burnt but he took a good, long pull and snapped it off the pad of his thumb and watched it arc over the water and heard it go *tsss* and saw it float there like a scratch on glass. Bob returned very slowly to the house.

Heather was drunk, or near enough to it. She'd poured her second tumbler of vodka, a hint of tomato juice stirred in as a formality - a nod to her biological need for food - at only seven in the morning. Heather had risen before the sun to do her hair and her makeup, heavy and dark as raccoon markings. Her face was now a screen print, maybe a rubbing, of the subtler version she'd worn thirty years ago when they'd met.

Thirty years since Bob found himself sleeping in an Air Force barrack in some throwaway cow pasture county in Great Britain. If you dissected a very fine whiskey and reduced it to its soggy, elemental parts, it would

375

smell just like that town. Heather had been another late blooming, chicken-legged teenager on a one-speed bicycle outside the pub. The tallish one who looked like a toothy Audrey Hepburn. Heather was bashful when Bob asked her to dance, though proved to be the better dancer. All the pilots assumed first pick of the local girls and good for them, but Bob had found her. Bob was too lanky for a pilot, his blood pressure too low. Bob was just a greaser-turned-flight-mechanic from a Maine lake town. He'd shot billiards and cruised drive-ins and, maybe, laconically, charmed a couple women - but he'd never gotten so lucky as this. He took Heather to a barstool and talked to her and Heather's rural accent in his ears was like a well-bred hen getting plucked. It filled out Bob's standard issue pants and she laid a hand right there, teasing him, looking away and back again with her big, wide, smoky eyes.

Heather robotically put his bacon and his coffee on, dropped two white planks down the toaster slots. She did it all with one hand because the other was clubbed around her drink. There was nowhere to go that day and the nearest neighbor was half a mile but as Bob walked into the kitchen Heather set down her medieval eyelash device and hung two glass bobbles from the worn slits in her ears. She said, "Coffee, Bob."

"Thank you, dear."

He pulled a porcelain cup, all flaking gold leaf and baroque filigree, from its place among the surviving tea service and half-filled it from the antique percolator. Reaching into an adjacent cupboard, Bob grabbed the opened bottle from a case of Bushmills and topped off his coffee with this. He took two ice cubes from the bin in the freezer and dropped one in his coffee to cool it a touch, the other in Heather's vodka. This was such an old gesture that even Bob couldn't remember whether it was affectionate or critical.

Heather gave an obligatory smile but didn't glance away from her affected newspaper-reading pose. A cigarette perched on the edge of a green glass tray, leaking a smoke trail through the air between them, gradually giving over to ash like an hourglass falling empty.

"That asshole Bush is sending more troops over," she told him, pronouncing 'asshole' using a soft A and a rounded-off L that sounded more like a W or like nothing at all. "Those poor boys ..."

"Poor boys," he scoffed. "Those boys are keeping your gas cheap, Heather."

"My brother says they pay ten pounds the liter, back home. They get by."

"Your brother works for BMW. He could pay twenty."

Bob sipped his coffee, glanced at the sports insert like a kid at his homework, topped off his cup again. He lit a cigarette and tried to enjoy the acidic warmth of hot whiskey in his stomach, but it would take a few more ounces to really help. He looked at his wife, seemingly engrossed in the front section, and imagined a dark, fist-sized cavity within his body. A round socket, with edges like a charred fire log left overnight in the rain. Where the infatuation had first caught, heating him in his bunk as Bob endured the breathlessness of other soldiers' farts and the rude, romanceless noise of other soldiers' jokes. The fluttering and panting of nights he'd taken Heather into the hay bales, put her skirt up and seen the long, pale slats of her thighs in the moonlight, smooth as sheets of paper.

Bob thought if he could stick a finger in there, the imagined cavity, it would feel wet and gnawed-at, like a melon rind. If every repressed emotion was a substance like flesh, he could mold an organ to fit that hole. Lust, pride, brief intervals of joy. His first panic at the sound of small artillery fire, maybe, and the broad, dull sorrow of his mother's death. A memory of diving from the high rock as a boy, narrow and beautiful, cutting the water like an angel of careless light.

"The kids are coming up today, don't forget," said Heather, eyes on her fingernails, maybe the faux-marble counter. Her hair rose off her forehead like a confection made in a lab.

"Okay." Taking a hat from the rack, taking his bottle. "I'll be in by noon."

Bob untied the boat and pushed it down the dock a few feet, cradling the half-full Bushmills in one elbow as he set his moccasin on a grip-taped gunwale. The boat dipped as he stepped lightly onto its deck, a bit of old reflex moving his hips just so. Bob could always get himself on or off a boat, however laden, however tipsy, whatever weather prevailed. He set his bottle in a cup holder and hit the ignition on the Crestliner. A red and white pleasure cruiser, it looked like the boat his dad had owned when boats looked like cars and cars looked like something from Flash Gordon. The engine lit up and Bob popped it into reverse with the gummy, rubber shifter. He backed the shining lozenge of a machine onto the lake and took a quick hit of Bushmills. Rocking and idling, the fifty horsepower Evinrude waiting for his command. The house already small on the hill. Heather might be up there, gazing down with a judgmental smirk, but probably not. Bob pushed the throttle forward and the boat surged, hugging an upholstered seat against his slight ass. The bow lifted and kicked up a white double-wake as he tore through the calm.

It was early enough that no one competed for the water. A couple of orange-vested hippies in kayaks entering the channel a mile away, but otherwise only Bob and the birds. He took a turn around the island just for sport, just burning some cheap gas from some war-stricken foreign oilfield. He enjoyed the feeling of inertia on his body as he cut the wheel from port to starboard, if those terms even applied on a tiny, land-locked pond like this one. Eventually Bob set out for the deep north end, the trout and salmon grounds, tilting the whiskey high and driving like a teenager.

The one rod was already fitted with a rattle-trap minnow and set in its holder, dragging the plastic bait at about five feet down and fifteen yards behind. Bob fumbled with the downrigger and the other pole, eventually getting his live bait to pull along, thirty feet down and also a good span from the noisy motor. No telling if the fish were sunning or laying low, so best to work both angles. It was more tackle than most guys would want to keep tabs on while driving, but it was Bob's method and he landed a handful of decent fish every season for the practice. *The Gazette* once ran a black-and-white of Bob with a trophy-sized pike and a smile on his face, but he hadn't bothered to clip out the photo and save it. He'd thrown the pike back alive, since the damned things were next to inedible.

The wheel was locked to troll him in a wide circle, letting Bob sit in the rear-facing passenger chairs and chain-smoke, sip his Bushmills, watch his poles. He could see the orange leaders flashing out beyond the riffle of his wake. He considered, not optimistically, what might be down there today.

Heather was most likely phoning up the propane guy, Harold, on the pretense that winter was coming and they'd need to lock in a decent price. "How's the bachelor's life?" Bob could hear her saying, cradling the receiver like a casual habit.

"Oh, I'll take care of ya, Heather," Harold would say. "I got a separate pricing sheet for beautiful fishing widows. Give Bob my best, if ya see him."

And the kids were coming. Bob and Heather had two daughters, but only one of them produced what anyone at the VFW would call a "family." They all piled into a wood-paneled station wagon at quarter-annual intervals - the Catholic daughter, the gruff factory worker husband, their precocious, mouthy kids - to drive two hours north and eat Bob's food and tear up the museum-like décor and just generally pry. Still, Bob loved his youngest daughter, his prettiest daughter, and he loved her kids. He was even getting on better with the thick-necked, brazen, son-of-an-Army-engineer guy she'd somehow married. They were all fine-and-well. What tried his patience was interacting with anyone while Heather held court. "Oh, Bob's

379

been out there, trapping raccoons like a sadist," she'd say. "Bob's got it in his head that we need a four-wheeler ... Bob's spending our money on ..."

The surface line jerked and Bob just caught the snap of the rod in his peripheral. He waited for the thing to bounce several more times before lifting the rod out of its brace and testing the weight of whatever was biting. Not a tremendous pull, but the fish gave good fight and Bob felt it in his arm, tightening his muscles and bulging his veins as he reeled. Bob had a tactile memory for fish, and he semi-consciously identified his quarry before it ever came into view. Smallmouth bass or yellow perch. A few more tugs, a tension adjustment on the reel.

Pickerel or yellow perch. The fish dove and Bob let it run for a moment, thinking, white perch or yellow perch.

When he landed the yellow perch, Bob let it dangle over the motor mount for a good minute. The ugly, useless animal hung by its jaw bone - a three-pronged hook having torn through the semi-translucent flesh of its gaping mouth. Spines rose from its back and around its gills, rising and falling, seeming to breath although the animal itself was drowning in air. Its eyes were like black marbles, each with a film of whitish organ sliding across and back over the surface, wiping at nothing, operating like broken elevator doors. The tail thrashed and subsided, thrashed and subsided.

Bob stuck a cigarette in his mouth and lit it, pulled a work glove onto his right hand. He grabbed the fish carefully by the fore-end, pressing its spines back against its own skin, and then worked the hook out of its jaw with a pair of pliers. He held it up, regarding the animal for a moment. Its gills sucked at the not-water, its eyes glazing in the unfiltered light. The yellow perch was a hapless thing and would strike at any bait.

Bob raised the fish up and then smashed it, brutally, against the case of his outboard motor. The perch's body went skipping off into the engine wake, later to be snatched by an osprey, but it left a slight mist of blood and brain matter on the outboard. This was Bob's grass roots environmental campaign, culling an invasive species. A junk fish. Bob had barely exhaled when the other rod started singing.

Again, the bait came up in the mouth of a yellow perch, and again Bob dislodged his tackle and then smashed its brains out. He took a good haul off the Bushmills and reset both rods, eyeing the ospreys who were now gathering, circling above. The morning was getting on, but little traffic came to that end of the lake. No kayakers in view, and the few houses on the waterfront sat dark and shrouded by trees. Again, the surface-riding lure was hit, and again Bob euthanized the idiotic perch that had struck it, taking his ill luck to heart and squinting through tobacco smoke. He was drunk, now, and beginning to revel in the rubbery bounce of fish-bodies off the motor. The downrigger brought one up, and then the surface rod again, and SMACK! he drove each spiny, flailing body against the metal housing, a whole harem of birds now picking up his gruesome leavings. The white enameled shell of the motor dripped with red and orange fluids. Reels whining and the bottle running low. Over bird-chatter Bob barely heard the downrigger drawing an entire spool of line.

The breeze froze, like a glass box had been lowered over the county. Bird cries died away and even the Evinrude coughed out and halted. The boat rode its own wake in one, final heave and then fell still. Yet the downrigger continued to squeal, as if a whale had hooked itself and run for the polar sea. One hundred yards of line. Two hundred yards of line.

Bob stubbed his smoke on his moccasin heel and looked for the shore. He couldn't seem to find it.

All at once the line stopped whirring and the lake surface frothed like spaghetti water. A wide bulge formed just twenty feet from Bob's Crestliner and bubbled and groaned, iridescent yellow and rising. The birds were already gone and the clouds dispersed and a row of great spikes rose from the troubled water like suspension bridge struts. Desiccated skeletons of men adorned them, hung like weeds, caught upon the cartilaginous barbs by their wrist joints and clavicles. Bob clutched his whiskey to his heart, for he knew the thing that rose from the lake was God and could only be God.

Its true mass finally showed above the pondweeds and shimmer of the water, hovering, too large to view all at a time. An armor of scales, each one the size and color of a rusted pickup truck, coated with cloudy mucus. Gills as large as barns. God's two eyes surveyed His kingdom independently as a chameleon's do, a hint of His duality, and His nictitating membranes sloshed away the lake water in torrents. His mouth opened and shut, opened and shut, with daylight shining through.

Bob set his bottle down on the bucking deck of the boat. He could see the downrigger line leading up into God's mouth, the hook stuck so preciously in an upper corner of God's lip. Bob thought of his grandchildren first, and then on back through the chronology of his life. His own kids, his wife, his years in the Air Force, and his childhood. When this was finished, he wondered why there wasn't more.

God raised a spiny fin, broad as an entire jet plane, and plucked Bob from the deck of his sports car of a boat. The deck flew away beneath Bob's feet, and the cold, bony structure that had grasped him tightened as his smallish mass began to slip. Bob looked down from that height, clutched in God's wet fin, upon the blood-and-brain-spattered Evinrude motor so very far below. The deity raised Bob to Its eye.

"Hey!" said God, in a small, far-off voice. The voice of a young woman. Bob began to detect that the world was turning in circles.

"Hey!" cried God, once more.

Bob's crotch was wet and cold, as if he'd pissed himself quite some time ago. His legs were splayed out in the rear of the boat and he'd slid almost completely from his backward-facing seat. The motor still chugged steadily but was wrenched all the way to port side, leaving the boat turning in tight, counter-clockwise doughnuts just fifty yards from shore. Bob's downrigger and poles were bent, clustered, fishing line having wrapped around them and the boat's wheelhouse and cinched all together in a taught, green web. An empty hook dangled before his face as Bob opened one eye, cautiously, squinting into the brightness of the lake going by.

Two kayaks panned through his field of view as the boat made another slow revolution. Two orange vests, casually unfastened to admit the breeze. Sun-ruddy faces that looked at Bob like a stumbled-upon cadaver.

"I don't know," he heard the girl say to her partner, as they both spun out of sight. "It might be too late to help him."

The Authors

Ridge Carpenter ("Yamanba" and "The Haunted Still") is a Seattle-based illustrator and strength trainer. His love of the supernatural developed in conjunction with his other childhood passions, reading and drawing. He continues to share all three interests with his two brothers (also illustrators), and until now their twice-yearly competitive ghost - story readings—usually held at Christmas and Walpurgis - had served as the only forum for his uncanny fiction. "Yamanba" and "The Haunted Still" are his first two published stories.

Barry Charman ("Palette") lives in North London. He has been published in various magazines, including *Ambit*, *Firewords Quarterly*, *The Literary Hatchet*, and *Popshot*. He has had poems published online and in print, most recently in *Leading Edge* and *The Linnet's Wings*. He has a blog: barrycharman.blogspot.co.uk

Kristin J. Cooper ("The Tattibogle") was born in Brisbane, Australia, and now lives in Aberdeenshire, Scotland where she writes stories, novels, and poetry in her spare time. In 2008 she wrote and co-produced the short film *Carnies* and went on to write film scripts for development and production. Several of her short stories have been published in horror and fairytale anthologies. She finds inspiration in myths, legends, fairytales, and the wild Scottish countryside, especially on cold dark nights by the fireside.

CL Dalkin ("A Brief Respite") is a school librarian living on the south coast of England with her son, husband, and very round cat. She stands on the beach every morning, no matter what the weather, and looks out to sea. She can't stop reading, and writing, and believes there is no known cure for this, other than to keep doing what she is doing. "A Brief Respite" won the 2016 Screw Turn Flash Fiction Competition.

Dessa ("Left of Heaven") is a musician, a writer, and a proud member of the Doomtree hip hop collective. She splits her time between Minneapolis, Manhattan, and a rented tour van. *My Own Devices,* her first hardcover collection of essays, will be published by Dutton Books in September 2018.

Janice Egry ("A Well-Urned Talent") writes poetry, short stories, non-fiction, children's stories, novels, and novellas, some of which have won prizes and/or have been published. She resides in Dutchess County, New York with her jazz pianist husband and two cats, Piccolo and McKenna. In "A Well-Urned Talent," the partial lyrics to the song "If You Could" ("If you could, would you be my love for all time...") are excerpted from a complete song of the same name by Donald C. Egry.

Rebecca Emanuelsen ("Wilbur") is a Michigan writer whose short stories have appeared in *Shimmer*, *Sugared Water*, and elsewhere. She is currently at work on a novel.

New York City native **Gene Bryan Johnson** ("Negroes Anonymous") has been a journalist, composer, interactive movie producer, and creator of documentaries exploring neuroscience and philosophy. He now lives in Mountain View, California, where, as managing partner of transmedia research and development at HazelEye MEDIA, he dreams about the day after tomorrow with his daughter, cultural industries scholar and singer/songwriter Rebecca Lee Johnson. GBJ has a degree in cultural reporting from Columbia University's Graduate School of Journalism and an undergraduate degree in humanities and creative writing from New York University. "Negroes Anonymous" won the summer 2016 Ghost Story Supernatural Fiction Award.

Carie Juettner ("Hindsight") is a teacher, poet, and short story author in Austin, Texas. Her work has appeared in *Daily Science Fiction*, *Nature Futures*, and *Hello Horror*, among other places. Carie was born on Halloween and has always had a passion for the weird, creepy, and unsettling. She invites you to read more of her work on her blog, Carie Juettner (cariejuettner.com).

Kevin McCarthy ("Holy Rollers") is originally from Minnesota, but now lives in Finland, which isn't too weird because he does enjoy snow and lakes and not talking to strangers. He recently graduated from the University of Helsinki with an MA in English philology, whatever that is. He teaches middle-school English and is currently writing a TV show about a b-team of socially inept paranormal investigators contracted to purify a possibly haunted historic hotel located on the shore of Lake Minnetonka.

Mindy McGinnis ("Solitude") is an Edgar Award-winning novelist who writes across multiple genres, including post-apocalyptic, historical, mystery, fantasy, and contemporary. Her titles include the Gothic historical *A Madness So Discreet*, which is set in an insane asylum, and a fantasy duology - *Given to The Sea* and *Given to the Earth*. "Solitude" won the 2017 Screw Turn Flash Fiction Competition.

Petra McQueen's ("Fog") writing has appeared in *The Saturday Evening Post*, *The Guardian*, *YOU* Magazine, *Writers' Forum*, *Cabinet des Fées*, and *Earthlines* among many other publications. She has won several prizes for her fiction, including first prize in the National Association of Writers' Groups Short Story Competition. She taught at Essex University and now runs a company offering creative writing events and assessments (thewriters company.co.uk). She is currently working on a novel.

Emma Murtagh ("Tongues") is a writer based in Galway, Ireland. She is a project manager at a non-profit and likes to write stories and poems in her spare time. Emma loves books and has a Master's Degree in Literature and Publishing from the National University of Ireland, Galway. Growing up, Emma was fascinated by Irish superstition and folklore and is working on a novel set in this world.

Melanie Napthine ("A Community Service Announcement") lives and writes in Victoria, Australia. She has won several national writing competitions, and was short listed for the Dundee International Book Prize in 2015. She is currently at work on a novel. In her professional life, she is a publisher at an educational publishing company.

Kurt Newton's ("The Coal Mape") fiction has appeared in numerous publications, including *Weird Tales, Space and Time, Dark Discoveries, The Best of Not One of Us, Year's Best Body Horror 2017,* and *Year's Best Transhuman SF 2017.* He is the author of two novels, *The Wishnik* and *Powerlines,* and several collections of poetry. He is a lifelong resident of Connecticut. "The Coal Mape" won the 2018 Screw Turn Flash Fiction Competition.

Robert Perchan's ("Compression: A Very Short Story") poetry chapbooks are *Mythic Instinct Afternoon* (2005 Poetry West Prize) and *Overdressed to Kill* (Backwaters Press, 2005 Weldon Kees Award). His poetry collection, *Fluid in Darkness, Frozen in Light* won the 1999 Pearl Poetry Prize and was published by Pearl Editions in 2000. His avant-la-lettre flash novel, *Perchan's Chorea: Eros and Exile* (Watermark Press, Wichita, 1991) was translated into French and published by Quidam Editeurs (Meudon) in 2002. In 2007 his short-short story "The Neoplastic Surgeon" won the on-line *Entelechy: Mind and Culture* Bio-fiction Prize. He currently resides in Pusan, South Korea. You can see some of his stuff on his website, robertperchan.com.

John Reaves ("A Ghost of a Smell"), a retired English professor, is the co-author of a nonfiction book published in hardcover by Henry Holt and in paperback by HarperCollins. He has published three other short stories, one of which won a national contest. He lives in the foothills of the Great Smoky Mountains with his wife, Candance W. Reaves, a poet.

Stuart Riding ("Kitsune") is a teacher, writer and nature-lover based in Edinburgh, Scotland.

Rebecca Ring ("A Nearly Perfect Five by Seven") was born in Colorado, came of age in California, married and had children in Quebec, and now writes and teaches in Utah. She has degrees in film and education and an MFA in Writing from Vermont College of Fine Arts. For the past seventeen years she has made annual visits to the cemetery with her fourth-grade students. To her knowledge, she has never lost one.

A.J. Rutgers ("The Salish Sea Zombie") is from White Rock, British Columbia, and has been a fiction writer for two decades. He won a Flash Writing contest for his story, "Farming," and for his story, "The Loon Spirit Totem," he placed second in a short-fiction writing contest in the on-line community "Becoming a Writer." He's currently at work on a novel titled *Mule*. Noting that Bob Dylan, in his acceptance speech for the Nobel Prize in Literature, spoke about the impact Herman Melville's *Moby Dick* had on his writing career, Rutgers says he intended "The Salish Sea Zombie" as "a humble salute to Bob Dylan and as an homage to Herman Melville." He adds, "As a fun aside I have included a homophone of a phrase and a palindrome that references *Moby Dick*. I hope the skilled reader will appreciate the puzzle." "The Salish Sea Zombie" won the fall 2017 Ghost Story Supernatural Fiction Award.

Scott Loring Sanders ("Moss Man") is the author of two novels, an essay collection, and a short story collection called *Shooting Creek and Other Stories* which includes "Moss Man." His work has twice been chosen for *Best American Mystery Stories*, noted in *Best American Essays*, and published in a wide array of journals and magazines ranging in scope from *Creative Nonfiction* to *Ellery Queen Mystery Magazine* to *North American Review*, among many others. He teaches creative writing at Emerson College in Boston and at Lesley University in Cambridge. For more information or to contact him, go to scottloringsanders.com.

JL Schneider ("Bubs & Johns") was a carpenter and an adjunct professor of English at a small community college in upstate New York. He won the 2015 *Fiction Southeast* Editor's Prize, and his fiction has also appeared in *Snake Nation*, *The Newport Review*, *The MacGuffin*, *International Quarterly*, *New Millennium Writings*, and *Bacopa Literary Review*, among other publications. He was nominated for a Pushcart Prize for fiction in 2013 and for nonfiction in 2014. Jeff Schneider died in January 2018. "Bubs & Johns" won the fall 2016 Ghost Story Supernatural Fiction Award.

Matthew Stephen Sirois' ("God Appears to the Fisherman") fiction and essays have appeared in *The New Guard Review*, *Split Lip Magazine*, *Necessary Fiction*, *The Ghost Story*, and elsewhere. His debut novel, *Near Haven* (Belle Lutte Press, 2017) received the bronze medal for Northeast Fiction from *Independent Publishers Magazine*, and is a Foreword INDIE Award finalist in both Literary and Science Fiction. Matthew lives with his wife and daughter in western Massachusetts, and works as a metal fabricator. Contact info and writing links can be found at matthewstephensirois.com.

Daniel Soule ("The Lostling") was an academic, but the sentences proved too long and the words too obscure. Although Northern Ireland is where he now lives, he was born in England and raised in Byron's home town, which the bard hated but Dan does not. They named every other road after Byron. As yet no roads are named after Dan - but several children are. He tries to write the kind of stories he wants to read and aims for readers to want to turn the page. Dan's work has been featured in *Number Eleven*, *Storgy*, the *Dime Show Review*, *Short Tale 100*, *Phantaxis*, and the horror magazine *Devolution Z*.

Maura Stanton's ("House Ghosts") stories have won the Nelson Algren Award from The Chicago Tribune, the Lawrence Foundation Award from The Michigan Quarterly Review, the Richard Sullivan Prize from the University of Notre Dame, and an O. Henry Award for 2014. She has published six books of poetry - including *Tales of the Supernatural* and *Life Among the Trolls*, three books of stories, and one historical novel, *Molly Companion*, set in Paraguay. She lives in Bloomington, Indiana. "House Ghosts" won the fall 2015 Ghost Story Supernatural Fiction Award.

Lisa Taddeo ("The Donegal Suite") is a 2017 recipient of The Pushcart Prize. She received her MFA in fiction as the Saul Bellow Fellow from Boston University. Her fiction has been published in The *New England Review*, *The Sun* Magazine, and *Esquire*, among others. Her nonfiction has been published in *Esquire*, *New York* Magazine, *Elle* Magazine, The *New York Observer*, *Glamour* Magazine, and *The Sun* Magazine. Her work has been included in *Best American Sports Writing* and *Best American Political Writing*. She is the winner of the William A. Holodnak Fiction Prize and the winner of the 2017 Florence Engel Randall Award in fiction. Lisa is currently at work on her debut nonfiction book for Simon & Schuster, and her first novel.

Ailsa Thom ("A Rational Explanation") has lived and traveled extensively in South America and Africa. Now living back in Scotland, she spends the free time between working and writing trying to tame the garden, and firmly believes that a night of salsa dancing is equivalent to a trip to the gym. She has had short stories published in *Litro* Magazine, *McStorytellers,* and *Flash Fiction Magazine*.

Rachel Wyman ("Guédé") is an interdisciplinary artist and dance/movement therapist based in Brooklyn, New York. Through dance, writing, and visual art, she explores bodily experience and the visible and invisible aspects of identity. "Guédé" won the summer 2015 Ghost Story Supernatural Fiction Award.

☽ Wyrd Harvest Press

Focusing on Folk Horror, Psychogeography, Hauntology, Visionary Pastoralism, Urban Wyrd, Occulture, folklore, history, curiosa, film, literature, poetry, art, photography and theatre.

100% of profits from FHR / Wyrd Harvest Press books sold in their online store is charitably donated at intervals to different environmental, wildlife and community projects undertaken by the Wildlife Trusts.

Other titles available (more to follow)

Folk Horror Revival: Field Studies - Second Edition (2018) ˜ A new and revised edition of the seminal tome *Folk Horror Revival: Field Studies*. A collection of essays, interviews and artwork by a host of talents exploring the weird fields of folk horror, urban wyrd and other strange edges. Contributors include Robin Hardy, Ronald Hutton, Alan Lee, Philip Pullman, Thomas Ligotti, Kim Newman, Adam Scovell, Gary Lachman, Susan Cooper and a whole host of other intriguing and vastly talented souls. An indispensable companion for all explorers of the strange cinematic, televisual, literary and folkloric realms.

Folk Horror Revival: Corpse Roads (2016) ˜ An epic collection of spellbinding poetry, focusing on folk horror, life, death and the eeriness of the landscape by many creative talents both living and departed. Accompanied throughout with atmospheric imagery by an impressive collection of contemporary photographers.

Carnival of Dark Dreams (2016) ˜ A visual day - trip into the depths of the jungle, the sands of the desert, to many haunted habitats and worse still into the darkness of the human imagination. But fear not, for captured, caged and presented for your curiosity by Dr. Bob Curran and Mr. Andy Paciorek are some of the deadliest, most grotesque, fearsome entities of world folklore. Roll up Roll up for the fright of your lives. Dare you visit The Carnival of Dark Dreams???

This Game of Strangers (2017) ˜ Prepare to taste the worm in the golden apple of Camelot as the evocative poets Jane Burn and Bob Beagrie peer behind castle walls and uncover the soiled sheets of the romance / betrayal of Lancelot and Guinevere. Slipping seamlessly from the lyrical to the modern, Bob and Jane draw us in like voyeurs to the clandestine passion and sometimes mundane (though always rich in language) details of the love affair between the most beloved of the legendary king. Prepare to read the classic tale of romance and bewitchment as it has never been told before. Illustrated throughout with atmospheric photography by several great artists.

North (2017) ˜ The eloquent words of two poets brought forth from the land, the lodestone and lodestar. All roads lead here. Join Tim Turnbull and Phil Breach as through poetry, prose and the atmospheric imagery of great photographers, they explore and invoke the physical and emotional landscapes. Head North my friends and don't look back.

Otherworldly: Folk Horror Revival at the British Museum (2017) ~
A transcript of the entire British Museum 2016 event, featuring
contributions by Shirley Collins, Gary Lachman, Iain Sinclair,
Reece Shearsmith and many more. A great keepsake for those
fortunate to be there at the superb event and a riveting read for
those who weren't but love the whole folk horror phenomenon.

Hares in the Moonlight (2017) ~ Written by accomplished singer
songwriter, Sharron Kraus. A tale of magic and adventure for
readers aged 8-12 in the tradition of Alan Garner and Susan
Cooper. Twins Lucy and Jay rescue a caged hare and then follow it
to a moonlit gathering of hares. They find themselves falling into
a world of shapeshifting and becoming hares themselves.

Wyrd Kalendar (2017) ~ Join Chris Lambert and Andy Paciorek as
they guide you through the twelve months of the year weaving
twelve illustrated tales of Magic, Murder, Terror, Love and the
Wyrd.

Folk Horror Revival: Harvest Hymns: Volume 1: Twisted Roots
(2018)
The Twisted Roots of Folk Horror music. An exploration of the
artists and their music who laid the foundations for future
generations of Folk Horror musicians. Taking in Murder Ballads,
Acid Folk, Occult Rock, The Blues and Traditional Folk Music as
well as Film Soundtracks Twisted Roots is a collection of articles,
interviews and album reviews from the likes of Maddy Prior,
Jonny Trunk, Sharron Kraus, John Cameron and Candia
McKormack

Folk Horror Revival: Harvest Hymns: Volume 2: Sweet Fruits
(2018)~
Blossoming and bursting from the Twisted Roots of Folk Horror

music; the second volume of *Harvest Hymns* explores how the damp and darkness and other superb strangeness influences the current crop of musical artists. Featuring interviews and essays containing the likes of Ghost Box, The Hare and The Moon, Mortlake Book Club, Boards of Canada, The Devil and the Universe, GOAT, English Heretic, Nathalie Stern, Hawthonn and many, many more; *Sweet Fruits* is the perfect dessert for all wyrd tastes.

The Wytch Hunters' Manual (2018) ~ "Thou shalt not suffer a witch to live" or so 'tis said. Within the binding of this hallowed tract, thy shalt findeth the means to cleanse the world of the maleficent curse that the devil, his imps and minions have issued. Praise be. Finding its way into the hands of Dr Bob Curran and Andy Paciorek, Wyrd Harvest Press now bring to the eyes of a modern readership the remaining fragments of the ancient, once thought forever-lost, book, 'The Wytch Hunters' Manual'. Within its pages can be found details of the tomes and tools that should be at the disposal of all professional witch-hunters as well as biographies of notable finders and prickers and their notable foes both earthly and hellish.

www.lulu.com/spotlight/andypaciorek

email: wyrdharvestpress@gmail.com